PRAISE FOR THE NOVELS OF
MARY BALOGH

SIMPLY PERFECT

"A warm-hearted and feel-good story . . . Readers will
want to add this wonderful story to their collection.
Simply Perfect is another must-[...] from this talented
author, and a P[...] *[...]nance Reader*

"Wit[...] [...] characterization
an[...] [...]etly sensual,
th[...] [...]t to a truly
[...]. —*Booklist*

SIMPLY MAGIC

"Absorbing and appealing. This is an unusually subtle
approach in a romance, and it works to great effect."
—*Publishers Weekly*

"Balogh has once again crafted a sensuous tale of two
very real people finding love and making each other's
lives whole and beautiful. Readers will be delighted."
—*Booklist*

SIMPLY UNFORGETTABLE

"When an author has created a series as beloved to
readers as Balogh's Bedwyn saga, it is hard to believe
that she can surpass the delights with the first
installment in a new quartet. But Balogh has
done just that." —*Booklist*

"A memorable cast . . . refresh[es] a classic Regency plot
with humor, wit, and the sizzling romantic chemistry
that one expects from Balogh. Well-written and
emotionally complex." —*Library Journal*

Then Comes Seduction

MARY BALOGH

A DELL BOOK

THEN COMES SEDUCTION
A Dell Book / April 2009

Published by Bantam Dell
A Division of Random House, Inc.
New York, New York

This is a work of fiction. Names, characters, places, and incidents
either are the product of the author's imagination or are used
fictitiously. Any resemblance to actual persons, living or dead,
events, or locales is entirely coincidental.

Dell is a registered trademark of Random House, Inc., and the
colophon is a trademark of Random House, Inc.

ISBN 978-0-440-24423-3

Printed in the United States of America
Published simultaneously in Canada

www.bantamdell.com

OPM 10 9 8 7 6 5 4

Then Comes Seduction

1

JASPER Finley, Baron Montford, was twenty-five years old. Today was his birthday, in fact. At least, he amended mentally as he loosened the knot in his neck-cloth with one hand while the other dangled his half-empty glass over the arm of the chair in which he slouched, to be strictly accurate in the matter, *yesterday* had been his birthday. It was now twenty minutes past four in the morning, allowing for the fact that the clock in the library of his town house was four minutes slow, as it had been for as far back as he could remember.

He eyed it with a frown of concentration. Now that he came to think about it, he must have it set right one of these days. Why should a clock be forced to go through its entire existence four minutes behind the rest of the world? It was not logical. The trouble was, though, that if the clock were suddenly right, he would be forever confused and arriving four minutes early—or did he mean late?—for meals and various other ap-pointments. That would agitate his servants and cause consternation in the kitchen.

It was probably better to leave the clock as it was.

Having settled that important issue to his own satis-faction, he turned his attention to himself. He ought to have gone to bed an hour ago—or two. Or even bet-ter, three. He ought to have come straight home after leaving Lady Hounslow's ball—except that that would have put him in the house alone before midnight on his birthday, a damnably pathetic thing. He ought to have come after leaving White's Club an hour or so later, then. And that was precisely what he *had* done, he remembered, since here he was in his own familiar library in his own familiar house. But he had been unable to go straight to bed because a group of gentlemen had somehow attached themselves to him as he left White's and come home with him to celebrate the birthday that had already passed into history.

He wondered through the mist of alcohol clouding his brain—actually, it was more like a dense fog—if he had invited them. It was deuced forward of them to have come if he had not. He must ask them.

"I say," he asked, speaking slowly so that he would enunciate his words clearly, "were any of you *invited* here?"

They were all in their cups too. They were all slouched inelegantly in chairs except for Charlie Field, who was standing with his back to the fireplace, propping up the mantel with one shoulder and swirling the contents of his glass with admirable skill since not one drop of precious liquor sloshed over the rim.

"Were any of us—?" Charlie frowned down at him, looking affronted. "The devil, Monty, you practically *dragged* us here."

"*By* the bootstraps," Sir Isaac Kerby agreed. "We were all bent upon toddling home after we left White's to get our beauty sleep, but you would have none of it, Monty. You insisted that the night was young, and that a fellow suffered a twenty-fifth birthday only once in his life."

"Though turning twenty-five is nothing to get unduly maudlin about, old chap," Viscount Motherham said. "Wait until you turn thirty. Then you will have every female relative you ever possessed down to cousins to the second and third generations and the fourth and fifth removes admonishing you to do your duty and marry and set up your nursery."

Jasper pulled a face and clutched his temples with the thumb and middle finger of his free hand.

"Heaven forbid," he said.

"Heaven will refuse to intervene on your behalf, Monty," the viscount assured him. He was thirty-one years old and one year married. His wife had dutifully presented him with a son one month ago. "The female relatives will rout heaven every time. They are the very devil."

"Ee—nuff," Sir Isaac said, making a heroic effort to get the word past lips that looked as if they were paralyzed. "Enough of all the gloom and doom. Have another drink, Motherham, and cheer up."

"No need to stand upon ceremony," Jasper said, waving his arm in the direction of the sideboard with its impressive array of bottles and decanters, most of which looked seriously depleted. Good God, surely they had been *full* when they all arrived here two or three hours ago. "Can't get up to pour for you, Motherham. Something has happened to m'legs. Doubt they will support m'feet."

"What a fellow needs on his twenty-fifth birthday," Charlie said, "is something to cheer him up. Some new venture. Some exhilll . . . arrrr . . . What the deuce *is* that word? Some new *challenge*."

"A challenge? A dare, you mean?" Jasper brightened considerably. "A *wager*?" he added hopefully.

"The devil!" Charlie said, lifting a hand to grip the edge of the mantel against which his shoulder already leaned. "You need to get an architect to take a look at this floor, Monty. It ought not to be swaying like this. It's downright dangerous."

"Sit down, Charlie," Sir Isaac advised. "You are three sheets to the wind, old boy—maybe even four or five. Just watching you sway on your pins makes my stomach queasy."

"*Am* I foxed?" Charlie looked surprised. "Well, that is a relief. I thought it was the floor." He weaved his way gingerly toward the nearest chair and sank gratefully into it. "What is it to be for Monty this time, then? A race?"

"I did Brighton and back just two weeks ago, Charlie," Jasper reminded him, "and came in fifty-eight minutes under the agreed-upon time. It ought to be something quite different this time. Something new."

"A drinking bout?" Motherham suggested.

"I drank Welby under the table last Saturday week," Jasper said, "and there is no one in town who can hold his liquor like Welby—or *was*. Lord, I think my head must have swollen to twice its normal size. My neck does not seem quite up to the task of holding it up. Does it *look* twice its normal size?"

"It's the liquor, Monty," Charlie said. "It will feel even larger in the morning—the head, I mean. Mine too. Not to mention my stomach."

"This *is* the morning," Jasper said gloomily. "We ought to be in bed."

"Not together, though, Monty," Sir Isaac said. "We might cause a scandal."

There was a bellow of raucous and risqué mirth for this sorry attempt at humor—and then a collective grimace.

"Agatha Strangelove," said Henry Blackstone, rousing himself from a semicomatose state in the depths of a leather chair in order to contribute to the conversation for the first time in at least half an hour.

"What about her, Hal?" Sir Isaac asked gently.

Agatha Strangelove was a dancer at the opera house. She had luscious blond curls and ringlets, a pouting rosebud mouth, a figure that was overgenerous in all the right places, and legs that stretched all the way up to her shoulders—or so one wag had observed when she first appeared on the stage a month or two ago, and every man who heard him had known exactly what he meant. She was also very miserly in the granting of her favors to the gentlemen who crowded the green room after each performance begging for them.

"Monty should have to bed her," Hal said. "In no more than a week."

There was a small, incredulous silence.

"He *did* that the second week she was in town," Sir Isaac said, his voice still gentle, as though he were talking to an invalid. "Have you forgotten, Hal? It went into the betting book at White's on a Monday night with a one-week time limit, and Monty had her on Tuesday and Wednesday and Thursday nights, not to mention the days in between, until he had exhausted them both."

"Devil take it," Hal said in some surprise, "and so he

did. I must be foxed. You ought to have sent us home an hour ago, Monty."

"Did I invite you in the first place, Hal?" Jasper asked. "Or *any* of you? I can't for the life of me remember. London must be duller than usual this year. There don't seem to be any really interesting or original challenges left, do there?"

He had used them all up, dash it all. And he was *only* twenty-five. Someone earlier in the spring had been overheard to say that if Lord Montford was sowing his wild oats, he must be intent upon sowing every inch of every field he owned—and those of his more prosperous neighbors too, for two counties in every direction. He could not possibly be down to his last inch yet, could he? Life would not be worth living.

"How about a *virtuous* woman?" Charlie suggested, risking the perils of an undulating floor in order to cross the room to the sideboard to replenish his glass.

"What about her?" Jasper asked. He set down his empty glass on the table beside him. Enough was enough—except that he had probably reached that limit even before leaving White's. "She sounds devilishly dull, whoever she is."

"Seduce her," Charlie said.

"Oh, I say." Hal had been sinking back into his semi-coma, but he roused himself again at this interesting turn in an otherwise long-familiar line of conversation. "*Which* virtuous woman?"

"The most virtuous one we can think of," Charlie said with relish, having reached the safety of his chair again. "A young and lovely virgin. Someone new on the market and with a totally unblemished reputation. Lily white and all that."

"Oh, I say." But Hal, having drawn all eyes his way, could not seem to think of what he wanted to say. He was wide awake, though.

Motherham chuckled. "Now *that* would be something entirely new for you, Monty," he said. "A new star in your illustrious career of devilries and debaucheries." He raised his glass as if to toast his friend.

"He wouldn't do it, though," Sir Isaac said decisively, sitting upright in his chair and setting down his glass. "There are limits to what even Monty would do on a dare, and this is one of them. He would not seduce an innocent for all sorts of reasons I could name—which I will not do on account of the odd fact that my tongue and my lips and my teeth are all at odds with one another. Besides, he probably couldn't do it even if he *did* decide to try."

It was the wrong thing to say.

Seducing an innocent was the sort of thing no decent gentleman would even dream of attempting—or even one of society's most notorious hellions for that matter. There *were* limits to what one would take on for a wager, though admittedly they were few. Of course, those limits fluctuated, depending upon whether one were sober or inebriated. Jasper was very far from being sober—just about as far as it was possible to be without losing consciousness altogether, in fact. And *someone* had just suggested that there was *something* he could not accomplish even if he tried.

"Name her," he said.

"Oh, I say!"

"Ho, Monty."

"Splendid of you, old chap."

His friends had been given all the encouragement

they needed. They proceeded to trot out the name of almost every young lady who was currently in town for the Season making her debut. It was a lengthy list. Yet everyone on it was gradually eliminated for one reason or another, though none by Jasper himself. Miss Bota was Isaac's second cousin once removed, while Lady Anna Marie Roache was about to be betrothed to Hal Blackstone's brother's friend's brother-in-law—or something like that. Miss Hendy had spots and therefore did not qualify as lovely . . . And so on.

And then Katherine Huxtable was named.

"*Con* Huxtable's cousin?" Sir Isaac said. "Better not. He would veto her name in a moment if he were still in town and here with us tonight. Wouldn't like it by half, he wouldn't."

"He would not care a straw about it," Motherham said. "There is no love lost between Con and his cousins—for obvious reasons. If Con had only had the good fortune to be born legitimate, *he* would now be the Earl of Merton instead of the young cub who actually has the title. Miss Katherine Huxtable is Merton's sister," he added lest any of his friends not know it.

"She is too old anyway," Hal said firmly. "She must be twenty if she is a day."

"But ladies do not come any more innocent, Hal," Motherham pointed out. "Her brother has only just succeeded to the Merton title, and it was all thoroughly unexpected. By all accounts the family was living in a tiny cottage in a remote village no one has even heard of, as poor as church mice. And now suddenly the lady finds herself sister of an earl and making her come-out before the *ton* during a London Season. I would say she must be as innocent as a newborn lamb. *More* innocent."

"She undoubtedly has country morals too, then," Charlie said with a theatrical shudder. "Puritanical values and unassailable virtue and all that. Even Monty with all his good looks and legendary charm and seductive arts would not stand a chance with her. It would be cruel of us to pick her for him."

It was again the *wrong* thing to say.

No challenge was ever more exciting than one that was impossible to win. There was no such thing, of course, but proving it to himself as well as to those who wagered against him was the breath of life to Jasper.

"She is the golden-haired one, is she?" he said. "The tall and willowy one with the inviting smile and the fathomless blue eyes." He pursed his lips as he pictured her. She was a beauty.

There was an appreciative roar from his friends.

"Oh-ho, Monty," Sir Isaac said. "Been scouting her out, have you? You have a secret yearning for a leg-shackle, do you, her being an innocent and Merton's sister and all that?"

"I *thought*," Jasper said, raising one eyebrow, "the object was to seduce the woman, not marry her."

"I vote that we name Miss Katherine Huxtable as the lady to be seduced, then," Hal said. "It cannot be done, of course. Only matrimony will tempt females like her. And even *that* might not tempt her if you were the one offering, Monty, no offense meant, old chap. But you *do* have a reputation that scares off innocents. For once I will feel quite confident of making something back on my bet. It will be a veritable investment."

"By seduction," Sir Isaac said, "we mean full intercourse, do we?"

They all looked at him as if he had sprouted a second head.

"Stealing a kiss or pinching her bottom would hardly be a challenge worthy of Monty," Hal said, "even if the said kiss and pinch had to be willingly granted. *Of course* we mean full intercourse. But not ravishment, mind. That goes without saying."

"Then why say it, Hal?" Jasper raised both eyebrows and realized that they were all very, very drunk and were going to regret this tomorrow—or whenever after tomorrow their minds were restored to sobriety. He also realized that none of them, even when sober, would back off from the wager that was about to be made and would soon be written formally into a betting book at one of their clubs and opened to bets from any other gentleman who cared to risk his money. It was not in any of their natures to back off from a dare once it had been made and accepted.

Least of all in his.

They seemed to possess, he thought in a rare moment of moral insight, a somewhat skewed notion of honor.

But to the devil with conscience and with honor too for that matter. He was too drunk to be burdened with any notion that might further addle his brain.

"The wager is, then," Motherham said in summary, "that Monty cannot seduce Miss Katherine Huxtable into full sexual intercourse within the next...what? Month? Fortnight?"

"Fortnight," Charlie Field said firmly. "The outcome to depend upon our trust in Monty's word."

They proceeded to a discussion of the monetary details of the wager.

"Agreed, Monty?" Motherham asked when all had been decided upon.

"Agreed," he said with a careless wave of his hand. "Miss Katherine Huxtable will be bedded and enjoyed within the next fortnight. *And,* it might be added, *she* will enjoy it too."

There was a ribald burst of laughter.

Jasper yawned hugely. This was certainly something new for him. He had never done anything like this before. But there were no really interesting challenges left that he had not already taken on and won. This would at least be interesting. Also challenging.

The seduction of Agatha Strangelove had been neither really. It had basically been the other way around, in fact, except that it could not be said that he had exactly been *seduced.* Miss Katherine Huxtable was a rare beauty. He had seen her a number of times so far this spring and had even taken the occasional second look. She was the young Earl of Merton's sister, as someone had just pointed out. Her elder sister had recently married Viscount Lyngate, who was Merton's official guardian—and possibly Miss Huxtable's too. Now there was an interesting thought.

A formidable man, Lyngate.

As was Con Huxtable. And Jasper was not as sure as Motherham was that Con hated his cousins—at least *this* cousin. Jasper had met him one day driving her and another young lady about town, presumably showing them the sights, and—significantly—he had not stopped to introduce them. He had probably been protecting their innocence, an unlikely shepherd guarding the lambs from the wolf.

Con would very probably *not* be pleased with this wager or its inevitable outcome—for it was, of course, inevitable.

Which fact merely added titillation to the challenge, for Con was, of course, his friend.

The other men were preparing to leave, he saw. He was very glad that he was already at home, though even the thought of hauling himself to his feet and climbing the stairs to bed was daunting. He had better make the effort, though, or his valet would be in here within a half hour with a burly footman or two to carry him off to his bed. It had happened once, and Jasper had found it more than a mite humiliating. Perhaps that had been Cocking's intention. It had never happened again.

And so less than half an hour later, having seen his friends safely off the premises, he weaved his way upstairs to his rooms, where he found his valet awaiting him despite the hour, which was late or early depending upon one's perspective.

"Well, Cocking," he said, allowing his man to unclothe him just as if he were a baby, "this has been a birthday best forgotten."

"Most birthdays are, milord," his man said agreeably.

Except that he was not going to be able to forget it, was he? A wager had been made. *Another* one.

He had never lost a wager.

But *this* time?

For a few moments after he had dismissed his valet and crossed his bedchamber to open a window, Jasper could not remember what it was he had wagered upon.

It was something that even at the time he had known he would regret.

He did not usually look too closely at each year's new crop of young marriage hopefuls. There were often a few notable beauties among them, but there was also too much danger of being ensnared in some matrimonial trap—despite what someone had said earlier about the innocents not wanting to marry him. He was, after all, a wealthy, titled gentleman, two facts that could easily wipe out a multitude of sins.

But he *had* looked closely more than once at Katherine Huxtable.

She was more than ordinarily beautiful. There was also a very definite aura of countrified innocence—or naïveté—about her. But an air of good breeding too. And there were those eyes of hers. He had never seen them from close up, but they had intrigued him nonetheless. He had found himself wondering what was behind them.

It was most unlike him to wonder any such thing. He was a man of surfaces when it came to other people and even when it came to himself. He was not in the habit of looking within.

Perhaps part of the lady's appeal was the fact that she was Con Huxtable's cousin and Con had made a point of not introducing her to him.

Now he was pledged to seduce her.

Full sexual intercourse.

Within the next fortnight.

Devil take it! Yes, that was it. *That* was the wager. That was what he had agreed to do.

It was a sobering thought—literally. He felt as he climbed into bed as if he had progressed straight from deep drunkenness to the nauseated, head-pounding aftermath.

One of these days he was going to renounce drinking.

And wagering.

And sowing wild oats, or whatever the devil it was he had been sowing for more years than he cared to count.

One day. Not yet, though—he was only twenty-five.

And he had a wager to win before he set about reforming his ways. He had never lost a wager.

2

KATHERINE Huxtable was one of the most fortunate of mortals, and she was well aware of that fact as she took a brisk morning walk in London's Hyde Park with her sister Vanessa, Lady Lyngate.

Just a few short months ago she had been living in a modest cottage in the small village of Throckbridge in Shropshire with her eldest sister, Margaret, and their young brother, Stephen. Vanessa, the widowed Vanessa Dew at the time, had been living with her in-laws at nearby Rundle Park. Katherine had spent a few days of each week teaching the very young children at the village school and helping the schoolmaster with his other classes. They had been living a life of genteel poverty, which had meant that there was almost no money except for food and the essentials of clothing—and what Meg had been saving for Stephen's education.

And then suddenly everything had changed. Viscount Lyngate, a total stranger at the time, had arrived in the village on Valentine's Day, bringing with him the startlingly unexpected news that Stephen was the new Earl of Merton and owner of Warren Hall in Hampshire as well as other sizable and prosperous properties—and a huge fortune.

And *all* their fortunes had changed. First they had all moved to Warren Hall, the mansion and park that were

Stephen's principal seat, taking Vanessa with them. Then Vanessa had married Viscount Lyngate. And then they had all come to London to be presented to the queen and the *ton* and to participate in all the busy activities of the spring Season.

So here they were, she and Vanessa, walking in the park as if there were nothing better to do in life. It all felt shockingly decadent—and undeniably enjoyable too.

Suddenly they were in possession of all sorts of new and wonderful things—money, security, fashionable clothes, vast numbers of new acquaintances, and more entertainments than there were hours in the day during which to enjoy them. And suddenly for Katherine there was the prospect of a glittering future with one of the numerous and eligible gentlemen who had already shown an interest in her.

She was twenty years old and still unattached. She had never been able to persuade herself to fall in love when she lived in Throckbridge, though she had had a number of chances. The trouble was that she still could not here in London even though she genuinely liked a number of her admirers.

She had just admitted in response to a question Vanessa had asked that there was no one special among the gentlemen of her acquaintance.

"Do you *want* someone special in your life?" Vanessa asked with perhaps a thread of exasperation in her voice.

"Of course I do," Katherine admitted with something of a sigh. "But that is it you see, Nessie. He must *be* special. I am coming to the conclusion that there is no such person, that I am looking for a mirage, an impossibility."

Though she knew romantic love in itself was not an impossibility. She had only to consider her sister's case. Vanessa had been deeply in love with Hedley Dew, her first husband, and Katherine strongly suspected that she loved Lord Lyngate just as much.

"Or perhaps," she admitted, "there *is* such a person but I just cannot recognize him. Perhaps the fault is in me. Perhaps I was just not made for soaring passion or tender romance or—"

Vanessa patted her reassuringly on the arm and laughed.

"Of course there is such a man," she said, "and of course you will recognize him when you find him and feel all the things you dream of feeling. Or *after* you have found him, perhaps, as I did with Elliott. We were married before I knew how much I loved him—or that I loved him at all, in fact. Indeed, I have still only just admitted it to myself, and I am not at all sure it would not alarm him dreadfully to know it, poor man."

"Oh, dear," Katherine said. "This does not sound at all encouraging, Nessie. Though I am sure Lord Lyngate would *not* be alarmed."

They looked at each other sidelong and both chuckled.

But perhaps the fault really was in herself, Katherine thought in the coming days and weeks. Perhaps she had too rigid a notion of what the man of her dreams would look like or behave like. Perhaps she was just looking for love in the wrong places. In all the *safe* places.

What if love was not safe at all?

That startlingly unexpected and really rather alarming question occurred to her when she was at Vauxhall Gardens one evening.

Margaret and Stephen had just gone back to Warren Hall to stay, Margaret because she was upset over the recent news that Crispin Dew, her longtime beau, had married a Spanish lady while with his regiment in the Peninsula—though she would never have admitted it if confronted—and Stephen because at the age of seventeen he could not yet participate fully in the social life of the *ton* but could get back to his studies and prepare himself for Oxford in the autumn. Vanessa and Lord Lyngate had gone with them to spend a few days at Finchley Park, their home nearby. Although Katherine would have been more than happy to go too, she had been persuaded to remain in London for the rest of the Season to enjoy herself. So she was staying at Moreland House on Cavendish Square with Viscount Lyngate's mother and his youngest sister, Cecily, who was also making her debut this Season. The dowager Lady Lyngate had promised to keep a maternal eye upon Katherine.

But that eye was perhaps not quite as watchful as it ought to have been, Katherine concluded during the evening on which she and Cecily joined a party at Vauxhall Gardens organized by Lord Beaton and his sister, Miss Flaxley. Their mother had undertaken to take charge of the party of young people, and the dowager Lady Lyngate had decided upon a rare evening of relaxation at home.

It was a party of eight young persons, not counting Lady Beaton herself—and it included *Lord Montford* of all people.

Baron Montford was a gentleman who had been specifically pointed out to Katherine as one of London's most disreputable and dangerous rakehells. The warning had come from one of his friends and therefore someone who ought to know—from Constantine Huxtable, in fact, her wickedly handsome, half-Greek second cousin, whom she had met for the first time only recently when she had moved to Warren Hall with her family. Constantine had been obliging enough to take both her and his first cousin, Cecily, under his wing here in London, escorting them about town to see the sights and to meet new people whom he considered suitable acquaintances for them. No chaperone could possibly have been stricter on that point, though Katherine suspected that he knew any number of less savory persons and was perhaps even friendly with them.

There was Lord Montford, for example. That gentleman had approached them in the park one day, calling a greeting to Constantine as if he were his closest friend in the world. But Constantine had merely nodded to him and driven on by without stopping to make introductions. It had seemed almost rude to Katherine.

Baron Montford was mockingly handsome, if such a word could be used to describe a man's looks. Even if Constantine had not proceeded to warn her against him after that chance meeting, Katherine was sure she would have taken one look at him and known that he was a rake and someone best avoided. Apart from his good looks, the careless, expensive elegance of his clothing, the assured skill with which he rode his horse—all attributes of numerous gentlemen she had met during the past several weeks—there was something else about him. Something—*raw*. Something to which she could not put a satisfactory name even when she tried. If she had been familiar with the word *sexuality*, she would have known it as the very one for which her mind searched. He positively oozed it from every pore.

He also oozed danger.

"If I should see either of you so much as glancing his way at any time for the rest of the Season," Constantine had said after Lord Montford had ridden by and he had explained who the man was and why there had been no introductions, "I shall personally escort the culprit home, lock her in her room, swallow the key, and stand guard outside her room until summer comes."

He had grinned at each of them as he spoke, and both of them had laughed merrily and protested loudly, but neither Cecily nor Katherine had been left in any doubt that he would do something dire if he ever caught them consorting in any way at all with that particular friend of his.

All of which, of course, had piqued Katherine's interest—quite against her will. She had found herself stealing curious glances at Lord Montford whenever she saw him—and because they moved in largely the same social circles, that was often enough.

He was even more handsome than she had thought from that first glimpse in the park. He was tall without being *too* tall, slender without being thin, and firmly muscled in all the right places. He had thick, dark brown hair, which he wore rather longer than was fashionable, and there was one errant lock of it that was forever falling over the right side of his forehead. His eyes were dark and slumberous—though perhaps that was not quite the right word. They looked sleepy because he often kept his eyelids drooped over them, but Katherine had come to realize that the eyes beneath those lazy lids were very keen indeed. Once or twice she had even met their gaze and been forced to look beyond him on the pretense that she had not really been observing him at all.

Each time her heart had thumped rather uncomfortably in her bosom. He was not the sort of man one wished to be caught observing. It was at such moments that the word *mocking* leapt to mind.

He had a handsome, arrogant face with the right eyebrow often cocked higher than the left. His finely chiseled lips were usually slightly pursed, as if something rather improper were proceeding in his mind.

He was a baron and was reputed to be enormously wealthy. But his company was not courted by the very highest sticklers of society. Constantine had not exaggerated about his reputation for unbridled wildness, for taking on any mad and dangerous challenge anyone was willing to wager on, for hard, reckless living and wicked debauchery. Several matchmaking mamas, even some of the more aggressively ambitious ones, avoided him as though he had a permanent case of the plague. Or perhaps they avoided him more because they feared he would turn those keen, mocking eyes on them, raise his right eyebrow, purse his lips, and make them feel as if they were three inches high if they presumed to suppose that he might pay court to their daughters—or even dance with them.

He never danced.

Many ladies gave Lord Montford a wider than wide berth for another reason too. He had a way of undressing them with his eyes if they looked too boldly at him. Katherine knew it to be true—she had seen him doing it, though never, thank heaven, to her.

She was fascinated by him, if the truth were known.

Not that she had ever been even remotely tempted to try acting upon that fascination. But in unguarded moments she had often wondered what it would be like . . .

She had always stopped her wonderings before asking herself what she meant by *it*.

And now she was a member of a select party that included him, so she was doomed to spend a whole evening in fairly close proximity to him. The dowager Lady Lyngate would be horrified when she knew, for of course Cecily was here too, and Cecily was only eighteen years of age and was fresh out of the schoolroom. Constantine would be furious—except that he was not in London at the moment. He had recently purchased property in Gloucestershire and had gone off to see it. Lady Beaton was not too happy either if her stiff posture and rather sour facial expression were anything to judge by.

Katherine felt some sympathy for her because this was really not her fault at all. What could she have done when presented with a fait accompli, short of being very rude indeed? Miss Rachel Finley, another member of the party, was a particular friend of Miss Flaxley— and a close acquaintance of Cecily and Katherine too, even though she was a number of years older than them. Naturally, then, she was an invited member of the party—as was Mr. Gooding, her betrothed. But Mr. Gooding had had the misfortune to turn his ankle that very morning when jumping down from his curricle and was unable to set his foot to the ground as a consequence. Rather than cancel her plans for the evening, Miss Finley had done the best she could in the short time available to her. She had pleaded with her brother,

Lord Montford, to escort her instead—and he had been obliging enough to agree.

And here he was, and here they all were with no alternative but to act as if it were the most normal thing in the world to be sharing a box at Vauxhall with one of London's most notorious rakehells.

Katherine found herself wondering why he had agreed to escort his sister. He did not seem the sort of man from whom one would expect any deep filial feelings, and this was hardly the sort of company with which he usually consorted. None of the other gentlemen were particular cronies of his, though they all showed a tendency to eye him with awe and even hero worship, which was perhaps marginally better than open hostility. Or perhaps not. Why would any gentleman hero-worship a rake? But here he was anyway, looking sleepy-eyed and slightly amused, as if he were enjoying a private joke and not bothering to share it.

And what a joke it was! Gracious heavens! Cecily had fanned her face vigorously on his arrival and looked genuinely frightened.

"What shall we *do*?" she had whispered to Katherine on his arrival with Miss Finley. "Con said—"

There was, of course, nothing they *could* do.

"We must relax and enjoy the evening," Katherine had told her, just as quietly, "under the safe chaperonage of Lady Beaton."

After all, it was highly unlikely that Lord Montford would try to bear one of them off in among the trees to have his wicked way with them. The thought amused Katherine considerably, and she decided to follow her own advice and enjoy the evening and the unexpected opportunity it presented to observe the gentleman more closely.

Lord Montford had seated himself beside Lady Beaton and had proceeded to make himself agreeable to her, and even charming—with noticeable success. The lady soon relaxed and was laughing and even flushing with pleasure and tapping him on the arm with her fan. Everyone else gradually relaxed too and chatted among themselves and looked about with interest at their surroundings. There could be no more magical setting on a warm summer's evening than Vauxhall on the southern bank of the River Thames, one of Europe's foremost pleasure gardens.

Lord Montford had a light, cultured voice. He had a soft, musical laugh. Katherine observed him surreptitiously from the opposite corner of the box until he caught her at it. He looked at her suddenly, while she was biting into a strawberry. It was a direct, unwavering gaze, as if he had deliberately picked her out—though his eyes did dip for a moment to watch the progress of the strawberry into her mouth and the nervous flick of her tongue across her lips lest she leave some juice behind to drip down her chin.

He watched as she lifted her napkin and dabbed her lips and then licked them because she had dried them too much and his scrutiny made her nervous.

Oh, goodness, she ought not to have looked at him at all, she thought, lowering her eyes at last, and she would not do so again. He would think she was *smitten* with him or *flirting* with him or something lowering like that. She wished Margaret were here with her.

"Would you not agree, Miss Huxtable?" he asked her just as she was lifting another strawberry to her mouth.

The fruit remained suspended from her raised hand.

It amazed her that he remembered her name, though his sister *had* introduced them less than an hour ago.

All she had to do was the sensible and truthful thing—to tell him that she had not been listening to his conversation with Lady Beaton. But her mind was flustered.

"Yes, indeed," she said, and watched the smile deepen wickedly in his eyes while Lady Beaton looked at her in some surprise. She had made the wrong response. "Or, rather..."

And it struck her as if out of nowhere that it would be very easy indeed to fall head over ears in love with someone like Lord Montford. With someone forbidden, unsafe. Dangerous.

Definitely dangerous.

Or perhaps it was not someone *like* Lord Montford with whom she could fall desperately in love if she was foolish enough to allow herself to do it. Perhaps it was *precisely* him.

The thought caused a strange tightening in her breasts and an even stranger ache and throbbing that spiraled downward to rest between her inner thighs.

It was then that the thought occurred to her that perhaps love was not safe. That perhaps it was her very attempt to find it in safe places that had prevented her from finding it at all. That perhaps she would *never* find it if she did not...

If she did not *what?*

Take a leap in the dark? The very *dangerous* dark?

He held her eyes rather longer than was necessary before returning his attention to Lady Beaton, and the evening proceeded more safely and predictably and altogether more comfortably. Lord Beaton danced with Katherine in the space before the tiered boxes after they had all dined, and then, with another couple, they went for a short stroll along the grand avenue beneath the colored lamps that swayed magically in the tree branches overhead, dodging crowds of revelers as they did so.

Lord Beaton was one of Katherine's more persistent admirers. With just a hint of encouragement, she sensed, he would probably court her in earnest. And a very advantageous match it would be for her, considering the fact that at the beginning of the year she had been a lowly village schoolteacher even if her father *had* been a gentleman and grandson of an earl.

She had never given that hint of encouragement. She *liked* Lord Beaton. He was fair-haired, good-looking, good-natured, and . . . well, and ever so slightly dull. There was not the smallest suggestion of danger about him.

Which judgment, she realized, was far more of a condemnation of her than it was of him. His steadiness of character ought to be his strongest recommendation. Why had it suddenly occurred to her that perhaps she would like a dangerous man better? Or rather, that she would more than just *like* one particular dangerous gentleman? She had better hope that her strange, irrational theory was never put to the test.

It was, though.

After more dancing and feasting and conversing, they *all* went walking to fill in the time before the fireworks display. They proceeded again along the grand avenue, all talking amiably with one another, not in any particular pairings.

Until, that was, Katherine was jostled by a drunken reveler who could no longer walk a straight line, and found when she stepped smartly out of his way that Lord Montford was at her side, offering his arm.

"One needs a trusty navigator upon such a perilous voyage," he said.

"And *you* are such a navigator?" she asked him. It seemed far more likely that he was the perilous voyage. She did not know whether she should take his arm or not. She felt breathless for no discernible reason.

"Assuredly I am," he said. "I will steer you safely to harbor, Miss Huxtable. It is a solemn promise."

He smiled, and his eyes beamed good humor. He looked safe and reliable. He was behaving like a perfect gentleman, offering her protection from the reveling crowds. And she found that she *wanted* to take his arm.

"In that case," she said, smiling back at him, "I accept. Thank you, my lord."

And she slid one hand through his arm and felt—foolishly—as though she had never done anything nearly so daring and reckless and plain exciting in her whole life. It was a rock-solid arm. It was also warm. Well, *of course* it was warm. What had she expected? That he was the walking dead? She could smell his shaving soap or his cologne—a subtle, musky scent that was unfamiliar to her. It was very . . . masculine.

So was he. He was masculinity incarnate. She felt surrounded by it, enclosed in it.

Someone had robbed her of breathable air.

And here she was, behaving like a very green girl indeed just because a handsome, charming gentleman with a shady reputation had paid her some attention and offered his arm to steer her past the crowds. She was being ridiculous. *Silly* might be a better word.

"You must be missing young Merton and your sisters and Lyngate now that they have gone into the country," he said pleasantly, drawing her a little closer to his side. But she took no alarm from that fact. The crowds were very dense, and he was protecting her from them with some success. Indeed, she felt very safe indeed.

With a little thread of danger that caused her heart to thump away in her chest.

But—he *knew* her? He knew who she was, who her family members were? He knew that Meg and Stephen had returned to Warren Hall, that Vanessa and Lord Lyngate had gone with them to spend a few days at Finchley Park? She turned her head to look into his face. It was startlingly close to hers.

"But is it with sadness that you miss them?" he asked her. "Or is it with relief at being free to kick up your heels in their absence?"

That very safe smile in his eyes had developed an edge of wickedness.

This presumably was kicking up her heels. He must know that her family would not knowingly allow her within fifty yards of him unescorted. Not that she needed their escort. Good heavens, the very idea! She was twenty years old.

"I hope I do not need my brother and sisters to en-sure that I behave as I ought, my lord," she said, hearing the primness in her voice.

He laughed softly. It was enough to send shivers up her spine.

"Or Con either?" he said. "I have teased him so mer-cilessly about turning himself into a prim nursemaid since your advent in town, and Miss Wallace's, that he has turned tail and fled into the country to hide his mortification."

"He has not fled anywhere. He has gone into the country to see his new estate," Katherine told him. "It is in Gloucestershire."

"However it is," he said, moving his head a little closer to hers, "he is gone, and so are your brother and sisters and your brother-in-law."

He made it sound as if she had plotted long and hard to be rid of them in order to be free to allow this forbidden tryst. It was *not* a tryst. She had not even known he was going to be here. She had not—

But suddenly it *felt* like a tryst.

"I am staying at Moreland House," she explained to him, "with the dowager Lady Lyngate as my chaperone."

"Ah," he said. "The lady who is conspicuous in her absence this evening?"

"I am here—" she began indignantly, but she stopped when he laughed softly again.

"—under the chaperonage of Lady Beaton," he said, "who does not even appear to have noticed that we have fallen behind the group."

And so they had. Several people had passed them and were between them and their own party. She could see Lady Beaton's royal-blue hair plumes nodding above other heads in the middle distance.

"Miss Huxtable," he said, moving his head even closer to hers and turning it so that he could look into her face, "do you never feel even the smallest urge to live adventurously? Even dangerously?"

She licked her lips and found that even her tongue

was rather dry. Had he been reading her mind this evening?

"No, of course not," she said. "Never."

"Liar." His eyes laughed.

"*What?*" She felt the beginnings of outrage.

"Everyone wants some adventure in life," he said. "Everyone wants to flirt with danger on occasion. Even ladies who have had a sheltered, very proper upbringing."

"That is outrageous," she said—but without conviction. She could not look away from his eyes, which gazed keenly back into hers as if he could read every thought, every yearning, every desire, she had ever had.

He laughed again and lifted his head a little away from hers.

"Yes, of course it is outrageous," he agreed. "I exaggerated. I can think of any number of people, both men and women, who are staid by nature and would sooner die than risk stubbing a toe against even the smallest of adventures. You are not, however, one of those people."

"How do you know?" she asked him, and wondered why she was arguing with him.

"Because you have asked the question," he said, "instead of pokering up and staring at me in blank incomprehension. You have become defensive. You know that I speak the truth but are afraid to admit it."

"*Really?*" she said, injecting as much frost into the one word as she could muster. "And what adventure is it that I crave, pray? And with what danger is it that I wish to flirt?"

Too late she wished she had used a different word.

His head dipped closer to hers again.

"*Me,*" he said softly. "In answer to both questions."

A shiver of horrified excitement convulsed her whole body, though she hoped it was not visible. Everyone, she realized, had been perfectly right about him. Constantine had been right. Her own instincts had been right.

He was a very dangerous man indeed. She ought to pull her arm free of his *right this moment* and go dashing after the others as fast as her legs and the crowds would allow.

"That is ... preposterous," she said, staying instead to argue.

Because danger really was enticing. And not so very dangerous in reality. They were on the grand avenue at Vauxhall, surrounded by people even if their own party was proceeding farther ahead with every passing minute. Danger was only an illusion.

"I speak of your deepest, darkest desires, Miss Huxtable," he continued when she did not reply. "No true lady, of course, ever acts upon those, more is the pity. I believe any number of ladies would be far more interesting—and interest*ed*—if they did."

She stared at him. She glared at him—at least, she hoped she did. Her cheeks were uncomfortably hot. So was all the rest of her. Her heart was pounding so hard she could almost hear it.

"You most of all," he said. "I wonder if it has ever occurred to you, Miss Huxtable, that you are a woman of great passion. But probably not—it would not be a genteel admission to make, and I daresay you have not met anyone before now who was capable of challenging you to admit the truth. I assure you that you *are*."

"I am *not*," she whispered indignantly.

He did not answer. His eyelids drooped farther over

his eyes instead, and those eyes laughed. The devil's eyes. Sin incarnate.

Suddenly and so unexpectedly that she almost jumped with alarm, she laughed. Out loud.

And she realized with astonishment and no uncertain degree of unease that she was actually almost *enjoying* herself. She knew that she would relive this part of the evening in memory for several days to come, perhaps weeks. Probably forever. She was actually talking with and *touching* the notorious Lord Montford. And he was actually flirting with her in an utterly outrageous way. And instead of being paralyzed with horror and tongue-tied with enraged virtue, she was actually laughing and arguing back.

They had stopped walking. Although her arm was still drawn through his, they were standing almost face-to-face—and therefore very close together. The crowds of revelers flowed around them.

"Oh, how very wicked of you," she was bold enough to say. "You have quite deliberately discomfited me, have you not? You have deliberately maneuvered me into hotly denying a quality of which we all wish to think ourselves capable."

"Passion?" he said. "You *are* capable of it, then, Miss Huxtable? You admit it? How sad it is that a gentle upbringing must stamp all outer sign of it from a lady."

"But it is something she must display only for her husband," she said, and felt instantly embarrassed by the ghastly primness of the words.

"Let me guess." He was more than ever amused, she could see. "Your father was a clergyman and you were brought up listening to and reading sermons."

She opened her mouth to protest and shut it again.

There was no smart answer to that, was there? He was quite right.

"Why are we having this conversation?" she asked him, about five minutes too late. "It is very improper, as you know very well. And we have not even set eyes upon each other until tonight."

"Now *that*, Miss Huxtable," he said, "is a blatant bouncer for which you will be fortunate indeed not to fry in hell. Not only have you set eyes upon me before tonight, but you have done so quite deliberately and with full awareness on more than one occasion. My guess is that Con's warnings against me—I do not doubt he *did* warn you—have had the opposite effect from what he intended, as a man of his experience ought to have known. But before you swell with indignation and perjure your soul with more lies, let me admit that since I am aware of your observing me before tonight, then of course *I* must have been observing *you*. Unlike you, though, I have no wish to deny the fact. I have seen you with increasing pleasure. You must realize how extraordinarily lovely you are, and so I will not bore you by going into raptures over your beauty. Though I will if you wish."

He raised both eyebrows and gazed very directly into her eyes, awaiting her answer.

Katherine was fully aware that she had waded into deep waters and was by now quite out of her depth. But oddly she had no wish to return to safe waters just yet. He really *was* flirting with her. And he had noticed her before tonight just as she had noticed him.

How very foolish to feel flattered. As if she did not know better.

"I see, my lord," she said, "that you do not observe the rules of polite conversation."

"Meaning," he said, "that I do not endorse lies and other hypocrisies in the name of politeness? You are quite right. When I see a spade, I see no conversational advantage in calling it something else. Perhaps this is one reason many people of good *ton* avoid my company."

"*One* reason, perhaps," she said. "There are others."

He smiled fully at her and regarded her in silence for a few moments. For which she was very thankful. The smile transformed him into...Oh, where were there adequate words? A handsome man? She had already thought of him as being handsome. *Irresistible,* then?

"That was a very sharp and nasty retort, Miss Huxtable," he said. "And not at all polite."

She bit her lower lip and smiled.

"We are being a severe annoyance to all who are proceeding along this avenue," he said. "Shall we move on?"

"Of course." She looked ahead. Their party was right out of sight. They were going to have to walk quickly to catch up. This brief, strange interlude was at an end, then? And so it ought to be. She should be feeling far gladder about it than she actually was.

But he did not lead her in their direction. Neither did he turn back toward their private box. He turned her instead onto a narrower path that branched off the grand avenue.

"A shortcut," he murmured.

Within moments they were enclosed by trees and darkness and solitude. There were no lamps swaying from the branches here. There was an almost instant feeling of seclusion.

This encounter, Katherine thought, was taking a very

dangerous turn indeed. She did not for a moment believe that this was a short route back to the others. She ought to take a firm stand *right now,* insist upon being taken without delay back to the main avenue and on to Lady Beaton and safety. Indeed, she did not even have to be taken. She could go on her own. He surely would not stop her by force.

Why did she not do it, then?

Instead of taking any stand at all, she walked onward with him, deeper into a darkness that was only faintly illumined by the moon and stars far above the treetops.

She had never really known adventure—or danger. Or the thrill of the unknown.

Or the pull of attraction to a man who was forbidden.

And *definitely* dangerous.

And, for the moment at least, quite irresistible.

3

M ISS Katherine Huxtable was, as Jasper had expected, naïveté itself. A dangerous innocent.

And quite exquisitely lovely.

There was also something unexpectedly likable about her. She was not insipid, as he had also expected.

All of which did not matter one tittle of an iota, of course.

Her eyes—those deep, fathomless blue eyes, which had drawn him from his first sight of her simply because he could not see far enough into them to understand them *or* her—her eyes could fill with sudden laughter, and laughter also lifted the corners of her soft, kissable lips.

Her hair was not golden after all. It was actually a dark blond. It might have been nondescript, even mousy, if it had not been for the pure gold highlights that gave it sparkle and luster—and allure.

She was coltishly, girlishly slender, but she was well shaped too, by Jove. He favored women of voluptuous proportions when given the choice, but there was much to be said for slenderness and poise when he was not.

She moved with a natural grace.

It had been sheer good fortune that Rachel had been invited to join this party at Vauxhall tonight—just four nights after his birthday—and that the party was to

include none other than Miss Katherine Huxtable—
minus any of her family members. His discreet inquiries
had revealed to him that they had all gone off to the
country together, leaving her behind in care of Lyngate's
mother. It was neither luck nor chance that had
brought *him* here. It had cost him all of fifty guineas to
persuade an indignant Gooding to turn an ankle while
descending from his curricle this morning. It had taken
less effort, it was true, to persuade his elder sister to beg
him to escort her in Gooding's stead and even believe
that the whole idea had been hers. She had even
thanked him profusely, explaining that an evening at
Vauxhall was not something to be missed even if she
must go without her betrothed. She had missed so
much of life in London. She was twenty-six years old,
and this was only her second Season.

"What are brothers for," he had said magnanimously,
squeezing her shoulder, "but to support their sisters
when they have suffered a disappointment? I have been
assured, by the way, that Gooding's ankle is not actually
broken. I daresay he will be as fit as a fiddle again to
dance with you by the next grand ball, whenever
that is."

This was all great good fortune even if he *had* had
to do some fancy maneuvering and open his purse
rather wide. There was no place more romantic than
Vauxhall—to a lady's sensibilities—or more conducive
to seduction.

The trickiest moment had already passed. She had
not resisted being turned off the grand avenue. Young
ladies really ought to be educated more thoroughly in
the wicked ways of the world. If he ever had daughters—*if!*—he would make very sure to include it in the

compulsory subjects of their schooling. Reading, writing, penmanship, embroidery, dancing, watercolor painting, geography, and the Wicked Ways of the World.

He pressed Miss Huxtable's slim arm tightly to his side for a while, but when he turned them onto yet another path, even narrower and more secluded than the last, he was forced to release it and set an arm about her waist so that they could move along side by side. Single file was the only sensible way to proceed along this particular path, but who was being sensible?

Not Miss Katherine Huxtable, certainly.

She did not point out, as she sensibly might have done, that this was hardly a shortcut back to the rest of their party. Neither did she make any protest at the intimacy of his touch. She stiffened for a moment, it was true, but then she relaxed again.

"Mmm," he said softly. "You wear a perfume I have not smelled before."

It was even true.

"It is not perfume," she said. "I never wear any. It must be the soap I used to wash my hair this morning."

He smiled at the naïveté of her answer. And at its unconscious invitation. He stopped walking and drew her to a halt too. He lowered his face to her hair and inhaled. He could feel it soft and silky against his nose.

"Ah," he murmured. "And so it is. Who would have thought mere soap could smell so . . . enticing."

He felt her shiver.

"It is what I always use," she said.

"May I offer a word of advice?" he said, turning her slightly so that her hand had to come up to his chest to keep a little distance between them. "Never change that habit. That soap is more appealingly fragrant than any perfume."

"Oh," she said. "Do you think?"

"*I think*, Miss Huxtable," he said fervently, and he slid his thumb along the base of her fingers, closed his hand about hers, and lifted it high onto his shoulder, bringing her against him with the other hand as he did so. "Though sometimes I prefer not to. Sometimes there are better things to do."

He lowered his head to brush his lips across the warm, soft flesh between her shoulder and neck and then moved them upward. He flicked his tongue over the warm, sensitive flesh behind her ear and heard her inhale sharply and felt her curve her body more firmly into his as he blew softly into the cavity of her ear and then moved his mouth to cover hers.

Her lips were closed and pouted, and it occurred to him that this was possibly her first kiss. Her whole body trembled noticeably and sagged further against his. Her hands gripped both his shoulders.

He kissed her softly, waiting for her grip to loosen before touching her lips with his tongue and, when they parted, sliding it into her mouth. She inhaled slowly through her mouth as he did so, an unconsciously erotic move that had him harden into early arousal.

She tasted of strawberries and wine and woman.

He twined one arm about her slender waist and spread the other hand lightly over her buttocks.

"Beautiful," he whispered, his lips still touching hers. "Beautiful, beautiful."

Her eyes were closed. She pressed her lips softly to his.

"We ought not to be here like this," he murmured.

"You ought not to be here with me. *Especially* with me. You have been warned."

She had opened her eyes, and even though they stood in almost total darkness, it seemed to him that he could see the depths of trust and surrender there.

"I make my own decisions about people," she said.

Ah, foolish. Naïveté par excellence. He felt a strange twinge of tenderness for her.

"Do you?" He feathered kisses against her lips. "I am humbled. And unworthy. You are so very beautiful."

He spread one hand over the back of her head, angled his own against it, and kissed her with sudden and deep urgency, pressing her mouth wide with his own, ravishing it with his tongue.

Her arms came tightly about him.

"Ah," he whispered after several moments, "you tempt me."

She made a low sound in her throat but said nothing, and he turned her so that they were off the path and her back was against the smooth trunk of a tree. In the distance the orchestra at the main pavilion played a waltz tune and revelers laughed and called out to one another.

He made love to her with his hands and his lips, slowly, gently, patiently, almost worshipfully, so that she would not take sudden fright and flight. His guess was that she was experiencing a seething torment of emotions, including alarm and guilt. His guess was also that her inexperience with sexual desire would persuade her to delay one more moment before stopping him and then one more—until the time came when she would feel it was too late to stop him at all without appearing very foolish.

His task was to wait until that moment came and had passed.

And to fulfill her every dream of forbidden sensual delights during the moments that followed. He had always taken a great deal of pleasure in all the women he possessed, but it had also always been a matter of pride with him to *give* a great deal of pleasure too—even when there was a wager involved.

He moved his hands over her, easing her flimsy dress off her shoulders and down her arms, baring her breasts in the process. He fondled them gently, kissed them, suckled them. They were small but firm, warm, exquisitely silky to the touch. Her nipples were pebbled hard.

Her fingers twined in his hair while she pressed her head back against the tree trunk. She was breathing deeply and audibly.

Someone really ought to make a perfume out of that soap. That someone would make a fortune.

He stood against her, softly kissing her face and murmuring to her while his hands slid the fabric of her gown up her legs and he touched their firm, smooth warmth. He nudged one knee between her inner thighs until she moved her feet apart and his hand had access to the most private, secret, hot core of her.

She whimpered slightly when he touched her there, and he stilled his hand for a moment while he kissed her lips.

"Ah," he murmured to her. "So very lovely."

She was too. She was all slender, immaculate beauty. A girl in innocence, a woman in soft, warm allure. His hand played with her, teased her, scratched her lightly. He slid one finger part of the way inside her before withdrawing it. She was hot and slickly wet.

Ready for him.

Hot with mindless desire.

Aware too perhaps that it was too late now to behave as she ought and as she surely had done all her life until this moment when tempted by a practiced seducer.

As he fondled her with one hand and stroked into her mouth with his tongue, he used his other hand to open buttons and lower the fall of his evening breeches. He set his erection against her when he was ready and felt the familiar pounding, almost painfully pleasurable anticipation of penetration, vigorous action, and ultimate release.

Naked flesh against naked flesh. *There.* And soon to be...

He really did want her, he thought. This was not *just* about seduction. It was not *all* cold cynicism.

Whom was he trying to fool?

The question presented itself to him with cold verbal clarity at just the moment when he needed to be as mindless as she.

He had a sudden flashing image of himself tomorrow swaggering into his club to claim his prize after only five days. Seduction of innocence complete—full penetration, full intercourse, full submission. Full enjoyment. One devil of a fine fellow. No dare too daring, no wildness too wild, no debauchery too debauched for Baron Montford, fondly known to his admiring intimates as Monty.

Always and ever a winner.

And he had a companion image of Katherine Huxtable tomorrow, confronting the knowledge of what she had done, knowing herself ruined and alone and abandoned, the latest victim of a heartless, conscienceless rake. Knowing too that she had only herself to blame. She had been warned—even by him.

Though of course it would not be all her fault at all—or even nearly all. How could an innocent be expected to contend against his considerable experience?

He felt suddenly and viciously angry. He was not accustomed to *thinking* at such moments—especially such thoughts. He *was* heartless. He *was* without conscience. He *was* an unprincipled rake. And he had a wager to win.

He cupped her with one palm, his hand between her open, inviting heat and the instrument of her violation.

"Miss Huxtable," he said in a voice that sounded shockingly normal, "you are about to cost me several hundred guineas."

And his pride and reputation. He would be the laughingstock.

"Wh-at?" Her voice sounded bewildered. It was slightly high-pitched.

"That is what it is going to cost me for denying myself the ultimate pleasure of mounting you and slaking my lust on you," he said, enunciating each word very clearly lest she—and perhaps he too—not understand.

"What?" She had still not even begun to understand. Her voice was thin and bewildered.

"There has been a wager on the books in one of the gentlemen's clubs for the past four days," he told her bluntly, "hotly contested by a large number of the members, that I cannot seduce you before two weeks have passed—*seduction* meaning *full sexual intercourse*. Full penetration of your body. Which will *not* happen here tonight. Not now, not ever. *Not* because you have said no, Miss Huxtable, as you ought to have done with firm moral outrage as soon as I enticed you off the main path and every moment since then, but because *I* say no."

"What?" She could not seem to find anything else to say. But there was more alarm in her voice now.

He took a step back and let her skirts drop about her legs while he buttoned up his breeches again. He pulled the bodice of her gown none too gently up over her breasts since she had made no move to do it herself.

"This was all *planned,* Miss Huxtable," he explained with cold, brutal honesty. "Right down to Gooding's curricle accident, which prevented him from coming this evening and gave me the opportunity to take his place. This was all *planned* and would have proceeded without a flaw if I had not just now decided that a wager so easily won was a wager not really worth winning after all. You may take your virtue home to bed with you tonight with my compliments. Now we must make our way back to Lady Beaton's box before your reputation suffers serious damage after all. Even now I do not doubt you will have to endure her frowns."

All his anger was directed against her—outwardly at least. For the moment she was a convenient target for an emotion that was quite unfamiliar to him. He had not even assigned the word *guilt* to it yet and perhaps never would.

He *never* allowed himself to feel guilt over anything he did. He prided himself upon having no heart. No conscience. He had spent long years cultivating the reputation he had.

A desirable woman had been his for the taking this evening. So had the winning of a lucrative wager and the awed adulation of all his male acquaintances.

He had not taken any of it. For once in his life, he had not *taken*. Because he had *chosen* not to. Because he was bored with her, bored with himself.

Or so he chose to believe.

Truth to tell, he did not know why he had stopped. It was something totally new to his experience. And he was angry and frustrated.

"I do not believe you." She had her fingers spread over the bare flesh above her bosom, as if to protect her modesty—a gesture somewhat akin to shutting the stable door after the horse had bolted. Her voice was shaking. Her teeth chattered audibly after the words were out.

"Do you not?" he said curtly. "You think I am making polite small talk, Miss Huxtable? You were warned that I am a rake of the worst order. You ought to heed such warnings, especially when they come from someone like Con Huxtable, who knows me very well indeed. You ought to have known what was happening as soon as I singled you out for attention back on the grand avenue—or even sooner, when I gazed at you eating your strawberry in the box. And you doubtless *did* know—you surely cannot be such an innocent as to have been entirely ignorant of my intentions. But you thought you were strong enough and worldly enough to handle me, did you not? Women are prone to the belief that they can handle and even reform society's rakehells and tame them with love. Is that what you were envisioning with me this evening?"

She did not answer immediately. Her arms had fallen to her sides. At any moment he expected hysterics or tears. And damn it all, he was going to have to find a way of dealing with it. And why the devil was he being so brutal to her?

"No, not at all actually," she said. Her voice had stopped shaking. "I thought to take some pleasure from you, Lord Montford, since you are so very famous for giving it. Alas, that fame has been greatly exaggerated. You have disappointed me. I expected a great deal better of such a notorious rake. And why ever would I wish to reform you when you are a disappointment as you are, or tame you when you are already far too bland? I have no such ambition, you will be relieved to know. Yes, let us go back, by all means. There is nothing more to be gained from remaining here, is there?"

He was startled into a bark of laughter.

Well.

That was a masterly setdown if ever he had heard one.

There was perhaps considerably more to Miss Katherine Huxtable than he had ever suspected. But it was too late now to find out of what that *more* consisted. Not that he wished to find out. Quite the contrary. One thing he would do quite assiduously for the rest of both their lives was stay as far away from her as the size of the globe would permit. It would not be impossibly difficult, he supposed, since she would surely be just as determinedly avoiding him.

But good Lord! Devil take it!

Alas, that fame has been greatly exaggerated. You have disappointed me.

He suppressed the inappropriate urge to add a shout of laughter to the short bark that had already escaped him.

She had somehow restored his good humor. He had

not destroyed her, then. She had not collapsed in a quivering heap of weeping womanhood.

And why ever would I wish to reform you when you are a disappointment as you are, or tame you when you are already far too bland?

The devil! He really *did* like her.

Far too late.

"I will lead the way out," he said, stepping back onto the path. "Follow me closely."

"Not too closely, thank you very much," she said coolly, and stepped out after him. "I do not believe this evening will present any more dangers against which I may need your kind protection."

The minx!

And so they went single file after all.

4

CECILY was wide-eyed with admiration.

"You actually walked *alone* with Lord *Montford*," she stated when she appeared briefly in Katherine's dressing room soon after they had returned from Vauxhall. "I would have been *terrified*. I very nearly swooned when he appeared with Miss Finley. I do not know how she *dared* bring him even if he *is* her brother. Con will *kill* us, not to mention Elliott. And did you observe Lady Beaton when he first arrived? I thought her lower jaw would drop all the way to the floor of the box. One could only feel sorry for her, for there was nothing she could do about it, was there, unless she chose to make a scene. And that would have been worse than anything. Whatever did you *talk* about, Kate? My tongue would have tied itself in a dozen knots before I had gone ten paces."

"I do not remember what we talked about," Katherine told her. "We conversed on a number of different topics."

"Well, I do not care what anyone says about his reputation," Cecily said with a sigh and a marvelous lack of consistency. "I think he is by far the most handsome gentleman in the *ton*—not counting Con, of course. Oh, and your brother."

"Constantine *is* very handsome," Katherine agreed.

"It is his Greek heritage. Your brother is just as handsome. Indeed, they look a great deal alike."

Cecily's brother was Elliott Wallace, Viscount Lyngate, Katherine's brother-in-law.

"And I believe Stephen will have more than his share of ladies sighing over him when he is a little older," Katherine added.

After a little more conversation and a series of yawns, Cecily finally went off to bed—to Katherine's great relief. She really did not want to talk with anyone. She did not want to think either. She wanted to sleep, preferably for a long, long time.

She was forced to both think and talk the following afternoon, though, when the dowager Viscountess Lyngate returned from a drive in the park, where she had met and talked with Lady Beaton. She sat at tea in the drawing room with Katherine, Cecily having gone off to the library with one of her new friends and that young lady's maid. Lady Lyngate was only very gently reproachful.

"You are twenty years old, Katherine," she said. "Older and considerably more sensible than Cecily. I do not doubt that your behavior was above reproach last evening—it was not *your* fault, after all, that Lord Montford was of your party. It was most unfortunate that we had no advance warning. However, gossip is everyone's favorite occupation in London during the Season, and even the faintest possibility of impropriety can feed drawing room conversation for a week or more and seriously compromise a lady's reputation. It might be wiser in the future, my dear, to avoid Baron Montford's company altogether, or, if that is impossible as it was last evening, to remain with everyone else of your party *at all times* so that no one can have any reason whatsoever to couple your name with his. He really is beyond the pale of respectability, you know, charming as he can be when he sets his mind to it. But since you *did* walk with him last evening and allow yourself to lag behind the others — though I do blame Lady Beaton for not keeping a far more careful eye upon you — I do hope he was the soul of honor."

She looked inquiringly at her young charge.

"Oh, but of course he was," Katherine assured her.

"Of course." Lady Lyngate smiled. "He is, after all, a gentleman despite his shocking rakehell ways, and he knows how to behave in genteel company. I daresay his reputation is somewhat exaggerated anyway. No one can be quite as wild as he is reputed to be."

"No," Katherine agreed.

"This has *not* been a scold, Katherine," the dowager assured her. "It has merely been a word of caution from someone older and perhaps wiser in the ways of fashionable society than you. I have only your best interests at heart."

"I know you do, ma'am," Katherine said. "I appreciate your concern. It is very kind of you to care."

"Not at all," Lady Lyngate said, leaning forward in her chair to pat her hand. "You are missing your family, are you not?"

"Oh," Katherine said, and to her surprise and embarrassment tears filled her eyes, "yes, I am. I have never been separated from them for so long before now."

Even when Vanessa had been married to Hedley Dew and living at Rundle Park with him and his family, she had been less than a half hour's walk away, and one or more of them had walked the distance almost every single day.

The dowager clasped her hand and squeezed it.

"Perhaps," she said, "Elliott and Vanessa ought to have taken you with them after all. It is not even as though they are to miss all the rest of the Season, is it? They will be back here soon."

"They wanted me to stay here," Katherine said, dabbing at her tears with her handkerchief. "They wanted me to stay and enjoy myself. And of course I am doing just that."

"Of course you are," the dowager said kindly. "Was Vauxhall as lovely as ever?"

"Oh, even lovelier, ma'am."

Katherine longed for her sisters and brother with a gnawing ache. Yet she was glad they were gone from town. What would she say to them today? How would she stop herself from blurting out the whole sorry, sordid story to them? She needed time to recover.

It was pointless to ask herself what she had been thinking last evening. She had not, of course, been thinking at all. Or not rationally anyway. It was quite horrifying to realize how quickly and easily she could succumb to the seductive charms of a practiced rake and to the base cravings of her own body.

In her own mind she had even called it love.

She had thought herself gloriously, passionately in love with a dashing, dangerous man.

How gauche of her. How... *humiliating*!

She would have allowed him...

No, she would not. At every moment she had been about to stop him. She would have done so before it was too late.

No, she would not have done.

It had already been too late.

She had him to thank for the fact that she was not irretrievably ruined today—a fallen woman.

It had all been calculated, deliberate on his part. He had set out quite coldly and deliberately to seduce her. He had arranged to be of her party at Vauxhall, and he had plotted to draw her away from the others and onto that dark, deserted path—and then off it behind a tree. He had planned it all.

How easy she had made it for him. He had stopped only because it was *too* easy to offer any interesting challenge.

There was a written wager in one of the notorious betting books at a gentlemen's club. With *her* name in it. Her name was being bandied about by countless gentlemen of the *ton*. And perhaps today he would be amusing them all with an account of exactly what had happened.

Only one thought persisted in Katherine's brain as she sipped her tea and conversed with her hostess. She wanted to go home—preferably all the way home to Throckbridge. She wanted her old life back. It had been a serene and happy one. She wanted to go back there and marry Tom Hubbard, who had asked so many times that they had probably both lost count. But no, Warren Hall would be better. Meg and Stephen were there. And it was in the country, in Hampshire, far away from London.

"We are to be busy during almost every moment of every day for the next week and a half," the dowager was saying. "It is very gratifying, is it not? And both you and Cecily are swarmed by admirers wherever you go. It should be altogether possible to have both of you happily betrothed before the Season ends and perhaps even married before the autumn. Is there any very special gentleman, Katherine?"

Katherine set down her cup with a clatter and blinked her eyes so that they would not fill with tears again.

"I want to go home," she said.

She could not bear—she really could not *bear* the very real possibility that she would see Lord Montford again as soon as she set foot beyond the door. She could not bear to see him again.

Ever.

"Oh, you poor dear," the dowager said, getting to her feet to come and sit beside Katherine and set a comforting arm about her shoulders. "Of course you do. I have sensed it, but I did not realize just how homesick you are."

Despite herself Katherine had tears in her eyes again, and they were spilling over to run down her cheeks. She gave one hiccup of a sob.

But she need not have worried, even though it took three days of preparations before she was on her way back to Warren Hall in the comfort and safety of the dowager's own traveling carriage. Lord Montford did not come calling. Nor did he attend the one evening concert for which Katherine dared venture beyond the doors of Moreland House.

In fact, she did not see him again for three full years.

Jasper's public admission of utter and abject failure the morning after the Vauxhall debacle was greeted with stunned astonishment by all the gentlemen who were fortunate enough to be present when he made it. The initial silence was soon replaced, however, by delighted rejoicing by those who had wagered against him and by much mirth and hearty back-slapping and commiserations and witty, ribald comments.

London's most prolifically successful rakehell had been ignobly vanquished by an inexperienced country mouse, who had seen through his ruse in a flash and had led him almost literally down a garden path in Vauxhall, *not* in order to hurl her virginity at him in eager, panting surrender, but to deliver an eloquent and cutting scold that had forced him to concede that continuing the campaign for what remained of the two weeks would have been an exercise in futility.

The picture of a vanquished Monty hanging his head in mortification before the eloquence of a country virago was too delicious a one not to be revived again and again in male conversation during the coming days. Miss Katherine Huxtable herself soared in everyone's esteem. A dozen gentlemen declared themselves to be quite in love with her. Two declared themselves forever her slaves. One promised to offer her matrimony before the Season was out.

Jasper, even after the first burst of exuberance had subsided, was the recipient of a chorus of sage advice mingled with mock sympathy, much of it concerned with the sharp decline in certain accomplishments a man must expect to endure once he had passed his twenty-fifth birthday.

"One is well advised to spend half an hour of each day at the mirror in one's dressing room, plucking out gray hairs," one not particularly witty wag said.

"And he is not referring to your head, Monty," someone else added.

"Or one risks finding the *ladies* discovering one's gray hairs," a third voice said, "just when one has launched into the final phase of seduction."

"And he is not referring to your head, Monty," the same voice repeated.

And so it went on.

"You may not have to worry about gray hairs, Monty. There may never *be* a final phase ever again."

"Of course there will. But he will have to learn to concentrate harder to get it up."

"And to get it in once it *is* up."

"What you *really* need to learn, Monty, is to spot a country mouse from a mile away and run like the wind in the opposite direction."

"But the eyesight begins to dim once one passes one's mid-twenties."

"As do the legs. And other parts."

"Never mind, Monty, old chap. There is always the church as a career."

"And the monastery."

"All of London's courtesans are going to go into collective mourning, Monty. But perhaps they expected this if they knew your birthday was looming."

"I can afford to purchase a new pair of boots at Hoby's with my winnings. You can borrow them, Monty, if you wish, the next time you spot a mouse bearing down upon you looking as if it is about to pounce."

"How far did you get with her, Monty? I am almost disappointed with my winnings, dash it all. Whose prowess can we believe in if we must lose faith in yours? It is the end of an era, by gad, and it is not just the courtesans who will suffer. There should be a national day of mourning."

"Black armbands for everyone."

Jasper took it all with resigned good humor. He had no choice in the matter short of telling the truth, which was even more humiliating than the lie he had told. He did answer the question about how far he had got, though.

"I got absolutely nowhere at all," he said on a mournful sigh. "I did not accomplish even a squeeze or a tickle or a kiss—not even a peck on the cheek. She did take my arm, it is true, but only so that she could lure me off the main avenue in order to have some privacy in which to read me a scold the like of which I have not endured since I was in leading strings. My ears were all blisters within a minute. They are *still* ringing. It was all quite, quite lowering, as you might imagine. So lowering, in fact, that I have decided to creep off into the country in order to lick my wounds and rethink my seductive techniques. This is *not* the end for me. I shall return next year or so, like the phoenix, rejuvenated and better than ever. It is a solemn promise. Gentleman's honor and all that."

The vow was greeted with a guffaw of derisive laughter from a few and a rousing cheer of appreciation from most of those gathered about him.

He was quite serious about leaving. He really was going to withdraw to his country estate for a while. He was going to leave London for Miss Katherine Huxtable's use. He even persuaded himself that his motive was a noble one. It was to save her the pain and embarrassment of risking running into him at every social event she attended for what remained of the Season. If his mind touched upon the possibility that it was just as much to save *himself* the embarrassment of seeing *her,* he firmly quelled the thought.

But it was harder to deny the utter humiliation he felt.

She had been his for the taking. He had been within a whisker of taking her. With one forward thrust she would have been his, and his wager would have been won. He would have enjoyed the experience too. So would she. His reputation would have remained intact—indeed, it would have been enhanced.

She would have been ruined, it was true—but that would not have been his concern since she would not be able to cry rape. She had been more than willing.

But he had stopped. He could still scarcely believe that *he had stopped.*

A crisis of conscience was something quite unfamiliar to him—and it was something he had no intention of cultivating. It would be too deuced uncomfortable and would put far too many restrictions upon his freedom. It had not been conscience that had made him stop but boredom, just as he had told her. Seducing her had been too easy.

He almost believed it, God help him.

He returned home to Cedarhurst Park in Dorsetshire three days after the Vauxhall evening. What he needed, he had decided, was something new upon which to focus his mind and energies, something different, something to alleviate the boredom.

He found that something quite unexpectedly on his own estate, which had run so smoothly and so prosperously all his life under the capable management of three successive and excellent stewards that he had never felt the need to trouble himself over the details. But for the rest of that summer and on into the autumn and through the winter he did just that and surprised both himself and his steward by finding it all rather absorbing. He even discovered that he had ideas.

He would go back to London next year, though. Of course he would. Why would he not? Katherine Huxtable and his strange crisis of conscience and his humiliation before his peers soon receded in memory and became nothing more than ancient history. Indeed, they were soon utterly forgotten.

He told himself so quite frequently.

5

THREE YEARS LATER

MARGARET and Katherine Huxtable did not spend a great deal of time in London. They preferred their quiet life at Warren Hall, their brother's principal estate in Hampshire.

Margaret managed the household with as much capability as she had shown at their cottage in Throckbridge. Katherine worked with the vicar—and with Stephen's blessing—to set up a school in the village near Warren Hall under the tutelage of a reputable schoolmaster. She even helped out with the youngest children there sometimes—just as she had at Throckbridge before their fortunes changed.

She was also being courted by Phillip Grainger, a neighbor not many years her senior. She had rejected two marriage offers from him during the past two and a half years and had told him firmly the second time that she liked him exceedingly well but could never think of him as more than a dear friend.

He had pulled a rueful face and assured her that if he could not have her as a wife, then he would have to settle for her friendship. But sometimes he looked at her with more ardor than a friend ought, and sometimes she wondered if she would accept him should he offer a third time. She was twenty-three years old, after all. Most women her age had fixed their choice long ago.

She no longer believed in romantic love.

Oh, yes, she did. She had not become a complete cynic. But she did not believe in it for herself. She had tried—and failed—so many times to fall in love that she had given up even trying. Yet she wanted to be married. She wanted to be settled in her own home. She wanted children of her own. She certainly did not want to be a dependent of Stephen's all her life.

She could surely have a perfectly happy life with Phillip Grainger. Well, a *contented* life, anyway—and she suspected that contentment was much underrated. Perhaps it lasted longer than the euphoric happiness of romantic love. She liked Mr. Grainger. He would be good to her and their children. But perhaps accepting an offer from him, feeling as she did—or did *not*—would be unfair to him.

Sometimes she and Margaret went to Rigby Abbey in Northamptonshire to visit their sister Vanessa. She and Elliott no longer lived at Finchley Park. They had moved almost two years ago, after the sudden death of Elliott's grandfather, the Duke of Moreland. Elliott held the title now.

Their sister was a duchess.

They sadly missed her. They also missed Isabelle, their young niece, who had been born at Finchley Park. They had not yet seen their newborn nephew, Samuel, Viscount Lyngate.

It was partly to rectify that omission that they had decided to spend the last few weeks of the Season in London this particular year. The Duke of Moreland was in town for the parliamentary session, so of course Vanessa and the children were there too.

So was Stephen, who had just completed his studies and had gone straight to London after coming down from Oxford. He had urged his sisters to join him there to help him celebrate. He was almost twenty-one. Soon he would reach his majority and be fully independent of all guardianship. Soon Margaret would be free of the obligation she had taken on at their father's death eleven years ago to see all her siblings safely to adulthood.

They had been settled at Merton House on Berkeley Square for just one day when Stephen went out to spend the evening with a group of friends. One of them was Constantine Huxtable, their second cousin, of whom Katherine was inordinately fond, though she did not see him often.

Stephen had promised before going out that he would bring Constantine to the house during the evening if the opportunity presented itself. He did not do so, of course—Katherine and Margaret had not really expected that he would. Stephen was an affectionate and generally attentive brother, but he was also a young man, and young men often forgot everything but the pursuit of their own pleasure when they got together with one another.

Margaret retired early, still tired after their journey to town the day before and a lengthy, busy visit with Vanessa and the children during the day. Katherine read for a while longer and was just on her way upstairs to her room when she heard the front door below being opened and then shut.

She could hear Stephen's cheerful voice and the butler's more sober tones in reply. She leaned over the banister to listen, though she could not see down into the hall. And then she heard a deeper voice—Constantine's.

It was late. They had doubtless been drinking and probably intended to have another drink or two in the library. She ought not to go down. They would not be expecting her, and her appearance might embarrass them. Constantine was sure to be in town for a little while. She would see him tomorrow or the next day.

There was a burst of merry male laughter, more indecipherable chatter, and then silence. They had gone into the library and shut the door.

She would just say good night to Stephen, she decided suddenly, running lightly down the stairs, and greet Constantine before they started drinking again. She would stay only a moment.

The butler had already disappeared. Katherine tapped on the door and opened it without waiting for an answer. She smiled at Stephen, who was at the sideboard pouring liquor from one of the crystal decanters into a glass. He was still youthfully slim and graceful, and his blond hair was still as curly and unruly as ever. But he had developed during the last few years into a confident young man who was going to be devastatingly attractive to the ladies. Indeed, he probably already was.

"Stephen," she said.

And then she turned eagerly to their second cousin, who was standing with his back to the fireplace.

"Constantine." She hurried toward him, both hands outstretched. "Stephen was to have brought you here earlier to see Meg and me. I daresay he forgot to tell you. We have not seen you since well before Christmas. How *are* you?"

"Very well," he said, taking both her hands in his and kissing her cheek. "I need not ask you the same question, Katherine. You are obviously blooming with good health and are as lovely as ever. More so, in fact. A lady's beauty is supposed to fade with each passing year. Yours grows more vivid."

He was laughing at her, and she laughed right back.

"Oh, goodness," she said. "I did not come down to listen to such flatteries. I came merely to greet you. I will leave you now, you will be happy to hear. A lady knows when her presence will merely dampen...er, *spirits*."

She turned her head to laugh at Stephen and realized for the first time that there was someone else in the room too. Another gentleman, who was standing beside the oak desk close to the bookshelves, an open book in his hands.

She looked fully at him and their eyes met.

Oh.

Her stomach felt as if it had dropped three feet straight down. Her knees suddenly felt like jelly.

His right eyebrow lifted slightly to half disappear beneath the lock of dark hair that had fallen over his brow. His lips pursed. He inclined his head in a half-bow.

"Oh, I say!" Stephen exclaimed. "My manners have certainly gone begging. I do apologize. Kate, do you know Lord Montford? My sister, Katherine Huxtable, Monty."

"Miss Huxtable," he said in that light, pleasant voice she remembered so well—a voice that somehow wrapped itself about her spine and caused an inward shudder. "My pleasure."

Somehow she commanded her knees well enough to dip into a slight curtsy.

"My lord," she said.

Constantine cleared his throat.

"Allow me to escort you back upstairs, Katherine," he said, stepping forward and offering his arm. "Late though it is, I will pay my respects to Margaret if she is still up."

"She is not," Katherine told him. "And there is no need to escort me. I can find my way alone. Good night."

She smiled brightly at him and at Stephen and hurried toward the door, ignoring Lord Montford. Even so, Constantine was there before her and opened it for her to pass through.

"Good night, Katherine," he said. "I will call upon you and Margaret tomorrow, if I may."

"Night, Kate," Stephen said cheerfully.

Constantine did not shut the library door until she was on the staircase. She lifted a hand and smiled at him and scurried upward.

It had been three years. And yet every one of those years had just fallen away. It could have happened yesterday . . .

The shame of it.

The terrible humiliation.

The hatred—not all of it directed against him.

He had not changed one whit. He was as handsome and as elegant—and as mocking—as ever.

And just as dangerously attractive.

Thank *heaven* Meg had gone to bed already.

*   *   *

Not only had young Merton failed to inform Con that he was supposed to call on his female cousins during the evening, but he had also neglected even to tell him that they were in town. If he had done so, Jasper would have heard it too, and he would not have gone within a mile of Berkeley Square tonight or any other night.

But he *had* gone, so when Katherine Huxtable had come hurrying into Merton's library, all warm smiles and dazzling beauty and flushed animation, Jasper had been taken completely by surprise.

And he had been caught like a rat in a trap.

Waiting for her to see him. To react. To swoon quite away. To have a fit of the vapors. Or of hysterics. To point accusingly at him and appeal to her male relatives for protection and revenge.

None of which had happened.

What shook him more than anything else, though, was that he instantly remembered every detail of that evening as if it had all been yesterday, when in reality it had been . . . how long ago? Two years? Three? Four?

A long time ago, anyway.

He was supposed to have forgotten all about it, was he not?

That was the only wager he had ever lost, before or since. Not that he had really *lost* it. He might have won it with ease with a week and a half to spare. He *thought* he had long forgotten the whole sorry episode, but if he *had* forgotten, then why had he been so thunderstruck when she walked into the library?

He noticed that Con hurried her out of the room as fast as he decently could. He had always wondered if

Con had ever heard of that wager. Nothing had ever been said between them. He suspected that plenty would have been said, though—*and* done—if he had ever claimed victory.

Not that Con was anybody's angel. Far from it. But for some unfathomable reason he seemed fond of his second cousins even though they—or Merton, at least—had taken the title and properties and fortune that would have been his if his father had only married his mother two days sooner than he had. Before Con's birth, that was, instead of just after it, stranding him forever in the land of the illegitimate and unable-to-inherit. It was impossible to know how Con felt about not being Earl of Merton himself. He never spoke of it.

Perhaps secretly he hated Merton.

Jasper wondered after the evening was over if he should perhaps avoid the main entertainments for the rest of the Season, even the ones to which he had already sent acceptances, and confine his activities to the gentlemen's clubs and Tattersall's and Jackson's boxing saloon and other safe places where he could be certain to meet only gentlemen.

But that would be a craven thing to do. Good Lord, when had he ever hidden from anyone? Was he now going to hide away from a *woman* whom he had once kissed and fondled and *not* possessed? He could scarcely believe the idea had even occurred to him.

And what the devil was she doing still unmarried? She must be well into her twenties by now. And no one would ever convince him that she had not had legions of offers over the years. Con had been right about one thing even though he had been teasing her and deliberately flattering her. She *was* more beautiful now than she had been two years ago—or three or four or however the devil many years it had been. And she had been lovely enough even then, by Jove. She had lost that coltish look in the meanwhile, though she was still slender enough to cause a man to imagine spanning her waist with his two hands and drawing her . . .

Well. Dash it all.

He decided to honor the invitations he had already accepted, the next one being a grand ball given by the new Lady Parmeter, whose father was a wealthy cit and not a gentleman at all, and who had therefore been willing to invite anyone who was likely to attend.

Even him.

Not that anyone but the very highest sticklers ever pointedly excluded him, it was true, and those were fusty events that he would not have wanted to attend anyway.

Perhaps the Huxtable sisters would be too high in the instep to put in an appearance at the Parmeter ball. Or perhaps they had arrived in town too recently to have been invited at all.

The event was well attended as it turned out, a fact that was no doubt gratifying to Lady Parmeter. There was a crowd in the ballroom when he arrived somewhat late and looked about him after passing along the receiving line.

Almost the first persons he saw were the Misses Huxtable.

Of course.

There was somehow an inevitability to it all.

They ought to have been attracting no attention at all. Miss Huxtable herself was several years older than Katherine Huxtable—the Duchess of Moreland was their sister and between them in age, was she not?—and therefore ought to be dangerously close to being long in the tooth. Yet in reality she was as lovely as her sister, though she was much darker and more voluptuous of figure—more to his usual tastes, in fact.

They were both attracting a great deal of attention, and plenty of prospective dancing partners, a fact that must be somewhat disconcerting to the veritable army of very young ladies making their debuts and attempting to take the *ton* by storm and lead the most eligible bachelor off in leg shackles.

Jasper spent much of the evening in the card room, where he—and his money—were always welcome. He had little inclination to dance. Which was probably just as well. He still found that there were mothers who looked at him askance as if they thought he was about to lead their daughters to the middle of the dance floor and proceed to ravish them there.

Very often when he attended balls he spent the whole evening in the card room. He did not particularly enjoy dancing. Even less did he enjoy watching ladies and gentlemen of normal good sense mincing or cavorting about a floor trying to look elegant and graceful while at the same time attracting as much admiring attention as possible.

Tonight more than ever he had good reason to keep his nose well clear of the ballroom. But young Merton came looking for him just when he was finishing a hand and gathering in his winnings.

"Ah, there you are, Monty," he said. "You ought to be dancing. There are so many beauties out there that my eyes are dazzled."

He grinned cheerfully.

"And I suppose they all want to dance with you," Jasper said, getting to his feet and setting a hand on the boy's shoulder.

"Well," Merton said sheepishly, "I *am* Merton, you know."

"Which fact will endear you to every female heart until you finally marry the owner of one of them," Jasper said. "But those blond curls and that smile probably have something to do with it too."

The boy looked like an angel, in fact. Fortunately, he possessed enough spirit and firmness of character to save him from appearing either weak or insipid. Jasper genuinely liked him. And the boy was new in town. It was no wonder if he was attracting far more than his share of female attention.

"Come and meet Meg," Merton said. "My eldest sister. She did not come down to the library the other evening when Kate did."

Ah. *Now* what? Hide himself in another game? Accept the inevitable? He accepted the inevitable, largely because he did not like that word *hide.*

"My pleasure," he said with cheerful untruth, squeezing the boy's shoulder.

The orchestra was taking a break. Had it not been, of course, Merton would not have been at liberty to come to the card room. He was much in demand as a dancing partner—and it was definitely not just because he was the Earl of Merton. One had only to look at the smitten, worshipful faces of the very young ladies as he passed to understand that.

It all made Jasper feel like a wizened grandfather at the grand age of twenty-eight. Though his own sudden appearance in the ballroom was not going unnoticed, of course. His lips twitched with amusement—until he recalled where they were going. And if he had entertained any faint hope that Katherine Huxtable would not be standing with her sister, it was soon dashed.

She saw him coming and raised her eyebrows—and her chin. She raised her fan too and wafted it with furious enough vigor to cool an army had there been one standing directly behind her.

"Meg," Merton said with cheerful unawareness of anything untoward in the atmosphere about him, "here is Lord Montford. I promised to bring him along to introduce him. He is Con's friend—and mine too. It is a pity Con could not be here tonight. This is my eldest sister, Monty. She was like a mother to me for years after our parents died—and a better mother no fellow could ever desire."

He beamed affectionately at her as she curtsied.

"Lord Montford," she said.

Her eyes were as blue as her sister's. He had expected that they would be dark, to match her hair. She was indeed a rare beauty. They were a family of beauties, in fact—with the possible exception of the duchess, though she was no antidote either.

"Miss Huxtable?" He bowed. "Miss Katherine?"

She did not curtsy. And she was going to shake her hand right off her wrist if she did not stop fanning her cheeks with such desperate intent.

He turned back to her sister.

"May I hope to lead you into the next set?" he asked. He supposed Merton might expect it of him, and the lady had not recoiled in horror at the sight of him. Either she knew nothing of his notoriety or she was made of stern stuff, like her sister.

"Oh," she said, looking genuinely sorry, "I have already promised the set to the Marquess of Allingham, my lord. He asked me a while ago. But I am much obliged to you for your courtesy."

He inclined his head to her. He could decently fade away to distant parts now.

"Ah, here he comes," she said, looking beyond him and smiling a warm welcome at Allingham.

"I am to sit out with Miss Acton," Merton said a little ruefully. "She is not allowed to waltz, you know, as she has not yet been granted permission by any of the patronesses of Almack's. I had better go and find her. Excuse me, Meg? Kate? Monty?"

And he was gone.

So, within the next few seconds, was Miss Huxtable.

Which left Jasper stranded with the younger sister.

A waltz.

Hmm.

Distant parts—in the form of the card room—beckoned urgently.

"I have heard," he said instead of bowing and hurrying away as fast as he decently could, "that moving a single body part continuously, without rest, can cause rheumatics in later life."

She noted the direction of his gaze, and her fan abruptly stopped waving. Her arm fell to her side.

"*That,*" she said, "would be *my* problem, Lord Montford."

It was not a very witty or original response. But it was firm and spirited enough to show him that she had neither forgotten nor forgiven.

Neither fact surprised him.

"Unlike the infant Miss Acton," he said, "I daresay

you were granted permission to waltz an age ago, Miss Huxtable. Not that I wish to cast aspersions upon your advanced age."

"I am to dance the set with Mr. Yardley," she said.

"Yardley," he told her, "was called away from the card room half an hour or so ago and left at a trot. I believe his wife is in a delicate way and had reached a crisis in her...ah, confinement."

"Oh," she said, and looked mortified.

Perhaps she had not realized Yardley was married. He liked to keep the fact a secret whenever he could, being the consummate ladies' man. This was Mrs. Yardley's sixth confinement if Lord Montford had not missed one or two when he was not paying attention.

"You had better waltz with me instead," he said.

Was he quite insane?

"*Had* I?" Her eyebrows shot up, and her fan went to work on her cheeks again. "I think not, Lord Montford."

"It will appear that you are a wallflower if you do not," he said. "That is a nasty feeling for a lady, I have been told. Especially for ladies of a...ah, certain age."

"*Of a certain—*" Her nostrils flared, her wrist stilled, her bosom swelled, her eyes glared, and...she laughed. Suddenly, unexpectedly, and unmistakably with genuine humor. Memory caught at the edges of his mind.

"How absolutely outrageous of you," she said. "I think it is something I liked about you at one time."

"Until you did not like me at all," he said, tipping his head slightly to one side, his eyes fixed on hers.

"Yes, until then," she agreed. She was looking at him consideringly. "For a long time I thought you the embodiment of evil. But then it struck me that the very fact of your deliberately *not* winning your wager that night proved that there was a shred of decency in you."

He shuddered theatrically.

"That failure," he said, "has been a blot upon my reputation that clings to memory like a limpet. That fact, in addition to the humiliation of having someone think me *decent,* brings me to the very brink of despair."

"Oh," she said, closing her fan with a snap, "you need not worry unduly about that, Lord Montford. I certainly do not think you a *decent* man—only one who on a single occasion in his life did something *almost* decent."

He smiled at her.

"We had better waltz," he said. "You do not wish to be a wallflower, do you? And I do not wish everyone assembled here to see me publicly rejected after I have humbly begged for your hand in the dance."

He thought she would refuse and marveled over the fact that he hoped she would not.

Lord! Devil take it, he had avoided all thought of her for a number of years. She represented his greatest humiliation. The *only* humiliation, in fact. Without her, his glorious reputation would have remained unblemished. It was not a pleasant experience to be forced to admit publicly to all one's peers that one had failed to win a wager. Especially one concerning a woman—and a wager he might have won handily. It was not good for a man's pride.

"Oh, very well," she said briskly, sounding rather cross. "Why not?"

She obviously did not expect an answer. When he offered his arm, she placed her hand on his sleeve and allowed him to lead her onto the floor where all the other dancers were already assembled.

And so here he was, not only in company with Miss Katherine Huxtable again, but also about to *waltz* with her at a *ton* ball.

Whatever next, pray?

The world was about to end?

Pigs about to fly?

The moon about to turn to cheese?

6

KATHERINE had come to the ball with her brother and eldest sister despite considerable misgivings. What if *he* should be there too? She had no wish whatsoever to see him ever again. But such an attitude was cowardly, she had decided. Was *fear* to keep her cowering at home? After *three years*? She could not remain at home throughout her stay in London or avoid the capital for the rest of her life. It would be ridiculous.

Besides, even remaining at home had not protected her from encountering him, had it? He had invaded her home—or Stephen's, to be more accurate. He had been standing in the library as if he had had every right to be there. As he *had,* of course—Stephen had invited him.

And besides again, she *wanted* to attend the ball. Though she did not come to London often and did not crave all the myriad entertainments a Season had to offer, she did enjoy a taste of them now and then.

So she had come tonight, telling herself that it was not the type of event that would attract Lord Montford. And sure enough, when she arrived with Meg and Stephen, he had been nowhere in sight.

But then, just when she had felt assured of his absence, Stephen had mentioned that he was in the card room and that he hoped to entice him out of there long enough to present him to Meg, who had not yet met him. He was a particular friend of Constantine's and therefore of Stephen's.

It had all been very provoking. For how could she have protested and begged Stephen to leave him in the card room where he belonged? He would have wanted to know why. So would Meg.

She had been rather proud of her behavior when Lord Montford had eventually arrived with Stephen. She had remained aloof and slightly frosty without doing or saying anything that might catch her brother and sister's attention. Meg had been unable to accept his offer to waltz with her since she was to dance the set with Lord Allingham, Stephen had gone off to find Miss Acton, Katherine had expected Mr. Yardley to appear any moment to claim his set, and the ordeal was all but over.

She had acquitted herself well.

Why, then, was she now standing on the dance floor facing Lord Montford, about to *waltz* with him?

It all defied rational explanation.

She found herself enveloped in a scent so startlingly familiar that she almost expected to see Vauxhall Gardens spread about her instead of the Parmeter ballroom. It was something expensive and musky and utterly masculine—his shaving soap or his cologne. It was a smell that evoked memories of temptation and unbridled passion and humiliation, none of which powerful emotions she had experienced with such intensity either before that night in Vauxhall or since.

And none of which she had the slightest wish to experience ever again.

Lord Montford was just as handsome as she remembered him, with his tall, slim, elegant figure, his dark hair and arrogant eyebrow and lazy eyelids shading keen, mocking, intelligent eyes. Just as handsome, and just as attractive. And just as dangerous—if she were any longer susceptible to that sort of danger.

Which she was not.

The waltz was about to begin. The musicians had readied their instruments, and a slight hush had fallen on the dancers, who were taking their positions.

Lord Montford's right arm circled her waist, and his hand came to rest against the small of her back. It felt as if it were burning a hole through the satin of her gown. His other hand took hers in a firm, warm clasp. She tried to keep her fingers from touching his hand, but inevitably they curled inward to rest against the back of it. His shoulder beneath her other hand was all solid muscle—as she remembered its being the last time she touched it.

She felt half suffocated with the physicality of it all.

She had never really enjoyed waltzing. She had always found it a little disconcerting to be in close proximity to one gentleman for all of half an hour, and a little tedious to have to make polite conversation exclusively with him. Of course, she had always guessed that with the right partner the whole experience could be gloriously romantic.

Lord Montford was *definitely* not the right partner.

She glared at him, as if he had just verbally claimed that he *was*.

"I suppose," she said, "your intention is to lead Stephen astray while he is still young and foolish?"

Both his eyebrows arched upward.

"And make a degenerate rake of him?" he said. "But of course. Why else would I have befriended him? It could not possibly be because he is the cousin of one of my closest friends, could it? And *is* Merton foolish as well as being young? That does not say much for the upbringing your eldest sister has provided for him."

She had walked into *that* trap with wide open eyes.

"I ought to have chosen my words with more care," she said crossly. "I ought to have used the word *impressionable* rather than *foolish*."

"But is there any real difference?" he asked her. "Is not an impressionable man a foolish man? A weak man? Can I possibly corrupt your brother if he is determined to be incorruptible?"

"I do not know," she said. "*Can* you?"

He could easily have corrupted *her*.

It seemed that not a muscle in his face moved. But his eyes smiled suddenly and wickedly from beneath his heavy eyelids, a change that had an immediate and quite unwelcome effect upon her knees.

"But why would I wish to?" he asked. "Have you made me into the devil incarnate in your imagination, Miss Huxtable?"

"*Is* it imagination?" she asked him.

He chuckled softly. "But you have already admitted to having found a modicum of decency in me," he said. "The devil is surely incapable of anything remotely good. It is a contradiction in terms."

She was saved from having to frame a suitable reply when the music began at last and they started to waltz.

Ah.

And *ah* again.

Her mind was incapable of any coherent thought for the next few minutes.

She had not expected him to be graceful, to move as

if he had been formed specifically to waltz. Though she might have guessed it if she had ever paused to think about it. Such a man would always see to it that he did everything to perfection—riding, fighting, dancing, dicing, making lo—

There! She was thinking, after all.

But only deep down, where unconscious thoughts dwelled. The rest of her became the music and the rhythm and the swirling colors of gowns and candles and the sound of voices and laughter and the smell of a masculine cologne and the smile of lazy dark eyes.

And she had been perfectly right. The waltz *was* gloriously romantic when danced with the right m—

Thought was intruding again.

And with it came the rather horrifying suspicion that for several enchanted minutes she had not removed her eyes from his. And that her lips were curved upward into a smile. And that her cheeks were flushed and her eyes shining.

And that for several minutes she had been enjoying herself quite mindlessly and quite totally—enjoying waltzing and enjoying the company of a man who danced and twirled her about the ballroom just as if there were no floor beneath their feet.

A dangerous man.

Lord Montford, no less.

And she no better than the green girl she had been three years ago.

She let her smile fade and lowered her eyes. How could she *possibly* have been enjoying his company? What was she *thinking*?

She remembered him telling her quite bluntly and insolently and dispassionately about that ghastly wager.

And she wondered again, as she had a thousand or more times since that evening, why he had not completed what he had started and claimed whatever prize there was to claim. She had never wanted to believe—she still did not—that there might be some decency in him, that perhaps he was a man with some conscience. She preferred to believe the explanation he had given at the time—that she had been too easy a prey to be of any real interest to him. Would that have mattered, though, when there was a wager at stake?

"You still hate me," he said softly.

His voice sounded abject—suspiciously so. There was also surely the suggestion of humor in it. She *amused* him.

"Are you surprised?" She raised her eyes to his again.

"Not at all," he said. "You informed me on a certain infamous occasion that I had disappointed you. How can one *not* hate the person who disappoints one in such a way?"

He was definitely laughing at her. But her effort to think of some suitably cutting retort was thwarted when he twirled her about one corner of the ballroom, using fancy footwork that somehow persuaded her own feet to match it. She laughed with delight before she remembered that she was not delighted at all.

"I could teach you *not* to hate me, you know," he said.

She raised her eyebrows.

"Would that not be doing you a favor?" he asked.

"On the assumption," she said, "that if I did not hate you, I would be indifferent to you and would not glare at you every time we met? That would be convenient to *you*, no doubt."

"*Indifferent* to me?" He drew her to a halt for one of

the brief pauses between waltz tunes but did not release his hold on her. "Miss Huxtable, I doubt even I have the power to make you indifferent to me."

Her stomach was performing a somersault again. She could not seem to look away from those lazy eyes.

"I suppose not," she said with a sigh. "Dislike is not indifference, is it?"

He smiled openly and chuckled aloud.

"I could teach you not to hate me *or* dislike me," he said, speaking very low since the music had not yet started again. His eyes dipped to her mouth. "I could teach you to love me if I chose, Miss Huxtable."

She was startled almost speechless.

"Ha!" was all she could manage to say. It was half exclamation, half question.

"Was that agreement?" The music had begun again, a somewhat faster tune this time. He twirled her several times before she could answer. "You admit, then, that I could do it?"

"Never in a million years," she said when she could command her voice. It shook with indignation. "Never in a *billion* years."

"Would it take a billion and one, then?" he asked her. "How very tedious! And how very firm-minded of you. But I believe you underestimate me, Miss Huxtable."

"And *you* underestimate *me*!" she retorted so vehemently that the couple dancing by them both turned their heads to look. "You are about as likely to persuade me to love you, Lord Montford, as I am to persuade *you* to love *me*."

He did not answer. Which was horrible, really, as her words seemed to hang between them and follow them about the dance floor as they waltzed in silence to an exhilarating rhythm, and the growing heat between them made her more and more aware of him physically and more and more uncomfortable.

She quite understood why the waltz was considered fast among a large segment of society. *Fast* as in not quite proper, that was. It was quite the most improper dance ever invented. It was...it was nothing short of lascivious.

Their hands, clasped together, had turned hot and damp.

The faster tune did not last long. Soon, almost without a pause, the orchestra began playing something far slower and more...romantic.

Still they danced without speaking—until eventually he broke the silence between them.

"It *does* seem like an impossibility when phrased that way," he said just as if five minutes or so had not elapsed between her words and his answer. "I have never been in love, Miss Huxtable, and I never expect to be. Lust is far more amusing and satisfying. My falling in love is an absolute impossibility, I am afraid."

"As it is for me," she retorted hotly. "An utter, complete impossibility."

"It is so mutually impossible, in fact," he said, "that it sounds quite perfect for a wager, does it not?"

"A wager?" She looked at him with a frown.

"Oh, I know," he said with an exaggerated sigh. "A refined lady does not lay bets. And anyone who wagers against me, male or female, inevitably regrets it anyway. I never lose, you see."

"Except once," she said tartly.

He raised his right eyebrow. It half disappeared beneath that errant lock of hair.

"Except once," he agreed. "How obliging of you to remind me, Miss Huxtable. Though we both know, do we not, that I forfeited rather than lost that particular one."

"What wager exactly are we talking about now?" she asked him after a short pause.

Was it her imagination, or were they dancing somewhat closer together than they had been a little while ago? She tried to edge backward, but his hand was as firm as a wall against her waist.

"A sort of double wager, I suppose it would have to be," he said. "An interesting prospect. That I can make you fall in love with me for my part, that you can make me fall in love with you on yours."

"Ha!" she said again. "There is *no way on this earth* that you would win your part of the wager even if you were given a thousand years. Or a billion."

"And no way *in this universe* that you would win yours," he said pleasantly. "It is a wager made in heaven, Miss Huxtable, I do assure you. The only wagers worth taking on are the ones impossible to win, you see. All others offer no worthy challenge at all."

"As I did not in Vauxhall?" she said, and could have bitten out her tongue.

His eyes grew very lazy indeed, though a smile lingered in them.

"I told a shocking fib on that occasion," he said. "*That* was not the reason I stopped, Miss Huxtable, and ignominiously lost my wager."

"Oh?" she said. "What *was*?"

"Perhaps," he said, and his eyes mocked her again, "I was afraid I might fall in love with you."

"Ha," she said for the third time though it was a

word—or a syllable—not normally in her vocabulary. Her stomach was into its tumbling act again.

"I could not take the risk, you see," he said, and grinned again.

"What nonsense you speak," she said crossly. "You just claimed never to have been in love and to be quite incapable of loving."

"Perhaps," he said, moving his head a little closer to hers as they turned about a corner of the room again and for a fleeting moment Katherine saw Margaret smiling up at the Marquess of Allingham, "I have been in danger *once* in my life, Miss Huxtable, just as I have lost a wager once. Perhaps you found a chink in my armor that evening and can now find a way through it to my heart."

She stared at him.

"*If* I have one," he added. "I must warn you that I do not believe I have. But you may find yourself challenged by such a disclaimer."

"Nonsense!" she said again.

"You will not know," he said, "unless you try."

"But why would I want to?" she asked him. "What does it matter to me whether you have a heart or not? Or whether you are capable of love or not? Why would I wish to win such a ridiculous wager? Why would I want you in love with me?"

"Because," he said, "by the time you admit that you *do* want such a thing, Miss Huxtable, *you* will be in love with *me*. It will be of the utmost importance to you to know that your love is not unrequited."

He had the most wickedly sinful eyes. They could smile even when no other part of his face was doing so. They could even laugh. They could mock. And they could penetrate all her defenses until she would swear they could see into her mind and even deeper than that.

"If we both succeed," he said, "we can then proceed to live happily ever after. Reformed rakes are said to be the most constant of husbands, you know. And the most skilled and excellent lovers."

"Oooh!" She drew back her head and glared indignantly at him. "You are trying to *seduce* me even now."

He winced theatrically.

"I would really rather you did not use that particular word, Miss Huxtable," he said. "I tried it with you once, and you vanquished me."

"I did *not*!" she retorted, and blushed to the roots of her hair when she realized what admission she had been drawn into.

"Ah," he said, both eyebrows raised, "but you did. I did not proceed to the main feast on that occasion and thus have remained forever famished. We are straying from the point, however. Do we have a wager?"

However had she been drawn into such a conversation—with Lord Montford of all people? But then no other man could possibly talk thus.

"*Of course* we do not," she said scornfully.

"You are afraid, Miss Huxtable," he said. "Afraid that I will win, that you will not. And that you will go into a permanent decline and die of a broken heart, your family weeping inconsolably about your bedside."

She glared at him—and then laughed despite herself at the ridiculous mental image he had conjured.

"*That,*" she said, "is something you really must not flatter yourself into dreaming of, Lord Montford. You would be doomed to certain disappointment. I would not waste such an affecting deathbed scene on you."

He laughed too.

"And what if I *were* to agree to such a preposterous suggestion?" she asked him. "And what if I won *my* wager? You would never admit to being in love with me, would you?"

His eyebrows shot up. He looked astonished—and affronted.

"You are suggesting that I could ever be a liar, Miss Huxtable?" he asked her. "That I am not an honorable gentleman? But even if I did lie, you would soon know the truth. You would be able to watch me sink into a deep depression and become a mere shadow of my former self. I would sigh constantly and piteously and write bad poetry and forget to change my linen."

She could not stop herself from laughing again at the mental picture of Lord Montford in love.

"I would be perfectly honest and admit defeat in the unlikely event that it were true," he said. "Are we speaking hypothetically, though? Are you still determined to be craven and to refuse to engage in the wager?"

"Lord Montford," she said as they twirled again and the light from the candles in the wall sconces became one swirling band of brightness, "let me make myself clear. Despite my agreeing to waltz with you this evening and to engage in this quite improper and absurd conversation with you, I am not the green girl I was three years ago. Although I will be polite to you whenever I encounter you for the rest of the Season, and indeed for the rest of my life, I really have no wish either to see you or to converse with you again. Ever."

"Do I understand," he said after a short pause, "that that was a no?"

She looked at him, exasperated. *Why* was she finding

him ever so slightly likable? Why was she finding his company more stimulating than that of any of the worthy gentlemen she knew?

"It was a no," she said.

"You *are* a coward," he told her. "I shall be forced to engage in a unilateral wager, then—that I can bring you to love me . . . ah, let me see, before the summer is out. Before the first yellow leaf flutters to the ground."

Her nostrils flared.

"If I should hear," she said, "that there is another bet concerning me in any of the infamous gentlemen's betting books—"

"Ah, no," he said, smiling with sudden warm charm. "This will be a private wager between you and me, Miss Huxtable. No, pardon me—between *me* and me since you are unsporting enough to refuse to participate."

"I see," she said testily. "I am to be harassed, then, am I? For your private amusement? You must be very bored indeed, Lord Montford."

"Harassed?" He raised one eyebrow. "I would call it being wooed, Miss Huxtable."

"And left with a broken heart if you succeed," she said. "*Which* you will not, I am happy to say."

"But *I* might be left equally brokenhearted," he told her, moving his head slightly closer to hers as the waltz tune appeared to be coming to an end. "The other half of the wager is that you will cause *me* to fall in love with *you*."

She clucked her tongue.

"I would not waste my time even trying," she said. "Not even if I *wanted* you in love with me. Which I do *not*. In fact, it is the very *last* thing I want."

They had stopped dancing. So had everyone else. The dance floor was slowly clearing.

"But just imagine how it would be, Miss Huxtable," he said, his voice low, eyelids drooped over his eyes, those eyes fixed keenly on hers, "if we were *both* to win. We could have a grand wedding at St. George's in Hanover Square with every member of the *ton* in attendance and then proceed to a lifetime of sleepless nights, making babies and passionate love, not necessarily in that order."

Her nostrils flared again at the same moment as her knees threatened to disintegrate under her. Oh, how dared he?

"And how do you know you will *not* win my wager?" he asked her. "Many ladies have tried to woo me—or rather my position and wealth—and have failed. Perhaps *not* trying will have better success."

"If you choose to amuse yourself with such foolish delusions, Lord Montford," she said, turning away from him, "I cannot stop you. Nor do I have any interest in doing so."

"Ah, cruel heart," he said, taking her hand and setting it on his sleeve to lead her across the floor in the direction of Meg and Stephen. "Mine is already in danger of shattering into a million pieces."

She turned her head to look up at him and found him smiling down at her just as if they were engaged in the most trivial of social conversations.

Gracious heaven, had she really just been having such a conversation with *Baron Montford*? After all these years of demonizing him in her mind, had she just been almost *enjoying* matching wits with him?

He was going to lay siege to her heart—merely for

the pleasure of doing what she had told him was quite impossible.

It *was* impossible.

As impossible as it would be to capture his.

Ooh, if only it could be done. If only she could make him love her and then spurn him, laugh in his face...

"Was not that a lovely waltz?" Meg said as they came up to her. "You dance it very well, Lord Montford. So does Lord Allingham."

"It is possibly," Lord Montford said, "the most romantic dance the world has ever known, ma'am, especially when a man is privileged to dance it with one of the two loveliest ladies at the ball. Allingham danced with one, I with the other."

He spoke with warm charm and not a trace of mockery, but with enough humor not to sound ridiculously fawning. Katherine looked up at him reproachfully, and he took her hand from his sleeve with his free hand, bowed over it, and carried it briefly to his lips.

Sensation licked up her arm, down into her breasts, and on down to pool between her thighs. Well, she had never tried to deny to herself that he was impossibly attractive, had she? That did *not* make him lovable.

"Merton," he said to Stephen, who was grinning from one to the other of them with open good humor, "would you care for a hand of cards in the card room? But no, of course you would not. There are too many young ladies demanding your attention here. Stroll that way with me anyway."

He released Katherine's hand and did not look at her again as he walked off with Stephen.

"Oh, Kate," Margaret said as soon as they were out of earshot, "what a very charming gentleman Lord

Montford is. And exceedingly handsome. I do not believe he took his eyes off you even once while you danced."

"I have it on the most reliable authority," Katherine said, "from Constantine, in fact, that he is a shocking libertine, Meg. And is the Marquess of Allingham still devoted to you? How many times have you refused his hand?"

"Oh, only once," Margaret protested. "And that was three years ago. He does not seem to hold any grudge against me, though. He is a very amiable gentleman."

"Only *amiable*?" Katherine pulled a face.

They smiled rather ruefully at each other before having their attention taken by the arrival of their partners for the upcoming set of country dances.

7

JASPER was not as totally self-absorbed as his behavior in London often suggested. He was carelessly fond of his elder sister, Rachel, who was now married to Laurence Gooding and living in the north of England with him. But he had a deep affection for Charlotte, his young half-sister. So deep, in fact, that he sometimes suspected that she had perfected the art of winding him about her little finger whenever she wanted something badly enough.

She had wanted very badly indeed to come to London with him this year after Easter, and he had brought her. But there were strict conditions attached, one of which being that she spend her days glued to the side of Miss Daniels, her erstwhile governess, now her companion, who could be relied upon to see to it that she behaved with the proper decorum at every moment. Another condition was that she clearly understand that this visit was *in no way* a sort of premature come-out. She was still only seventeen years old.

Her eighteenth birthday was in August. Next year she would make her debut in society. All would be done right and proper when the time came. He was still not quite sure *how* it would be done since Rachel was adamant in her refusal even to *think* about coming to London for a full Season in order to sponsor her half-sister when she had her own home and husband and family to occupy her days. And Aunt Florrie, his mother's only sister, was an invalid and living somewhere in Cornwall. The only other possibility—Lady Forester, Charlotte's Aunt Prunella on her father's side of the family—was really no possibility at all. He would rather keep Charlotte as a permanent resident of the schoolroom than hand her over to the tender mercies of that particular lady. By next year he would have to think of something—some decent way of launching Charlotte into society and onto the marriage mart.

But he had brought her to town this year, bowing to her wheedling arguments that it would be to her advantage *next* year if *this* year she learned her way around London, got to know which were the best dressmakers and the best shops, acquainted herself with all the best galleries and museums and libraries—he had pursed his lips at that particular argument—and perhaps called privately upon a few older ladies who had been their mama's particular friends.

Charlotte was his mother's daughter by her second husband, who had died when she was not quite eight. Their mother had survived him by only five years.

Jasper lay awake thinking about Charlotte's upcoming birthday the night after the Parmeter ball, his fingers laced behind his head, his legs crossed at the ankles. Or, to be more accurate, he was thinking about her birthday *party*.

It was no new thought. He had promised even before bringing her to town that she might have some sort of birthday celebration in August, after she returned home. She had concocted a happy scheme of inviting all the young people of the neighborhood for miles around to a day of frolicking in the park and an evening of charades and country dancing in the drawing room. He had been quite prepared to indulge her. One's young sister turned eighteen only once in her life, after all.

And since that was so, he thought now, then perhaps something altogether grander than her idea would be more the thing. Something far more lavish.

His generosity of spirit did not arise entirely from a selfless motive, of course. There was another.

He gazed up at the pleated silk of the canopy over his head.

He must be mad. Not that *that* was any new realization.

What the devil had got into him? Why ever had he even asked her to waltz? Because she had looked so prunish?

Probably that had been it.

And why had he spent the half hour of their dance trying to wheedle her into agreeing to a double wager with him? Just to see if she could be goaded? She almost had been too, by Jove. Her interest and her pride had certainly been piqued. But she had got cold feet at the last moment.

Why had he then proceeded to pledge himself to winning his side of the nonexistent wager? Only to prove to them both that he could?

No doubt.

Did he *want* her in love with him, though? Of course he did not. The very thought alarmed him. It would be embarrassing for him and possibly painful for her. For all his sins, he had never set out deliberately to hurt anyone. Though he had almost done just that on their first encounter, of course.

Was *that* what had made him stop?

Damnation! What *was* it about the woman?

But he knew the answer. Of all the females he had ever known, she was the only one who had ever been able to hold her own with him verbally. He could still remember that masterly setdown she had given him at Vauxhall when she must surely have been just about expiring from shock and humiliation. She had kept pace with him earlier this evening too.

And you *underestimate* me! *You are about as likely to persuade me to love you, Lord Montford, as* I *am to persuade* you *to love* me.

Ah, yes, that was what had done it.

The woman was irresistible.

He still did not want her in love with him, though, did he?

But he did want her to admit … oh, that she was *infatuated* with him, perhaps.

He was attracted to Katherine Huxtable, an admission that surprised him since he never allowed himself to be attracted to any female he had no hope of bedding. What would be the point, after all, since he was certainly not looking for a leg shackle? He *was* attracted to Miss Huxtable, though—a strange fact when he remembered how assiduously he had avoided even thinking of her for the last three years. *Was* it as long ago as three? She had said it was, and women were usually good at such details.

Odd to think that he might have had her with the greatest ease three years ago. Would he still want her this year if he had had her then? Of course, this year it would not be nearly so easy. For one thing, she would now know what he was up to. For another, she was older and wiser. She was no green girl, she had said earlier. And he believed her.

It was unlikely that she could ever be persuaded to admit that she loved him—or even that she was infatuated with him. As far as he was concerned, they were one and the same thing anyway. But of course, she would be too stubborn to admit either.

He had suggested an unwinnable wager.

A quite irresistible one, in fact.

Which perhaps explained why his thoughts had strayed to Charlotte's birthday and the idea of giving her a party on a far grander scale than he had hitherto intended.

He lay awake for a while longer, plotting and planning and yawning.

It would be diabolical, he decided just before falling off to sleep. But he would not be taking away from her even one iota of her power to tell him that he had lost his wager, would he? She could say no even before that question arose, in fact, and put an end to the wager before it started.

Like a soggy firework.

She would *not* say no. He would see to it that she did not.

He had a wager to win, by Jove, and he never lost a wager. Not even that once. Not really.

"I have been thinking, Char," Jasper said at breakfast the morning after Lady Parmeter's ball, "about your birthday."

She glanced up from her plate.

"*Have* you, Jasper?" she asked rather warily.

She looked very different from Rachel and him. She was golden-haired, hazel-eyed, small, and dainty. And she seemed to have grown overnight from a girl into a young lady—one who was already turning heads on Bond Street and in Hyde Park. Male heads, by thunder. He had caught a few young bucks at it one morning and had stared them into bumbling confusion without even having to resort to the use of his quizzing glass. If he had to crack a few heads together, he would not hesitate to do it.

She was *seventeen*, for the love of God.

Charlotte was also shy, modest, eager, impulsive, occasionally given to excited chatter—a bewildering mix of contradictory characteristics, in fact.

"I have been thinking," he said again now, "that it might be a good idea to have more than just neighbors at Cedarhurst for your birthday. A few of the new acquaintances you have made in town might perhaps be persuaded to join you there for a week or two. You will turn eighteen only once, after all. Why not have a full-blown house party for the occasion?"

She had made some acquaintances even though she had attended no *ton* parties. She was not the only young person languishing in London under the stricture of being slightly too young to attend any real social events.

She leaned slightly toward him across the table, her cheeks flushed and her eyes shining.

"Oh, Jasper, I would like it of all things," she said. "Might I ask Miss Clement and the Misses Dubois? Even perhaps Lady Marianne Willis?"

"I can think of no objection to any one of them," he said, trying to recall who their parents were—friends of his mother's, probably, or friends of friends. Her companion would have made sure that all were thoroughly respectable. "What do you think, Miss Daniels?"

"Miss Clement and the elder Miss Dubois have already made their come-out," she said, "and so will be valuable friends for Charlotte to have next year—though rumor has it that Miss Dubois is about to be betrothed. Miss Hortense Dubois and Lady Marianne will be making their come-out with Charlotte next spring. I think the idea of a house party a splendid one, my lord. It would be a good idea to invite some young gentlemen too, perhaps, and possibly a few slightly older guests who are more established in society."

Jasper nodded his agreement. She had taken the words out of his mouth.

"But what gentlemen will we invite?" Charlotte asked, leaning back in her chair. "And what older people? I know hardly *anyone*. It is most frustrating to be seventeen and more than ten months and yet—"

Her brother held up a staying hand.

"You and Miss Daniels may discuss the guest list between the two of you," he said. "I have other things to do this morning. Miss Daniels is to have the afternoon off to call upon the Reverend Bellow's sister, is she not? It would be a pity for you to be confined alone to the house on such a fine, warm day, Char. I will come home for luncheon and then take you out with me, shall I?"

"With *you*, Jasper?" She beamed at him, her complaints about the frustrations of her age instantly forgotten.

"The young Earl of Merton is a friend of mine even though he has only just come down from Oxford and has not quite reached his majority," he said. "He is a cousin of Con Huxtable's. His sisters have recently joined him here in town. They grew up in the country as daughters of a clergyman before Merton inherited the title. They are both older than you, but their friendship would certainly do you no harm at all. They are, in fact, just the sort of slightly older, more established members of society Miss Daniels just spoke of. We will perhaps call upon them at home this afternoon. I have an acquaintance with them, and I believe you will like them."

"Oh, Jasper," she said. "I will look forward to it ever so much. I will be with *you*. I could not possibly be happier."

Sometimes he felt uncomfortably unworthy of such unconditional worship. That was especially true today, for of course he had an ulterior motive in the planned visit—*and* the planned house party—despite the fact that he really did believe the Huxtable sisters would be kind to Charlotte and would not look askance at being called upon by someone so young.

"Charlotte," Miss Daniels said, setting her napkin down beside her plate and getting to her feet, "we had better go up to your sitting room and put our heads together over this list. How many guests are there to be, Lord Montford?"

"A dozen?" he suggested. "*Five* dozen? As many as the rooms at Cedarhurst will hold? As many as you and Charlotte can persuade to come?"

"Carte blanche, in other words?" She smiled at him. "I believe we can make do with carte blanche, can we not, Charlotte?"

"Oh, this is going to be the *best* birthday ever," Charlotte said as she followed her companion from the room. "And you are the *best* of brothers, Jasper, and I love you." She hugged him about the neck and planted a noisy kiss on his brow as she passed his chair.

Before next Season was out, he thought ruefully as the door closed behind them, her thoughts were going to be stuffed full of beaux, and *Jasper* was going to be relegated to the role of rather dull elder brother. But those beaux had better be worthy of her, by thunder!

He hoped the Huxtable sisters would be at home this afternoon.

He drummed his fingertips on the table, pursed his lips, and stared off into the middle distance.

She still used the same soap for washing her hair. He had noticed that last evening as soon as he started to waltz with her. He had not realized before how powerful the sense of smell could be in evoking memories. Not all of them unpleasant, strangely enough.

He had better stop woolgathering, he decided, and take himself off to White's to read the morning papers and find some congenial companionship to fill in the rest of the morning hours. He had already looked through the post and decided which invitations to accept and which to reject. He had set aside the fortnightly report from Cedarhurst to read later.

Before he could rise from the table, however, and follow his sister and Miss Daniels from the room, his butler arrived on the scene, a card on a silver platter in his hand and a look of open disapproval on his face.

"The gentleman hopes to see you immediately, my lord," he said as Jasper took the card from the tray. "*Or sooner.* His exact words, m'lord."

Jasper was given no chance to read who it was who had such an urgent need to see him. The visitor did not wait in the hall to be properly admitted. He strode into the breakfast parlor almost on the butler's heels.

Jasper raised one eloquent eyebrow.

"Clarrie!" he said with heavy irony. He did not get to his feet. "This is an unexpected pleasure. Come in and make yourself at home. No need to stand upon ceremony here."

Clarence Forester—*Sir* Clarence since the demise of his father eighteen months or so ago—hated almost more than anything else in the world to be called Clarrie. Hence Jasper had never called him anything else all their lives. He was Aunt Prunella's beloved only son, Charlotte's cousin, and a weasel of the first order. Jasper noted his expanding girth and thinning fair hair and florid complexion. It had been a while since he had seen the man. He was not maturing well though he could not be a day older than twenty-five.

"My dear mama and I arrived in town yesterday," Clarence explained, eyeing an empty chair as though he thought it might collapse beneath him if he sat on it and then lowering himself onto another. "We came with all the speed we could muster as soon as we heard."

"All the way from Kent?" Jasper asked. "Pour Sir Clarrie some coffee, if you will be so good, Horton. He looks in dire need of sustenance. Sprang your horses, did you, old boy? That was rash of you. Sprung horses have a tendency to become lame horses if they do not have very skilled hands at the ribbons."

"Sir *Clarence,* that is," Clarence said pointedly in the direction of Horton. "And bring me some porter instead."

Jasper nodded when Horton looked his way.

"We have *heard,*" Clarence said, leaning back while

his glass of porter was being set down in front of him, "though I am sure you will correct me if we heard wrongly as we surely must have done, Jasper. We have *heard* that you have brought Cousin Charlotte to London."

Jasper looked politely at him.

"All of which goes to prove," he said agreeably, "that your ears are in fine working order, Clarrie. Were you worried about them?"

"She *is* here, then?" Clarence asked.

"Body and soul," Jasper agreed. "Mind too, I daresay. Charlotte is nobody's genius, but Miss Daniels has educated her as well as she is able, and she is an admirable woman. They have even visited a few token galleries and museums together since coming here. I have been vastly impressed."

Clarence drew an audible breath and swelled alarmingly. There was a thin mustache of porter on his upper lip. It made him look slightly rakish.

"It *is* true, then," he said. "I hoped desperately that it was not. So did Mama. She said so all the way here in the carriage. 'I do *hope*, Clarence,' she said a dozen times if she said it at all, 'that this *is* a wild-goose chase we are on, unlikely as it seems when Jasper is involved.' I have been forced to believe a number of painful and wicked things about you in the past number of years, Jasper, try as I have to be charitable toward a man who is my uncle's stepson. I know he was as fond of you as if you had been his own flesh and blood even if you did try his patience almost every day of your life. But this beats all. This puts you beyond the pale. This merits a visit to my great-uncle Wrayburn, much as I hesitate to disturb the peace of the old gentleman. Mama is prostrate with distress."

"That must be uncomfortable for her," Jasper said, folding his napkin and setting it beside his plate. "Perhaps if you were to prop up her head with some pillows, Clarrie? Or her feet? Or both? Do you have enough pillows?"

Dash it all—Aunt Prunella in town. And Clarrie. Two for the price of one. Charlotte would be wishing she had stayed at Cedarhurst. Especially as they were after her blood. No, correction—it was *his* blood they were after.

"Your tone of levity does you no credit, Jasper," Clarence told him. "It never did. Uncle, alas, trusted that you would grow up given time. I knew you never would."

"It is always an enormous satisfaction, is it not," Jasper said lazily, "to be proved right? Especially when it is something nasty that one has predicted. If it *is* nasty to accuse me of being an eternal boy, that is. Perhaps you meant it as a compliment? As a suggestion that I have discovered the fountain of youth, perhaps? I shall choose to take your words as a compliment, old boy, and thank you from the bottom of my heart. You had better refill Sir Clarrie's glass, Horton. It is dry."

"Sir *Clarence*," Clarence said through his teeth. "You *must* know, Jasper, that it is quite shockingly unseemly to bring a young girl to town when she has not yet made her come-out. It is enough to give any high-stickler heart palpitations and a fit of the vapors, and Mama is the highest of sticklers."

"You had better not let Charlotte hear you refer to her as a girl, Clarrie," Jasper said kindly, "especially a *young* girl. She considers herself a young lady now—with good reason, I might add. But you and your mama might decide with some relief that you have indeed been dashing after a wild goose. When you ask around, as you surely will, you will discover that Charlotte has not been seen at any *ton* events or done anything else that is remotely inappropriate to her age and circumstances. *I* may know no better, old chap—you are quite right about that—but Miss Daniels certainly does. I would warn you not to try taking her to task for any imagined improprieties. She is to be a clergyman's bride before Christmas, and the Reverend Bellow may take it into his head to excommunicate you or some such unfortunate thing if you offend her. It is true that he is the most amiable, mild-mannered of gentlemen, but there is no saying what effect an insult to his beloved might have upon him. *I* would not wish to put the matter to the test myself."

Clarence dashed the back of his hand over his mouth, obliterating the rakish mustache.

"You make a joke of everything, Jasper," he said. "Charlotte is of impeccable lineage, and she is a considerable heiress. It is quite imperative that she not be seen in public until after she has made her curtsy to the queen next year. You have quite recklessly flouted the terms of Uncle's will. I am here to see that you do not continue to do so. Great-Uncle Wrayburn will see to it also once I have had a word with him."

"You will give him my regards when you call?" Jasper said pleasantly.

Throughout the visit he had been wondering why Charlotte's aunt and cousin had suddenly exerted themselves on her behalf when they had not done so anytime during the past ten years since the death of her father or even the last five since the death of her mother. The greatest interest Lady Forester had ever shown in her niece was a lengthy letter twice a year—at Christmas and on her birthday—to admonish her to be good and virtuous and to listen to her governess more than to anyone else in her life. Jasper, the implication had always been, was the *anyone else* in her life.

He thought he understood now, though. Clarence had mentioned that one telling detail about Charlotte's being a *considerable heiress.* And come to think of it, she had read out one passage of her aunt's letter last Christmas—the paragraph in which Lady Forester had mentioned hearing from dear Rachel and had proceeded to assure Charlotte that if her sister would not bring her out after her eighteenth birthday, *she* most certainly would. Indeed, it was something she had always intended, something Charlotte's dear *papa* had always intended if her mama should happen to be deceased when the time came. In the same paragraph she had mentioned that dear Clarence was eagerly looking forward to becoming reacquainted with his cousin and that he was now a fine figure of a young man and quite ready to settle down once he had met a lady worthy of him.

Charlotte had made Jasper promise that she would never be turned over to her aunt and cousin, whom she disliked almost as much as he did.

The trouble was that although Jasper was Baron Montford and always had been, his father having predeceased his birth by one month, and although he was owner of Cedarhurst Park, where his mother and her second husband had lived until both their deaths and where Charlotte had always lived, and although he was Charlotte's half brother and closest male relative—despite all those facts in his favor, he was not in fact her sole guardian. His mother's second husband had neither liked nor trusted him, and while he had bowed to his wife's persuasions sufficiently to name Jasper in his will as one of Charlotte's guardians until her fortune became her own either at her twenty-first birthday or on her wedding day, whichever came first, he had also insisted upon naming two other gentlemen as joint guardians—his own uncle, Seth Wrayburn, and his brother-in-law, Sir Charles Forester. Clarence had inherited one third of the joint guardianship on his father's death.

All of which meant that any two of the guardians could outvote the third on any matter concerning Charlotte's life and well-being.

Jasper had always taken comfort from the fact that Seth Wrayburn, an elderly, indolent hermit, had never once shown even an ounce of interest in either Charlotte or Clarence or indeed any of his family. Or in Jasper himself for that matter.

"Mama," Clarence said now, "is quite prepared to sacrifice her time and energy and independence in order to give Charlotte the respectable home she needs and the proper preparations for her come-out that she suspects are being sorely neglected. It is something I daresay you are prepared to agree to, Jasper, since you must wish what is best for your half sister. I will forgo my visit to Great-Uncle Seth if you will agree to relinquish her into my care and Mama's tomorrow. One does not wish for any dissension among her guardians, after all, and I daresay you will be glad to be free of the responsibility. What do you say?"

He attempted to look jocular, and merely looked ridiculous instead.

Jasper had the very nasty suspicion that the *worthy lady* Clarence was supposedly looking for was going to be Charlotte. She was his first cousin, it was true, and a union between them would be distasteful even if not illegal. She was also very rich—and Clarence's father had liked to play deep at the tables but had lacked either skill or luck. What he had probably *not* lacked at his death was debts.

Jasper's brow was creased in thought, and Clarence's manner became almost sprightly.

"I can see no flaw in your argument, I must confess, Clarrie," Jasper said. "Except that I do indeed wish what is best for Charlotte and quite fail to see how I might fulfill that wish by relinquishing her into your care and your mama's. Forgive me if I am being dense. Perhaps Wrayburn will understand better. Perhaps you had better pay him that call after all, old chap. I do not doubt he will be delighted to see you. In the meanwhile I find myself unable to sit here exchanging pleasantries with you any longer, despite the fact that you are my *almost*-relative. Are you ever thankful for the small mercy inherent in that *almost,* Clarrie, as I am? I have to be busy this morning."

"Boxing at Jackson's or looking over horseflesh at Tattersall's, I suppose," Clarence said scornfully.

"Dear me," Jasper said, getting to his feet, "nothing so strenuous, Clarrie. Spare me, old chap. I daresay we will see you *and* your mama within the next few days though I must warn you—with regret—that we plan to be from home on that particular day."

"I did not *name* a day," Clarence pointed out.

"Ah," Jasper said, "did you not? We plan to be from home that day anyway. You found your own way in, old chap. Be so good as to find it again on the way out, will you? It is so very tedious to have to walk all the way to the front door merely to see a guest off the premises when it is so much easier to proceed immediately upstairs."

He inclined his head courteously and preceded Clarence from the room. He went up the stairs without looking back.

The nonchalance of his movements was not quite matched by the grimness of his thoughts, though.

Seth Wrayburn was an unknown quantity. He always had been.

One could only hope that he would recognize a prize ass when he saw one—even if that ass *was* his greatnephew.

8

KATHERINE was in the drawing room with Margaret when the butler came up with a visitor's card on a silver salver. They already had one visitor—Constantine had been with them for almost half an hour, having returned with Stephen from a long morning spent together at Tattersall's. They were not expecting anyone else. Indeed, they had been about to go walking in the park when the men had arrived.

"It is Lord Montford," Margaret said after lifting the card from the tray. She looked directly at Katherine and raised her eyebrows.

"Monty," Stephen said gladly. "Oh, show him up by all means. He was at the ball last evening, Con. Did I tell you?"

"Was he?" Constantine said. "I suppose he spent all evening in the card room relieving a few of the other guests of their fortunes."

"Not *all* evening," Stephen said. "He actually danced once."

Oh, please, Stephen, say no more.

Katherine wished fervently that she could obliterate that dance from both fact and memory. It had kept her awake half the night. She had been able to think of little else all day. Goodness, she had almost been goaded into agreeing to that ridiculous and horribly improper wager he had suggested. She could not *believe* she had almost agreed. With *Lord Montford* of all people.

But just imagine how it would be, Miss Huxtable, if we were both to win. We could have a grand wedding at St. George's in Hanover Square with every member of the ton in attendance and then proceed to a lifetime of sleepless nights, making babies and passionate love, not necessarily in that order.

Oh!

And now, just as those words were popping into her mind for surely the dozenth time—at a conservative estimate—since they had been spoken, he was stepping into Stephen's drawing room, looking handsome and immaculately elegant. He was escorting a young and exquisitely pretty lady.

Oh, how dared he come like this after last evening—and after three years ago. Except that he had declared last evening that he had a wager to win, and he could not do that without contriving meetings with her.

He bowed and the young lady curtsied deeply.

"Miss Huxtable," he said, focusing his attention—and his charm—upon Margaret. "I have come to tell you how delighted I was to make your acquaintance last evening, even if I was not fortunate enough to secure a dance with you. And I have been presumptuous enough to bring my young half sister, Charlotte Wrayburn, with me in the hope that you will allow me to present her to your notice and Miss Katherine Huxtable's."

He oozed respectability and perfect good manners, Katherine noticed in some indignation.

"But of course." Meg hurried across the room, reaching out her right hand to the girl as she went. "Miss Wrayburn. How delightful! Meet my sister too, and our brother, the Earl of Merton. And our cousin, Mr. Constantine Huxtable."

The girl blushed and made a series of curtsies as Meg indicated each of them in turn.

"I have not yet made my come-out," she explained, "because I am not quite eighteen. But Jasper and Miss Daniels, my companion, have said that it is unexceptionable for me to make a few carefully selected acquaintances this year."

"And since I wished to call here anyway," Lord Montford said, "and Miss Daniels is otherwise occupied this afternoon, I suggested that Charlotte accompany me."

"I am delighted you did, Monty," Stephen said, smiling and bowing. "I shall be sure to reserve a set with you at your come-out ball next spring, Miss Wrayburn — well in advance and on the strength of a prior acquaintance."

She laughed and blushed.

"Charmed, Miss Wrayburn," Constantine said with a smile.

"And I am delighted too," Margaret said. "Do come and sit here beside me, Miss Wrayburn. Constantine, pull the bell rope beside you, if you will, and I will have more tea and cakes brought up. Lord Montford, please have a seat."

Katherine, who had got to her feet on the entry of the visitors, sat down on the half of the love seat she had been occupying before. Before Constantine could pull the bell rope and rejoin her on the other half, Lord Montford took it. And as he did so, he looked at her for the first time since he had entered the room — with a very direct, very intense, very...sizzling glance that was hidden from all the other occupants of the room.

It was a glance quite deliberately intended to discompose her, of course, and announce to her that he had not for a moment forgotten last evening or his determination to win his wager.

Neither his shoulder nor his thigh touched her own after he had seated himself, but she could *feel* both, and her heart raced, half with indignation and half with an awareness of his physical proximity even stronger than she had felt last evening when they had actually been touching.

"I trust, Miss Huxtable," he said, turning his head to address Katherine, "you enjoyed the ball last evening?"

"I did, indeed, my lord, I thank you," she said. *Despite the fact that one particular waltz ruined it,* she would have added if there had not been the chance that someone else might have overheard the words.

"So did I," he said. "It is always a pleasure, is it not, to discover some of one's dearest friends at any social entertainment."

His manners were impeccable. His eyes smiled. Only she, who was looking into them from the distance of a mere foot or so, could see the merriment and the mockery lurking in their depths. He was enjoying himself.

Miss Wrayburn, who was at first blushing and silent, soon relaxed under the combined kind ministrations of Meg and Stephen, and chattered happily upon any topic that was suggested to her. Katherine smiled warmly at her.

"Ah," she said as Margaret poured the tea and Stephen offered the cakes, "so you have a love of the country too, Miss Wrayburn. So do I. Much as I enjoy the occasional visit to London, I am always more than happy to return home."

She talked determinedly about Warren Hall and even about Throckbridge. She talked about Isabelle and Samuel, her niece and nephew, and about Vanessa, her sister. She did not monopolize the conversation—that would have been discourteous—but she did talk more than she usually did.

And at every moment she was aware of the man who sat almost silently at her side and at whom she did not once glance. But she *knew* he was amused. She *knew* he was aware of her awareness and was deliberately causing it. *How* he did it she did not know, but after sitting beside him for ten minutes or so she felt as if her left side were on fire and as if her heart were running a footrace uphill against a stiff wind.

She deeply resented all this. *Why* had she not simply refused to dance with him? But she had done so, had she not? And had danced with him anyway?

Lord Montford, she concluded, was a master puppeteer, and she was his helpless marionette.

It was a thought that made her bristle and turn her head to glare at him. He was looking politely back at her, a benign smile on his lips.

"Your sister being the Duchess of Moreland," he said.

"I suppose you have not met her," Katherine said, turning back to Miss Wrayburn. "Perhaps we may have the pleasure of taking you to call on her one day. She would enjoy that, and I am sure you would like her. She has the sunniest nature of us all, does she not, Meg?"

The girl was delightful. Even so, it was perhaps not the best of ideas to prolong their acquaintance with her since she had the distinct misfortune to be a half sister to Baron Montford. The words had been spoken now, though.

"A *duchess*," Miss Wrayburn said, looking suddenly nervous again. But then she smiled brightly. "I would indeed like it."

"And perhaps," Meg said, "you would care to accompany Kate and me on a walk in Hyde Park tomorrow afternoon, Miss Wrayburn—if you do not have other, more interesting plans, that is."

"Oh, I do not," the girl assured her, leaning forward in her chair. "I am not *out* yet and have been hardly *anywhere* except to a few shops and galleries. And I have met hardly *anyone* except ladies as old as my mother, though some of them do have daughters like me, it is true, and sons. Walking in the park with you sounds very interesting indeed to me. I will come. *May* I, Jasper? I do hope it will not rain."

"I shall escort you, Char," he said, "if the company of a male will not offend Miss Huxtable and her sister. I will certainly be the envy of every other gentleman in the park when I am seen with three of the loveliest ladies in town."

They had, of course, Katherine realized, played *right* into his hands. He must have hoped for just this sort of chance to see them—or *her*—again. He had not even had to exert himself beyond coming here to introduce his young sister.

"*Jasper!*" Miss Wrayburn laughed gleefully. "How silly you are."

"What?" he said. "I ought to have said with *two* of the loveliest ladies, then, Char? I have overlooked all sorts of imperfections in your appearance, have I, because you are my sister and I am partial to you?"

He spoke to the girl with a lazy affection in his voice, Katherine noticed grudgingly. She did not want to discover that there was any goodness in him.

"You have certainly not, Monty," Stephen said. "There are no imperfections in either my sisters or yours. And not *all* the other gentlemen will envy you. You are not to be allowed to have the pleasure of walking with the ladies entirely to yourself. I will come along too."

"That will be lovely, Stephen," Katherine said. "It always gives me the greatest pleasure to walk on your arm and watch all the young ladies expire with envy as they pass."

She was aware, even though she did not look directly at Lord Montford, that he pursed his lips and looked amused.

"I would come too," Constantine said, "but I have another commitment for tomorrow, alas."

Lord Montford rose to his feet and raised his eyebrows in his sister's direction, and they proceeded to take their leave.

"I shall look forward with the greatest of pleasure to tomorrow afternoon," he said as he bowed over Meg's hand. He favored Stephen and Constantine with an affable nod. He ignored Katherine, whose hand Miss Wrayburn was shaking.

Except that he had somehow conveyed the message that the words spoken to Meg were intended for her.

Oh, *how* did he do it?

And was it just her imagination? Was she being ridiculous?

She knew she was not.

He had set himself the task, purely for his own amusement and because he was a very bored gentleman indeed, of making her fall in love with him.

Even though she had assured him it could not be done in a billion years.

That assurance, of course, had merely goaded him on.

"It was a *waltz* Monty danced last evening," Stephen said after the visitors had left. "With Kate. He dances as well as he seems to do everything else. I could not waltz, alas. I was obliged to sit out with Miss Acton because she has not yet been granted permission to waltz."

Constantine was looking steadily at her, Katherine was aware. She turned her head and smiled more fully at him.

"And Monty brought his half sister to call upon you this afternoon," he said to her, shaking his head slightly, "even though she has not yet made her come-out. I can remember warning you against him once a long time ago, Katherine. Nothing has changed, you know. Monty is one of my closest friends, but if I had a sister, I would not allow her within five miles of him unless she had a chaperone chained to each wrist."

She laughed.

So did Stephen.

"Constantine!" Margaret said reproachfully. "Lord Montford is a gentleman. His manners are more than pleasing. And his fondness for Miss Wrayburn is to be commended."

"I am no green girl, Constantine," Katherine said— just as she had said last evening to Lord Montford himself.

"I suppose not," Constantine admitted. "I forget

that by now you are almost elderly, Katherine. You are ... what? Three-and-twenty? Do remember, though, that he is not safe company for any unescorted lady."

"And you *are*, Constantine?" she asked with a laugh.

He winced deliberately. "Sometimes," he said, "it takes one rakehell to recognize another. *Not* that I am making any admissions that might incriminate me."

She loved him dearly—he was a second cousin they had discovered late in life. He had always been kind to them. Yet she was aware that she really did not know him at all. He hardly ever came to Warren Hall, and he was not often in London either—neither were they, of course. He had a home and estate in Gloucestershire but had never invited them there or told them anything about it. And he had a long-standing quarrel with Elliott, Duke of Moreland—his first cousin and her brother-in-law—that had somehow drawn Vanessa in too a few years ago. Neither of them spoke to him whenever they could decently avoid doing so. Katherine had no idea why. There was, in fact, an intriguing aura of mystery surrounding Constantine that was, she supposed, part of his appeal.

Was he a rakehell? He was a friend of Lord Montford's and every bit as dashing and handsome as he was, even if his looks did narrowly escape perfection because of his nose, which had been broken at some time in the past and not quite straightened afterward. Though actually the bend in his nose made him look more attractive than perfection would have done.

"Enough of this," Margaret said firmly. "You will stay for dinner, Constantine? Bar the doors, Stephen, lest he say no."

"Coercion succeeds with me every time," Constantine

said. "But so does a friendly invitation. I will be delighted to stay."

And so, Katherine thought, she was surely doomed to another disturbed night. She was to go walking with Lord Montford tomorrow—and Meg and Stephen and Miss Wrayburn. She must make a determined effort to walk with one of *them*.

She must also pray very fervently that it would rain tomorrow.

The five of them went walking as planned the following afternoon, which was fortunately fine, even sunny, after a damp, unpromising morning. Jasper walked with Miss Huxtable while Merton had Charlotte on one arm and Miss Katherine Huxtable on the other. After they had all spent a while down by the Serpentine, admiring the swans and watching a young boy sail his small boat on the water under the eagle eye of his nurse, they walked back again with Merton between Charlotte and his eldest sister and Jasper with the younger.

As he had planned from the start, of course. One must never be too obvious in such pursuits, but one must be relentless. He had maneuvered the exchange without any of the others even suspecting that maneuverings were going on. Except, perhaps, Katherine Huxtable herself. She favored him with a tight-lipped but otherwise expressionless stare as she took his arm.

"Miss Wrayburn is charming," she said almost vengefully.

"But sometimes anxious about how she will be received," he said, inhaling to see if he could catch a whiff of that soap smell again. He could. It was faint but unmistakable. It must be the most seductive scent ever invented.

She looked very fetching too in a sage green, high-waisted walking dress with a straw bonnet adorned with ruched pale green silk about the crown and ribbons of a matching color beneath her chin. Her hair looked very golden beneath its wide brim.

"Oh, but she need not be anxious with us," she said. "There is no reason to be. We are very ordinary people."

"Indeed?" He looked down at her with raised eyebrows, but she was being quite serious. "One wonders, then, what *extraordinary* people would be like. One might need an eye shade just to look at them."

She clucked her tongue and raised a reproachful face at the same time.

"That was a compliment, was it?" she said dryly. "Thank you, my lord, on behalf of Stephen and Meg."

"Charlotte is very taken with you," he said quite truthfully. "And with your sister," he added to be fair. "She is flattered by your kindness and condescension in taking notice of her."

"It is hardly condescension," she said. "We were very ordinary mortals indeed just a few years ago and living in a small cottage in a small country village. I was contributing to our meager income by teaching at the village school a few mornings a week. The most glamorous events in our lives were the infrequent village assemblies and the annual summer fete at Rundle Park, the manor of Sir Humphrey Dew. Our circumstances have changed since then, but we have not, I hope. I liked us as we were."

Was she deliberately making herself sound dull? He felt a wave of amusement.

"I believe, Miss Huxtable," he said, dipping his head a little closer to hers, "I would have liked you then too. Did you dance about a maypole on the village green every spring, by any chance? There is nothing more enticing than the sight of a lovely woman weaving her ribbon about the pole, dipping and swaying and flashing her ankles as she goes."

"No maypoles." But she laughed suddenly. "And no flashing ankles."

He felt enveloped by sunshine and warmth and noted with some surprise when he glanced upward that the sun was hidden behind clouds. It amazed him that he had tried to forget her for three whole years, that his memories of her had not been pleasant ones. That, of course, was because his memories of her had been all tied up with memories of humiliation.

"No maypoles or flashing ankles," he said. "How very sad. Though perhaps not. Perhaps the males of your village from the age of twelve to ninety were thereby saved from unutterable suffering at your hands—or should I say rather, at your *ankles*."

"I wonder, Lord Montford," she said, though her face still laughed, "if you have any skill or experience with *ordinary* conversation."

"But of course I have," he said, all astonishment. "I am a gentleman, am I not? You wound me with your assumption that I have none."

"But I have never heard any evidence of it," she said.

"Would you say," he said, looking upward, "that those clouds overhead presage more rain to come later? I would say not. You will observe that they are white and fluffy and really quite benign. And there is blue sky beyond them. My prediction is that in one hour's time, or even less, the sky will be a pure blue and we will bask in the bliss of it for a short while before the pessimists among us start to worry about tomorrow. Have you noticed how good weather invariably brings on the prediction that we will have to suffer for it with some shockingly infelicitous storm in the near future? Have you ever heard anyone do the opposite? Have you ever heard anyone on a day of cold sleet and arctic gales gloomily predict that we will suffer for this with blue skies and sunshine and warmth at some time in the future?"

She was laughing out loud.

"No, I never have," she said. "But is this *ordinary* conversation, Lord Montford?"

"The topic is the weather, is it not?" he said. "Could anything be more ordinary?"

She did not answer, but she continued to smile.

"Ah," he said, "I understand. You did not mean *ordinary* at all, did you? You meant *dull*. Yes, I am capable of dull conversation too, and will demonstrate if you wish. But I must warn you that I may fall asleep in the middle of it."

"You need not worry about that," she said. "I would be asleep before you."

"Ah, an interesting admission," he said, moving his head a little closer to hers, "and one I may use to my advantage at some future date."

"You would be unable to," she said. "You would be asleep too."

"Hmm. A thorny problem," he admitted.

"Besides, Lord Montford," she said, "you cannot make me fall in love with you while I am asleep, can you? And

I assume that is what this is all about? This visiting me with your sister? This walking in the park with us?"

"While you are asleep?" he said, moving his head even closer to hers.

And actually, in his attempt to arouse her interest in him, he was arousing himself to no small degree. The idea of making a sleeping woman—all warm and languorous in the depths of a soft mattress—fall in love with him had a very definite appeal. Good Lord!

"Miss Huxtable, you are quite—"

He got no further. They had progressed by this point to a more public part of the park, and the daily promenade had begun—vehicles of all descriptions, horses, pedestrians, all jostling for space on the crowded thoroughfares, all vying for attention. For the purpose was less to acquire air and exercise than it was to see and be seen, to show off new bonnets and new mounts and new beaux, to see and criticize other, inferior bonnets and mounts and beaux. It was the *ton* at play.

And one garishly ostentatious open barouche, which was almost abreast of Jasper and Miss Huxtable, was slowing and then drawing to a halt. Its occupants peered down at them with frowning disapproval—or at him, actually.

Lady Forester and Clarence, by thunder!

He had been hoping to avoid them for what remained of the Season, though it was admittedly a forlorn hope when they had come up from Kent for the precise purpose of displaying their displeasure with him and snatching Charlotte out of his wicked clutches.

He had not even told Charlotte about their arrival in town. Why distress her before it was strictly necessary?

"Lady Forester?" He touched the brim of his hat to

the lady. He had not called her Aunt Prunella—or even Aunt Prune—since he was a boy. She was no aunt of his, for which fact he would give daily thanks if he were a praying man. "Clarrie? How do you do? May I have the pleasure—"

But apparently he might *not* have the pleasure of introducing Miss Katherine Huxtable to them—or her sister and brother either.

"Jasper," the lady said in awful tones and with a swelling of the bosom that he remembered well, "I will see you *in my own home* tomorrow morning at *precisely* nine o'clock. Charlotte, step away from that man's side *this minute* and come up here to sit beside me. I would have expected *you* to know better even if your half brother does not. I *thought* you had a respectable governess."

"Aunt *Prunella*!" Charlotte exclaimed with a gasp and a look of open dismay.

"Oh, I say!" young Merton exclaimed at the same moment, indignation in his voice.

"Clarence," his mother said, "get down this instant and assist Charlotte."

"You had better stay where you are, Clarrie, old boy," Jasper advised. "It would be a waste of effort to hop down here only to have to hop right back up again. And you stay where you are too, Char, with Miss Huxtable and the Earl of Merton. You are not footsore, are you?"

"N-no, Jasper," she said, her eyes as wide as saucers.

"Then you do not need a ride," he said. "She does not need a ride, ma'am. But thank you for stopping and offering. I shall do myself the honor of calling upon you in the morning, then. I may be four minutes late as the clock in the library, by which I invariably time myself, is four minutes slow. Or do I mean early? I have never quite worked it out. Which *do* I mean, Miss Huxtable?"

He glanced down at Katherine on his arm.

"Late," she said. "You would be late. Or *will* be late as I suppose it has never occurred to you to have the clock set right."

"It would be too confusing," he said. "I would not know *where* I stood. Neither would my servants."

"Jasper," Lady Forester said in tones that clearly had Clarence quaking in his boots and not sure whether he should stay where he was and incur her undying wrath or whether he should hop down and risk Lord Montford's, "I *will not* be spoken to thus in your usual insolent vein. Charlotte—"

"Clarrie," Jasper said conversationally, "you are holding up traffic, old boy. I daresay there are curricles and phaetons and barouches backed up all the way to the gates and out into the street, not to mention other vehicles. You had better move on before this good coachman behind you decides to get down from his perch and knock your hat off. He is already purple in the face. So are his passengers. I shall see you both at precisely four minutes after nine tomorrow morning. Good day to you."

And Clarence, after a nervous glance back at the vehicles behind him, gave his own coachman the signal to move on.

"Oh, Jasper," Charlotte said when they were out of earshot, "you will not allow Aunt Prunella to take me away, will you? She would not stop sermonizing from dawn to bedtime. It would be like going to prison. I really do not think I could *bear* it."

"There, there, Miss Wrayburn," Merton was saying, patting her hand.

"I am *so* sorry," the elder Miss Huxtable said, sounding deeply distressed, "if my invitation to Miss Wrayburn to come walking with Kate and me this afternoon has caused a problem. Is it because she is not yet out? But even children and young people need air and exercise at some time of the day, surely."

"I daresay," Merton said, "it is because I invited myself to come too. I suppose the very highest sticklers might argue that Miss Wrayburn ought not to be seen in company with me until after her come-out. I do beg your pardon, Miss Wrayburn, and yours too, Monty. I did not think."

"I cannot imagine," Jasper said, "that even the queen herself could take exception to a young girl strolling in a public park with her brother and guardian and three of his friends, two of whom are ladies older than herself. I will certainly not have any of you chastising yourselves for a nonexistent fault. I shall set Lady Forester right on the matter tomorrow morning. And no, Char, you will not be thrown into the lions' den with Aunt Prunella and Clarence. Not under any circumstances."

"But Clarence is one of my *guardians*," she reminded him. "He always was pompous and horrible. I hated him when he was a boy and I am sure I still hate him. He has turned downright ugly too. He is *fat*."

Which blunt words spelled doom for any courtship Clarence might hope to mount with his cousin.

"We will not bore Lord Merton and his sisters with our private business any longer, Char," he said firmly. "And we had better stroll onward before we invite a wider audience."

Which they proceeded to do—in a rather deafening silence punctuated by small bursts of bright, stilted conversation.

"This," Miss Katherine Huxtable said when they arrived back at the gates, loosening her hold on his arm and including the others close behind them in her remarks, "has been a lovely afternoon, has it not? Thank you very much indeed, Miss Wrayburn and Lord Montford, for accompanying us."

She and her brother and sister were going one way and he and Charlotte were going the other, so they all took their leave of one another with a flurry of cheerful farewells, just as if that damnably melodramatic interruption had not occurred.

And how many people had witnessed the scene? *Not* that he cared the snap of his fingers what the gossips might say about him. But there *was* Charlotte to think about. Good Lord, what the devil had her aunt been thinking of, exposing her thus to the public gaze and censure? She could not possibly have waited until tomorrow morning to read him a scold in the privacy of her own drawing room?

"Jasper," Charlotte said, her small hand tucked beneath his arm, "what will Aunt Prunella say tomorrow? What will she *do*?"

"Let *me* worry about that," he said, patting her hand. "Or not."

"But you know what Papa said in his will," she said, her voice thin and high-pitched with misery.

Her father had stated that she must be brought up and housed until her marriage by his sister, her aunt, if her mother should die and there were ever any question of neglect or impropriety in the way Baron Montford handled her upbringing.

"Your papa also appointed three guardians," he said, "and fortunately Clarence is only one of them."

"But if Great-Uncle Seth were to take his side," she said, "then Aunt Prunella would take me away and there would be nothing you could do about it. Oh, I wish now I had stayed at Cedarhurst."

"Great-Uncle Seth is too lazy to move out of his own shadow," he told her. "He has never made any secret of the fact that he resented being named guardian by his own nephew—especially when that nephew had the effrontery to predecease him. I am sorry, Char. I ought not to talk about your papa in that careless way. But you need not worry about Great-Uncle Seth."

"But I *do,*" she said. "He has only to say the word—" She did not complete the thought.

"It won't happen," he said, guiding her across the road and skirting about a pile of manure that the crossing sweep had not yet cleared. "I promise. I'll go and call upon your great-uncle in person if I must, though he won't like it above half."

"Will you?" she said. "Do you think—"

"Let's talk about something more cheerful," he suggested, patting her hand. "Do you like the Huxtables?"

"Oh, exceedingly." She brightened immediately, and then she turned a laughing face his way. "You like Miss Katherine Huxtable."

He looked at her sharply.

"I like them both," he said. "They are Merton's sisters, and they are genteel and charming, not to mention beautiful."

"But I think you *like* Miss Katherine Huxtable," she

said with an impish smile from beneath the brim of her bonnet. "You scarcely took your eyes off her while we were walking back through the park."

"We were *conversing*," he said. "It is polite to look at the person with whom you are having a conversation. Did Miss Daniels never teach you that?"

But she only laughed.

"And I think," she said, "*she* likes *you,* Jasper."

"Never tell me," he said, recoiling in feigned horror, "that she was looking at me too while we talked. How very brazen of her."

"It was the *way* she was looking," she told him. "But I daresay *all* ladies like you. Are you going to marry one of these days?"

"One of these very *future* days, perhaps," he said. "Maybe. Probably. Possibly. But not in the foreseeable future."

"Not even," she asked him, "if you were to fall in love?"

"I would marry immediately if not sooner were *that* to happen," he said. "I would be so startled I would not know what else to do. As startled as I would be if I were to hear that hell had frozen over."

"I wish," she said with a sigh, "you were not such a dreadful cynic, Jasper."

"And what do you think of Merton?" he asked, smiling down at her.

"He is exceedingly handsome and amiable," she said. "He looks like a god. I daresay everyone is in love with him."

"Including you, Char?" he asked.

"Oh, no," she assured him. "I would not be so foolish. It would be like pining for the sun. I shall look for someone altogether more . . . *possible* with whom to fall in love. But not yet. I want to be at least twenty before I marry."

"Elderly, in fact." He grinned fondly at her. He had not realized how practical she was, how unsure of herself, how underestimating of her own charms. There was no reason in the world why the daughter of a wealthy baronet, sister of a baron, could not aspire to the hand of an earl.

But definitely not yet.

"Perhaps," he said, "love will take you by surprise one of these days."

"I hope so," she said, smiling brightly at him. "When I am old enough to be quite sure that love is what it is. And I hope it happens to you too, Jasper. Falling in love, I mean."

"Thank you," he said, patting her hand again. "But let me see, is it a blessing or a curse you are bestowing?"

She laughed.

"I have an idea," she said suddenly, gazing up eagerly into his face. "A *wonderful* idea. Miss Daniels says we should try to add a few more names to the guest list for my house party. I think we ought to invite Miss Katherine Huxtable, Jasper. Oh, and Miss Huxtable too. After all, you will need some congenial company as well as I will."

"And since I am an elder and those two ladies are elders too," he said, "we can congenially entertain one another? About a crackling fire to keep our aged bones warm in July, perhaps?"

"Miss Katherine Huxtable was twenty when her brother succeeded to the title," she said. "She mentioned it when we were walking to the Serpentine. And that was three years ago. She is not so very old, Jasper, though it is surprising that she is not already married. Especially when she is so beautiful. Perhaps she has been waiting for someone special. I admire her for that."

"Char," he said, looking sidelong at her, "you are not *matchmaking* by any chance, are you? I warn you it is an impossibility."

"Is it?" She gave him a wide-eyed, innocent look.

He had, in fact, just got *exactly* what he wanted without having to try very hard at all. Katherine Huxtable still had to accept the invitation, of course.

"Then I will have to play this game too," he said with a sigh. "If the Misses Huxtable are to be invited, Char, then it would be quite ill-mannered not to invite Merton too."

She turned her head sharply to face front again until the poke of her bonnet hid her flushed cheeks.

"Oh, would it?" she said. "But I daresay he has far more interesting things to do."

"Probably," he agreed. "Let's find out, shall we?"

And to the devil with the fact that perhaps she really ought not even to be acquainted with Merton yet. What strange gothic notions some people had. Good Lord, Aunt Prunella and her ilk would probably have young girls locked in a high tower with their spinning wheels if they had their way.

9

JASPER'S visit to Lady Forester and Clarence the following morning proceeded much as he had expected. He was very careful to time his arrival so that he was knocking on their door at precisely four minutes after nine, and they kept him waiting in the visitors' parlor for fifteen minutes.

Touché.

He was *not* invited to sit down when they did arrive.

There followed a tirade—delivered by the lady—in which Jasper was accused of every excess and vice known to man and a few unknown ones too and a demand that he relinquish control of Charlotte to her aunt before she was corrupted beyond hope of reform.

"If she is not already," Clarence was unwise enough to add.

Jasper had deliberately armed himself with a quizzing glass for the occasion, an affectation with which he did not usually encumber himself since his eyesight was excellent. He raised it to his eye at that moment and directed it at Clarence, particularly his ostentatiously tied neckcloth. Good God, even a dandy would shudder.

"Perhaps it might be wise, Clarrie," he said, "to allow your mama to do the talking for you. You would not particularly enjoy having me rearrange that knot at your neck, old chap, although it is in dire need of rearrangement, I must say."

He lowered the glass before looking politely back at Lady Forester.

And she proceeded to tear apart the good name of Merton and his sisters, who might appear blameless in the eyes of the *ton* but who did not deceive *her,* the vulgar upstarts. They certainly did not know how to behave if they had all seen fit to be seen in public with *him* and—far worse!—in company with a young schoolgirl who had no business being seen in public at all until after she had made her curtsy to the queen.

"And for either one of the sisters to allow Charlotte to walk *on the arm* of the Earl of Merton was the outside of enough and merely confirms me in my conviction that they are brazen hussies," she added. "I took quite a nasty turn at the realization that that very young girl in the park was *my niece,* my dear dead brother's daughter. Did I not, Clarence? My maid was forced to burn feathers to revive me after we arrived home."

"It is to be hoped that none of them were your best evening plumes, ma'am," Jasper said, all concern.

"They are vulgar and quite long in the tooth," Lady Forester said. "I suppose no real gentleman will have them. And the earl is doing himself no favor behaving as he does. And he is your *friend,* I understand."

Jasper bowed and smiled.

"I really must be on my way," he said. "This has been a delightful half hour, but I have other matters to attend to and so will not, alas, be able to sit down and take refreshments with you. No, no—you must not bother to offer them. Charlotte, by the way, will be remaining at my home and under my protection and her companion's guidance. Good day to you both."

He reached for his hat from the table where he had set it down since the servant who had opened the door and ushered him into the parlor had not offered to take it.

"She will not be there for long, Jasper," Clarence said with spiteful relish. "I called upon Great-Uncle Seth yesterday afternoon after escorting Mama home."

Jasper paused, his hand on his hat.

"Ah," he said. "That must have been a pleasant experience for you both, Clarrie. Did he offer to kill the fatted calf in your honor?"

"I was able to apprise him of the truth concerning Charlotte," Clarence said. "He agreed with me that something really must be done."

"Clarence," his mother said sharply, "there was no need to say a word about that visit to Jasper. It is none of his business. He has never shown any interest in Charlotte's family, including Uncle Seth."

"He ought to know, Mama," Clarence said, "that his carelessness regarding my cousin will not be tolerated any longer, that soon she *will* be living here with us, where she will be properly prepared for her debut into society and for a respectable marriage."

"You would be *well* advised, Clarrie," Jasper said as he fixed his hat on his head and crossed the room to let himself out, "to listen to your mama and allow her to speak for you. Always. For she *always* knows best."

A minute later he was striding down the street.

Another visit, it seemed, was in order, and he had Clarence of all people to thank for alerting him to the necessity of making it without further delay.

Poor Seth Wrayburn! Having two visitors descend upon him in as many days was going to be a severe trial to him.

But some things could not be helped.

When Miss Wrayburn and Miss Daniels called at Merton House later the same morning in the hope of finding the Misses Huxtable at home, they were admitted immediately and shown up to the drawing room, where they discovered not only those ladies but also the Duchess of Moreland, their sister, and her two young children. The duke was downstairs in the library with the Earl of Merton, whom he still considered his ward and his responsibility though he had loosened the leading strings considerably during the past year.

Margaret and Katherine had been telling Vanessa about Miss Wrayburn and how they liked her—and how upset they had been at the encounter with Lady Forester, her aunt.

"It had just not occurred to either of us, or Stephen, that perhaps there was something improper about inviting her to walk in the park with us, had it, Kate?" Margaret had said.

"That is because there *was* nothing improper about it, you silly goose," Vanessa had assured her. "Good heavens, who *is* this Lady Forester? I have never heard of her, but she sounds remarkably silly. I must ask Elliott. He knows everyone."

They had talked too—inevitably—about Baron Montford. Meg had given it as her opinion that he had a partiality for Kate, and Katherine had protested that he was a notorious libertine and had a partiality for *any* lady who was willing to spend a few minutes tête-à-tête with him.

"Now, Lord Montford I *do* know," Vanessa had said, her eyes twinkling. "We sat together at supper during someone's ball earlier this year and talked for all of ten minutes exclusively with each other. He did not show the *smallest* sign of partiality for me and so I must contradict you on that, Kate. I found him charming and amusing—and quite gloriously handsome."

"And *I* walked all the way to the Serpentine with him yesterday," Margaret had added, "while Kate was with Stephen and his sister. He was amiable and interesting and showed not the *tiniest* sign of partiality for me."

Katherine was quite glad of the interruption.

Miss Daniels made her curtsy to them when Miss Wrayburn presented her and found a chair near the door when invited to be seated. Margaret introduced Vanessa, and Katherine watched Miss Wrayburn's awed expression disappear within moments when Vanessa behaved in a very unduchesslike way and smiled and talked to her and explained that she *must* stand and rock like a boat in a stiff breeze in the hope that young Sam would soon lose his battle with sleep.

"He is very stubborn," she said. "His papa insists that it is a trait he has inherited from me. I know that the opposite is true, of course."

Miss Wrayburn tiptoed forward to peep into the baby's face, and then she smiled at two-year-old Isabelle and sat beside her.

Margaret poured the tea, and they all conversed comfortably for several minutes until the gentlemen joined them and more introductions had to be made.

Sam was still fussing.

"I suppose it did not occur to you, Vanessa," Elliott said, scooping the baby up out of her arms, "to summon his nurse from the housekeeper's sitting room and instruct her to take him away somewhere else."

"No, it did not," she admitted, her eyes laughing into his as he crossed the room to stand close to the window, the baby's head held to his shoulder with one hand.

Isabelle had jumped to her feet at the arrival of the men and was standing in front of Stephen, holding up her arms. He laughed and lifted her high onto his shoulder. She sat there chuckling and clinging to a fistful of his curls.

"I am delighted to meet you, Miss Daniels," he said. "And I am delighted that you have come again, Miss Wrayburn."

"I came for a very particular reason," Miss Wrayburn said, flushing and moving forward to the edge of her seat. "I am going to be eighteen in August. Jasper has said I may have a house party for the occasion at Cedarhurst Park—it is in Dorsetshire. He has told me I may invite as many guests as I wish—for two whole weeks. Miss Daniels and I have made all sorts of plans for everyone's entertainment—picnics and excursions and wilderness walks and croquet and dances and boat rides and riding and...and charades and cards and... Oh, and all *sorts* of things. It is going to be the most wonderful time I have ever had in my life."

She smiled eagerly from one to the other of them.

"And the most wonderful time everyone else will have had too, of course," she added.

Miss Daniels looked pointedly at her.

"*And,* Charlotte?" she said softly, making a beckoning

gesture with one hand. "Of what concern is this to Miss Huxtable and her sister and brother?"

"Oh." Miss Wrayburn looked mortified and then laughed too—a light, youthful sound. "I want you to come, Miss Huxtable, and you too, Miss Katherine, and you if you will and if you do not have other more exciting plans, Lord Merton, though I daresay you do. I want you all to be among my houseguests. *Will* you? I would like it of all things, I do assure you. Please say yes."

Jasper has said I may have a house party . . .

Was he deliberately luring her to a place where he would have plenty of opportunity to be tête-à-tête with her?

How very clever of him.

Or was she reading too much into this invitation?

"It sounds very delightful," Margaret was saying. "But are you quite sure you wish to have us among your guests, Miss Wrayburn? Your aunt did not appear to consider us suitable companions when she saw us with you yesterday."

The girl flushed.

"She did not even know who you *were*," she said. "She wants to have me live with her now that I am almost grown up and no longer a nuisance of a child. She wants to control my fortune and have me marry Clarence. I would rather *die*."

"Charlotte, my *dear*," Miss Daniels said reproachfully.

"Well, it is *true*," the girl said. "And you yourself said, Danny, that it was quite unexceptionable for me to walk in the park with the Earl of Merton and his sisters and Jasper himself. Besides, this party is to be held in the *country*. At Jasper's home and mine. Nothing could be more respectable. Aunt Prunella has *nothing* to say in the matter. Please come."

She looked as if she were almost in tears.

Elliott had turned from the window—Sam was fast asleep against his shoulder, his mouth open.

"*Stephen* is no suitable escort for Miss Wrayburn?" he said. "In a public park with her brother and his sisters in attendance? How very peculiar."

"It is because I am not yet *out,*" Miss Wrayburn explained. "My aunt believes that I ought to remain hidden in the schoolroom until my presentation to the queen."

"Well," Stephen said, swinging Isabelle to the floor at her insistence—she came to sit on Katherine's knee. "I *do* have exciting plans for those weeks in August, Miss Wrayburn. I plan to spend them at Cedarhurst Park in Dorsetshire—as the guest, I believe, of Baron Montford, my friend. And by happy chance it seems that you are to have a birthday while I am there."

"Oh." The girl clasped her hands to her bosom and beamed at him. "Oh, how *splendid*. Jasper will be *so* pleased. And I am too."

"I believe," Margaret said, "it is quite proper for Kate and me to accept your invitation, Miss Wrayburn. We would be delighted to come, would we not, Kate?"

The decision had been taken from her, then, had it? Katherine did not know if she was glad or sorry.

"Absolutely," she said, smiling at Miss Wrayburn. "I shall look forward to it."

And she knew she would even though she really ought not.

Miss Wrayburn beamed at them all.

"I am *so* glad," she said. "Oh, thank you."

A few minutes later Miss Daniels rose, and Miss Wrayburn followed suit and took her leave of them all.

"She is indeed a delightful girl," Vanessa said when they had gone. "It is very kind of her brother to arrange a party in the seclusion of the country for her. It is a ridiculous notion that girls ought to be left in the schoolroom until the very moment of their come-out. *Then,* of course, they know no one and are gauche and blushing and uncomfortable. Miss Daniels told me which other guests have been invited to Cedarhurst. Most of them—both ladies and gentlemen—are very young indeed. Stephen is going to seem like an elder statesman. But of course it is right too that a few older guests be invited—for Lord Montford's sake."

She looked pointedly at Katherine and laughed.

Katherine busied herself with amusing Isabelle and pretended not to notice.

Mr. Seth Wrayburn lived in London all year long, even during the heat of the summer when the beau monde deserted it en masse for the greater comforts of the countryside or the relative coolness of the seaside.

He lived on Curzon Street, which was in a fashionable enough neighborhood for a gentleman of his rank. He had nothing to do with fashions, however, and nothing to do with the beau monde either. Or with anyone else for that matter except his valet and his butler and his chef and his bookseller.

The best company a man could ever desire, he had always said—when forced to say anything at all, that was—was his own. At least a man could expect a little intelligence and sense from himself.

He was *not* pleased to be presented with a visiting card the very day after being bothered with another. He had been forced to admit Clarence Forester the day before because that fool had sent up the verbal message with his card that it was a matter of life and death concerning Charlotte Wrayburn, who happened to be not only Seth's great-niece, but also his ward. He had never been pleased with that latter connection, but he had not contested the terms of his nephew's will when he might have done so with some success immediately after his death—a man surely could not be forced to take on the guardianship of a girl in whom he had no interest whatsoever, after all. But it was probably too late now.

He had admitted Clarence, albeit reluctantly, expecting to have his ears assailed with an affecting story about how his great-niece was at her last gasp on her deathbed or a lurid tale about how she had eloped with the groom after climbing out of the schoolroom window down knotted sheets while her governess slept—or some other such dire event over which he supposed he would be expected to exert himself.

Though what he could be expected to do to stop the girl from dying or to set her back in the schoolroom when she had been wed and bedded by the groom he could not imagine. Nor did he *want* to imagine.

As it turned out, Clarence had bored him exceedingly and at great length and had confirmed him in his long-standing conviction that he himself had been born into the wrong family—and a parcel of nincompoops at that—more than seventy years ago and had been made to suffer for it ever since.

But since Clarence had demanded action in that pompous way of his and had raised some issues that probably could not be ignored much longer, Mr. Wrayburn sighed deeply when he lifted Jasper's card from the butler's tray and read the name written there.

"There is no message to accompany the card?" he asked. "No life-and-death situation? No warning that the sky is falling or the great trump of doom blowing from the heavens to summon us all to judgment?"

"None, sir," his butler assured him.

"Show him up, then," Mr. Wrayburn said with another sigh. "At least he is no blood relation. That is some consolation. Small enough, it is true, but *some* nonetheless."

His nephew's stepson strode into the room a minute or two later, looking fashionable and virile and altogether too full of energy for his own good. He held up a hand as he came.

"Do not get up, sir," he said. "No need to stand upon ceremony. Do remain seated."

Since Mr. Wrayburn had made no move to rise to his feet, and never did when in company, he snorted, especially as he detected a gleam of amusement in the younger man's eyes.

"Impudent puppy," he muttered. "Still raking your way through life, I hear?"

"You *hear*?" Jasper raised one eyebrow as he helped himself to a seat. "From the lips of Clarrie, I suppose?"

"You would call him a liar, then?" Mr. Wrayburn asked him.

"Probably not," Jasper said, grinning, "though he always had an impressive gift even as a boy for embellishing every story he told—to his own aggrandizement and my debasement. He was and is a weasel—apologies to you, sir, since he *is* your great-nephew."

"Through an unhappy accident of birth," the old man said. "You must help yourself to a drink if you want one, Montford. You will dry up like a desert if you wait for me to get up to pour it for you."

"Sounds painful," Jasper said. "But I am not thirsty. I daresay Clarrie informed you that I am a shockingly unsuitable guardian for Charlotte?"

The old man grunted.

"Did you or did you not know that she was cavorting about the park with young Merton the day before yesterday when she ought to have been in the schoolroom reciting the multiplication tables?" he asked, not without irony.

"Charlotte can recite even the thirteenth times table without pausing for breath or making one mistake," Jasper said. "I know. I worked it all out on paper one day—and she was right, by Jove. She is *not* still in the schoolroom. She is seventeen years and ten and a half months old, and her governess has acquired the new name and expanded duties of companion. And yes, I knew she was in the park with Merton. I was with them, and so were his sisters, both older than he."

Mr. Wrayburn snorted again.

"I suppose," Jasper said, "Clarrie conveniently omitted those pertinent details?"

"And did you or did you not," the old gentleman continued, "observe Prunella fainting dead away at the sight of such impropriety involving her beloved niece? And gashing her head open as she fell so that traffic was held up for half a mile behind them?"

Jasper chuckled aloud.

"I almost wish I *had* seen it," he said. "Dash it all,

it must have happened when I turned my head or blinked."

"And is it or is it not true," Mr. Wrayburn continued, "that Merton's sisters are no better than they ought to be?"

Jasper sobered instantly.

"Now *that* is a baseless lie," he said with uncharacteristic grimness. "And if Clarrie is spreading such vicious untruths about them, then—"

"Spare me." The old man held up a hand. "If you are fool enough to slap a glove in the face of that idiot, Montford, and to ruin your own life by putting a period to his, then have the goodness to do it without feeling the necessity of giving me a full preview, if you please. The thing is that according to that infernal will of my nephew's, you were not to take Charlotte anywhere beyond the bounds of Cedarhurst without the express consent of either Forester or myself. You have done it anyway. And people like Prunella are bound to cut up vaporish about such things as the girl wandering in the park on the arm of an earl for all the world to see when she has not yet been fired off into society—even if her brother and his sisters *were* with them. It was all the provocation she needed to orchestrate an assault on my peaceful haven here. It is all a parcel of nonsense, of course, and tries my patience to the utmost limit, but if I ignore the complaint and Charlotte ends up flying off to Gretna Green with this earl or someone else less eligible, then I am going to have to endure another visit from Clarence—and probably from Prunella as well. And I am going to be made to feel that I have neglected my duty to make sure that both Charlotte and her fortune are delivered safely to some suitably sober and worthy and dull husband when the time comes."

"Clarrie," Jasper said.

"Eh?"

"I am convinced of it," Jasper said. "Lady Forester has not cared a tupenny toss for Charlotte all these years. But now her eighteenth birthday and her fortune are looming on the horizon, and Forester senior died with a veritable mountain of unpaid gaming debts, and Clarrie is fortunately still single and in a position to recoup the family fortunes by marriage to the right woman."

"His own first cousin," Mr. Wrayburn said in open disgust. "It makes perfect sense, though. One could not expect any other woman to have him, after all, could one? I will exert myself to deny my permission for such a match, Montford, as I am sure you will. *Devil* take my nephew for naming me as guardian to the girl. As foolish as every other member of the family, is she?"

"Not at all," Jasper said. "I am inordinately fond of her."

Mr. Wrayburn grunted. "At least she can recite the thirteenth times table," he said. "I doubt Clarence can say the second without using his fingers and toes and wondering why he has run out when he arrives at eleven times two."

Jasper chuckled.

"Here is the thing," the old gentleman said. "I'll state it once, Montford, and then you may do with it as you will. It is time for my luncheon and my nap and I never postpone either. You may keep the girl with you over the summer and winter—you have my vote on that. But you are not in any position to bring the girl out next spring, if Clarence is to be believed—your other sister, whose name I cannot recall at the moment, is married and breeding often enough to decline the honor of organizing and supervising young Charlotte's come-out. So Prunella is going to have to be the one for the task."

"But, sir—"

Mr. Wrayburn held up a hand again.

"There *is* a solution," he said. "It is as clear as the nose on your face, Montford, but I am not going to advise it. I never took that road myself and would not wish it upon my worst enemy. It would be a solution for Charlotte, though, if you are determined to offer her one."

"You are suggesting," Jasper said, "that I *marry*?"

"You do not listen well," the old gentleman said. "I am suggesting no such thing."

For once Jasper was speechless.

"You have the summer and the winter with Charlotte—with my blessing," the old man said. "*Provided,* that is, you do not force my hand. Your excesses and debaucheries, all enumerated in lurid detail by my esteemed great-nephew yesterday, are of no interest to me, and I am fully aware that more than half of what I was told was exaggeration or baseless innuendo or outright fabrication even if I am not sure *which* half. But be careful nevertheless. I *am* Charlotte's guardian, and if something about you surfaces that suggests it would be downright irresponsible to leave the girl in your charge, I may be forced to act. Don't force me, Montford. I would *not* be amused. Close the door quietly behind you as you leave, will you? I abominate loud noises and sudden drafts."

Jasper got to his feet.

"You would deliver Charlotte into their clutches—" he began.

"What I *would* do," Mr. Wrayburn said testily, "is have my home back to myself, Montford. I *like* you. You stood up to my fool of a nephew all through your boyhood though some of your exploits almost made even *my* hair stand on end. And you are no namby-pamby, sniveling idiot. It always seemed markedly unjust to me that you were not my relative instead of all the others. But like it or not—and I do *not* like it, I assure you—I am one of Charlotte's guardians. And when I am called upon to assert my third of the guardianship, I shall do so according to what I consider to be her best interests, even if those are only a choice between the devil and the deep blue sea. Go away now. I have a sore throat from doing so much talking."

Jasper went.

With much food for thought to digest.

10

KATHERINE was at a garden party in Richmond the next time she encountered Baron Montford. It was two days after she and Margaret and Stephen had accepted their invitation to Miss Wrayburn's birthday celebrations.

It was a crowded event. A large number of guests were in attendance, taking tea on the wide paved terrace before the house or moving about the lawns that stretched between the terrace and the River Thames or boating on the river. This was the home of Mr. and Mrs. Adams, who were renowned for their lavish entertainments — and for the beauty of their gardens, which at this particular time of the year were laden with flowers, all in varying shades of purple, magenta, and pink. Flowers of the same shades hung from baskets across the front of the house and bloomed in large pots along the terrace.

It was a dazzling and glorious display — and a quite irresistible one to Katherine, who was always alternately drawn to crowded social events and pulled toward solitude, preferably in a setting of natural beauty. She mingled happily with the crowds for well over an hour. But then she was assailed with the familiar need to get away from it all, to be by herself even if only for a short while.

Margaret had been borne off to one of the boats by

the Marquess of Allingham, Stephen was in the midst of an animated group that consisted largely of young ladies and their twirling parasols, Vanessa and Elliott had stepped inside the house with Mrs. Adams, and Katherine was free to make her way to a pretty little glass pavilion that faced onto a rose garden.

It was a warm day when the sun was out. But there were some clouds too and a noticeable breeze, and it was during a particularly lengthy cloudy period that Katherine stepped inside, goose bumps pebbling her bare arms. The glass walls and roof had trapped the heat of the sun, and she sat down gratefully on a wrought iron seat and prepared to enjoy the roses and the warmth for a while before conscience inevitably drove her back outside to be sociable.

She was immediately aware of the heady scent of the roses, and peace seeped into her soul as she breathed in their fragrance.

Her solitude did not last long, though.

After what could have been no more than a scant five minutes, she became aware of someone striding away from the crowds on the terrace and moving in her direction. When she turned her head to look, she could see that it was Lord Montford, dressed elegantly in a dark green coat, which molded the muscles of his chest and arms, with buff pantaloons, which did the like for his legs, and shiny Hessian boots. No gentleman ought to be allowed to be so handsome—especially when he was someone of whom one could only disapprove, to say the least.

He had not been at Lady Cranford's concert last evening. And he had not been here so far this afternoon. She had been glad of it on both occasions. There was something about him that never failed to ruffle her calm.

And she had *so* wanted to be alone for a little while longer.

It was not to be. His eyes met hers through the glass, and it was clear that she was indeed his destination. A glass pavilion did not, alas, provide an effective hiding place. Not that one ought to be looking for one at a garden party.

She resented the way her heartbeat quickened.

He stopped when he was in the wide doorway and propped one shoulder against the wooden frame. He crossed his arms over his chest and one booted ankle over the other. It was the way she would always remember him, she realized, apparently indolent, his eyes alert but half hidden beneath lowered lids, one eyebrow half cocked, one lock of dark hair down across his forehead.

"This has to be deliberate," he said. "The dress to match the flowers, the straw hat to add a delicate rustic touch, the glass-walled retreat to suggest both the desire for solitude and the subtle invitation to have that solitude interrupted, the relaxed, graceful posture—it *has* to be deliberate."

Only he could be so outrageous as to suggest such a thing—*even if it were true*.

"But of course it is deliberate," she said. "You do not think I would attend a garden party, do you, without first consulting with the hostess to discover the color of the flowers in her garden and the existence of a glass pavilion within full sight of the terrace and lawns in which I might arrange myself for full pictorial effect. *Of course* it is deliberate."

Her dress was a deep rose pink muslin. Paler pink rosebuds adorned the crown of her wide-brimmed hat.

He chuckled—a lazy, seductive sound.

"Then you have succeeded beyond your fondest hopes," he said. "I am only surprised that gentlemen are not queued up outside for the pleasure of spending a few moments paying homage to you. But I have only just arrived. Perhaps they have been paying court to you since the party began and are only now all finished. *May* I?"

He advanced inside the pavilion and indicated the empty half of the seat beside her. He did not wait for her permission. He sat down, and she was instantly aware that the seat was not very wide at all. She could feel his body heat even though he was not touching her. She could smell his musky cologne.

"Do have a seat, Lord Montford," she said crossly. "There is no need to feel that you must remain standing in my presence."

He chuckled again.

"Prickly, Miss Huxtable?" he said. "Have I done something to offend you? Or said something?"

"*You?*" she said. "The soul of propriety? Tell me, was the idea of inviting me to Cedarhurst Park for two weeks in August yours or Miss Wrayburn's?"

"Good Lord!" he said. "The day I plan the guest list for an eighteenth birthday party, Miss Huxtable, is the day someone really ought to put a bullet in my brain. It would save me from the misery and ignominy of being hauled off to Bedlam."

Which did not really answer her question, did it? But it was not worth pursuing.

"This is a lovely garden," she said. "It makes me miss

Warren Hall. And Throckbridge too. There is nothing more desirable than being in the country, is there? Do you miss Cedarhurst Park?"

"I hated it with a passion for at least the first twenty-five years of my life," he told her.

"Oh, why?" she asked in surprise, turning her head to look at him.

"I suppose," he said, "because it was the visible symbol of my captivity."

"Captivity?" She frowned at him. "I would say very few people are freer than you, Lord Montford. You must have everything you could possibly need or want."

He smiled that lazy smile of his.

"Your brother is a fortunate man, Miss Huxtable," he said. "Not because he unexpectedly inherited the earldom of Merton at the age of . . . what?"

"Seventeen," she said.

". . . at the age of seventeen," he said, "but because he had all those years before it in which to be free to live his life as he chose."

"We lived in a small cottage after our father's death," she said indignantly. "Meg had to use all her ingenuity to make ends meet so that we could eat and clothe ourselves."

"And Con Huxtable is a fortunate man," he said. "He somehow managed to get himself born two days before his father, the old earl, could procure a special license and marry his mother. And so, though he grew up as the eldest son of the house, he could never inherit, and he knew it from the start."

That touched her on the raw.

"That was *fortunate?*" she said. "It was surely the worst thing that could possibly have happened to him.

The knowledge that it *did* happen has dampened Stephen's pleasure in his good fortune, I know. He has not enjoyed benefiting from someone else's misfortune."

"Your brother was free to dream until the age of seventeen," he said, "and when the news of his inheritance came, then it must have seemed like a dream come true. Con has always been free to dream."

"And you have not?" She was frowning again.

"I was my father's eldest and only son," he said. "He died before my birth. I was born with the title Baron Montford. Cedarhurst and all the rest of it have always been mine."

"Most people in your circumstances," she said sharply, "would spend their lives counting their blessings."

"I suppose they would," he said softly. "What I have always counted a blessing, Miss Huxtable, is that I am not and never will be *most people*."

"Well, *that* is certainly true," she conceded, clasping her hands tightly in her lap.

She would need time to think through ideas that had never occurred to her before now, though. What *was* freedom? It certainly was not poverty. That put horrible shackles upon people. She and her family had never been so poor that they must fear for their next meal, but even so she knew poverty well enough to be sure that there was no freedom in it. But in wealth and position and privilege? Were they not the very epitome of freedom? Was it not almost sinful to hate being owner of a grand house and estate and master of a fortune?

But if one had everything one could ever need or want, what was left to dream of? That question had never occurred to her before now.

Someone else had left the terrace and was approaching the pavilion, she noticed with her peripheral vision. She turned her head to look. It was actually two gentlemen—she recognized one of them as Sir Isaac Kerby. They had stopped walking by the time she looked, though. The other one had his right hand raised as if in acknowledgment of something or someone, and they both turned back toward the terrace without coming closer.

Katherine turned her head the other way in time to see that Lord Montford had one hand partly raised too and one eyebrow lofted above the other.

A signal must have passed between him and the other gentlemen. He did not want their company?

She noticed too that his other arm was spread along the back of the seat behind her shoulders though it was not touching her at all. He was turned slightly toward her.

"We all need to dream," she said.

"Ah, but I prefer not to," he said, his eyes heavy lidded again and half smiling and resting fully on her, "whenever there is a more congenial activity to keep me awake. At the moment I can think of nothing more congenial than sitting here tête-à-tête with you."

Good heavens, he made it sound as if they were indulging in a secret lovers' tryst. She ignored the alarmingly unexpected shiver of physical awareness that tightened her nipples and settled between her thighs.

"No, you misunderstand," she said firmly. "Indulging in dreams—*waking* dreams—is essential to us. As essential as eating or breathing. As essential as hope. It is through our dreams that we do our hoping."

"Stop dreaming, boy, and find something useful to do," he

said in the mock tones of a stern parent or tutor—his own from long ago, perhaps?

"I would be more inclined to tell my children the opposite," she said. "Stop being fruitlessly busy and *dream*. Use your *imagination*. Reach out into the unknown and dream of how you can enlarge your experience and improve your mind and your soul and your world."

He chuckled softly.

"And of what does Miss Katherine Huxtable dream?" he asked her. "Love and marriage and motherhood, I suppose?"

He did not get the point at all, did he? He might be intelligent, but there was no spark of the dreamer in him. Perhaps because there had never been anything to dream of that he did not already have. But that was absurd.

Oh, *how* absurd it was!

"Of flying," she said impulsively. "I dream of *flying*."

She did not, of course. Not literally, anyway. But there were no real words for dreams—even most of the ones that came at night while one slept.

"Ah," he said, a mocking gleam in his eye. "A worthy activity to replace doing something useful."

"Through the blueness of the sky and the rushing freshness of the air," she said, ignoring him. "Close to the sun."

"Like Icarus," he said. "To have the wax of your wings melt for your presumption and to hurtle back to the earth and reality."

"No," she said. "*Not* to fall. Dreams do not recognize the possibility of failure. Only the desire, the *need,* to fly close to the sun."

She was making an utter cake of herself, of course.

She did not often try talking of such things, even to Meg or Nessie. Dreams were very private things.

He drummed his fingers against the wrought iron back of the seat beyond her shoulder, looking at her with narrowed eyes while she tried to focus her mind on the roses again.

"What is so mundane about your life that you wish to escape it?" he asked her.

He was turned almost entirely toward her now, and he was looking fully at her.

"Oh, I do not wish to *escape*," she said, exasperated, "only to ... to go beyond what I already have and know and am. It is hard to explain. But is it not the way of all humans?"

"Is it?" he asked softly.

"I think we all yearn to expand our ... our souls into something ... beyond," she said. "I wish there were words. But you *must* have felt it too?"

"The need for God?" he said. "I was taken to call upon him every Sunday of my growing years, Miss Huxtable. But though my privileged backside was comforted by the cushions in the family pew, my mind was tortured by a whole lot of tedious and confused double-talk about love and judgment, forgiveness and damnation, heaven and hellfire. It all taught me to avoid such a confused and confusing God and be quite thankful never to look beyond myself."

"Oh, you poor man," she said, turning her head sharply again and tipping it to one side so that she was suddenly aware of his arm, less than an inch away from her ear. "You did not get the point at all, did you?"

"On the contrary. I believe I got it very well indeed," he told her. "It was explained very clearly to me—

repeatedly. Apparently I was headed for judgment, damnation, and hellfire. I was incorrigible. Beyond hope."

He grinned at her and she shook her head.

"What clergyman told you *that*?" she asked indignantly. "My father would have given *him* a piece of his mind."

"No clergyman," he said. "There are other persons in a lad's life who speak with even more authority for the deity."

She gazed at him. Was he talking about his *father*? But his father had died before his birth. His tutor, then? Or his *step*father, Miss Wrayburn's father?

"What is so mundane about your life as it is?" he asked her again.

"It would be ungrateful to call it mundane," she said. "By most standards it is anything but. It is just that sometimes when I am alone—and I *love* to be alone—I feel a welling of something, of a knowledge that is only just beyond my grasp, of a great happiness that is just waiting to be embraced. Sometimes I try to express the feeling through poetry, but even poems require words. You may laugh at me now if you wish."

He smiled, but he did not immediately say anything. She found herself gazing rather uncomfortably into dark eyes that were only inches from her own. She was aware again of his cologne.

She spread her fingers across her lap.

"*Do* you dream of marriage?" he asked her. "Do you dream of finding happiness *that* way?"

"Yes, I dream of marriage," she said, "and of children and a home of my own. There is not much else for a lady, is there? Even now I worry about being a burden upon Stephen all his life. I am twenty-three years old."

"You must have had numerous offers," he said.

"Some," she admitted. "Good offers from good gentlemen."

"But—?" He raised his eyebrows.

"I want him to be very special," she said, looking back toward the rose garden. "Heart of my heart, soul of my soul. It is foolish to wait for him, I know. Very few people actually do find that one unique mate we probably all dream of finding. But I have never yet been able to persuade myself to settle for less."

She was assailed suddenly by a sense of unreality. Was she actually having this conversation with *Lord Montford,* of all people? However had they got onto such a topic?

She almost laughed.

"He is a fortunate man," he said without any apparent irony, "or will be when he finds you. It will be a love to move mountains."

She turned her face to him again and really did laugh this time.

"I believe it is more likely," she said, "that he will run ten miles without stopping. Men do not think of love and marriage as women do. I have learned *that* in my twenty-three years. How would you react if I told *you* that you were heart of my heart and soul of my soul?"

She could have bitten out her tongue as soon as the words were spoken.

He regarded her from beneath half-closed eyelids.

"I believe," he said, "I might feel my heart beat faster and my soul stir to life from its long-dormant state."

She bit her lip.

"Or I might also," he said, moving his head a little

closer to hers so that for one startled moment she thought he intended to *kiss* her, "claim to have won my wager."

She smiled again. He held his composure for a moment longer, and then he smiled too—slowly and lazily.

"But you are *not* going to say it?" he asked her.

"I am not," she agreed.

"Not yet," he said. "But you will."

She laughed softly. No man had ever flirted with her. She had never flirted with any man. Until she met Lord Montford, that was. And why did it happen with him—every time they met? Why did he do it? Why did she allow it?

His gaze had moved beyond her again; and he raised his hand once more and executed a mock salute and a half-wave with it before turning his attention back to her.

"The esteemed Sir Clarence Forester," he explained, "and his even more esteemed mama. They are no longer coming this way, you will be pleased to know. Probably they saw that Charlotte was not here and lost interest. They will doubtless search for her elsewhere in the garden and on the water—a sad waste of time, of course, as she is not here."

"They have been here all afternoon," she said.

They had pointedly avoided an introduction to Meg, Stephen, and her. Katherine had been made to feel as if going walking in Hyde Park with Miss Wrayburn the other day really *had* been a wicked impropriety. It was quite ridiculous. Even Elliott had said so, and he knew about such things.

"Have they?" he said. "That must have been pleasant for all the other guests."

"You really do not like them, do you?" she said. "And yet they are your aunt and your cousin?"

"Not *mine,*" he said decisively. "Only poor Charlotte's. Lady Forester is her father's sister and Clarence her cousin."

"Your stepfather's relatives," she said.

"My mother's second husband's, yes."

"You did not like him either?" It was a very impertinent question, she thought too late.

"He was godly and righteous and without sin," he said with a smile. "He was also without humor, wit, compassion, or joy. He married my mother just before my first birthday and died just after my eighteenth. I will say no more. He *was* Charlotte's father. And I would not spoil this very pleasant half hour with you, Miss Huxtable."

Had it been that long? Half an hour? Gracious! She had not meant to be away from the main party for more than fifteen minutes at most. And how must it look to anyone who had noticed them sitting alone here together for so long? Though they *were* in a glass pavilion and fully visible from both the terrace and the lawn.

She got to her feet and brushed her hands over her skirt. He had not moved. He still sat at his ease on the wrought iron seat—oh, goodness, it really *was* narrow—his arm stretched out along the back of it.

"I daresay Meg is back from her boat ride with the Marquess of Allingham," she said. "I must go and find her."

"You must do what you must do, Miss Huxtable," he said, his eyes smiling at her from beneath hooded lids again. "I shall remain here for as long as the fragrance of your hair lingers and is not overpowered by the less enticing scent of the roses."

"Oh." She laughed. "How absurd."

"Life is full of absurdities," he said. *"Fortunately,"* he added softly.

Katherine hurried away, feeling as if he had caressed her. How did he *do* that, without even touching her? There was something about his voice, something about his eyes . . .

I believe, he had said when she had asked how he would react if she told him he was heart of her heart, *I might feel my heart beat faster and my soul stir to life from its long-dormant state.*

She smiled.

I might also, he had added, *claim to have won my wager.*

She chuckled aloud.

There was no point in denying that she had enjoyed the last half hour.

And then she spotted Vanessa and Elliott, who were drinking wine on the terrace with another couple, and waved to them as she went to join them.

11

T H E first inkling of trouble to come came to Jasper early the following morning when he went for a ride in Hyde Park despite the fact that the clouds were low and a misty drizzle was threatening to turn into an out-and-out rain. He had Rotten Row almost to himself, though Isaac Kerby and Hal Blackstone were there too, riding together.

They stopped when they saw him and waited for him to come up to them.

"Ho, Monty," Hal called by way of greeting, "finding it hard to sleep at night, are you? Love is said to do that to a man."

He grinned at Isaac, who grinned right back. As if something mightily witty had just been said.

Jasper raised one eyebrow.

"*Love?*" he said. "Affecting *my* sleep?"

"I have been telling Hal," Isaac said, "about how Charlie and I were cruelly rebuffed yesterday at the Adams's garden party."

Jasper reined in his horse until it was moving at the same snail's pace as theirs.

"Rebuffed?" he said. "*Cruelly?*"

They chose to be further amused.

"You see, Isaac," Hal said, "love makes a man blind. He did not even *see* you."

"Ah," Isaac said, "then it must have been a fly he was wafting away, Hal, and Charlie and I were not after all being sent to perdition because Monty was smitten by the lady's charms."

Oh, the devil! Jasper realized suddenly what they were talking about.

"You would have to agree with me, Hal," he said, "that Miss Katherine Huxtable is considerably prettier than either Charlie or Isaac. We admired the roses together. And I had an excellent sleep last night, thank you kindly."

"Half an hour or longer to admire the roses," Isaac said. "Did you count every petal on every single bloom, Monty? You had any number of people speculating—I heard them. It *is* most unlike you, you must admit, to seek out the lone company of any lady—*in* public. A word of advice, old chap. If you are not looking for a leg shackle, you had better count rose petals entirely alone in future. Or not at all unless you want all your friends believing that you are touched in the upper works."

"It is a sorry state of affairs," Jasper said, "when a man may not enjoy the company of a lady at a social event without risking a marriage trap."

And yet all his adult life he had deliberately avoided just the sort of ridiculous speculation that he had apparently aroused yesterday. He must be more careful in the future.

"But the same lady with whom you waltzed at the Parmeter ball?" Isaac said, coming after him. "*That* must have been a sight worth seeing, Monty. I wish I had been there. I did not even know you *could* dance."

"And the *same* lady, Monty," Hal added, "with whom you walked the length of the park just a day or two after the ball? And the *same* lady who is to spend two weeks of the summer at Cedarhurst?"

"Ah, you know about that, do you?" Jasper asked.

"Merton mentioned it when I ran into him last evening," Hal explained.

"Then you also know," Jasper said, "that Merton himself and the eldest Miss Huxtable are to be at Cedarhurst too—all of them as guests of my sister."

But his friends would only laugh.

He really *must* be more careful, Jasper decided. He had been enjoying the challenge of flirting with Katherine Huxtable so much that he had been neglecting the caution he had practiced for years. That very caution was his potential downfall now, of course. It was apparently so unusual to see Lord Montford spending more than thirty seconds at a time with any lady of *ton* that everyone and his dog sat up and noticed when he *did*.

It was not a problem that weighed heavily on his mind, though. Any incipient gossip would soon die down when he stayed away from the lady.

The fresh morning air—even the water droplets against his face—felt invigorating. He looked forward to another day of pleasurable activities, beginning with this ride along an unusually empty Rotten Row. He urged his mount to a gallop, and his friends fell into place on either side of him.

The first inkling of trouble came to Katherine via Constantine. He came to call upon her and Margaret the afternoon following the garden party. They had stayed at home because the weather had turned. Fine drizzle had alternated with heavier rain all morning, and the clouds had begun to break up only when the afternoon was too far advanced for them to make plans for an outing.

They were glad they had remained at home when Constantine came. They both enjoyed his company and had it all too infrequently. He took tea with them and stayed for half an hour before getting to his feet to leave.

"The sun is trying its best to shine at last," he said, looking toward the window. "I brought my curricle with me. I can take only one passenger, I am afraid, or I would invite you both to take a turn about the park with me."

"Thank you, but I would refuse anyway, Constantine," Margaret said. "I find riding in sporting vehicles pure terror. I need a barouche or a gig or a closed carriage in order to feel safe."

He stood smiling down at her.

"I will borrow a barouche one day, then," he said, "and come back for you, Margaret. Would you care to ride up with me today, Katherine, or are you trembling in your slippers too?"

She had looked wistfully at the sunshine beyond the window when he had drawn their attention to it. She hated to spend a whole day indoors.

"I would love to come," she said. "Give me a moment to fetch my bonnet."

A short while later they were bowling through the park, and Katherine was happily admiring the scenery and observing the crowds from her high perch beside Constantine.

"I understand," he said, "that you are to be Monty's

guest at Cedarhurst Park for two weeks in August, Katherine."

"Yes, indeed. Meg and Stephen and I are all going," she said. "But we are to be *Miss Wrayburn's* guests at a house party in celebration of her eighteenth birthday."

Why was she feeling defensive?

He maneuvered the curricle past the crowd of vehicles and pedestrians making the usual afternoon circuit. Soon they were on a long path that was relatively secluded.

"Katherine," he said, "at the risk of sounding like a fussy chaperone, I must warn you to be very careful. Monty is dangling after you for some reason known only to him, and it is extremely unlikely that he has matrimony in mind. He never does."

She felt a shock of indignation and...humiliation?

"Oh, this is really *quite* unnecessary, Constantine," she said. "Is this why you brought me out here this afternoon, away from Meg? Because you feel somehow responsible for me? I have no idea why you would feel any such way when I have both Stephen and Elliott to protect me should I ever be in need of protection. And is it also because you do not trust me? I am twenty-three years old. I have learned a thing or two about life during all those years. I have certainly learned how to spot a—a *rake*. I know Lord Montford has a reputation for being one, and I would have known it for myself even if you had not told me so a long time ago. I am well able to handle any improper advances he may make toward me. He has not made any."

"Not even three years ago?" he asked, causing her stomach muscles to clench. "I was not in London at the time, but I *know* you handled that situation very well indeed, discerning his intentions immediately and drawing him aside to deliver a scold and a blistering set-down. He confessed all to his peers the very next day. Had he not, or had he in any way succeeded in what he had set out to do, I doubt he would be living now to boast of it and harass you again."

Her heart felt suddenly as if it were beating at double time. He *knew* about that long-ago wager? Had known all this time? But he did not know the actual details of what had happened. Had Lord Montford lied in the retelling of that night's events, then? Had he made her seem entirely blameless, even heroic? Had he made himself seem rather ridiculous?

"If you know about all that, then you ought to trust me now," she said, somehow finding her voice. "I do not need a lecture from you, Constantine. Besides, you are Lord Montford's friend. Do you not trust *him*?"

"Monty may feel that he has something to prove after that colossal failure," he said. "It embarrassed him so much, by the way, that he left London afterward and stayed away for more than a year. He can be very charming when he chooses to be, Katherine. I have known him a long time, remember."

"Perhaps," she said, "he is merely being amiable."

"Monty," he said, "*never* dances. Yet he waltzed with you at Lady Parmeter's ball. He *never* strolls in the park with a lady on his arm. Yet he strolled all the way to the Serpentine and back with you."

"And with Meg and Stephen and his sister," she said indignantly. "How foolish this is, Constantine."

But he had not finished.

"And he sat for a whole hour with you in a secluded pavilion at the Adams's garden party yesterday," he said.

"I was not there myself. But even allowing for the fact that reports can be exaggerated and it might have been half an hour and the pavilion and its occupants might have been fully visible to every other guest in attendance, nevertheless you *were* alone with Monty—and sitting very close to him—for quite long enough to attract attention. Some reports even have it that his arm was about your shoulders."

...for quite long enough to attract attention...

Some reports...

She felt suddenly cold.

"I would not have expected you to listen to idle gossip, Constantine," she said. Her voice was all breathless and shaking.

"One cannot help listening," he said, "when one is in a place where people all around one are constantly talking. I was in such a place last evening. I do not pay heed to ninety-nine out of every hundred snippets of gossip I hear. But when one of those snippets concerns a cousin of mine, and one of whom I am fond, then I do take notice."

"It is wicked and ridiculous gossip," she said. "What about all the other gentlemen I danced with at Lady Parmeter's ball? Is anyone gossiping about them? And what about the fact that Meg walked one way to the Serpentine on Lord Montford's arm while I walked with Stephen and Miss Wrayburn? Is anyone gossiping about Meg? And we were together no longer than half an hour yesterday in a pavilion made entirely of glass a mere few yards from the terrace and lawn where most of the other guests were congregated. Meg was out on the river with the Marquess of Allingham for longer than I was sitting with Lord Montford. Is anyone gossiping about them? And Lord Montford did not have his arm about my shoulders. It was draped across the back of the seat because it was narrow. He did not once touch me."

"I can understand your anger, Katherine," he said, turning the curricle onto a path that would take them back onto the main thoroughfare. "But I am not sure you understand the *ton*. Gossip does not have to be based on pure truth. It is built upon half-truths and perceptions and exaggerations and speculations and the human tendency to think the worst of others and even to enjoy thinking it. And Monty has been behaving out of character, you know. He never singles out any lady at any social event. The fact that he has done so now more than once with the same lady accounts for the notice everyone is taking. Unfortunately, you are the object of his attentions. I will have a word with him—he really ought to know better and doubtless does. His trouble is that he does not care a fig what the *ton* thinks of him. Please do be careful. Not of your virtue—I *know* that is safe. But of your reputation. Monty is trouble, Katherine, even if he *is* my friend."

They had emerged from the cover of trees. The sun was now shining in earnest, and Katherine raised her parasol above her head.

"This was all very unnecessary, Constantine," she said, "but I will remember that it comes from your concern for me. And I always appreciate that. How I wish we had known each other from childhood on as we ought to have done since we are cousins. I would have known Jonathan too. I am sure I would have loved him."

Jonathan had been Constantine's younger brother—

his legitimate brother and Earl of Merton for a while after their father's death. He had been handicapped and had died at the age of sixteen, leaving Stephen the title and properties and fortune. Constantine had once described his brother as pure love.

He turned his head and grinned at her.

"Anxious to change the subject, are you?" he asked. "Very well, then. Yes, you would have loved Jon, and he would have adored you. All of you."

Katherine relaxed and tried to enjoy the rest of the outing.

But part of her was almost numb with shock.

There was *gossip* about her. About her and Lord Montford of all people.

And she was at least partly to blame. She might have said no when he asked her to dance at Lady Parmeter's ball. She might have insisted upon taking Stephen's arm for the walk back through Hyde Park from the Serpentine and left Lord Montford to escort Meg or his sister. She might have told him yesterday quite firmly that she wished to be alone in the pavilion. Better yet, she might have got to her feet, bidden him a civil good day, and left him there.

Oh, yes, she was at least partly to blame. For she had actually been finding his company amusing and his conversation witty and stimulating, much as she disapproved of him and told herself that she wanted to have nothing to do with him. Much as she knew very well that he was up to no good.

She must indeed be more careful. She must have nothing whatsoever to do with him while she remained in London, and when she went to Cedarhurst Park—how she *wished* now she were not going—she must remain with Meg or Stephen or Miss Wrayburn or one of the other guests *at all times*.

But all resolves to be more careful came too late.

Trouble hit with full force for Jasper the following day. He had spent the evening at home, a rare thing for him. He had accepted an invitation to the Clarkson soiree, but it was sure to be one at which Katherine Huxtable would also be making an appearance, and it seemed wise to stay away. He could have gone, of course, and made a point to the would-be gossips by staying far away from her all evening, but that would have been a flat bore, and he chose never to endure boredom when it could be avoided altogether.

So he had delighted Charlotte by remaining at home with her all evening.

He was taken quite by surprise the following morning, then, when, on his arrival at White's Club to read the papers he was greeted by a veritable army of friends, acquaintances, and the merely curious.

"Ho, Monty," Viscount Motherham called out by way of greeting, "we all guessed that you would have run for the hills by now as fast as your legs would carry you."

"Splendid courage, old chap," Barney Rungate said. "I did not guess any such thing. I would have wagered on your sauntering in here as you have just done as though nothing had happened."

"*Courage?*" Charlie Field said. "More like a death wish, Rungate. Is it not a mite suicidal to be still in town this morning, Monty? I would have thought even Cedarhurst unsafe territory. Or even the hills, for that matter. Does the American wilderness beckon, perhaps?"

"You are a dead goner, Monty," some unidentified voice said mournfully. "No doubt about that."

"With the key word being *dead*," someone else added. "I believe the Duke of Moreland and the Earl of Merton and Con Huxtable are after your blood, Monty, to mention only three."

Ah! What now?

Jasper raised his eyebrows and pursed his lips.

"Where the devil have all the papers gone?" he asked. "Has Norton taken them all again? And have I perchance missed something interesting? Three gentlemen turned vampire, for example?"

"Monty," Charlie Field said, clapping a hand on his shoulder, "never mind the papers, old boy. Those three would probably have found you by now and relieved you of a pint or two of blood each if they had not considered it of greater importance to go after Forester first. He is your cousin, I believe?"

Ah!

Jasper went very still. He did not even correct the misconception.

For the first time he felt a powerful premonition of disaster.

"I am devastated," he said languidly. "*Forester* is deemed of greater importance than I? What has he done, pray, to merit such a distinction? Or said?"

"It is more what someone else has been saying, Monty," Motherham explained, "though no one seems to know *who,* and understandably no one is owning up to having loose lips and saying it. But *someone* has told Forester about that infamous wager you lost a few years ago. A few dozen men knew about it, of course, but not a one of them ever broke the code of a gentleman's honor to spread the word outside our own circle, especially as the reputation of an innocent lady was at stake. Not a one until now, that is. But *someone* told Forester, perhaps because the man is your cousin and whoever it was assumed he already knew."

Jasper stared at him, all pretense of languorous unconcern abandoned. It was far worse than anything he might have expected.

"And—?" he said softly.

"And Forester spent all evening yesterday at Clarkson's telling everyone who would listen," Motherham continued. "Except that he changed a few details and cast aspersions on the lady's honor and on your word that you had failed to win the wager. He has been saying that her behavior this year indicates that she did not spurn you on that occasion, Monty, and has not spurned you on any occasion since then either."

"It's a disaster, old chap," Charlie said unnecessarily, slapping him on the shoulder again. "You know that gossip is like the contents of Pandora's box. There is no recalling it."

"It is going to be parson's mousetrap for you if you do not make a dash for the hills now or sooner," Hal said. "I would dash for the hills if I were you."

"It is going to be the end of all matrimonial hopes for the Huxtable chit if you do that, though, Monty," Barney Rungate said. "And probably for her sister too. Even Merton may find himself not so well received for a while. It's a devilish thing. I wonder if Moreland and Merton and Con will toss for it to see who gets to put a bullet between Forester's eyes—before coming after you, that is. However did you get yourself saddled with someone like Forester for a cousin? It's dashed hard luck. And what the devil have you done to offend him that he has dreamed up *this* sweet revenge?"

Jasper had recovered some of his famous ennui. He even managed a yawn behind one hand, though admittedly that was probably overdoing things just a little.

"My mother had the misfortune to marry his uncle," he said. "He is not my cousin, and I would be obliged never again to hear that he is. I believe he has taken exception to being called *Sir Clarrie* instead of Sir Clarence. It is, I suppose, provocation enough for a vicious attack upon a young lady who has done nothing to offend him and is entirely innocent of all charges against her. I trust everyone here is convinced of that fact?" His voice had gone very quiet.

There was a murmured swell of assent.

"Whiter than snow, Monty," Charlie said. "There has never been any doubt of that. Not here, anyway. But it will be another story in almost every drawing room in town, old fellow. I believe Lady Forester was with her son last evening and confirmed everything he said. Until she had a fit of the vapors, that was, and had to be carried out to her carriage. I hear it was a most affecting sight."

"Well," Jasper said, looking around the room. "If Norton has made off with every paper, there is no point in my remaining here, is there? I will have to look for something else to amuse me. I believe I shall go weasel hunting."

Nobody asked what he meant by that. Nobody tried to stop him. And though Charlie Field slapped him on the shoulder again and even squeezed it reassuringly, no one offered to go with him.

Within two minutes he was striding down the street.

Two gentlemen who were approaching the doors of White's took one look at his face and thought better of attempting to greet him and commiserate with him.

Trouble came with full force to Katherine while she was in the breakfast room with Margaret. They had sat talking rather longer than usual, reminiscing pleasantly about their years in Throckbridge. They were to meet Vanessa later to shop on Bond Street and had just agreed that they must go and get ready if they were not to be late.

Before they could even rise from their chairs, however, the door opened abruptly and Vanessa herself rushed in. Her eyes focused immediately upon Katherine.

"Oh, thank heaven!" she exclaimed, hurrying toward her. "You did not leave home early for some reason."

But before Katherine could get to her feet to hug her sister and comment upon her strange appearance here so early, she became aware that Elliott, Duke of Moreland, was also in the room, looking dark and forbidding, to say the least.

And Vanessa was looking rather as if she had seen a ghost.

Katherine surged to her feet, as did Margaret.

"Nessie," Katherine said, terror clutching at her heart. "The children?"

Vanessa shook her head, but it was Elliott who answered.

"I ought to have spoken to you after the garden party, Katherine," he said, striding farther into the room, "though as it has turned out, I would have been too late even then. Your name has become inextricably linked with that of one of London's worst rakes, I am afraid."

Oh, *this* again! She did not pretend to misunderstand.

"Lord Montford?" she said. "There *is* some gossip, is there not? It is all very foolish and very baseless. Constantine warned me about it yesterday, and Meg and I stayed home from the Clarkson soiree last evening just to be on the safe side. It will doubtless blow over like yesterday's wind once—"

"Oh, Kate," Vanessa said, possessing herself of both Katherine's hands and squeezing them rather painfully, "what has that man *done* to you? Why did you not *tell* us?"

"D-done to me?" Katherine looked from her sister to Elliott in some bewilderment and mounting alarm. "What do you mean? He has done nothing except dance with me and sit with me at the garden party. What exactly is being said?"

Margaret, she could see, had both hands pressed to her bosom.

Elliott sighed audibly. "We were not at the soiree last evening either," he said. "We were at a private dinner instead. But Montford's aunt and cousin *were* there for an hour or so, quite long enough to spread rumors that I hope *are* just rumors. Though even unfounded gossip can do considerable harm to your reputation. Katherine, did you meet Lord Montford three years ago soon after coming to town for the first time? Vanessa and I put our heads together on the way here and wonder if it might have been during that week when we went into the country with Margaret and Stephen and left you in my mother's care. Did you meet him then?"

Katherine felt her head turn cold. If she could have trusted her legs sufficiently, she would have sat down on her chair again. But her knees seemed to be locked beneath her.

"Cecily and I had been invited to join Lady Beaton's party at Vauxhall," she said. "Miss Finley—now Mrs. Gooding—brought her brother without first asking Lady Beaton because Mr. Gooding had sprained an ankle."

"Kate," Vanessa said—she was still clutching Katherine's hands, "what did he *do* to you?"

"Kate?" Meg's voice was unnaturally high pitched.

"He did *nothing*," Katherine said.

"Did he *try* to do something?" Elliott asked, looking keenly at her.

She opened her mouth to deny it. But clearly this was not the time for lies or evasion. Some trouble was brewing—and that was probably a colossal understatement—and it was going to be necessary that her family know the truth.

The tension in the room was thick enough to be sliced with a knife.

"He had made a wager," she said. "It was in the betting book at one of the gentlemen's clubs—I do not know which. He was to seduce me within two weeks. He had persuaded Mr. Gooding to sprain his ankle, and then he had persuaded his sister to allow him to escort her instead."

Elliott's blue eyes were boring into hers. Both Meg and Nessie were standing as still as statues.

"And?" Elliott asked, his voice rather like a whip. "Did he succeed?"

Katherine shook her head.

"No," she said, her voice a mere whisper of sound. "No, he did not. And he went back to his club and said so. He did not claim victory. And he was not lying. He did *not* win that wager. He did nothing to me."

She could not after all bear to tell the full truth.

Vanessa had one hand pressed over her mouth. Margaret was weeping with choking sobs, which she was trying to smother.

"Forester—Sir Clarence Forester," Elliott said, sounding suddenly weary, "will be answering a few of my questions as soon as I have found him—he was not at any of the clubs when I tried them earlier. Whatever grudge he may have against his cousin, his manner of taking revenge is *unpardonable*. Then I will need a few answers from Montford himself. Maybe he did not win his wager, Katherine—indeed, I trust your word that he did not—but I have to dispute your claim that he *did* nothing. He took on that dastardly wager, did he not, and set about winning it?"

Margaret spoke up.

"Sir Clarence Forester and his mother are the pair who stopped us in the park," she said, her voice trembling, "and made us all feel so very dreadful as if we had done something *wrong*. *They* are the ones who have done wrong—vicious, deliberate, irreparable wrong. What has Kate ever done to deserve their spite? Oh, if I could *just* get my hands on them."

"I'll do it for you, Margaret," Elliott said grimly. "In the meanwhile, you had best stay in the house here, both of you. There is much—"

The door crashed open again and Stephen strode in, his hair a halo of unruly curls about his head after a morning ride, his eyes wild, his face as pale as his shirt.

"I am in time, thank God," he said, fixing his eyes on Katherine. "You are on no account to go out this morning, Kate. There is a damned scoundrel and liar loose on the town and I have just drawn his cork. I would have done more, but the sniveling bast— The sniveling coward ran away. He took a purple nose and a bloodied shirt with him, though, by thunder. I know this is all a pack of lies, Kate—Monty is a friend of mine and you are my sister. But even so—"

The door did not crash open again for the simple reason that Stephen had not shut it behind him. But Constantine, when he appeared in the doorway, looked as if he would have come through the door without opening it if it had stood in his way.

"Constantine," Katherine said, holding up one shaking hand. "If you have come here to tell me that you told me so, I shall first scream very loudly and then slap your face very hard."

And she burst into tears to her own terrible chagrin. Soon she had four arms about her, and Meg and Nessie were murmuring words of comfort when really there was no comfort to be found.

"Forester is a clever bastard," Constantine said. "By the time I appeared at his door a short while ago, he had his mother stationed there instead of a servant, and short of planting her a facer, which I was sorely tempted to do, I could not get in. If she is to be believed, Forester met with an accident this morning at the hands of a large gang of fierce footpads and lost a courageous battle against them."

"They were me, Con," Stephen said.

"Glad to hear it," Constantine said. "It's the first good news I have had all morning. I missed that damned soiree last evening. Oh, sorry for the language, Margaret. Sorry, Vanessa and Katherine. But now I have seen that Katherine is safely at home, I'll pay Monty a little visit."

"You can safely leave that to me," Elliott said stiffly, and Katherine looked up to see the two of them—first cousins who had grown up like brothers and who looked more like twins—glaring at each other and almost squaring off.

"Oh, *stop* it!" she cried. "It is not Lord Montford who has been spreading spiteful stories—and untrue ones too if they claim that he won that ridiculous wager all those years ago. He did not win it because he *chose* not to pursue it. He told me about it and...and we had a laugh over it. I do not suppose he is enjoying this scandal any more than I am. It is all stupid and ridiculous, and I will not have everyone bloodying everyone else's nose and fighting one another to be the one to defend my honor and all the other stupid *stuff* that goes by the name of manly honor. I will not have it. Do you hear me, Stephen?"

She had risen to her feet again. Her sisters stood at her sides, silent sentinels.

"I hear you, Kate," he said. "But it is not—"

"And do *you* hear me, Elliott?" she asked.

"Loudly and clearly," he said. "But—"

"And *you*, Constantine," she said, "do *you* hear me?"

He shrugged with both shoulders and both hands.

"And I will not have you and Elliott carrying on your *ridiculous* feud in my presence or Meg's," she continued, unable to stop, it seemed now that she had started. "I have no idea what it is about, and I do not want to know. I do not *care*. Men are *so* foolish. Take your quarrel elsewhere if you must. *Shoot* each other if you must. But not here. Now go away all of you. *All* of you. I want to be alone. No, better yet, I shall go up to my room—alone."

She swept past them all, her chin up.

She neither knew nor cared what they decided to do about her predicament or about the two men who between them had brought her to this.

She was ruined.

She was in no doubt about that.

And, as she had admitted to herself when she was with Constantine in Hyde Park, she was at least partly to blame.

She had thought herself far more grown up and worldly wise this year than she had been three years ago. But she had fallen prey to the practiced charms of a rakehell just as easily this time as last. It would be useless to deny it.

And now she was ruined.

She did not stop to consider that perhaps the punishment far exceeded the crime.

12

BY the time Jasper arrived at the house where Lady Forester and Clarence were staying, they had already left it and were presumably bowling along the highway to Kent as fast as wheels would turn or horses gallop.

He did briefly consider going after them, but unfortunately there were more pressing concerns to keep him in London.

He did, though, have the satisfaction of hearing from one of the recently hired, newly dismissed servants, who had not yet left the house—a man who clearly felt no loyalty whatsoever to his erstwhile employers. Clarence, it seemed, was taking home with him a purple, bulbous nose and two black eyes, which he had claimed—the servant had paused to look both skeptical and contemptuous though his questioner was a grim-looking gentleman—which he had *claimed* came from a gang of ruffian footpads. At least her ladyship had claimed it since Sir Clarence himself had not been saying much of anything.

Even that news, though, was only marginally satisfying to Jasper. Either Moreland or Merton or Con Huxtable had done what he ought to have done—except that *he* would have considered a bulbous nose and two black eyes a mere preliminary to a more complete drubbing.

Those same three men were doubtless still breathing fire and brimstone and plotting to do the like to him.

He returned home to change into clothes more suitable for a morning call and discovered Charlotte in tears in the library. Miss Daniels was not having a great deal of success consoling her. There was an open letter on the desk.

"What has happened?" he asked from the doorway.

What *now?*

"Jasper!" Charlotte looked up sharply and it was obvious to him from the redness of her eyes and face that she had been crying for some time. "Aunt Prunella is going to have me fetched to Kent. Great-Uncle Seth has said I must go there, that you are an unfit guardian for me. It is not true, is it? You have not d-debauched Miss Huxtable."

Oh, Lord!

"Charlotte, *my dear,*" Miss Daniels said, looking excruciatingly embarrassed.

"It is not true," Jasper said grimly, only thankful that he was not quite lying. "But that is the story Clarence put about last evening and that is what everyone believes today. Have you heard from Great-Uncle Seth himself?"

He glanced at the letter.

"N-no," she said. "From Aunt P-Prunella."

"Then it is probably wishful thinking on her part that he will agree with her," he said. "I had better go and see him again, though. He will not like it above half and neither will I, but it must be done. Go and dry your eyes, Char, and wash your face. Tears are not going to solve anything and they threaten to transform you into a gargoyle."

"Everything is *ruined*," she said, fresh tears running down her cheeks. "Everyone will suddenly discover that they cannot come to my party after all or if they *do* come, *I* will not be there to receive them. Aunt Prunella will have dragged me off to Kent and I shall die. I shall simply *die*, Jasper."

"The thing is, Char," he said, "that you will not, and would not even if all that were to happen—which I do assure you it will not while I have life and breath in my body. But I have to go. Why I learned of all this only this morning when the whole world knew it last evening I will never know. Remind me never to stay home of an evening again. But I am off."

"What must *Miss Huxtable* be suffering this morning?" she asked him. "I am being very selfish, am I not? What of *her*?"

As if he had not thought of that for himself!

"I am off," he said firmly, and strode from the room— and from the house—without stopping to change his clothes after all. And his main purpose must be postponed for a short while.

He was admitted at Seth Wrayburn's house. He would not have been at all surprised if the door had been barred against him, but it was not. He found the old gentleman in a towering rage, though.

"God damn it all to hell, Montford," he said as soon as he saw him, "what the devil is this all about and why do I have to be dragged into it? If I had known the trouble it would be to see one chit of a girl safely to adulthood, I would have hauled that will off to court and flatly refused to be her guardian."

"I do not blame you in the least for being annoyed," Jasper said, strolling farther into the room. "Clarrie has been spreading vicious lies about town, seconded by Lady Forester, and they have left enough damage in their wake to clog a river. However—"

"Where there are lies," Mr. Wrayburn said, "there is usually at least a modicum of truth, Montford. I suppose there *was* once a wager? Concerning young Merton's sister? The most obscene, disgusting wager ever written into a betting book? And I suppose you *did* try your damnedest to win it?"

He glared at Jasper and waited for an answer.

"I am afraid so," Jasper said. "But she repulsed me in no uncertain terms—sent me away with a flea in my ear. She is blameless in all this."

"I *hope*," the old gentleman said, "she gave you a good swift kick in the arse too, Montford—or somewhere where it would hurt even more. Give me one good reason why I should leave my ward under your care."

"Because they are damned liars," Jasper said. "And sending Charlotte to live with them is unthinkable."

"Clarence is a fool," Mr. Wrayburn said, "and Prunella is a crashing bore. I do not doubt they are both liars too, but then most people are. But they *are* respectable. You are not."

"I will be setting this mess all right in the course of the day," Jasper told him. "After I leave here, I will be paying Merton a call and then his sister. There *is* only one thing to do, and by God I will do it."

"*If* she will have you," Mr. Wrayburn said. "She will be a fool if she does."

"I am not sure," Jasper said grimly, "she has much choice."

The old gentleman picked up a cane from beside his chair and pointed it at his visitor like a weapon.

"If you can smooth over this confounded scandal, Montford," he said, "and I did say *if*. *If* you can do it, then I will inform Prunella that she may disturb my peace again only on a matter of undisputed life and death concerning her niece. If you cannot, then Prunella can have the girl and give her a decent firing off next year and find a decent husband for her, though I can assure you that he will not be Clarence. And under those circumstances I will hear from *you* only on a matter of undisputed life and death concerning your sister. I trust I have made myself clear? I trust that you will not be sauntering in here again, trying to look nonchalant, within the next day or two. I trust you are not planning to make a habit of calling upon me. If you do, you will start finding the door shut and locked and my butler deaf."

"You will not be hearing from me," Jasper said firmly. "Soon I will be at Cedarhurst—with Charlotte. And by next year I will have made appropriate arrangements for her come-out that will not in any way involve Lady Forester or inconvenience you."

"God damn it all," the old gentleman said, "I hope so. I sincerely hope so, Montford. I have no particularly avuncular feelings for Charlotte, but I would not wish any girl upon those two fools—unless there is no alternative. Good day to you."

Jasper made his bow and left.

What must Miss Huxtable *be suffering this morning?* ... *What of* her?

Charlotte's words echoed in his head.

What, indeed?

He was, he supposed, going to find out pretty soon. But another voice replaced Charlotte's in his head, and try as he would he could not dislodge it as he walked. The words kept repeating themselves over and over—in the voice of Katherine Huxtable.

I want him to be very special. Heart of my heart, soul of my soul . . . I have never yet been able to persuade myself to settle for less.

He was about to attempt to persuade her to settle for considerably less.

To borrow a phrase from Seth Wrayburn—*God damn it all to hell.*

Katherine was in her bedchamber when Stephen came back home soon after noon. She was sorting through drawers. A maid would pack her things later—and Margaret's. They were going home to Warren Hall tomorrow—back to peace and sanity. She could hardly wait.

She ought never to have come. She would certainly not come again. Not for a long, long time, anyway. The thought cheered her.

Margaret was sitting on the side of the bed, watching. They were not doing much talking. But there was comfort in being together.

Margaret too had said she wanted to go home, that she longed for it, pined for it, was only really happy when she was there, would never want to leave again once she was home.

The fact that it was *Stephen's* home and that he was all but grown up and would surely take a wife and start a family within the next ten years at the longest was not spoken between them. Certain bridges were best crossed when one arrived at them.

Neither of them had yet written to Miss Wrayburn to excuse themselves from attending her house party in August. It would be done before they left tomorrow, though.

Stephen had gone with Elliott and Vanessa, doubtless to confer on what was to be done about the scandal. Katherine did not care what they decided. There really was nothing to be done. He was looking very pale when he appeared in the doorway of the bedchamber after tapping on the door and being bidden to come in.

Katherine smiled at him and continued to kneel on the floor, the contents of a lower drawer of the dressing table in piles about her.

"Monty—*Montford* found us rather than the other way around," Stephen said. "He came to Elliott's."

Katherine sat back on her heels.

"I do not suppose he is amused by all this," she said.

She *hoped* he was not. She had no illusions about him, but she did not believe he was a totally conscienceless rogue. She had had proof of that three years ago.

"It was as much as I could do," Stephen said, his hands curling into fists at his sides, "to keep from planting him a facer, but I was at Vanessa's house and our niece and nephew's house and it would not have been at all the thing."

"Besides," Margaret said, "this was all Sir Clarence Forester's doing, Stephen. Try as I will, I cannot be sorry that you punched him in the nose. I so hope it is still sore."

"Apparently," Stephen said, stepping inside the room, "it is twice its normal size, and both his eyes have turned black."

"Good," Margaret said fiercely. "Oh, and I always thought I was a pacifist."

"Kate." Stephen turned his attention on her and drew an audible breath. "He wants to call on you here this afternoon."

"Sir Clar—?" Her eyes widened. *"Lord Montford?"*

"I would far prefer to plant him a facer," he said. "And Elliott would far prefer to slap a glove in his face and run him through with a rapier. He said it to his face, too. But the thing is, Kate, that neither of those things can be done without making things ten times worse for you. It would be assumed that the lies Forester has spread were the truth. Elliott pointed that out when I had Montford by the throat, and I had to agree with him when I stopped to consider. It was strange, come to think of it, that Monty did not try to defend himself."

Katherine got slowly to her feet and brushed out her skirt.

"Why is he coming here?" she asked. "To apologize? It is three years too late for that. It is Sir Clarence who should be apologizing, anyway, but if you ever let *him* come within one mile of me, Stephen, I'll—"

She could not quite think what she would do, but it would certainly be something quite violent and quite unladylike. And *she* was a pacifist too.

"He is coming to make you an offer, Kate," Stephen said.

"What?"

"Oh, no, Stephen!"

She and Margaret had spoken simultaneously.

"You are allowing him to come here—into your own home, to *offer* for me, Stephen?" Katherine said, her voice on the edge of hysteria. "*Elliott* is allowing him to come?"

His face and his voice were clouded with youthful misery.

"The thing is, Kate," he said, "that it is the only thing that would set everything right. The gossips would be satisfied if Monty were seen to do the right and honorable thing. And they would have nothing else to say about you if you were married to him."

Katherine inhaled sharply.

"And I am to give up my freedom," she said, "and marry a r-rake just to satisfy the *gossips*? I am to win back respectability by stooping so low and ensuring my own lifelong misery? A respectability I have done *nothing* to forfeit? And you *condone* such warped reasoning?"

"Oh, Stephen," Margaret said, "you cannot have permitted Lord Montford to call here on such an errand. Not after what he did to Kate—or tried to do—three years ago when none of us were here to defend her. You *cannot*. And Elliott cannot have done so. I do not believe it."

"The thing is that he has been dangling after Kate again this year," Stephen said. "I cannot see that there has been anything improper about it. I would have said something if I had thought so. So would you, Meg. Nessie would have said something, and Elliott *certainly* would. And there has been nothing improper in the way Kate has allowed him to dance with her and walk with her and sit with her. I actually thought a courtship was developing, and I was *pleased* about it, God help me, because Monty was my friend and I didn't think his reputation signified if he had fallen for someone as good as Kate. But they really have been favoring each other and everyone has noticed. *You* noticed, Meg. But what looked innocent and even romantic before last evening suddenly looks different in light of what happened, or nearly happened three years ago."

"You *cannot* believe, Stephen," Margaret said, and she was on her feet too now, "that Kate has ever done anything whatsoever that is improper. I have spent time with the Marquess of Allingham this year because we have a former acquaintance and like each other. Is there gossip about *that*? Am I now expected to marry him or risk ruin and ostracism?"

"Allingham has an impeccable reputation, Meg," he said with a sigh. "Besides, he has never made a wager that he could seduce and ruin you."

"I do not *want* to see Lord Montford," Katherine said decisively. "My answer is no. You can inform him of that, Stephen, and save him the effort of coming here. I daresay he will be vastly relieved. So will I when the carriage has left London behind tomorrow."

He ran the fingers of one hand through his hair, leaving his curls more rumpled than ever.

"I knew you would refuse," he said, "and I don't blame you. I would in your place. I told Elliott you would refuse, and he said of course you would. But the thing is that perhaps you ought at least to see Monty and listen to what he has to say. If it is known that he made the offer but that you refused, then perhaps things will look a little better for you. I am not sure they will, but—"

"I am not interested in things looking better," she said. "I am not interested in *things* at all, Stephen. And I do not care what anyone thinks. I want to go home. I want my life back. I want to forget that any of this happened."

"But it did happen," he said. "And I don't think you will forget. I doubt anyone else will either."

"Kate." Margaret had sat back down. She was paler than ever. "Stephen and Elliott are right, you know. You have done no wrong in any of this. *We* know it. But the truth does not seem to matter in this new world we moved into three years ago when Stephen inherited the title. Only respectability matters. Lose that, and it seems you lose everything. Perhaps you ought to see Lord Montford and listen to his offer and then refuse it. Elliott has considerable influence. Good heavens, he is a *duke*. And Stephen is an *earl*. Together they can put it about that you behaved with the utmost propriety but that you had the courage to declare your innocence of all wrongdoing and to refuse to take the easy way out. They can put it about that you have withdrawn to the country in righteous indignation rather than that you have crept off there in disgrace. I daresay you will not ever want to come back here—I am sure *I* will not—but at least you will leave the door open for a return if ever you should want it."

Katherine gazed reproachfully at her.

"Besides," Margaret added, "if you refuse to receive Lord Montford, Kate, it might be perceived that Elliott and Stephen could not bring him up to scratch, that they were unable to defend your honor as they ought."

"And they defend my honor by marrying me to a heartless scoundrel?" Katherine said.

She was being unfair. He was *not* that. It was Sir Clarence Forester who deserved that description.

But her brother and sister had said their piece, it

seemed, and had nothing to add. They looked at her, both faces still pale with misery.

And all this was not just about her, Katherine realized suddenly. This was about *all* of them. Even if she could go slinking off back to Warren Hall, or even all the way back to *Throckbridge* and somehow pick up her life where she had left it off there soon after Valentine's Day more than three years ago — and it was a big *if* — but even if it could be done, she would be leaving Meg and Stephen and Nessie to live with the consequences of this horrible scandal.

And she was not entirely blameless.

Her family was, though.

She still could not see quite how she could help her family by seeing Lord Montford this afternoon. She really, really did not want to do it. She never wanted to see him again.

But Stephen thought she ought. So did Elliott.

And so did Meg.

"Very well, then." She looked defiantly from Meg to Stephen. "I will receive Lord Montford this afternoon and I will listen to what he has to say. I will say one word in reply — *no*! But I will see him."

"I do think you ought," Stephen said. "Though my knuckles still itch to go at his face."

"Kate," Meg said, twisting her hands in her lap. "Oh, Kate, I let you down. I ought to have stayed with you in London three years ago, and what happened then would not have happened. Neither would everything that has happened this year."

Katherine closed the distance between them, grabbed her sister about the shoulders, and hugged her tightly.

"Meg," she said, "you have been the best of sisters. The *very* best. I am *not* going to have you blaming yourself, even if I have to *marry* Lord Montford to prevent it."

Not that it was going to come to that.

But the very idea of Meg trying to shoulder the blame, as she always did when something threatened any one of them!

13

IT had occurred to Jasper that since Merton had not yet reached his majority, it might be more to the point to speak to his guardian first. But when he had arrived at Moreland House late in the morning, he had found the two men together.

It was just as well. It had been a dashed uncomfortable interview, but at least it did not have to be repeated once it was over.

No punches had been thrown and no gauntlet dashed in his face, though both men had looked murderous enough and Merton *had* grabbed him by the neck when he first appeared in the ducal library and raised his fist. Jasper had expected a bulbous nose to match Clarence's—and had had no right to defend himself, by Jove.

The ensuing interview had been brief, hostile, deuced uncomfortable, and relatively civil. And the result of it was the afternoon call he was about to make.

Was there any way he could have predicted all this twenty-four hours ago? Would that damned weasel have dared open his mouth last night if *he* had gone to that infernal soiree instead of leaving the field clear for Katherine Huxtable—who also had not been there?

But dash it all, there had been rumblings of gossip

even before Clarence had orchestrated them to a veritable roar.

Hell and damnation! His mind followed up that mild beginning by dredging up every foul word and phrase he had ever heard or uttered. When he had covered the list, he went back through it again for good measure.

He felt not one whit better when he arrived outside Merton House.

He half expected that he would be tossed from the door by some burly footman hired for that express purpose and that that would be that—reprieve, freedom, and a guilt that would doubtless nag at him for at least the next decade or two.

Damnation!

When had he developed a conscience? At Vauxhall on a certain memorable occasion? It was a dashed uncomfortable thing. He did not like it at all.

He was not tossed from the door or even informed politely that he must go away as Miss Katherine Huxtable had decided not to see him within the next billion years or so.

He was admitted and shown into the library just as if this were any afternoon social call—the same library where he had seen her for the first time in years when she had let herself into the room to greet Con.

A fateful evening, that. If he had not accepted Merton's invitation to come here for a drink... If she had stayed upstairs and been content to wait a day or so before seeing Con... But fate had been playing one of its fiendish little games. He might as well add that if he had not invited his friends back to *his* house on his twenty-fifth birthday, then he would not be here now.

And if his father had not met his mother... Or his grandfathers his grandmothers...

But there was no time to go all the way back to Adam and Eve with his reflections upon the vagaries of fate, and no time to collect his thoughts and rehearse one more time the words he must speak. He discovered in some surprise that she was in the room before him.

Alone.

She was standing in front of one of the long windows, between the desk and one of the bookcases—in almost the exact spot, in fact, where he had stood that evening, feeling rather like a rat caught in a trap. She was not even standing with her back to the room, pretending to admire the view. She was facing the door. Her eyes were fixed steadily on him.

She was dressed in white muslin, an unfortunate choice today, perhaps, as it offered no contrast to her pale complexion. Her hair had been brushed ruthlessly back from her face and twisted into a knot behind her head.

She certainly did not look like a lady preparing to receive her suitor.

She held her hands clasped loosely in front of her. She did not smile.

Of course she did not smile.

She did not say anything either.

It was all a trifle disconcerting.

He advanced farther into the room.

"One thing I have to admit about Clarence Forester," he said, "is that he has a certain degree of intelligence. He always did. He always knew unerringly just how best to avenge himself against any insult or worse I happened to toss his way. He is, in fact, quite ruthlessly vicious."

"Lord Montford," she said, "let me save you time. My answer is no—unequivocally and irreversibly."

"Is it?" He took a couple of steps closer.

"You have done the honorable thing," she said. "You called upon my brother and brother-in-law this morning, and now you have called upon me. A proposal of marriage is to follow, I understand. It may remain unspoken. My answer is no."

"Ah," he said. "You will not allow me to make amends, then."

"There has been nothing this year for which to make amends," she said. "I have danced with you—once. At a ball, where the whole purpose was for ladies and gentlemen to dance with each other. I have received you and your sister with my own sister and brother in my brother's drawing room here. I have walked with you— once—in Hyde Park with our relatives. I have sat talking with you in a glass pavilion at a garden party, whose primary function was that guests converse with one another in the setting of the garden."

She had been counting off their meetings on the fingers of one hand.

"Ah," he said, "but there was also Vauxhall three years ago."

"Where *nothing* happened," she said, jerking her chin higher. "You need not make amends for that, Lord Montford. We both know that I was not innocent in that sordid encounter."

"Because you would have capitulated to the practiced arts of an experienced and determined seducer?"

he said. "You were as innocent as a newborn babe, Miss Huxtable. You must allow me . . ."

"I was twenty years old," she said. "I knew the difference between right and wrong. I knew that what was happening was wrong. I knew you were a notorious rake. I chose to ignore what was right because I wanted the excitement and self-gratification of what was wrong. The wager was . . . disgusting. Naming *me* as its victim was more so. But I might have said no as soon as you offered me your arm when we were on the grand avenue with the others. I did not say no either then or later, and so I am as guilty as you. You do *not* have to make amends. You may go away now, satisfied in the knowledge that you have at least done what society demands of you today."

"Even if you had refused to take my arm that evening and made it quite impossible for me to win my wager," he said, "the wager would still have existed, Miss Huxtable. It would still stand in the books. Clarence would still have found out about it and told the whole world with the implication, of course, that we became lovers that night and resumed the liaison this year."

"I cannot control what people choose to believe," she said, color in her cheeks at last. "I do not *care* what they believe. I am going home to Warren Hall tomorrow—where I belong and where I am happy."

He could turn and leave. He had come. He had made an effort to set things right. Good Lord, he had been prepared to take on a leg shackle for the sake of her reputation. She did not want him—hardly surprising. She would not have him—for which she was to be commended. He had even tried adding a little persuasion, but she was still adamant.

He could leave.

He could be free.

And perhaps things would not be too drastically bad for her after all. Merton and Moreland would put it about that he had offered and she had refused. Perhaps the *ton* would assume that she must be innocent if she was prepared to do something as foolhardy as refuse him. Perhaps they would forget in a year or two or ten and she could return.

He could be free.

If he did not marry, though, Charlotte would suffer. She would have to go to Lady Forester. Seth Wrayburn had made it clear that he would have no option but to give his vote to Clarence and Jasper's vote would count for nothing.

And if he did not marry Katherine Huxtable, she would be permanently ruined. He was fooling himself if he chose to believe otherwise just because he wanted to. The *ton*, with its rather peculiar notions of morality, would take back to its collective bosom a lady who had lost her virtue to one of its wildest rakehells provided she married him when caught out. It would never forgive a lady who was courageous enough to declare her innocence by saying no to the said rakehell and thumbing her nose at society's opinion.

"Are you quite sure scandal will not follow you even to Warren Hall?" he asked her.

"If it *does*," she said, "it will be my problem to deal with, Lord Montford, not yours."

"And your sister's problem too?" he asked her. "And your brother's? Are you sure the scandal will not touch them also?"

Those large eyes of hers grew luminous and she

turned pale again. He knew he had touched a weak point.

"This is all so *ridiculous,*" she said then, her voice somewhat thinner and higher pitched though she still had not moved. "*So* ridiculous! Why should my freedom be curtailed by the *ton*? Why should yours? Why should my family be affected by what I have done — or *not* done?"

"Welcome to the beau monde, Miss Huxtable," he said softly, raising one eyebrow. "Are you only now discovering for yourself what I told you not so long ago? That there might be wealth and comfort and pleasure in privilege, but that there is precious little freedom?"

"*Will* Meg suffer?" she asked, looking very directly at him. She had moved at last. Her arms had fallen to her sides. And her hands were fidgeting with the sides of her skirt. "And Nessie? And the children? And Stephen? Oh, surely not. It would be so absurd. And so unfair."

He clasped his own hands loosely behind his back.

"Will *Miss Wrayburn* suffer?" Her eyes widened.

He pursed his lips but did not answer. There was nothing to say that she did not already know.

"Your aunt wants to have Miss Wrayburn under her own roof," she said. "She wants to prepare her for her come-out next year. She thinks you an unsuitable guardian. But are you *not* her guardian? *Can* your aunt take her away even after this scandal?"

"Charlotte's father appointed three guardians," he explained to her. "Clarence's father, now Clarence himself, me, and Mr. Seth Wrayburn, Charlotte's great-uncle. Her fate on any matter can be decided by any two of the three of us."

"And where is Mr. Wrayburn?" she asked.

He pointed downward.

"Here in London," he said. "He is a recluse. He is not amused at the flurry of activity in which he has been involved during the past week. He does not like either Clarence or his mother, and has always preferred to leave things as they are with Charlotte living with me. But he is annoyed with me today. He gave me an ultimatum when I called on him this morning."

It did not take her long to understand.

"Miss Wrayburn can remain with you," she said, "provided you squash the scandal and silence the gossips by marrying me. Is *that* the ultimatum?"

"More or less," he said.

"More or less?"

"More rather than less," he admitted. "He did suggest a few days ago that if I do not want Lady Forester in charge of Charlotte's come-out next year I had better marry so that my wife can sponsor and chaperone her instead. Today, though, he indicated that my choice of bride has been narrowed to one candidate."

"Me."

He pursed his lips again.

"This is why he did it, then, is it not?" she said. "Sir Clarence Forester, I mean. He did it so that Mr. Wrayburn would have no choice but to grant custody of Miss Wrayburn to his mother."

"Charlotte is very rich," he said, "or will be on her marriage. And Clarrie is very poor and very single."

"He means to marry her." Her voice was flat. And then she laughed suddenly, though there was no hint of amusement in the sound. "I always imagined that when I finally gave serious consideration to a marriage proposal, I would have only myself to consider—and the man who was making the proposal. Did I like and respect him? Did I have an affection for him? Did he like and respect and have an affection for me? Would I have a reasonable expectation that we could be happy together for the rest of our lives? Was there—oh, was there that extra spark of.... of what? Of romance, of magic, of...of...of *love*?"

"And you cannot answer any of those questions in the affirmative now?" he asked her. "*None* of them?"

She shook her head slowly.

Double damnation! He did not need this. But then, neither did she.

"I am being asked," she said, "to think of what *other people* will think of me—some of them people I do not even know, all of them people I do not even care about. I am being asked to think about the good name of my sisters and brother, of my niece and nephew. I am being asked to save *your* sister from a fate that seems quite unthinkable. I am being asked to marry, not *for* something, but to prevent a whole lot of things. Marriage ought to be about only the two people concerned and their feelings for each other. Instead it is about a whole society. Society does not care if we will be happy or miserable, does it? It does not care that we will certainly be miserable."

Will be? As opposed to *would be*?

"Are you so sure," he asked her, "that we would be miserable together, Miss Huxtable?"

Suddenly she was hurrying across the room toward him. She stopped when she was no more than a foot away and glared directly into his eyes. Her hands, he noticed, had balled into fists at her sides.

"It *is* a mask," she said. "It is how you hide from the

world. *Open your eyes.* Look fully at me. And tell me we would be happy together—for a lifetime."

He felt jolted by her sudden anger. And rather shaken by her accusation that he wore a mask, that he was afraid, perhaps, to face the world with wide-open eyes.

He obliged her and gazed steadily back at her.

"I *want* you," he said curtly. If it was honesty she was asking for, then by God she would have it. "And you want me. You cannot deny that, Miss Huxtable. I would not believe you."

She laughed again—that harsh sound that was not really a laugh at all.

"You want to go to bed with me," she said, and suddenly her pale cheeks flamed with color. "And I want to go to bed with you. Very well, I will not deny it. It is a fine recommendation indeed to marriage, Lord Montford. We are certain to be blissfully happy for the rest of our lives. We will be married. We may go to bed with each other as often as we please without incurring any future scandal. Thank you. All my misgivings have been blown away."

He had not been feeling even one faint spark of amusement since walking into the house—not since he had stepped into White's this morning, in fact. But he smiled now—slowly and with genuine amusement.

He wondered how often in the future she would be tortured with embarrassment at the memory of talking so explicitly of going to bed with him.

"It would be one consolation for being forced into marriage, you must confess," he said. "Making love at night, during rainy mornings, during the sleepy afternoons, out in the woods at any time of the day or night, in the bottom of a boat, underneath—"

"Stop it!" she commanded. "Stop it this minute. And *open your eyes.* Marriage is *not* sex, Lord Montford."

Roses bloomed in her cheeks again. Scarlet ones. And they flamed rather than bloomed.

He smiled again and said nothing. He did not open his eyes.

"You do not understand, do you?" she said. "You do not understand about friendship and companionship and mutual respect and togetherness and affection and—and l-*love.* It is inconceivable to you that a man and a woman can share any of those things and need them all if the marriage is to be a decent one. You think it is nothing but s—" She lost her courage with the second mention of the word.

"—ex," he completed for her. "Is a marriage only friendship and respect and affection, then? It sounds yawningly dull to me. How are children to be begotten?"

Roses turned into flames in her cheeks and she swallowed awkwardly.

"You just do not understand," she said.

And he supposed he did not. Except that he did like her—it was not *all* lust he felt for her. He even—yes, he did—felt a certain affection for her. He certainly liked her better than any other woman he had ever met. Perhaps even as well as he liked and was fond of Charlotte. But was not the fact that they wanted to bed each other the best consolation they could find for being forced into marrying each other?

Apparently not.

You just do not understand.

"Then perhaps," he said abjectly, "you can make it your mission in life to *make* me understand, Katherine."

Her eyes widened.

"I have *not* given you permission to make free with my name," she said.

He let his eyes smile alone this time.

"And yet," he said, "you speak of our marriage as something that *will* happen. Am I to address you for the rest of our lives, then, as *Lady Montford*?"

He watched her swallow again.

"I have not said I will marry you," she said.

"Indeed," he said, raising his eyebrows, "I do not believe I have even asked you, Miss Huxtable. May I, though? Ask, that is?"

Something happened to her eyes. They grew larger and deeper and bluer, and for a moment he had the sensation of falling into them. Then they filled with tears and she lowered her eyelids over them and looked down at the carpet between them.

"I do not *want* to marry you," she said, "and you do not want to marry me. Why should we be forced into what neither of us wants? No, do not answer that. We have dealt with all the reasons why and will start to talk ourselves in circles if we continue."

He heard her inhale slowly.

"Very well, then," she said, "you may ask."

He took her right hand in both of his. It was limp and cold. He warmed it in his own.

"It will not be so bad," he said, trying to console himself as well as her, "if we choose not to let it be. The expectations of society and our concern for the well-being of our family may force us into marrying, Miss Huxtable, but they cannot force us into being miserable forever after. Only *we* can do that. Let us *not* do it. Let us make each other happy instead."

Good Lord, where were the words coming from? What the devil did he know about making a woman happy? What the devil did he know about making *himself* happy, for that matter? What *was* happiness?

But what else was there to say? Except . . .

"Miss Huxtable," he said, dipping his head a little closer to hers, "will you do me the great honor of accepting my hand in marriage?"

The dreaded words that surely inhabited every single man's nightmares.

Spoken at last.

Perhaps he ought to have made a complete ass of himself and gone down on one knee. Too late now.

Her head came up again, and her eyes met his from only inches away. They were still huge and bright with unshed tears.

"It would seem," she said, "that I have little choice, Lord Montford."

Loverlike words indeed.

"Is that a yes?" he asked, his eyes fixed on her lips. He forced a smile, which he hoped was neither twisted nor mocking.

"Yes," she said. "It is a yes."

"Thank you," he said, and he moved his head closer in order to kiss those lips.

Except that she turned her head aside, leaving his mouth half an inch from her ear.

Leaving him feeling like an ass after all.

Ah. Well.

"Perhaps," he said, "we had better—"

He did not complete the thought. There was a tap on

the door and it opened before either of them could re-
spond.

"Kate," Merton said, all pokered up and looking very
aristocratic and older than his twenty years, "is everything all right? You said you would be back upstairs
within five minutes."

He did not even look at Jasper. Neither did the elder
Miss Huxtable, who stood in the doorway at her
brother's shoulder. Nor did the Duchess of Moreland,
who was behind them.

An affecting family tableau.

"It has taken longer than I expected," Katherine
Huxtable said. "But we have finished now and you might
as well all come inside and congratulate us. I have just
accepted a marriage offer from Lord Montford. He is
my betrothed."

They all looked suitably stunned. Obviously it had
been understood that their sister would say a quick no
before his offer was even made and that she would be
back with them within minutes of his arrival.

Then her sisters rushed into the room to catch her
up in a hug—whether of congratulation or commisera-
tion was not evident—and Merton advanced upon
Jasper, his mouth set in a grim line, his hand outstretched.

"I am to congratulate you, then, Montford," he said,
all arctic frost.

Not *Monty* any longer?

Jasper set his hand in that of his future brother-
in-law.

Lord! He was an affianced man, soon to be a married
man. There was an unfamiliar ball of something that
felt like panic in the pit of his stomach. But it was too

late now to run for the hills. He was a dead goner, as someone had predicted at White's this morning.

Clarence Forester had better watch his back, by thunder, if he ever plucked up the courage to leave the safety of his home in Kent again.

And his front too, by God.

She might have married Tom Hubbard or one of a number of other suitors she had had when she still lived in Throckbridge, Katherine thought, and lived a worthy life of contentment.

She might have married Phillip Grainger almost any time since she had moved to Warren Hall and lived a worthy life of contentment with him.

But she had held out for that elusive something called romantic love, and now she was to marry Lord Montford, who did not know the meaning of either romance or love. She had no illusions about him. He was incapable of commitment.

And how could *she* commit herself to a man who did not take life at all seriously? One who was willing to wager that he could make her fall in love with him for the sheer amusement of tackling an impossible challenge? One who thought that physical desire and going to bed with each other were the only ingredients necessary to a good and lasting marriage?

They were pointless thoughts. She was betrothed to him anyway.

In one month's time they would be married. The nuptials were to be at St. George's in Hanover Square with as many of the *ton* present as could be persuaded to remain in town after what would normally be the end of the Season. If she were a wagering person, she would bet that that would be a large number. They would not be able to resist witnessing what they had collectively forced upon two people who had become victims of the vicious gossip spread by one of their own.

What a farce it all was! If it were not also tragic, she would laugh until the tears ran down her cheeks.

Elliott, who had remained upstairs in the drawing room when the others came down to the library, had thought it was best to have a proper society wedding instead of a quiet ceremony by special license. He had said so after they all went upstairs to break the news of the betrothal to him. Stephen had agreed with him. So had Meg and Nessie.

So had Lord Montford.

Katherine had not expressed an opinion. She did not care when or where they married.

She was sitting now, half an hour later, staring into the empty fireplace in the drawing room while her family talked about her with false heartiness. They talked with one another, having given up trying to comfort her and draw her into the conversation. Lord Montford had left.

And then the butler appeared with a visitor's card on his tray.

Whoever could be calling at this hour, so late in the afternoon? She would go up to her room, Katherine decided, and avoid whoever it was. She had had quite enough for one day. This was surely the final straw.

"Miss Wrayburn is calling with Miss Daniels," Margaret said, looking across the room at Katherine.

Katherine sighed. There was to be no escape yet.

"Let them come up, then," she said, and stayed where she was.

Did Miss Wrayburn know about the betrothal? Already? Or had she merely heard about the gossip and scandal?

A minute later she had her answer when the girl came hurrying into the room with a bounce in her step, all bright, happy smiles. She beamed about at everyone, but it was Katherine who was the focus of her attention. She came across the room, her hands outstretched, as Katherine got to her feet.

"Oh," she said, "I am *so* happy I could burst. I have never been happier in my life. You are going to be my *sister,* Miss Huxtable. May I call you Katherine, please? And you must call me Charlotte."

Katherine took her hands and smiled. Her facial muscles did not seem quite to belong to her.

"I would prefer *Kate,*" she said. "My family calls me that."

"And I am to be your family," the girl said, laughing. "I am to be your sister, Kate. And I will be able to live with you and Jasper until I marry. You will be able to bring me out next year, and I will not have to worry about Aunt Prunella ever again."

"No, you will not." Katherine squeezed her hands.

"I am happy for myself," Charlotte said, biting her lip. "How selfish of me. But I am even happier for Jasper and for you. I have known for *ages* that you love each other. I have seen it in your faces. I know you are going to be happy forever."

Katherine merely smiled.

Charlotte released her hands and turned to look about at everyone else in the room.

"We are *all* going to be family," she said. "Is it not wonderful? I had to come immediately as soon as Jasper came home to tell me, though Miss Daniels did not think it was quite the proper time to make a call. You *will* forgive me, will you not? I am almost family already, after all. Next month I will be."

"There is absolutely nothing to forgive, Miss Wrayburn," Stephen said. "Do please have a seat, Miss Daniels."

"We will consider you a part of our family from this moment on," Vanessa said, getting to her feet to hug the girl. "May I call you Charlotte too?"

"And yes," Margaret said, "it is indeed wonderful."

"I am almost *glad* Clarence has been such a beast," Charlotte said as she took a seat between Margaret and Vanessa. "Jasper might not have come to the point before the end of the Season, and we might all have had to wait another year before he did. By that time I would have been with Aunt Prunella. Even so, Clarence *is* a beast, and I apologize to all of you for the fact that he is my cousin. I heartily wish he weren't. But no matter. Soon I am to have a whole new family."

Had they all been so young and innocent once upon a time?

Katherine sat down and continued to smile.

Someone was happy, anyway.

At least *someone* was.

Jasper also had a visitor late in the afternoon—a mere quarter of an hour after Charlotte had gone dashing off to Merton House like a kitten with two tails, in fact. He had not stopped her. This was a strange day for all of them, and if she was filled to the brim with exuberance, then why stop it from spilling over? She would surely be forgiven at Merton House.

He was sitting at his desk in the library, though there was nothing on its surface except pens and ink and a large blotter. He had one elbow propped on the desk-top and his thumb and forefinger pinching the bridge of his nose.

He was trying his hardest not to think. There was no point in thought. It was a useless effort, of course.

It will not be so bad if we choose not to let it be. The expectations of society and our concern for the well-being of our family may force us into marrying, Miss Huxtable, but they cannot force us into being miserable forever after. Only we can do that. Let us not *do it. Let us make each other happy instead.*

Lord! He ought to hire himself out as a three-handkerchief speech writer. He would have the whole nation awash in sentimental tears.

But the trouble was that he must act upon those words, like it or not. His salad days were over. His wild oats had all been sown. He was going to be that dullest of dull fellows—a married man.

Such gloomy thoughts were interrupted when Horton scratched discreetly on the door, opened it quietly, and was then swept aside by the very visitor he had obviously come to announce.

Con Huxtable strode into the room, obviously in a black humor, looking like grim Greek thunder, and Jasper got to his feet and strolled about the desk.

Con did not stop until his face was an inch away from Jasper's.

"Do come in, Con," Jasper said. "No need to wait to be announced."

Con grabbed him by the neckcloth with one hand and hoisted upward. His face moved half an inch closer so that they were almost nose-to-nose.

Ah. *This* again.

Jasper did not allow his heels to leave the floor, but his breathing was somewhat restricted. He did nothing to free himself though he might have done so with some justification, since Con was neither her brother nor her brother-in-law. Or her guardian.

"I suppose," Con said, "you have offered her marriage."

"I have," Jasper said.

"And has she accepted?"

"She has."

Con backed him against the desk until the top of it, which overhung the side, dug painfully into his back. He still did not resist. A man must be allowed to defend his female relatives even if they were only second cousins.

"If I should hear one word," Con said through his teeth, "*one word* about you mistreating her or making her miserable or dishonoring her by continuing with your raking, I'll... I'll..."

Jasper raised his eyebrows. The main physical difference between Con Huxtable and Moreland, he realized for the first time, was the color of their eyes. They could easily pass for brothers, almost twins, but Con's eyes matched his dark Greek coloring. They were such a dark brown at the moment that they might easily be mistaken for black. Moreland's were a surprising blue.

"So help me, Montford," Con said, still between his teeth, "I'll put your lights out."

"Fortunately for me—or for *you*, Con," Jasper said,

"since I daresay you would not enjoy an appointment with the hangman, you will never be called upon to put your threat into effect. Tell me, did you always know about that wager?"

Con released him suddenly and took one step back. His nostrils flared.

"I knew," he said curtly. "You would have been a dead man if you had won it."

"And yet," Jasper said, "it is only now that you choose to demonstrate your righteous indignation? Three years after the fact?"

"Some things are best not spoken of," Con said. "Sometimes it is best not to stir up gossip, especially when it will swallow up an innocent—as it has now."

"Courtesy of Forester," Jasper said. "Do have a seat, Con, or pour yourself a drink, or pace the carpet. I find my eyes having a hard time focusing at such close range."

"Merton has a powerful arm," Con said, stepping back. "He almost certainly broke Forester's nose. Both his eyes are black today from the impact."

"You have seen him?" Jasper said, crossing to the brandy decanter in order to pour them both a drink.

"One of the servants left behind obviously felt no need to be loyal or closemouthed," Con said. "I suspect he had not been paid."

"That will teach him to take employment with someone of Forester's ilk," Jasper said, turning with both glasses in his hand. "Katherine Huxtable is to be my bride in one month's time—as soon as the banns have been read. Banns have been judged more proper than a special license under the circumstances. The nuptials are to be celebrated at St. George's, of course. You will be my best man if you will, Con."

14

KATHERINE'S prediction proved quite correct. Although by the time of her wedding day it was July and the Season was officially over and normally the *ton* would already have made a mass exodus for their country estates or Brighton or one of the spas, a significant number of them remained in town to attend the event.

Baron Montford was actually getting married. No one could resist seeing it happen, especially since the circumstances surrounding it had been so very scandalous. And everyone had always considered Katherine Huxtable to be so very proper and so very respectable. It was hard to picture her as the bride of such a notorious rake, poor lady. Though of course she had brought it all entirely upon herself by allowing him to dangle after her this year despite that shocking wager of three years ago. She was fortunate indeed that he was willing to do the decent thing. It would have been entirely in character if he had abandoned her to her fate.

The Duke and Duchess of Moreland were to host a wedding breakfast at Moreland House following the nuptials. The bride and groom were to leave for the country immediately after for a brief honeymoon before the arrival of the houseguests who had been invited to Cedarhurst Park to celebrate Miss Wrayburn's eighteenth birthday. Those guests were the envy of the *ton.* They were to have all the pleasure of witnessing the early progress of such an unlikely union.

But for now it was Katherine's wedding day.

She was wearing a new pale blue muslin gown that fell in soft folds from its high waistline to the silver-embroidered hem. Similar embroidery trimmed the short puffed sleeves and the modestly scooped neck.

Her new straw bonnet was lavishly trimmed with blue cornflowers and was held in place beneath her chin with wide blue silk ribbons.

The white gold chain about her neck with its faceted diamond pendant, which to her mind resembled a large teardrop, had been a betrothal gift from her bridegroom.

She wore long white gloves and silver slippers.

She knew she was looking her best. She needed to. Today had very little to do with her except that following it she would be married forever after to Lord Montford. No, today was all about respectability, belonging, accepting the rules and conventions of society. She was a member of society whether she liked it or not. She had been ever since Elliott, still Viscount Lyngate at the time, had ridden into Throckbridge to inform Stephen that he was the Earl of Merton. She owed it to her family to fit into society as best she could.

And when all was said and done, her family was all that really mattered. She loved them. She was doing this primarily for *them,* though they would be perturbed if they knew it. All of them at one time or other during the past month had found time for a private tête-à-tête with her and had urged her to put an end to the betrothal and wedding preparations if she really did not want to marry Lord Montford. Each had offered his or her undying support if she made such a decision.

Margaret and Vanessa were in her dressing room now. They had both stopped in the doorway to exclaim with admiration and assure her that she looked beautiful.

"And we were quite right about the color," Meg said, coming closer to take Katherine's hands in her own— with a painfully tight grip. "It is the very best color and shade for you. It matches your eyes and flatters your hair. Oh, Kate, are you quite, *quite* sure . . ."

Meg had even offered to move somewhere in the country with her if she wished—far away from London and Warren Hall and even Throckbridge. They would be quiet and happy together in a small cottage for the rest of their lives, and the beau monde could go to Hades—Meg's own words.

Poor Meg! This was all harder on her than on anyone else with the possible exception of Katherine herself. She had given years of her life since their father's death—all of her youth and most of her twenties, in fact—to the care of her brother and sisters. She had even given up Crispin Dew, the man she had loved and perhaps still did. Her one goal had always been to see them well settled in life. But more important even than that, she had wanted to see them all *happily* settled.

Katherine smiled and returned the pressure of Meg's hands.

"*Of course* I am sure, silly goose," she said, as she had said numerous times before. "I was horribly embarrassed by all those foolish stories a month ago, it is true, and I was terribly angry at having my hand so forced. And of course I was not best pleased with Lord

Montford either since in many ways—though not in *every* way—he was the cause of it all. But that is all in the past now, and I am well content with what has come of it. I am twenty-three years old and eager to marry at last—and I am to do it with the man of my choice. I really am *enormously* fond of him, you know."

She was overdoing it. That word *enormously* especially did not ring at all true. But Meg was looking reassured nonetheless.

"Then I am content too," she said, tears brightening her eyes. "And I *do* believe he has a regard for you too, Kate. Oh, I *think* so, and I thought it even before all this nastiness happened. I will forgive him all his sins against you if this turns into the love match I dream of for you."

Vanessa took Meg's place and hugged Katherine tightly.

"You know," she said, "I did not at all love Elliott when I married him, and he *certainly* did not love me. How could he when *I* was the one who proposed marriage to *him,* poor man. I believe he could barely tolerate me, in fact."

She laughed merrily and stepped back.

Elliott had been looking about him for a bride when he first assumed guardianship of Stephen, and being an unromantic soul at the time, he had fixed his choice on Meg for pure convenience's sake. But Meg had been waiting for Crispin Dew, who had gone off to war. Nessie had known, though, that Meg had a strong sense of family duty and was very likely to say yes to Elliott purely because she would think the marriage in the best interest of her family. And so Nessie, in a grand gesture of self-sacrifice, had proposed to Elliott before he had a chance to propose to Meg. And he had married her.

"But now," Nessie said, her rather plain face suddenly beautiful with animation, "we not only love each other dearly, we are also deeply *in* love. If there is the will to love, Kate, then love itself will follow in lavish abundance. I promise."

"But I already *do* love Lord Montford," Katherine protested. "And he loves me."

She was overdoing it again.

"Of course." Vanessa's smile suggested that she knew it but that she was filled with hope anyway. "*Of course* you do. Oh, I *so* want you to be happy. I want *both* my sisters to be happy. And Stephen too, though he is far too young to worry about yet."

She blinked back tears and laughed again.

And then Stephen himself appeared in the doorway, looking splendidly handsome and very grown up in black and white.

"Kate," he said, coming inside and reaching out his hands to take hers in a strong clasp, "my favorite sister, I would feel bound to say if you were not all three my favorites. I wish I could have been an *older* brother so that I could have offered some of the care and protection that you all always gave me. I wish I did not have to give you up so soon. But Monty is a decent man despite everything. I am convinced of it. There is nothing vicious about him. I could never have been his friend if there had been. He will treat you well."

"*Of course* he will." She laughed at his earnestness. "And soon your friend will also be your brother-in-law."

"I thought I had better come up," Elliott said from the doorway, "to remind you all that we are expected at

St. George's sometime today. It occurred to me that perhaps you had forgotten."

Katherine remembered seeing him for the very first time at a Valentine's assembly in Throckbridge, the evening before he came to their cottage to break the news to Stephen. She had thought him—every lady present had thought him—the most handsome man she had ever set eyes upon with his dark good looks, which she had learned later came from his Greek mother—except for his blue eyes. Now he was Nessie's husband and Isabelle and Sam's father, and she could see him only as someone very dear.

Oh, Nessie *had* been fortunate in her choice.

"I am *not* going to deliver a sentimental speech or offer any sage words of advice, Katherine, you will be relieved to know," he said. "It would all make us later still. But I must say that you look very fetching indeed."

"Thank you, Elliott." She took a few steps toward him and he opened his arms. She went into them and they hugged each other.

Did all brides feel that they were saying a final goodbye to all who were nearest and dearest to them? Was it natural?

She stepped away from Elliott and smiled about at all of them, only slightly watery-eyed even though she felt as if there were a great lump in her throat.

"If this is to be the happiest day of my life," she said, "and I am determined that it *will be*, then let it begin in earnest. Off to church with all of you."

A minute later she was alone with her brother, and the dressing room seemed very quiet and empty—all her belongings had been packed and taken away earlier. She took his hand in hers and held it tightly. It was as if *she* no longer belonged. As she did not. This would never again be her room or her home.

Stephen patted her hand.

"You *were* my favorite, Kate," he said, slightly shame-faced. "You *are* my favorite. You are closest to me in age, and you were my playmate and my friend and confidante. Be happy."

"I have every intention of being the happiest woman in the world," she assured him.

But she bit her upper lip as she smiled and then blinked back tears when he raised her hand to his lips.

"Oh, Stephen," she said, "I *will* be happy. Wait and see."

His family members were sitting in the pews behind him—Rachel with Gooding, Charlotte, an uncle—his father's brother—and three cousins, his offspring, all of whom Jasper had rarely ever seen because they had stopped coming to Cedarhurst after his father's death and his mother's remarriage. It had been Katherine's idea that they be invited, enthusiastically seconded by Charlotte, though they were not her relatives.

Indeed, both ladies had even insisted upon inviting Uncle Stanley and the cousins to Cedarhurst too for the birthday celebrations, and they had agreed to come.

His *family*. His blood relatives. His support group of persons who loved him unconditionally. Jasper's lip curled slightly as he sat beside Con Huxtable in the front pew. Though he had no real cause to feel cynicism—not unless he directed it at himself too. He might have made an effort to establish closer family ties after the death of his mother's second husband. Or after her death.

He had not done so on either occasion.

It had been too late by then.

He wondered suddenly—as he had stopped doing years and years ago—how different life might have been if his father had not tried jumping that particular hedge that day but had ridden up to the gate as any sane man would have done. Pointless wonderings, of course. His father *had* jumped. And died.

He felt an unfamiliar constriction in his throat and snapped to attention. Good Lord, if he was not careful, he was going to find himself weeping for his lost childhood on his wedding day. Now *that* would give the gossips something to talk about.

If he was not mistaken, the bride was late. A fine thing it would be if she failed to turn up.

A spectacular catastrophe.

Jasper, who had made it his business until one month ago never to worry about anything, felt a knot of sudden anxiety in the pit of his stomach and wished he had not eaten any breakfast. But wait a minute. He had *not* eaten breakfast, had he? He wished he had, then.

But even as he wished it and even as he wished his valet had not throttled him with the knot in his neckcloth this morning, Con looked back over his shoulder and nudged Jasper's elbow, and they both stood. There was a stir at the back of the church, and the whole congregation—dash it all, it was large!—was looking back to catch a first glimpse of the bride.

The clergyman was taking his place at the front.

She had come and he was dry-eyed and all was well.

Jasper inhaled slowly and forgot to exhale when he

caught sight of Katherine. Good God, she was beautiful. It was no startlingly new revelation, of course. He
had thought it on his very first sight of her more than
three years ago. He had thought it every time he had set
eyes on her since then.

But today she was his bride. Soon she would be his
wife. His baroness, by Jove.

And today she was . . . well, she was beautiful.

Dash it all, why was the English language so inadequate to one's needs on occasions like this?

He was glad he had worn a dark blue coat with pale
gray breeches and white linen rather than the black and
white that were more fashionable. Black had seemed
just too funereal for the occasion. Now they would
match each other.

Would they?

Match, that was?

He had promised her he would make her happy, had
he not? Or had he only said that he would try not to
make her miserable?

There was, he supposed, a difference.

But dash it all, this large congregation, most of
which had put in an appearance only out of morbid curiosity, would *not* go away thinking him unhappy. Or her
either, if he had any say in the matter.

As she approached on Merton's arm, he fixed his
eyes on her. He remembered to open them wide and
drank in the sight of her. And he smiled slowly at her.

She was looking at him too through the fine veil that
fell from the brim of her bonnet and covered her face.
There was color in her cheeks—or so it seemed.

And then, while everyone in the front seven or eight

pews could still see her face, she smiled back at him, and it seemed that she must have brought the sunshine in with her from outside. But was it not cloudy out there?

They smiled at each other—a bride and groom anticipating the advent of happily-ever-after in just a few minutes' time. It was a grand charade that they played.

An accelerated heartbeat was not necessary for a charade, though, was it? No one could see it.

His heart thumped out a merry tattoo in his chest anyway.

Good Lord, she was his *bride*.

He was about to be *married*. Forever and ever, amen.

They turned together to face the clergyman.

"Dearly beloved," he began.

She must have washed her hair recently. He could smell that soap smell that had always been more enticing to him than any perfume.

He could feel her body heat though they did not yet touch.

He felt a sudden and unwelcome wave of remorse. This ought to be the happiest day of her life. Devil take it, it *ought* to be. But only the happiest so far. There should be happiness abounding in her future.

The clergyman had said something and Merton was holding out her hand. Giving her away when he really ought to be clasping that hand tightly and whisking her off somewhere far away where she would be safe—from him. And happy—without him.

Jasper took her hand in his own.

And her very life into his safekeeping.

For the rest of both their lives.

It was a far more profound moment than anything he could have anticipated.

Devil take it!

"And what God hath joined together, let no man put asunder."

It was done, then. Already. So soon. There was no going back now.

They were married.

Strangely, though Katherine had been concentrating hard on the words of the nuptial service, making it all very real to herself, as she must, part of her mind had drifted back to that evening at Vauxhall.

She remembered the pull of forbidden attraction she had felt toward him then. And how their eyes had met and held while he was talking with Lady Beaton. And how her heart had turned over. She remembered the leap of excitement she had felt when he offered his arm later, during their walk, and the thrill she had felt when he spoke to her in a manner no man had ever spoken before. She remembered how that foolish, innocent young girl had fallen headlong in love with him, with the danger of him and the raw masculinity of him, and how she had followed him willingly to her doom because she had decided that love was not safe but that it must be pursued at all cost.

Finally she knew the cost. She was paying it.

Even though she had tumbled right back out of love with him on that same long-ago evening.

Except that some of her fascination with him had lingered on into this year, and she had given in to it and so sealed her doom.

Even today...

Even now...

She turned her head and found him smiling at her as he led her forward to the communion rail.

Ah, even now she found him more attractive than any other man she had ever known. And handsome too, of course. He looked plain...*gorgeous* in his wedding clothes. And he was her husband.

She should be the happiest woman in the world.

She remembered all the people sitting in the pews behind them—looking at them. Including her family. Whom she loved. Who loved her.

She smiled back at him.

Not long after, it seemed, the communion service was over, the register had been signed, and they were on their way out of the church, her arm drawn through his, the organ playing a triumphant anthem, everyone nodding and smiling—or simply looking. And she smiled and smiled. So did he.

As they reached the outer doors and stepped out through them, Katherine became aware that the church bells were pealing joyfully and that a crowd of the curious had gathered about the open barouche that awaited them on the square. Someone set up a halfhearted cheer, and other voices joined it.

Despite herself she felt a welling of...something. Not joy exactly. But *something*. Some sense of completion. Perhaps relief that it was finally done and there could be no further temptation to call everything off and run away.

Lord Montford hurried her in the direction of the carriage and handed her inside before joining her there and giving the coachman the signal to start just as the congregation began to spill out through the church doors.

The crowd parted to let the horses and barouche through.

It had been a cloudy morning. It had looked as if it might rain at any minute. But at some time while they were inside the church, the clouds had moved off and the sun was beaming down on them from a clear blue sky. The air was warm without being oppressively hot.

It was a perfect summer day.

A perfect day for a wedding.

He was sitting across the corner of the seat beside her, looking at her, his eyes half closed, his mouth half smiling.

"Well, Katherine," he said softly.

She looked back at him—at her new husband.

"Well, Jasper," she said.

It was the first time she had spoken his name even though he had invited her to do so all of one month ago.

The half-smile became a full one.

"Lady Montford," he said.

"Yes."

They could *choose* not to be miserable, he had said on that same occasion one month ago. Had he also phrased the idea in a more positive way? She could not remember. Could they choose to be happy?

Was it possible? Was Nessie right?

But even if it *was* possible, they would both have to commit themselves to the choice, would they not? What if *she* chose to be happy, and *he* chose to carry on with his life just as if nothing had changed?

"I suppose," he said, "we had better reassure our

families, had we not? Not to mention everyone else who has remained in town just for this."

And even as she looked inquiringly at him and felt the barouche jolt into motion, he moved away from the corner in order to lean across her and set his lips to hers.

She jerked back her head, realized what he had said, and . . . smiled dazzlingly at him.

"But of course," she said, and touched a hand to his shoulder as she raised her mouth to his again.

As he kissed her, his lips slightly parted, his mouth warm and moist and knee-weakeningly sensual, she could hear applause and laughter and a few whistles and more cheering mingled with the sound of the church bells.

All the sounds of a wedding.

All the sounds of happiness.

It had been a very crowded and a very grand wedding breakfast indeed. Jasper did not believe he had smiled so much before in his life. It had really been quite wearying. Katherine had smiled without ceasing too.

The happy bride and groom.

But finally they had extricated themselves. He wanted to get as far as Reading tonight. They had bidden their farewells to guests, hugged and kissed their family members, dealt with tears — Charlotte had cried all over them both even though she would be joining them at Cedarhurst in just a couple of weeks' time. In the meanwhile she was going to stay at Warren Hall with Miss Huxtable, whom she insisted upon calling her sister.

The farewells had all been said. The smiles had all

been smiled, the tears all shed. They had just left London behind.

Jasper settled himself more comfortably in his traveling carriage and looked at his wife beside him. She was quietly gazing out through the window on her other side. She was still wearing both her bonnet and her gloves, though different ones from this morning. She had changed into traveling clothes before leaving. Her hands were set quietly one atop the other in her lap. She looked relaxed.

A little *too* relaxed.

He wondered if she was looking forward to the coming night.

Their wedding night.

There *were* compensations for some of life's unpleasant experiences.

He reached out and took one of her hands in his. He peeled off her glove, one finger at a time, and tossed it onto the seat opposite to join his hat. He set her hand palm-down on top of his. It was slender and pale-skinned and warm. Her palm was smaller than his, her fingers not quite as long.

She did not move it though she had turned her head to look down at it.

He eased his fingers between hers and moved their clasped hands to rest on his thigh.

She did not resist. Neither did she cooperate.

Of course she was not looking forward to tonight. Marriage was not about sex to her, was it? She had said so the day he proposed to her. Women were funny that way, and Katherine seemed funnier than most. She dreamed of love and hearts of hearts and souls of souls.

She was like an alien creature.

She was also, dash it all, his wife.

And she *had* admitted that she wanted him.

He hated the remorse he always felt in relation to her. He was not a man given to guilt and conscience. He was who he was, he did what he did, and anyone who did not like it—or him—could go hang for all he cared.

But on one infamous occasion several years ago he had crossed an invisible but very real line from recklessness into depravity, and though he had crossed back over that line before irreparable harm had been done, nevertheless . . . Well, irreparable harm had been done anyway. The fact that they were sitting here in this carriage together, man and wife, but without a word to say to each other, was proof enough.

And he would, he supposed, have to carry remorse with him to the grave. Not remorse for himself, for the fact that he had been forced to take on a leg shackle today. That he could and would live with. He was a gentleman, after all, and he had always known that sooner or later he must marry and produce an heir.

But the point was that *she* had taken on a leg shackle too today. And for that fact he would always feel guilty. For it really was a shackle. She would not have chosen him in a million years if she had been given a free choice. Sexual desire alone was not enough for idealistic, romantic ladies like Katherine Huxtable—or, rather, Katherine Finley, Baroness Montford.

He almost hated her.

A fact that made him feel even *more* guilty.

He wanted his wedding night, nonetheless. He could scarcely wait for Reading and their hotel room and the consummation of their marriage. He had come to realize lately that slim, curvaceous ladies were far more to his taste than more obviously voluptuous ones.

And these thoughts brought with them more guilt again. He ought not to be thinking of his own sexual pleasures but of how he could make her *happy*.

He wished someone in the course of history had thought of striking that word and all its derivatives from the English language—*happy, happier, happiest, happiness*. What the devil did the words really mean anyway? Why not just the word *pleasure*, which was far more...well, *pleasant*.

"You know," he said, "it may not be as bad as you think."

Had he not said that to her on another occasion? When he proposed marriage to her, perhaps?

"*It?*" She turned her head and looked at him with raised eyebrows. "My marriage?"

"Actually," he said, "it is ours, is it not? *Our* marriage. It may not be so bad."

"Or," she said, "it may."

He pursed his lips and considered.

"Or it may," he agreed. "I suppose we get to decide. Will we be happy or will we not? It will be one or the other, I suppose."

"Is life all black and white to you, then?" she asked him.

"As opposed to varying shades of gray?" He thought again. "I do believe it is. Black is the absence of all color. White is the presence of all colors. I suppose life must be one or the other. On the whole, though, I think I would prefer color to its absence. But then black does add depth and texture to color. Perhaps certain shades of gray *are* necessary to a complete palette. Even unrelieved black. Ah, a deep philosophical question. *Is* black necessary to life, even a happy life? Could we ever be happy if we did not at least occasionally experience misery? What are your thoughts on the matter?"

"Oh," she said with a sigh, "you can turn any topic into a convoluted maze."

"Did you expect me, then," he said, "to tell you simply that I prefer gray to either black or white? I would abhor a gray life. No real misery but no joy either, only endless placidity and dreary depression. Indeed, I must absolutely banish gray from my own particular palette. Never tell me you are a gray person, Katherine. I will not believe it."

She smiled slowly—and he guessed unwillingly—at him.

"Ah," he said, "this is better."

"Will we ever have a sensible conversation?" she asked him.

He raised his eyebrows.

"That," he said, "is for you to decide. I have tried to provoke a discussion on one of life's deepest mysteries—the necessity of darkness in our lives as well as light—and you accuse me of having a convoluted maze for a mind. If you would prefer to discuss the weather, by all means let us do so. There are endless possibilities in that particular topic. If I should snore in the middle of the discussion, you may nudge me awake."

She laughed.

"Better and better," he said, half closing his eyes as he gazed at her.

If his eternal punishment was a beach to be cleared, he thought, perhaps one grain of its sand would be lifted every time he made her laugh in what remained of both their lives. But it would still take a million years.

Perhaps even a billion.

Perhaps it would be impossible.

But the thought brightened him. *Nothing* was impossible.

15

THEY stopped for the night at the Crown Inn, the best hotel in Reading, and took the best apartments there. Katherine could not fault either the private dining and sitting room or the spacious bedchamber adjoining it, with its wide, canopied bed.

They ate dinner—she even forced down some food—and talked at great length about the weather. At least, *he* did. She did not do much talking herself, but she did a great deal of laughing, despite herself, while he regarded her with those lazy, half-closed eyes of his and pursed lips.

He could be utterly absurd and vastly amusing. But she had always known that. It had always been a part of his appeal. Those facts did not make him into the man to whom she would have wished to find herself married, though. She had pictured someone altogether more serious, more romantic, more . . . loving.

She was afraid for the future and tried not to think of it. The future would come soon enough.

She was alone now in the bedchamber. He had told her that he was about to make an ingenious excuse to go downstairs for a while so that she might have some privacy in which to prepare for bed. Then he had proceeded to do just that—he thought he had detected a spot of fluff on the rump of one of the horses during the journey and would not be able to settle for the night until he had gone down to the stables to check and to remove the fluff if it turned out that he was correct. And off he had gone, the absurd man, after she had laughed at him again.

But she was not laughing now. She had undressed and washed and donned the silk and lace nightgown that was one of her new bride clothes, purchased during the past month—Stephen had insisted and had even threatened to take her shopping himself if she refused to go with Meg and Nessie. She felt half naked—which was silly really when the nightgown was no more revealing than either of the two dresses she had worn today. It was just that it *was* a nightgown, she supposed.

She was terribly aware of the large bed that was occupying much of the room, its blankets and sheets neatly turned down for the night. And of the relative quietness of the inn—even the distant sounds of voices calling and glasses and silverware clinking only served to emphasize the silence of the room. And of the darkness beyond the wide window. Their rooms were at the back of the inn and therefore away from all the light and bustle of the yard.

She sat down in an armchair beside the window. She should, she supposed, go to bed. Or she could get a book out of her valise. But she would be quite unable to concentrate upon it, and she would look a little silly when he came to join her. He would *know* that she was not, in fact, reading.

Oh, she hated this. She *hated* it.

A wedding night should be something magical, something shared, something . . . romantic.

The trouble was that she was strongly attracted to

him, that part of her really *was* aching with the anticipation of what was going to happen here when he returned. But part of her despised her own need, which
was entirely physical. A woman *ought* to despise any attraction to a man that did not involve her heart. She did
not love him—she could never love a man who lived life
so carelessly and aimlessly to say the least. And he certainly did not love her. She doubted he was capable of
loving anyone with a steady and enduring devotion.

But they were married. Surely *any* feeling, even just a
physical attraction, was better than nothing. Was not
that what *he* had said a month ago to console her for the
forced marriage?

She rested her head against the back of the chair and
relived the day in her mind—getting dressed this morning, hugging her family, arriving at the church with
Stephen, walking along the central aisle with him, and
seeing Lord Montford waiting there for her, his eyes
fixed on her and then slowly smiling, the exchanging of
vows, the shiny new wedding ring sliding onto her finger, the...

"Hey."

The voice was soft and low, and Katherine opened
her eyes to find herself looking up at her husband. He
had a hand on each of the arms of her chair and was
leaning over her, his face only inches from her own.

Had she been *sleeping*?

He had removed his boots, she could see, and his
coat and waistcoat and neckcloth. He was still wearing
his shirt and pantaloons.

She lifted one hand without thinking and brushed
back the lock of dark hair that was forever falling across

the right side of his forehead. It fell back again as soon as she took her hand away, and he smiled and kissed her.

Very lightly and very briefly on the lips.

All her insides turned to jelly.

"I was mistaken," he said. "No fluff. Now I can rest in peace."

She had not heard him coming back into their apartments.

"I just closed my eyes for a moment," she said. "It has been a long day."

"You are not going to plead *exhaustion,* Katherine, are you?" he asked. "On our *wedding* night?"

"No, of course not," she said.

"And is it," he asked her, "desire or duty that prompts that reply?"

She opened her mouth to give him an answer and closed it again.

His eyes bored into hers. He was still looming over her, waiting for a reply.

"Duty," she said. "You will not find me undutiful, my— *Jasper.*"

"Ah, will I not?" He straightened up and held out a hand, palm up.

She set her own in it and got to her feet.

It was *not* just duty. It ought to be, but it was not.

He tugged slightly on her hand and she came against his full length, her hands splayed against his chest. She could feel him instantly, hard and male, from her shoulders to her knees. She could feel the bulge of his manhood pressed to her stomach.

His hands slid hard down her back. One remained against her waist. The other spread across her buttocks and pulled her even closer.

She tipped back her head.

"It *will be* desire, Katherine," he said, and it seemed to her that his voice and expression were fierce, with none of the usual lazy humor. "Before I lay you on that bed and mount you, it will be desire more than duty."

She had offended him, perhaps even hurt him. Hurt his pride. He prided himself on his seductive powers, on his sexual prowess. Perhaps he thought, foolish man, that in those things alone lay all his claim to manliness.

"You had better see to it, then," she said, "that actions match words, Jasper. I do not want to be disappointed—again."

The fierce look was gone instantly. The humor was back in his eyes, and he laughed aloud.

"You minx," he said. "You saucy minx, Katherine."

And his mouth was on hers again, open and demanding this time, not subtle at all. She opened her mouth against the onslaught, and his tongue pressed deep inside her mouth so that for a moment she gasped for air.

And then one hand came up to the back of her head and tipped it to one side, and his tongue ravished her mouth slowly, pulsing in and out, curling to stroke the roof of her mouth with exquisitely light strokes until she moaned and one hand gripped his shoulder while the fingers of the other twined in his hair.

She could feel with her stomach that he was hard and big.

His hands were stroking over her then, his palms firm, his fingers gentle and sensitive, rousing every nerve ending as they went—over her shoulders, down her arms to her elbows to her hands, over her breasts, lifting them in the cleft between his thumbs and forefingers, circling her nipples with his thumbs and then pressing lightly on them through the fabric of her nightgown until they were hard and aching, down over her waist and hips, in to her stomach, down to cup her between her legs, down the outsides of her thighs, up behind to circle and caress her buttocks, lifting her slightly so that he could rub his hardness between her thighs.

His mouth had followed his hands—down over her chin, along her throat, down to the cleft between her breasts.

And her own hands had not been idle—or her body. She explored the magnificent hard, muscled length of him, pressing her palms to him, teasing him, caressing him with her fingertips, rubbing her breasts against his chest, her stomach against his.

After just a few minutes they were both hot and clammy. They were both breathing raggedly and audibly.

He had caught hold of the sides of her nightgown just above the knees, she realized suddenly, and was sliding it upward over her body. She raised her arms and he lifted it all the way off and dropped it to the floor beside them.

She was naked then, and the candles still burned on the dressing table. She did not care. She moved back against him and wrapped her arms about his neck and kissed his lips.

But he moved his head after a minute or so and kissed a hot, moist path down to her breasts again. He feathered kisses around one nipple while he circled the other with the tip of one finger, and then he licked it, inhaling through his mouth so that she felt a rush of cool air. She gasped, and he sucked the nipple into his mouth and suckled her while he rubbed a thumb over the other nipple.

She was so raw with desire that she could only lean into him for balance and throw back her head almost in agony and clutch his hair with both hands.

Her legs were weak. Up inside, where no man had ever been, she pulsed and throbbed with a need so intense it was indistinguishable from pain.

She let out a long breath on a ragged sigh. It sounded almost like a sob.

He lifted his head and kissed her softly on the mouth. One of his hands had gone down to cup over the throbbing place. And memory returned on a rush of sensation, the memory of his doing that once before and then . . . Stopping.

Not this time. Please, not this time.

"Please," she murmured against his lips. "Please."

He was looking down at her then with his lovely heavy-lidded eyes.

"Tell me you want me," he whispered, rubbing his nose lightly across hers. "Tell me, Katherine."

And for a split second she considered pulling away, breaking the spell, putting an end to this as he had done that other time. For he had promised she would desire him before he took her to bed, and he had fulfilled his promise—with the greatest ease. Just as he could have won his wager at Vauxhall if he himself had not decided to put an end to it.

Was this all a charade to him? Another easy conquest?

And did it matter?

She was his wife. This was their wedding night. She owed him surrender even if this were indeed no more than duty. But she wanted him. Oh, yes, she did. She did not care about anything else. She would think again in the morning.

Only a split second had passed—a jumble of thoughts that did not even have time to articulate themselves verbally in her mind.

"I want you," she whispered back.

Please don't stop. Not like that other time. Please don't stop.

He backed her the couple of feet to the side of the bed. She sat down on it, and then lay down and gazed up at him. But he had bent over her and kissed her open-mouthed as he pulled his shirt free of the band of his pantaloons. He broke the kiss for the moment it took to pull the shirt off over his head, and then resumed it while he undid the buttons at his waist and removed his pantaloons and drawers.

He came onto the bed with her, looming over her, his hands braced on either side of her head, his knees straddling her legs.

He was gazing down into her eyes and it occurred to her that he had not thought of blowing out the candles. Or perhaps he had. Perhaps he had left them burning deliberately. She did not care.

She lifted both hands and cupped his face with them. She touched her thumbs to his lips, moving them outward lightly from the center to the corners.

"I want you," she whispered again.

He kissed her, and his weight bore down on her, and his legs came between her own and pressed them wide until by sheer instinct she bent them at the knees and lifted them to twine about his, and she felt him position himself hard and hot against the most sensitive part of herself, and then . . .

Ah, then.

He came slowly in and in until there seemed nowhere else to come, and she clutched his back in fear of
pain. And the pain came, sharp and terrifying—and was
gone almost before she had felt it. And he came in and
in until she was stretched and filled and aching with
need from the crown of her head to the soles of her
feet.

"The consummation, then, my wife," he murmured
against her lips.

Her mind did not quite grasp the words.

He had moved his head to the pillow beside her, and
he was withdrawing slowly from her, and then—before
she could protest—pressing in again.

It amazed her that she could be twenty-three years
old, that she could have grown up in the country surrounded by animals both wild and domestic, that she
had known the basic facts of life for as far back as she
could remember, and yet that she had never really
known...

Ah, she had never *known*.

It went on for what seemed a very long time, the
wonderful riding rhythm, the firm thrust and withdrawal, the hot wetness that she could even hear, the
aching, the need, the pleasure, the pain, the ... But, there
were no words.

There were no words.

And then his face was above hers again and some of
his weight had been lifted off her. He had braced himself on his forearms to look down at her.

And the rhythm changed. It was slower and deeper.
His face glistened with sweat. She bit her lower lip and
then frowned slightly.

Pleasure had become pain pure and simple.

And then the rhythm quickened until it became ... unbearable.

She closed her eyes very tightly and pressed her head back into the pillow. She untwined her legs from about his, braced her feet against the mattress, and lifted, strained into the pain.

And ...

Oh, *and*.

It shattered into a million pieces and revealed itself to be what it had been all along. Peace. Beauty.

Pure, beautiful peace.

She was aware that his weight had come down on her again, that he was pumping hard into her, that after a few moments he held still, straining into her until she felt a lovely gush of liquid heat at her core.

But it was all peace. All beauty.

Until, after a couple of minutes, he disengaged his body from hers and moved off her to lie beside her and pulled the bedcovers up over them.

She was suddenly damp, cold, uncomfortable, bereft.

Bewildered.

Herself again. Though not quite that. Not yet.

She turned over onto her side, facing away from him. She needed to get herself back. She needed ...

She was aware of him turning onto his side too—away from her.

Why had peace given place so soon to turmoil? To two separate solitudes?

Because peace had been without thought? Without ... integrity?

How could she have felt like that without love?

Was love essential?

Did it even exist—the love she had dreamed of all her life?

If it did, it was too late now for her to find it.

Must she make do with this instead, then?

Only this?

Pleasure without love?

Despite the troubled turmoil of her thoughts, she finally fell into a sleep of sheer exhaustion.

Jasper did not sleep. He lay staring at the door leading into their private sitting room. It stood slightly ajar.

The candles were still burning. He did not bother to get up to extinguish them.

He had known that she lied—duty rather than desire, indeed! He did not know why he had even asked the question. Just to see if she would be honest with him, he supposed.

And then she had challenged him with just the sort of defiant spirit she had shown at Vauxhall. She had challenged him to *make* her desire him.

He half smiled despite the fact that he was feeling very far from amusement.

It was something he was good at, something he excelled at—making women desire him, that was. He *ought* to excel at it—he had had enough practice, by God.

And so he had made her desire him until she was mindless with need. He had not had to use all his skills, either, or even nearly all. Which was just as well—they would simply have shocked her and killed her desire. But he had used enough. He might even say that he had gone coldly about arousing her, except that it had not been cold at all. He had aroused himself too. Or, to be more fair, *she* had aroused him.

He had worked on her until she had admitted that she wanted him, until she had begged.

Please ...

And then he had taken her slowly and thoroughly—all the way to completion. He had surprised even himself over that. He had never before had a virgin. He had heard that it was impossible to bring a virgin to the ultimate completion her first time.

He had done it with Katherine.

And he had proved a point. He had vanquished her just as he might have done at Vauxhall if he had chosen. Despite all her scruples and misgivings about him and her marriage to him, she was like clay to mold in his hands when it came to sex.

Which made him one devil of a fine fellow.

His peers would clap him on the shoulder, slap him on the back, roar with mirth and appreciation if he could only tell them.

Monty, the ultimate Lothario.

He stared relentlessly and sightlessly at the door.

But Katherine Finley, Baroness Montford, had a mind of her own and a morality of her own—and dreams of her own even if he could make her temporarily forget all three with his lovemaking.

He had felt her withdrawal as soon as he drew free of her body. And she had turned onto her side to face away from him just as he had been about to slide his arm beneath her head, amuse her a little with some nonsense to make her chuckle, and tease her into admitting that her wedding night had been the most enjoyable night of her life.

As soon as he was sure she slept—it was a dashed long time—he folded back the covers on his side of the bed and eased himself out so as not to wake her. He went to stand naked at the window.

If he was at Cedarhurst now, he would have gone out for a brisk gallop on his horse, darkness be damned. But he was not there, and it would be considered more than a trifle odd if he were to abandon his bride to go cantering off into the night—he stayed here often enough that the innkeeper had realized that she *was* his bride.

He would not expose her to the ridicule that was bound to follow such a move. Not to mention the fact that he would be the laughingstock.

Damnation! And devil take it! He would not forgive Clarence for this even if they both fried in hell for a thousand years and the only way out was through forgiveness.

And then he stood very still.

Either she had not been deeply enough asleep when he got up or he had made more noise than he realized getting out of bed. She had made no discernible sound or movement, but there was a quality to the silence that made him realize suddenly that she was awake, and sure enough, when he turned his head to look, he could see that her eyes were open.

"The candles are still burning," she said. "You must make a pretty sight for anyone who is out there looking up."

There were a dozen answers he might have made. Instead he made none but reached up and jerked the curtains closed. He made no move to cover himself. And she made no move to look away.

"I suppose," he said, "you believe there ought to be more than lust."

It came out as a bad-tempered accusation.

"And you do not," she said, neatly turning the tables on him. "It is a fundamental difference between us, my—*Jasper.* It is a difference we must learn to live with."

It irritated him no end that his name did not come naturally to her lips, that even after marriage this morning and sex tonight she still had to stop herself from addressing him as *my lord.*

"Or not," he said.

She gazed at him.

"Is there an option?" she asked him.

"If I cannot bed you without feeling the necessity of loving you first and wooing *your* love," he said, "and if you cannot enjoy the aftermath of a bedding when it has been simply lust, then pretty soon we are going to be sleeping in very separate beds, Katherine. Probably in different houses since my appetites tend to be healthy ones. Though probably in your vocabulary that would be *unhealthy* ones. I enjoy sex."

"Yes," she said. "I do not doubt it."

He sat down on the chair where she had been sitting asleep when he came into the room earlier. It was unlike him to be bad-tempered with a woman. To accuse and complain. This was a fine way to start a marriage.

He tried again.

"I find that I like you," he said, "that I enjoy your company and your wit, that I admire your beauty and desire your body. I am even prepared to attempt affection and fidelity. But I cannot offer what you call love because I really do not know what the word means in the context of a relationship between a man and a woman. And I certainly cannot expect *you* to love *me* or even to like me particularly well. Not after what you have been forced into and with whom. This whole marriage business is looking to be impossible, in fact."

Not a great attempt. Worse than before, except that his voice sounded less like a petulant grumble.

"I have just realized something about you," she said. "It is something I had not even suspected until tonight, and it is a complete surprise. You do not really love *yourself*, do you? You do not even *like* yourself particularly well."

Good Lord! He stared at her transfixed, his fingers drumming on the arm of the chair.

"What poppycock are you speaking now?" he asked her, and irritability was back in a heartbeat.

"And I never expected to hear the word *impossible* on your lips," she said. "A workable marriage is *impossible*? *Love* is impossible—on *both* our parts? I thought, Jasper, that it was a matter of supreme pride with you to win a wager."

"It is kind of you to remind me of the only one I lost," he said.

"You did not lose it," she said. "You chose a more courageous and honorable outcome—which you, of course, interpreted as a humiliation. But it is not of *that* wager I speak."

He laughed softly.

"The one I made at Lady Parmeter's ball?" he said. "*That* was no wager, was it? A wager of one with no takers, no prize for a win, no forfeit for a loss, no time limit?"

"Those facts did not deter you before we were embroiled in scandal," she said. "You were quite determined to make me fall in love with you. It is why you pursued me so relentlessly after that waltz. And you *do* have a taker—me. And there *is* a prize—me. And a forfeit too—the loss of me. And a time limit—the end of the house party."

He gazed at her, speechless for once. But he felt good humor clawing its way back into his being. Trust Katherine not simply to be tragic.

"I will wager against you," she said. "I say it cannot be done, that you can *never* persuade me to love you, that it is indeed impossible. That it would be a waste of your time to try. But you are the man to whom all things are possible, especially those things that seem quite out of reach. Well, *I* am out of reach. Totally. Make me love you, then."

Tempting. But there was a problem.

"I would have nothing to offer in return," he said. "Not anything that would be of value to you, anyway. I am not a romantic, Katherine, and if I ever pretended to be I would simply make an ass of myself."

"That," she said, "is something for you to work out for yourself."

They stared at each other for a long time. The candles began to flicker. They had almost burned themselves out.

He felt a smile nudge at his eyes and tug at his lips. He could *never* persuade her to love him, could he? It would be a waste of his time to try, would it?

"But one thing," she said. "If the wager is to become a real one, then we will raise the stakes."

He raised his eyebrows.

"No love," she said, "no sex."

"Forever?" he asked.

"Until after the end of the wager," she said. "And then we will see."

A month of celibacy? And a new bride only once tasted? That was raising the stakes sky-high.

But the smile took possession of him. Impossible, was it?

An impossible wager.

They would see about that!

He got to his feet and moved toward her, his right hand extended.

"Agreed," he said.

And she set her hand in his and they shook on it.

"The couch in the sitting room had better be as comfortable as it looks," he said.

"Take a pillow," she advised.

He did so and then turned and walked out of the bedchamber.

The candles flickered one more time and died just as he was closing the door behind him.

The couch had been very comfortable to sit on. But it was too narrow and too short for a bed. He lay wedged against the back, his feet elevated over one arm, his head propped over the other.

It was not a position conducive to sleep even if the wheels of his mind had not been turning at breakneck speed—mostly with the same unwelcome thought.

He was, by God, going to have to offer something in return for her love, which he would, *of course,* win. And he very much feared that only one thing would do. Devil take it, but *he* was going to have to fall in love with *her.* And he might as well tell himself quite firmly now that it was impossible or he would never feel challenged enough to do it.

It was impossible.

There!

Now it would be done. He would fall in love.

Lord, how the devil could he ever have thought this couch *comfortable*?

...heart of my heart, soul of my soul...

He grimaced.

Devil take it! Were there *bricks* in this pillow?

He was going to fall in love with her.

His own private wager with himself.

Impossible?

Of course.

But doable?

Of course!

And then he had an inspired idea. He moved off the couch, lay down on the floor with the pillow beneath his head and his coat over his arms, and addressed himself to sleep.

Comfort at last.

His legs were cold.

16

"AND one *more* thing," Katherine said just as if they were in the middle of a conversation, when in reality they had been traveling all afternoon in virtual silence.

He was lounging at his ease across the corner of the carriage seat beside her, one booted foot propped on the seat opposite, his arms crossed over his chest, his eyes closed—looking indolent, but not asleep. Indeed, she suspected that he was watching her, though how he could be doing that with his eyes closed she was not sure—except that he was a man who scorned impossibilities.

He was also a man who had made no move whatsoever all day to woo her love and win his wager. She had got up this morning and steeled herself for a day of blatantly seductive wiles. Instead he had talked pointedly about the weather for a time during the morning, had remarked finally that if he could not coax a smile out of her he might as well get some sleep since he had had precious little last night, had folded his arms, and had closed his eyes.

He looked wondrously attractive, of course, all relaxed, slumberous male, though he was *not* sleeping. He was taking up more than half the carriage interior. She had to keep her feet and knees tight together and hold her legs rather stiff to avoid brushing his knee when the carriage swayed, as it did almost every moment.

She had ignored him. Though she could draw no real satisfaction from doing so while he pretended to sleep. She wished he would wake up so that he would know himself ignored. Of course, she *had* stopped herself from laughing over some of his more absurd comments on the weather. She spoke in order to wake him, though that, of course, involved *not* ignoring him.

He opened his eyes.

"And one *more* thing," she said again.

"*Another?*" he said. "Is this one more thing to add to the one more thing you mentioned a few moments ago? *Two* more things, in fact?"

She looked reproachfully at him.

"Charlotte is thrilled at our marriage," she said. "And I do not think it is just because now she has someone to sponsor her come-out next year and no longer has to fear that she will be sent to her aunt. She genuinely loves you and wants you to be happy. She thinks you will be happy with me. She thinks we are in love."

His eyes half smiled at her. It was really quite disconcerting the way he could do that without moving a muscle in the rest of his face. His eyes, she thought suddenly, could very well be her downfall—if it were possible for her to fall, that was, which it was not.

"That is one thing," he said. "*Is* there another?"

"Yes, there is," she said. "I come from a close-knit family. We all love one another dearly. We rejoice in one another's joys and grieve with one another's miseries. It is of great importance to my sisters and brother to see me happily married, to see us in love with each other.

Yet at the moment they are full of doubts. They fear that we do not love each other and never will."

"That is two things," he said, his voice lazy, as if he really had just woken up from a deep sleep. "Interesting things. Things to give me all the incentive in the world to win my wager and you all the reason you need to capitulate and let me do so."

"You did not hear me clearly," she said. "I said that it is important to our families that *we* love *each other*— *both* of us, not *me* adoring *you*, and *you* proceeding with life as usual."

"You want to make it a double wager, after all, then, Katherine?" he asked her, his smile catching at the corners of his eyes and curving his mouth upward. "You want to make me love you? I may even give you a sporting chance of winning."

"What I *do* want," she said, wishing he would sit up properly so that he would look less . . . less . . . Well, less *something,* "is that we put on a good show for the weeks of the house party. That we convince Charlotte and Meg and Stephen that ours really *was* a love match—or *is,* anyway. For we love them as much as they love us. I *know* you love Charlotte even though you deny being capable of any such emotion. And I owe more to Meg than I can ever say and love her more than I love anyone else in the world. I love Stephen dearly too. He is a good brother. He might have drifted from us in the past few years and concerned himself only with the pleasures life has to offer a wealthy, privileged young man."

"As I did when I left home?" he asked.

"I will *not* be distracted," she said. "Though of course, if the boot fits, then it ought to be worn. But we must agree to make them all as happy as we possibly can while they are at Cedarhurst with us. We can do that by appearing to be happy with each other."

"And after Miss Huxtable and Merton have returned home?" he asked. "We will keep up the charade for Charlotte, will we? Until she marries or for the rest of our lives if she does not?"

That was the weak point in her plan, of course. Pretending to an affection for each other for two weeks, while the house party was in progress, ought not to be impossibly difficult. But after that?

"We will think of that when the time comes," she said.

"We will not need to worry our heads over the problem if there *is* no problem by that time," he said. "You must work diligently over your half of the wager, Katherine, as I am working diligently over mine."

He looked sleepy again.

"I do not *have* half the wager," she protested.

"Then what is the point of me winning my half?" he asked her. "Why would I want you in love with me if I do not love you in return? Why would you want to love me if I do not love you?"

"I do not *want* to love you," she said.

His eyes moved lazily over her and she felt suddenly as naked as she had been last night in the candlelight— something she definitely did not want to think about today.

For she had realized something this morning—well, last night after he had withdrawn to the sitting room, to be more accurate. She had realized that in cutting him off from the physical side of their marriage for a whole month, she had cut herself off too. And she had been rather dismayed to discover that it was not a pleasant prospect. It *ought* to be. There should be no lust in marriage—only love.

There *could* be love if she took up half the wager and won—and if he won his half.

How absurd! She felt thoroughly cross.

"I think, Katherine," he said, "you just told a whopping fib. But perhaps you do not even realize it yet. Of course you want to love me—I am your husband. And of course you want me to love you—you are my wife."

Oh, she thought suddenly, he was at work already, was he not? The grand wager-winner? And already he was having some effect upon her. There was a sudden ache in the region of her heart—a fact that, once noticed, made her even more cross.

"Oh, go back to sleep," she said. "Or back to *pretending* to sleep."

But he took her left hand in his instead.

"We are almost there," he said.

"Home?" She looked through the window beyond his shoulder, but all she could see was fields on the other side of the hedgerows lining the road.

"Cedarhurst," he said with slight emphasis.

His fingertips were at the base of her little finger and then sliding lightly along it to the tip. Why was she feeling it in her *throat*?

"Do you still hate it, then?" she asked him. "Is it not home to you? Where *is* home, then?"

He moved his fingertips to her third finger, and they closed about her wedding ring and turned it slowly. He had pursed his lips, and his eyelids had drooped over his eyes as he watched their hands.

"If you intend always to ask multiple questions, Katherine," he said, "you must expect my mind to become more and more addled as our marriage progresses. You will end up with the village idiot for a husband."

She might have laughed, but she did not do so. She wanted answers. A man who hated the home he had always owned but who had nowhere else to call home was someone alien to her. Her husband, in this case. How very little she knew him. Yet she had married him yesterday and shared the intimacy of the marriage bed with him last night. To her, home had always been at the very center of her existence, whether that was the vicarage while her father had still been alive, or the cottage to which they had gone after, or Warren Hall, where they had moved three years ago.

"No, I do not hate Cedarhurst," he said. "Yes, it *is* home if it must be labeled at all. The word *home* is rather like the word *love,* is it not? Impossible to define and therefore essentially meaningless?"

"Those words are impossible to define precisely because they *are* words and can only symbolize concepts that are brimful of meaning," she said. "They symbolize emotions that are too deep for words. But we have to *use* words because they are one of the primary ways by which we communicate. And so we have to label something vast and fathomless and beyond value with totally inadequate words like *home* and *love.* Just as white encompasses all the colors and all the shades of all colors—as you pointed out to me yesterday."

He drew her ring off over her knuckle and then pressed it back into place before sliding his fingertips along the finger itself and moving on to the middle finger. A smile played over his lips, though his eyes were still hooded.

And now she was feeling it in her *breasts*.

"I remember telling you once," he said, "that you are a woman of great and extraordinary passion, Katherine. One day you will learn to direct that passion toward another person instead of to ideas—toward *me*, I would have to say, since I certainly could not countenance my wife directing it toward any other man, could I?"

He looked up into her eyes, his smile lazy and just a little lopsided. And now her *breathing* was suffering.

He looked down at their hands again as his fingertips stroked along her middle finger, causing sensation in her lower abdomen. She firmly ignored it. This was all quite deliberate on his part—to arouse her physically, but very subtly, so that she would fall in love with him. He did not understand at all.

"But to answer your third question," he said, "there *is* nowhere else. Nowhere else I call home, I mean. Cedarhurst is it, for better or worse."

"Like marriage," she said.

"Like marriage," he agreed, looking up into her eyes again. "When I spent almost a year at Cedarhurst a while ago, I took the first tentative step toward making it mine."

"What was that?" she asked him.

"I will show you when we arrive," he said, his fingertips tracing a path down her forefinger. And her inner thighs were aching.

What was going to happen when he got to her thumb?

It did not happen.

"Ah," he said suddenly, at the same moment as she became aware of houses appearing beyond the carriage windows.

They were passing through a village. There was a tall church spire a short distance ahead.

He lowered his foot to the floor and straightened up on the seat at last to gaze out. He raised a hand to a few people who stood on the street watching the passing of the carriage. And everyone raised a hand in return, Katherine noticed. A few people smiled too. All looked glad.

An interesting reaction to a landlord who did not spend a great deal of his time here and who even found it difficult to admit that this *was* home, that he did not actively hate it.

She looked curiously at him as they left the village behind and turned onto what she guessed was the driveway to Cedarhurst. It was broad and tree-lined, though she could see lawns stretching away to either side beyond the trees and water glistening far off to the left.

And then she saw the house up ahead, a grand, solid, square gray stone edifice. The front seemed all windows, the longest on the ground level, slightly smaller ones on the floor above, and smaller ones yet on the top floor below the roof with its stone balustrade decorated with stone statues. There was a massive columned portico in the center of the front facade with wide marble steps leading up beneath it to the front doors.

Below the steps were two wide terraces, one below the other, and below *them* there was a huge and magnificent square garden sunken below ground level and surrounded by low walls over which spilled banks of yellow and red wallflowers in glorious profusion. The garden itself, Katherine could see as the carriage made its way past it on the left-hand side, was arranged in perfect parterres with graveled walks, low box hedges, beds of flowers and herbs, statues — and a stone sundial at the center.

She said not a word because *he* did not. He sat beside her, looking out, and he had changed completely. She sensed a tension in him.

But this was *home*. Not just his, but hers too. She was Baroness Montford of Cedarhurst Park. The reality of it had still not quite sunk in despite yesterday, despite last night, despite now.

And yet she felt a tugging at her heart while seeing her new home for the first time — something she could not remember feeling on her arrival at Warren Hall more than three years ago. A sense that her life, all her future hopes lay here. And the house was beautiful. The sunken garden was so lovely that it brought the ache of tears to her throat.

Of course, she was seeing it all at its best. The sun was shining. There was not a cloud in the sky. And it was summertime.

"Ah," he said, breaking a lengthy silence, and he sounded more himself again. "You see how one's every actions have repercussions, Katherine? I thought it wise to send word to the housekeeper that I would be bringing a new baroness home with me today as well as a houseful of birthday guests within the next two weeks. And the servants have contrived a way of catching an early glimpse of you without having to peep from forbidden windows or about forbidden screens or doorways."

The upper terrace had come into full view. The carriage was about to turn onto it. In neat rows, looking more like clothed statues than real people, Cedarhurst's large staff was lined up on the steps, the menservants on one side all in crisp black, the maidservants on the other side, also in black, with white mobcaps and white aprons that fluttered in the breeze.

"A welcoming reception," Jasper said, sounding half exasperated, half amused. "I hope you are up to it."

Katherine remembered that the same thing had happened at Warren Hall when she and her sisters arrived there with Stephen. They had all enjoyed it enormously. Stephen had stopped to have a word with everyone.

"Of course I am up to it," she said, nevertheless feeling her stomach flutter rather uncomfortably. "I am your wife, am I not? The new mistress of Cedarhurst?"

Unbidden, there was a stirring of excitement at the realization that that was precisely who she was.

"My love." He was still holding her hand in one of his, she realized as the carriage drew level with the house steps and one of the men, presumably the butler, stepped forward to open the door and set down the steps. "I never did reply to your *and one other thing*, did I? I agree to your every demand. How could I not when I became your lifelong slave yesterday—entirely from inclination, I must add. And what could be more to my inclination today and every day for the foreseeable future than displaying to my servants, my family and yours, and my friends and yours that I adore you?"

She turned a look of reproach on him, but his head was bent over her hand as he raised it to his lips, the picture of the devoted and besotted bridegroom while every servant from the butler on down to the boot-boy gawked through the open door at them.

She laughed instead.

Trust him to make a joke of it all.

And to look impossibly handsome and—ah, yes—*romantic* as he did so. She probably imagined the sigh that passed through the ranks of the maids, but it would not be surprising if she had not.

He would give her a tour of the house later, Jasper decided, perhaps tomorrow. She had shown no eagerness to see everything at once. She had shown no eagerness at all, in fact. Not about the house or park, anyway. She had said nothing as they approached and he had sat tensely beside her.

What had he expected? Enthusiasm for the home that had been forced upon her?

And did it matter to him what she thought?

Did *Cedarhurst* matter to him?

He had brought her up to the drawing room after they had inspected the servants. They had walked up the house steps on one side and then back down them on the other—greeting first the maids and then the menservants.

She had smiled warmly at each of them in turn, repeated their names when his housekeeper or his butler presented them to her, and had a word with each.

So had he, actually. It had rather surprised him to see so many old faces—not necessarily old in years, but old in service at Cedarhurst. Did they *like* working here? Were they well paid? But had he not given the order to raise their wages after the death of his mother's second husband? And again after his mother's death?

He had remembered with some surprise as he greeted them all that he had liked most of these people when he lived here—even loved a few of them. They had fed him in the kitchens and washed and bandaged his scrapes and sometimes washed *him* and his clothes and polished his shoes before his mother's second husband could see the mud or lake water on them. They had even mended rents in his clothes. They had listened to his stories, some of them extremely tall tales. The gardeners and grooms had sometimes disciplined him themselves rather than complain at the house about his transgressions, sometimes setting him to work with a brush or hoe, occasionally even giving him a swift walloping when he really deserved it. Sometimes they had lied for him, claiming not to know where he was rather than have any of his favorite haunts and hiding places discovered.

It was strange how one could forget huge chunks of one's life. Those haunts . . .

The tea tray and a plate of cakes had followed them into the drawing room. Katherine poured their tea but did not take any of the cakes.

"I do hope," she said, "I will remember at least some of their names and that I will learn them all soon. There are so many of them."

"There is no need," he said. "They will not expect it of you."

And yet, he thought, he knew almost all the servants by name without ever having made a determined effort to do so. And he believed he might remember the names of those who were new—but only because there were not many of them and most of them bore a family resemblance to former or current servants.

"But I expect it of *myself*," she said. "Servants are people."

He was always amused rather than irritated by her occasional lapses into primness—a product of her upbringing in a country vicarage, he suspected.

After going back down the steps outside the house while talking with the menservants, she had stood on the terrace, looking up at them all and laughing. The breeze had been wafting the brim of her hat, and the sunlight had caught the gold highlights in her hair. And she had addressed them all with similar words to the ones she had just spoken to him.

"Please forgive me," she had said, "if I do not remember all your names the next time I see you. But if I *still* cannot remember one month from now, then I will neither deserve nor expect your forgiveness."

There had been a ripple of laughter, and Jasper's guess was that his whole large staff had fallen instantly in love with the new baroness.

He had been rather charmed himself.

She did not sit down in the drawing room. She walked over to one of the long windows and stood looking out, sipping her tea as she did so.

He went to stand a little way behind her.

"I think," she said, "that is the loveliest garden I have ever seen."

She was looking down at the parterres.

He closed his eyes briefly, and some of the tension that had been tightening his shoulders and neck since they had turned onto Cedarhurst property eased out of him.

"Is it?" he said.

For a moment he thought she had nothing else to say about it, that she had just been making a polite observation couched in rather lavish praise.

"It is so perfectly constructed," she said, "with such geometrical precision. Is it exactly square? Do you know? It must be."

"Down to the last quarter of an inch," he said.

She laughed softly, thinking that he joked.

"Something so very man-made ought not to be beautiful too, ought it?" she said. "Such a ruthless taming of nature? But it is. Perhaps it says much about humankind's place in the world. We can impose order and precision upon nature, but we cannot destroy any of its loveliness or enthusiasm."

"Enthusiasm?" he said.

"Look at the banks of wallflowers spilling down over the walls," she said. "They are exuberant even though they have been confined to the perimeter of the garden. They give notice that they can be tamed but not destroyed, that they are in no way less powerful than the men who put them there and who see to it that they remain there without encroaching upon the parterres."

He laughed softly, and she turned her head to look at him.

"Oh, very well," she said. "Laugh at me. I do not mind."

"The rest of the park," he said, "has been laid out according to the theories of Capability Brown and his ilk. There are rolling, tree-dotted lawns and a lake, and a wilderness walk winding through the trees on the far side of it and up through the wooded hills behind the house. All carefully constructed to look artfully natural or naturally artful—I am not sure which is more appropriate. The object, of course, is to make the park look like a piece of wild, unspoiled nature when in reality it is no such thing. The lawns came almost to the very doors until a few years ago."

"Just a few years?" She turned her head to look back outside.

"The terraces are newly constructed," he said. "So is the parterre garden. Last year it looked better than the year before, and this year it looks better than last year."

She was looking at him again, and this time he felt that all her attention was on him.

"Is this that first tentative step you spoke of in the carriage earlier?" she said. "The first step to making Cedarhurst your own?"

"It is one very tiny step, is it not?" he said, raising one eyebrow. "And it took so much energy that I doubt I will ever take another."

"This is *your* work," she said.

"I did not heft a shovel," he said. "At least, I *did,* but my contribution to the actual manual labor was minuscule, Katherine. I might have damaged my manicure."

"And I suppose," she said, "the design was yours too."

"Not at all," he said. "I lay no claim to artistic vision—or mathematical genius for that matter."

Though he *had* insisted that the square be exact, even down to the final quarter of an inch.

"Come," he said, "I will show you something—if you have finished your tea, that is."

She drained off the last mouthful and crossed the room to set her cup and saucer on the tray—to save a servant from having to retrieve it from the window ledge, he supposed. Another relic of the vicarage, where presumably there were no servants, or very few?

He led her from the room and into the east wing of the house, where their apartments were—the two east-facing bedchambers, large and square, the dressing rooms on the far side of each, and the private sitting room between.

He ought perhaps to have taken her to her own bed-chamber first since she had not even seen it yet. Or at least to the sitting room, where she could be comfortable and quiet during the morning hours whenever she wished. But he took her straight into his own bed-chamber.

He had had it completely redecorated and refurnished after his mother's death—though it had not been used for years before that. He would have gutted the room with fire if he could, but actually the changes he had made had obliterated the presence of his mother's second husband. Everything was dark blue and gray and silver now.

"This is my room," he said. "Not yours too, you will be relieved to know. And there is a whole spacious sitting room between us and probably a lock on your bed-chamber door to keep out the wolf."

"You have made a wager with me," she said. "I will trust to your honor. Even if there is a key, I will not turn it."

"Something," he said, "you may live to regret."

It was going to be devilishly difficult living up to that condition of celibacy she had added to the wager last night and he had agreed to in a moment of madness— just because it had added another element of the seemingly impossible to the challenge.

"This is what I brought you here to see," he said, indicating the large painting that hung over the mantel in its gilded, old-fashioned frame.

"Oh, yes," she said, and she moved closer to it.

"In a fit of desperate boredom a few years ago," he said, "after it had rained steadily for days on end, I made a foray into the attic storage rooms and discovered this, its face to the wall. It is a view from the house a century or more ago. Before the parterres were destroyed in the name of modernity and the artfully natural look. I fell in love."

She whisked around, her eyes alight with merriment.

"*Did* you, indeed?" she said.

He shrugged.

"As you so eloquently explained earlier," he said, "many words merely symbolize what cannot be expressed verbally. Clichés do the same thing when one is too lazy even to try to find original words. I knew immediately when I looked at this painting that if I were ever going to live at Cedarhurst, this is what I must look out upon from the drawing room or from the front steps of the house. And so I gave the necessary orders. Sometimes it is a great advantage to have both power and wealth."

She was looking at the painting again.

"But here," she said, "there is only one terrace with the parterres below it. And they are not sunken. They are not surrounded by a wall and banks of flowers."

"For very pride's sake," he said, "I could not just make a slavish copy. I had to add *something* of my own."

"Or something of yourself," she said, more to herself than to him. "Adding a lower terrace and sinking the garden below ground level are brilliant adaptations."

"Are they?" he said. He felt absurdly pleased. "How kind you are, Katherine."

She clucked her tongue and turned to face him again.

"I *thought* so from the sound of your voice," she said.

"You have retreated behind your usual disguise to deceive me into thinking that you do not care. This garden was not just one small, tentative step, was it? It was a bold stride to assert your personhood."

He grinned at her—though he actually felt as far from being amused as he had ever felt. He felt rather exposed, actually. And slightly foolish. Perhaps he ought not to have brought her here.

"There must be a wonderful feeling of seclusion and peace in that garden," she said.

"It is my hope," he said, "that you will find both there in the coming years, Katherine. Though I hope too that your desire for seclusion will not always exclude me." He raised his eyebrows.

She gazed at him without speaking for a few moments.

"I realize," she said, "that I dug a deep hole for myself last night when I made that wager with you. For the next month I will not know when you speak sincerely or when you speak merely to win the wager."

He almost fell in love with her then. Her eyes looked sad.

He smiled slowly, deliberately drooping his eyelids again just because he knew it would annoy her and make her forget to be sad.

"*That,*" he said, possessing himself of her right hand, "is the challenge of the game, Katherine. The *fun* of the game, if you will. And there is a third alternative, you know. Perhaps I speak from both sincerity *and* a determination to win my bet."

"Hmm," she said, a quirk to her lips.

He raised her hand to his lips and kissed her palm.

Then he folded her fingers one at a time over the spot he had kissed.

"Keep it safe," he said. "It is a small token from someone who adores you."

She laughed softly.

"You are a rogue," she said. "You really are."

"Come," he said. "I will show you your own apartments."

She liked the parterre gardens. No, she *loved* them. And she got the point of them. Beauty and peace. He had never assigned those actual words to what he had done to his home, but they were perfect.

That was *exactly* what he had tried to impose upon a place that had always belonged to him yet had never been quite his.

17

"T H E housekeeper—Mrs. Siddon," Katherine said at breakfast the following morning, determined to use names from the start so that she would not forget them, "sent word to my room that she is willing to show me the house this morning if you need to be busy with your steward—Mr. Knowles, I believe?"

"Hang Knowles," Jasper said. "Or rather, since I cannot think the man guilty of any capital offense, hang the idea of my spending my first morning at home with him and the account ledgers. I would rather spend it with you. I will show you the house myself."

And they spent the bulk of the morning wandering from room to room while Katherine became aware of just how grand a mansion Cedarhurst Park was—and of how surprisingly knowledgeable he was about it.

She was awed by the state apartments on the ground floor, where he took her first, and their gilded splendor. She gazed at carved friezes and elaborately painted coved ceilings, at heavy velvet draperies and brocaded bed hangings and wooden floors so shiny that she could almost see her face in them when she leaned forward, at elegant, ornate furnishings. She was amazed at the size of each room, particularly the ballroom, which was vast.

"Is it ever used?" she asked as they stepped inside the double doors. "Are there ever enough people to fill it?"

French windows stretched along much of the wall opposite. There was a small balcony beyond them, she could see. The wall on either side of the doors was all mirrors. If one stood in the middle of the room, Katherine thought, one would have the impression of doors and light and openness stretching in both directions.

"Not by London standards," he said. "Nothing that could be called by that flattering term *a great squeeze*. But there used to be a Christmas ball to impress all the local gentry for miles around. There was even once a tradition, I have been told, of inviting everyone to Cedarhurst—not just the gentry but *everyone*—for a summer fete and ball in the gardens and the ballroom."

"You have been *told*," she said. "You do not remember those fetes, then?"

"Oh, goodness me, no," he said. "We were of far too great a consequence to continue *that* vulgar tradition. Besides, worse than being vulgar, it was sinful. Evil. The work of the devil."

Who were *we*? She did not ask. But she could guess that he spoke of his stepfather.

"And are *you* of too great a consequence?" she asked him.

"To revive the tradition?" he asked her. "It sounds like a great deal of hard work, Katherine. I am not sure I am up to it."

"You do not need to be," she said. "You have a wife now."

He grimaced.

"Thank you for reminding me," he said. "That fact

caused me a rather restless night, you know. I suppose you slept like the proverbial baby?"

"I slept very well after the long journey, thank you," she lied. She had actually been terribly aware that it was the second night of her marriage but that her bridegroom was sleeping—or not sleeping—alone just two rooms removed from hers when just the night before...

"As I thought," he said, "cruel heart."

And he looked soulfully at her and then grinned.

"Perhaps," she said, "we could revive it for Charlotte's birthday and give her a party that will be grander and more memorable than anything she has imagined."

"The fete?" he said, raising both eyebrows. "The ball? This year? In less than one month's time?"

"Why not?" she said, suddenly caught up in the excitement of such a wildly *impossible* scheme. "It would be a wonderful way to involve the whole neighborhood and countryside in a joint celebration of Charlotte's growing up and our marriage."

He looked at her and cocked one eyebrow.

"I have an alarming suspicion," he said, "that I have married an enthusiastic wife. Do tell me I am wrong."

She laughed.

"I think it would be a splendid idea," she said. "If *you* will agree, that is."

He raised both eyebrows.

"*If* I agree?" he said. "I am merely the master here, am I not—as I always have been? *You* are the mistress, Katherine. You will do as you please."

Oh, she would indeed. But although he had spoken with the sort of lazy irony that was characteristic of him, there was something about the words themselves that caught her attention and made her look more closely at him—you *will* do as you please rather than you *may* do as you please.

"You are not *merely* the master here," she said. "You *are* the master. It must be what you wish too."

"To run three-legged races and egg-and-spoon races all afternoon and taste two dozen fruit tarts and view twice that many embroidered cloths and handkerchiefs before naming a winner and have my ears murdered by the shrieking of children at play?" he said with an elaborate shudder. "And then to trip the light fantastic all evening in a succession of vigorous country dances? Katherine, you know how much I love to dance."

And yet she had the curious impression that he was pleased, that he *wanted* the fete to be revived. It was his stepfather who had put an end to a tradition that had been upheld by his father and grandfather and perhaps even generations before that. Now he could restore it.

"We might allow one waltz," she said. "I might even be persuaded to reserve it for you."

He raised one eyebrow.

"Ah. Well, in that case," he said, "I capitulate on everything. Organize this fete and ball by all means. I will waltz with you at the latter so that you will not be a wallflower—a dreadful fate for a lady, or so I have heard. You will doubtless call upon me if you need my assistance with anything else."

"Oh, I will," she assured him, smiling. "Are we going to call upon your . . . upon *our* neighbors soon?"

"*We?*" He grimaced.

"Of course," she said. "You must introduce me. It is surely expected, though I suppose some people will think it more appropriate to come here to pay their respects to us. That is what happened after Stephen went to Warren Hall. Let us forestall them and go call on them. It will give you a chance to show everyone how much you love me, how much we love each other. It will help us to begin our life here on the right footing."

She had woken this morning full of energy and full of hope, though hope for exactly *what* she did not know. Perhaps their marriage need not be the dreadful thing she had imagined during the month before their wedding, when she had seen very little of her betrothed and had never been alone with him.

"And so it will," he said, his eyes suddenly amused. "It will be done, then. But why are we standing here in the ballroom doorway when there is far more to see? The gallery is at the far side of the state rooms, but it is full of ancient family portraits which can be of no interest whatsoever to you. I will show you some of the family apartments you have not yet seen."

"But I would like to see the gallery," she said.

"Would you?" He looked surprised.

It was long and high-ceilinged, a companion piece to the ballroom at the other side of the main floor, though narrower. It ran the full width of the house with windows at both ends to provide light. There were marble busts in every second alcove, cushioned benches in the others. The floor gleamed. The walls were hung with portraits. It would be the perfect place for exercise in rainy weather.

Katherine walked from one to the other of the paintings while Jasper explained who the subjects were and what relationship they bore to him. She had not realized how ancient a family the Finleys were. There were portraits reaching back to the fifteenth century.

"You know everything about all these paintings and the history of your family," she said. "I am surprised—and impressed."

"Are you?" he said. "But they are exclusively mine, you see. And I spent a great deal of time up here as a boy."

She wondered if he realized how much he had revealed to her in those few words.

They moved on until they came to the final two portraits.

"My mother," he said of the first. "And my father."

His mother, brown-haired and dressed in the fashion of twenty years or more ago, was plump and pretty and placidly smiling as she sat at an embroidery frame, a small dog like a bundle of fur at her feet. Katherine could see no resemblance to either Jasper or Charlotte—or Rachel.

His father, on the other hand, looked very much like Jasper even down to the mockingly raised right eyebrow. He was slender and dark and handsome. And he was about the same age in the portrait as Jasper was now.

"It was painted only a few months before his death," Jasper said. "A few months before my birth."

"How did he die?" she asked.

"He broke his neck," he told her, "jumping a hedge on a wet, muddy day. He was in his cups—a not unusual state with him, apparently."

"I am sorry," she said.

"Why?" he asked. "Did you cause him to drink? Or to

jump that hedge when apparently there was an open gate not twenty yards away?"

"Sorry for *you*," she explained.

"Why?" he said again. "He was no loss to me. I never knew him. Though I resemble him to an uncanny degree—or so I have always been told. In looks and every other imaginable way."

She turned away from the portrait to look at him. There was, she realized with sudden shock, a world of pain locked up in this mocking, careless, rakish man she had married. Perhaps it had not been such a good idea to have insisted that they come in here. Or perhaps it had. He had spoken with unaccustomed bitterness. Was it worth trying to penetrate his defenses?

"Ah, those eyes," he said, cupping her chin with one hand. "They are what first drew me to you, you know, in those long-ago days when I dared not admire any respectable lady lest her mama snare me in her net and whisk me off to the altar. But I would not have been able to resist your eyes, Katherine, even if you had been surrounded by half a dozen mothers. Do you know how deep, how fathomless, they are, how they draw in the beholder to . . . Ah. To what? To your soul? To rest there in peace?"

With the pad of his thumb he traced the seam of her lips, sending shivers downward into her breasts and her womb and her inner thighs.

His voice was soft, warm with sincerity. So were his eyes.

He was a very dangerous man indeed.

Not that she must resist loving him. It had occurred to her that if she was bound to him for life she must try to feel a deeper fondness for him than she did. But she *would* resist dancing to his tune. She would love if and when she *chose* to love, not when he had tricked her into a mindless infatuation.

"I suppose," she said, smiling against his thumb, "you took one look at me—or at my *eyes*—and fell instantly and irrevocably in love with me. And this was before the Vauxhall evening, I take it?"

"Ah, Katherine," he said, his voice and eyes openly mournful now, "I was not wise enough to fall in love with you then and so prevent the disaster of Vauxhall. What *is* it about your eyes, though? Is it that they reveal or hint at a person well worth knowing? Someone whose love is well worth courting? Someone who is well worth loving?"

She felt more like crying than thinking of a suitably spirited retort.

"You are going to have to do considerably better than that, you know," she said. "A Cheltenham tragedy will not do it."

"Ah. Will it not, cruel heart?"

He removed his hand and grinned at her.

"And you are *not* your father, Jasper," she said. "You are yourself."

For a moment his eyes looked curiously bleak despite the grin. Then he took her hand in his and raised it so that he could kiss the inside of her wrist.

"I am, as you say, myself," he said. "A fact for which I am remarkably thankful, especially at this moment."

He raised her hand and set it on his shoulder. He took a half step forward and slid his other arm about her waist, so that they were lightly touching along their full length.

He was, she supposed, going to kiss her. Their wager

had not forbidden kisses, had it? But she could not bear to be kissed at this precise moment. Her emotions were feeling rather raw.

"It would be desirable," she said, "for us to concentrate upon becoming friends before we even think of love."

"*Friends?*" He chuckled. "After this month is over, Katherine, I intend to take you to bed every night and all night—and often during the days too. I would find it inordinately embarrassing to take my *friend* to bed. *Con* is my friend, and Charlie Field and Hal Blackstone and half a dozen other fellows. All male. I believe you might find me a mite impotent if I got into bed with you and then discovered that I had got in with my *friend*."

She could not help laughing.

"Is it easier, then," she asked him, "to make love to your enemy?"

"Enemy be damned," he said. "Pardon my language. I would rather make love to my *lover*, Katherine. To *you*, since you are my wife and sex is one of the definite advantages of being married, provided one can tolerate one's wife."

"And provided she can tolerate her husband," she said.

"Neither of which *provideds* poses any problem in this particular marriage," he said. "*Do* they?"

He waited for her answer. And there was no witty response to that particular question, was there?

"No," she said.

He smiled slowly, his eyelids drooping over his eyes, which focused on her lips.

"I do not suppose," he said, "I can persuade you to forget the one condition of our wager, can I?"

"That it will take you one month to win my love?" she said. "Oh, very well, then. We will make it five weeks if you feel you need more time."

He threw back his head and laughed, startling her.

"You minx, Katherine," he said. "I adore you. Do you know that?"

"You would have to define the word *adore*," she said.

He leaned forward again and kissed her—on the tip of her nose.

"The wager will remain as it is, then," he said. "We will make up for lost time when the month is over. But we are wasting a lovely day standing here. Come and sit in the parterre garden. You have not even smelled it yet—all those herbs."

And he took her hand in his and laced their fingers together before leaving the gallery with her and descending the stairs and stepping out onto the upper terrace.

Just like lovers.

Or newlyweds.

With nothing to care about but their absorption in each other.

They spent an hour or more in the garden, first strolling along the graveled walks, examining the statues, admiring the flowers, and the neatly clipped hedges, smelling the herbs, reading the time by the sundial, and then sitting on one of the seats that were half hidden against the banks of wallflowers.

They breathed in the mingled scents of sage, mint, lavender, and myriad flowers, and Katherine closed her eyes and sighed with what sounded very like contentment.

Jasper had never really understood what had drawn him to that old painting in the attic to the extent that he had almost instantly determined to restore the parterres as they had been a century ago, with adaptations of his own. If he had thought of it at all, he would have given a negative reason—the artificiality of such a garden beyond the front doors and directly below the drawing room windows would have horrified his mother's second husband and therefore must be recreated. Perhaps his decision to make it a *sunken* garden and therefore very difficult to remove and obliterate at any future date had been a final act of defiance to the hated memory.

But a positive had come out of that negative motive. The garden was both beautiful and peaceful, though he had never thought of that latter fact until Katherine had used the word.

Strange that, when the garden was in full view of the house and of any carriage approaching it.

"Is solitude necessary for peace?" he asked her.

She opened her eyes.

"Perhaps not," she said, "if one is in harmony with one's surroundings and any companion with whom one shares them."

"But not someone who talks a great deal?" he said.

She smiled.

"Is this," he asked her when she said nothing, "another case of wearing the boot if it fits?"

"No," she said. "I am feeling perfectly at peace even when you talk. I love it here."

"Do you?" he asked her. "Here in the garden? Or here at Cedarhurst?"

"Both," she said.

"And with present company?" he asked her.

"You remind me," she said, still smiling, "of a little boy seeking approval."

Good Lord!

"Whereas in reality," he said, "I am a big, bad boy wondering if he dares steal a kiss—if kissing is permitted, that is. *Is* it?"

"In full view of the house?" she said. "And any servants who happen to be peeping out at us? It is said that servants know their employers better than anyone else, that there is no hiding anything of significance from them. How long will it be before they know us and our marriage as well as we do? Even as long as a month?"

She had not answered his question about kissing.

He was feeling remarkably contented, considering the fact that he had got married just two days ago under the worst possible circumstances and agreed on his wedding night to a whole month of celibacy.

It felt surprisingly good to be home.

With Katherine.

Despite what he had said in the gallery about friendship with women, he had the odd feeling that he could become comfortable with Katherine's companionship.

Comfortable?

Companionship?

Peace was shattered in a sudden surge of panic.

Good Lord and devil take it, he was *a married man*.

And if *that* realization was not terrifying enough, there was the added conviction—it suddenly occurred to him and took him completely by surprise—that he did not really approve of adultery. One reason he had hated that viper of a second husband of his mother's with such intensity was that for all his piety and righteousness he had kept a mistress not twenty miles away and had visited her regularly twice a week from the time of his marriage until his death.

Oh, yes, Katherine had spoken a greater truth than she realized just a moment ago. Servants did indeed know all there was to know about their masters—or, in this case, about their master's stepfather and self-appointed guardian.

No, dash it all, he did *not* believe in adultery.

Comfort and companionship would be *something,* he supposed. But there was going to have to be more. There was going to *have* to be. He was definitely not cut out for either celibacy or a companionable, decorous exercise of his marital rights once a week or so.

"This," she said, indicating the parterres, "was what you described as your first tentative step to making Cedarhurst your own. And it was a magnificent step. What will your second be, Jasper? And your third?"

"*Must* there be a second and third?" he asked with a sigh. "Have I not exerted myself enough for one lifetime?"

"Is everything about the house and the park perfect, then?" she asked him. "Are you content to live with everything as it is for the rest of your life?"

"Well," he said, "since moving into the east wing—*and* exerting myself to refurbish my bedchamber, I would have you know—I have been dissatisfied with the sight of the long stretch of lawn below my window.

There is nothing to look at but grass and trees in the distance. But I can hardly have parterres put there too."

"Probably not," she agreed. "I had the same thought, though, when I looked out of my window this morning. There ought to be flowers down there so that they can be smelled from the bedchambers. And seen, of course. A rose garden, perhaps, though I would prefer to keep a rose garden small rather than have it fill that whole space—a rose *arbor* rather than a full garden."

"With an apple orchard beyond it," he said. "There is no orchard in the park. I always rather like seeing trees planted in straight rows like soldiers."

"And blooming in the spring," she said, turning a glowing face his way. "Oh, there is nothing more magical."

"And heavy with fruit in the late summer," he said. "To be plucked at will."

She jumped to her feet and reached out a hand to him. "Let us go and look," she said. "Let us go and see if it will be possible to have both. Though I am sure it will."

He looked up at her and her outstretched hand and felt something in his soul shift. Perhaps it was nothing more than an easing of guilt. Maybe marriage would suit her after all, even with a man she would not have chosen in a million years if she could have made a free choice. And even without someone who could be heart of her heart and soul of her soul. As soon as the month was over, he was going to start working on giving her babies. She would surely be a wonderful mother— one who would enjoy her children. Had she not taught young children at that village in which she had grown up?

And before the month was over he was going to be able to look her in the eye without even having to make use of what she called his mask and tell her that he loved her. Even if he did not know quite what he meant by the words, he was going to say them. And mean them too as far as he was able.

He stood up and took her hand in his, lacing their fingers together.

"Very well, then," he said with a sigh. "But you are not envisioning me with a shovel in my hands, digging holes for the apple trees, are you, Katherine?"

Ah, he loved to see her laugh.

"No, of course not," she said. "I picture you wielding an axe and a saw, making and erecting trellises and arches for my rose arbor."

"Good Lord," he said. "And *yours,* is it?"

"And remember," she said, "that you will be taking yet another step toward full independence at the end of the month. You will be hosting a revival of the Cedarhurst fete and ball."

"I am going to be running a three-legged race, am I?" he said, looking at her sidelong.

"Definitely," she said.

"With you as a partner?"

"*Must* I?" she asked him.

"You must," he assured her.

"Oh, very well, then."

"And I am going to be judging embroidered angels and flowers, am I?" he asked.

"I will do that," she told him. "You may taste the fruit tarts."

"Hmm," he said. "And waltz with you during the evening?"

"Yes," she said.

They strolled along the terrace in the direction of the east side of the house just like a contentedly married couple.

A mildly panic-provoking thought.

18

KATHERINE went down to the servants' quarters after luncheon while Jasper went in search of his steward. And she had a word with the housekeeper and the cook and the butler. They must be consulted, after all, before she proceeded further with plans for the fete. It was upon them that much of the work would fall—and they already had a houseful of guests to prepare for.

They were indeed alarmed at her initial suggestion. A grand fete and ball *in one month*?

But as soon as she had assured them that the bulk of the planning would be hers and that most of the work would be shared among whichever neighbors could be persuaded to take on the task, they became almost instantly enthusiastic, even excited—and comically offended that she should try to release them from some of the work.

"But I am going to be in charge of the food, mind," the cook declared in a voice that brooked no contradiction. "I don't mind a bit of help with the planning and even the cooking, my lady, but I am going to be in charge."

"I never thought for an instant that you would not be," Katherine said, smiling. "Indeed, I hoped you would be, Mrs. Oliver, as I suspect the kitchens here would collapse if ever you were to abandon them."

"And I will be in charge of decorating the house and ballroom," Mrs. Siddon said, "and ordering the supplies. You will find any number of people, my lady, who will be only too eager to help out and give you ideas and even set them into effect, but I must be in charge of the house."

"And happy I am to hear you say it," Katherine assured her. "But I will see to it that you get all the help you need."

"I will speak to Benton myself, my lady," the butler said. And lest she not remember who that was, "The head gardener, my lady. He will want to supply all the flowers for the ballroom from the kitchen gardens and the greenhouses."

"I was so hoping he would," Katherine said. "And I would be much obliged if you would ask him."

"And I will be in charge of the food tables," he said as if he thought she might argue, "and the footmen serving at them."

"Oh," she said, "how very kind you are, Mr. Couch."

"It will be just like old times," Mrs. Oliver said with a sigh. "Ah, the fete at Cedarhurst was always the best day of the whole year. It was always good, clean fun for everyone, I don't care what anyone says to the contrary. It was *not* the devil's own work. The very idea!"

"The last one was less than a year before Lord Montford died," Mrs. Siddon said. "Less than a year before his present lordship was born. Bless my soul, how quickly time does fly. Though there have been long, dreary years in between, there is no denying."

"Those days," the butler said, "are like something out of another lifetime."

"And now they are to be resurrected," Katherine

said. "Oh, I *do* want the fete to be as it always was—with some new touches too. I want it to be perfect and something everyone will want repeated every year for the rest of their lives."

"The people you need to speak with, my lady," Mrs. Siddon said briskly, "are . . ."

And she listed an impressive number of mostly older people in the neighborhood. Mrs. Oliver and Mr. Couch added the names of some younger people, who maybe did not remember the fetes but who would be only too delighted to plan a new one.

They could not go visiting at all during the rest of that day as Jasper needed to be busy with the steward, though he did come and fetch her from the drawing room during the afternoon so that she could join him, Mr. Knowles, and Mr. Benton on the east lawn. They spent an hour out there, discussing what was wanted and needed, pacing back and forth across the grass to see how large the orchard could be and where exactly the rose arbor should be situated.

It rather intrigued Katherine to see Jasper without any of the artifice he affected in London and kept up most of the time when alone with her. With the two men he was all seriousness, all business, all energy and intelligence. And he clearly knew a great deal about land and drainage and plants and sunshine and shade and everything else one needed to know to be a successful gardener.

He knew the house and he knew the park. He knew all of his ancestors pictured in the gallery. He might have hated Cedarhurst for most of his life, but he had not neglected it or his duty to it.

She found it all a little disconcerting. And reassuring too. She could *like* this man.

The rest of the afternoon she spent in the making of lists of things that would need to be done if the fete and the ball were to be a success. Something of this magnitude would usually take a whole year to plan, she guessed. But there was only one month.

It was a daunting, exhilarating thought.

Perhaps, as Jasper had assured her on more than one occasion, this new life would not be so bad after all.

They spent much of the next three days calling upon the neighbors, some of them in the village, some in the countryside around. Jasper had known them all as a boy, though only a few of them had been deemed worthy of being officially visited or of being invited to visit or dine. He had played with some of their children whenever he could steal away to do so, and indeed some of those children were now grown up and settled with families of their own.

He had enjoyed genial relations with everyone since growing to adulthood. But he had not spent a great deal of time here, except that one year when the disaster of the Vauxhall wager had driven him home. He had never had any problem getting along with his neighbors.

It had not dawned upon him, though, until now that these people were *his* people, that they shared a background and heritage and memories with him, that they had known him most of his life, that they were, in fact, fond of him.

They were all eager to meet his wife, and it struck Jasper that word of the scandal that had precipitated them into marriage had undoubtedly arrived here. But rather than looking upon him with disapproval and Katherine with suspicion, everyone seemed more inclined to take their own to their collective bosom and let the world beyond their neighborhood go to the devil.

It was clear to him that they all fell in love with Katherine almost as soon as they met her. She had beauty, of course, and charm and a way of dressing that was smart and elegant without in any way suggesting that she was trying to put on town airs. Her roots were in a country village. These might not be people she knew, but they were people with whom she could identify. And they recognized that in her and respected it and liked her the better for it.

And she had a way of showing interest in everyone, of deflecting attention away from herself and onto them. She listened to their stories, their woes, their triumphs, their jokes, their reminiscences of the past and always responded appropriately.

And of course—he might have expected it—she had only to mention the idea of reviving the Cedarhurst summer fete and ball for everyone to exclaim with delight and offer to help in any way they could. The older people remembered the fetes as the high point of the year and had wondered when his lordship intended restoring them.

"It had not occurred to me," Jasper explained more than once as they moved from house to house, "since the last one happened before my birth. Now that my wife is determined to revive it, however, I am all enthusiasm."

For which pronouncement he was always favored

with a dazzling smile from Katherine and fond nods of approval from his neighbors.

The younger people could not *wait* for the revival of something they had heard spoken about with happy nostalgia so often down the years.

Before the three days of visits were over, they had seen everyone there was to be seen and had drunk more cups of tea and consumed more cakes than Jasper had done in a decade. And the fete was well on the way to becoming a reality. Mrs. Ellis had agreed to head a committee to organize games for the children, Mrs. Bonner had volunteered to look after the needlework contests, Mrs. Penny had been unanimously declared the best one to be in charge of the baking contests, and Mr. Cornell had been persuaded by his wife and four daughters and a sister-in-law—he had not stood a chance, poor devil—to form a committee to plan games and activities for the men.

"And an ale-drinking booth will not suffice, Cornell," Jasper had said with a straight face.

All the ladies had laughed heartily at the witticism but had then assured Cornell that indeed it would not.

And the Reverend Bellow, Miss Daniels's betrothed, would take it upon himself to prepare a blessing to be delivered at the opening of the fete.

"For it has been brought to my attention, my lord and lady," he said in the gentle, serious manner that had endeared him to all his parishioners, "that the old fetes were sometimes described as being the devil's work—which a community celebration of the joys of summer and neighborly fellowship is assuredly *not*. But it will be just as well to let everyone know that the Lord's blessing is upon such innocent amusements."

"Oh, thank you, Mr. Bellow," Katherine said. "We had hoped you would do something like this, had we not, Jasper?"

"Indeed," Jasper said, raising his eyebrows.

It was all done, then. They had established themselves with their neighbors to such a degree that he guessed social life at Cedarhurst would be active for years to come. They were to reestablish the summer fete, probably as an annual event. They were expecting a houseful of guests and two weeks of frolicking. And there was to be an apple orchard planted at the east end of the house and a rose arbor beneath their private sitting room. They had been married for a little less than one week.

If he could have seen into the future just six weeks ago, Jasper thought, and seen this, he would have wept. Or got thoroughly foxed.

He actually felt remarkably cheerful.

Of course, there was still a three-legged race to be run, which might be quite entertaining if it was Katherine's leg that was to be bound to his own.

And fruit tarts to judge—but country ladies were always the very best of cooks.

And country dances to be jigged. Hmm.

And a houseful of mostly very young persons to entertain. Plenty of giddiness and giggling to be expected there.

And a wager to be won.

And love to be fallen into. But he already liked her very well indeed. And he already desired her—a thought best avoided for the next three weeks or so.

He had never been very good at celibacy—not since

he had lost his virginity at the age of eighteen, exactly one day after leaving Cedarhurst.

Though come to think of it, he had been celibate for almost a year when he had come back to Cedarhurst after Vauxhall.

Jasper spent a full morning with his steward. He looked strangely attractive when he set off for the home farm, clad in what looked like an old, somewhat ill-fitting brown coat and drab breeches that bagged slightly at the knees and top boots that had seen better days.

Katherine spent the early part of the morning in conference with Mrs. Siddon and the rest of the morning writing long-overdue letters to Margaret and Vanessa. It felt good to relax a little after the busyness of the past few days, though there was, of course, much to be done for the house party and the fete. She had no intention of leaving everything to the servants and the neighborhood committees. But today she was going to take off just for herself.

She changed into fresh clothes after a late luncheon taken alone since Jasper had not returned from the farm, and stepped outside. Her first plan was to go down into the parterre garden to sit. But she had not yet seen any other part of the park except from a distance, and the lake was not far away.

She walked past the stable block and down the sloping, tree-dotted lawn beyond it until she came to the lakeside. The lovely summer weather was still holding. There was scarcely a cloud in the sky or a ripple of a breeze. She opened her parasol, glad she had thought to bring it with her.

She went and sat on a little wooden jetty that jutted out into the water of the lake not far from a boathouse, her knees drawn up, one arm clasped about her legs, the other holding the parasol at an angle to shield her eyes from the sun. She was surrounded on three sides by water, which was glassy calm and a shade darker than the blue of the sky. Opposite her was a grassy bank, a wooded slope above it, and a little thatched stone cottage farther to the right, which she suspected was a folly, since it looked far too small to be a real habitation. Beside it, a waterfall fell like a ribbon over the steep bank. She could even hear it from where she sat—a peaceful, rural sound. A family of ducks swam across the water, a row of little ducklings in hot pursuit of their mother, leaving V-shaped trails behind them.

Behind her were the sloping lawn, the stables, the terraces and the house, and, behind it, in a great horseshoe arc, low, tree-covered hills.

There was something very special about Cedarhurst, something that spoke to her soul. She could sit just here forever, she believed, not reading or painting or doing anything useful, not talking, not even thinking. Just *being*. A part of it all. Solitude had always been something she had actively sought out whenever she could. There was never quite enough of it. Perhaps here she could find both a busy life to keep her mind off the negative aspects of her marriage and peace too.

And perhaps eventually there would be more solitude than she had ever wanted. She had not really looked beyond the next few weeks. What would happen after the house party was at an end and all the guests had returned home? Would he remain at Cedarhurst? Or would boredom soon drive him away, to return again for brief, unsatisfactory visits down the years? What could she offer that would keep him here with her, after all? And did she *want* to keep him with her?

But she would not think of such things today. And not here.

She lowered her parasol, lifted her face to the warmth of the sun, and closed her eyes.

"A perfect setting and a perfect pose," a voice said from so close by that Katherine realized he must be standing on the bank behind her. "Even the lemon-colored muslin dress and pale blue sash and your wedding bonnet are perfect."

His voice was soft, amused.

Katherine looked back over her shoulder. Jasper was propped indolently against a post that had been driven into the bank, his arms across his chest. He had changed into a dark green form-fitting coat with buff-colored pantaloons that molded his muscled thighs like a second skin, and shiny Hessian boots crossed at the ankles. His neckcloth was white and crisp and tied in a neat, unostentatious knot. His shirt points were high but not dandyish. There had never been anything of the dandy about Lord Montford.

"Oh, dear," she said, "is it so obvious that I dashed down here to observe the surroundings and then dashed back to the house to dress accordingly—just as I did with the Adamses' garden party? Ought I to have worn just any old rags instead? And sat beside the rubbish heap?"

His eyes regarded her lazily from beneath the brim of his tall hat.

"The trouble is," he said, "that I am not sure it would make any difference. Katherine in rags beside a rubbish heap would doubtless look just as dazzling as Katherine dressed in blue and yellow by a blue lake with blue sky and sunshine overhead."

She hugged her knees and smiled at him.

"I *always* fall head over ears in love with flatterers," she said.

"Ah, do you?" he said. "But not with those who speak from the sincerity of a pure, adoring heart? How cruel of you."

She half wished she had not grown to like him so much. One ought not to like a man who had flatteries and deceits at his fingertips—or at his tongue's end. But then, he always spoke them with humor and perhaps no real intention of deceiving her. He seemed to enjoy the game for its own sake.

"I suppose," he said, "I will not make nearly as romantic a figure sprawled on the bank as you make perched on the jetty, but I will try my best notwithstanding."

And he sat down on the bank, reclined on one side, tossed aside his hat, propped one elbow on the ground, and cradled his head in his hand. He looked lazy and relaxed and impossibly handsome. Katherine turned to face him so that she would not have to keep her head turned over her shoulder. She raised her parasol again—it was pale blue to match her sash and the ribbons and cornflowers in her bonnet.

"Not so romantic, perhaps," she agreed. "But a tolerably pretty picture nonetheless."

"*Pretty?*" He lofted his right eyebrow. "Tell me you chose the wrong word, Katherine, or I shall dive into the lake without further ado and sit sulking on the bottom until I am well and truly drowned."

She laughed.

Laughter was the last thing she had expected of the days following her wedding. But she had been doing a great deal of laughing during the past week, she realized. But of course, he always had been able to provoke laughter in her.

"*Handsome,* then," she said. "There, you have had your compliment for the day."

They sat looking at each other. Somewhere behind her the family of ducks she had been watching earlier were having a conversation in which all seemed to be quacking at once. In the grass unseen insects were whirring and chirping. From the direction of the stables came the occasional, distant clang of a hammer upon metal. All the sounds that had accentuated the peace of this particular place in the park just a few minutes ago now drew attention to the silence between them.

Jasper plucked a blade of grass from beside him and sucked on it while he gazed at her with narrowed eyes.

And she wanted him—sharply and shockingly.

"What would you be doing now," he asked her, "if you had not married me? If that scoundrel Forester had not stirred up scandal and forced you into it?"

"I would be at Warren Hall preparing to come here," she said, "with Meg and Stephen."

"And afterward," he said, "what would you have done?"

"Gone back home to Warren Hall," she said. "Lived there quietly until someone suggested leaving again—to go and visit Nessie and Elliott and the children, perhaps, or to go to London."

"Your eldest sister will miss you," he said.

"Yes."

"Why is she not married?" he asked her. "She is several years older than you, is she not, and just as beautiful in her own way. Rumor has it that Allingham made her an offer, which she refused. Is she holding out for love, as you were doing?"

"She *was* in love," she said, "with Crispin Dew of Rundle Park near Throckbridge. Nessie married his younger brother, but he was consumptive and died within a year. She knew when she married him that he was dying. She loved him dearly, and he her."

"Three romantics," he said, "and only one got her wish. But even she married a dying man. There is a lesson for you somewhere in all that, Katherine."

"Nessie and Elliott love each other dearly too," she said.

"But the elder Dew did *not* love your eldest sister?" he asked.

"He *did*," she said. "They would have married when she was very young, and I daresay they would have been happy for a lifetime. But my father had died and Meg had promised to look after us until we had all grown up and could look after ourselves. She refused to marry Crispin until much later. But he would not wait. He joined a regiment and went off to war and married a Spanish lady and broke Meg's heart. You may laugh now, if you wish. Women are very foolish."

"They frighten the devil out of me if you want the truth," he said.

"Well, that, at least," she said, "is a positive sign. With the devil gone, there is hope for you."

He chuckled softly and sucked on his blade of grass again.

"Selfless love," he said. "The supreme virtue. Or is it?

In choosing you and your sister and brother rather than love, did Miss Huxtable perhaps doom a decent man to a life that can never bring him the happiness he might have had with her?"

She was instantly indignant. Trust Jasper to take the man's part. Crispin might have had the patience and fortitude to wait. The wait would be almost over by now—Stephen was almost twenty-one.

"Do not people who selflessly choose the path of servitude to one or more individuals often neglect other paths and other individuals who need them just as much?" he asked her.

"Like a nun going into the convent and leaving a family bereft of her presence?" she said.

His eyes smiled.

"That would be one illustration, I suppose," he said, "though I confess I would not have thought of it myself."

"Or a mother so devoted to her children that she would neglect her husband?" she said.

He pursed his lips and tossed the blade of grass aside.

"That would be the husband's fault for not paying enough attention to pleasuring her," he said.

And *trust* him to give a sexual slant to what was really an interesting topic.

"Or a mother so devoted to her husband, then," she said, exasperated, "that she would neglect her children."

"There could never be such a mother, could there?" he said softly.

"No."

He sat up, crossed his legs, draped his wrists over his knees, and squinted out over the water.

And she realized something. There *could*. Be such a

mother, that was. His *own* mother? Had that happened to him?

"Miss Daniels," he said in what seemed like a complete change of subject, "has been Charlotte's governess, more lately her companion, since she was four years old. They have both been very fortunate. They are extremely fond of each other. And now, when Charlotte is ready to spread her wings, Miss Daniels is to marry the local vicar."

"And Rachel?" she said.

"The world was a wide and wicked place," he said, "and so Miss Rachel Finley of Cedarhurst Park remained at home. And then she remained because she was in mourning—and then because our mother had collapsed so almost completely that she needed a constant companion. And then there was the mourning again for her death. Rachel was twenty-four when she finally had a Season and made her come-out. Shocking, was it not? She was fortunate to meet Gooding. He is a thoroughly dull dog, but he is of steady character and fortune, as dull dogs tend to be, and I suspect they have an affection for each other."

Katherine had lowered her parasol again so that she could hug both legs.

And what of *him*? How had his mother neglected him? Had she been so besotted with his stepfather?

He was looking directly at her again, his eyelids drooping, a lazy smile in his eyes. But there was a tension about his shoulders and arms that told her more than ever that he wore that look as a mask when he did not wish to reveal too much about himself.

"Are you in love with me yet?" he asked her. "Can we

dispense with the next three weeks? I have already told you more than once that I adore you."

It was not a serious question—or a serious declaration. He just did not want to pursue the line the conversation had taken. She realized that.

"I am not, and will never be, even one modicum of one iota in love with you, Jasper," she said. But she was half smiling at him.

He set one hand over his heart.

"A modicum of an iota," he said. "I am trying to picture such an entity if it *can* be observed with the naked eye. Is it like a grain of sand? *'To see the world in a grain of sand'*?"

He was quoting *William Blake* at her. How could he possibly appreciate such gloriously mystical poetry when he knew nothing of dreams?

"A grain of sand," he said, "or a modicum of one iota will be quite enough to work on. I am delighted to hear you admit that such a seed exists."

"You are famous for not listening," she said. "I said it did *not* exist."

He raised both eyebrows.

"There is no such thing as one modicum of one iota?" he said. "You disappoint me. But I believe there must be. If there were not, you would not have mentioned it or you would simply have been making yourself sound foolish. And if it exists, then I am left to hope. Nothing that exists ever quite disappears, you know. Or is lost. If it is lost, it is merely because someone is too lazy to look for it. Despite what you may think of me, Katherine, I am *not* lazy. It is just that I conserve my energies for what is of importance to me. I will find that modicum of an iota and will build it from a grain of sand into a whole glorious sand castle with towers and turrets and a liveried bugler standing on the battlements blowing out his hymn of triumph. Is *hymn* the right word? But you understand my meaning. You *will* love me and bow to my adoration, my sun goddess."

She was laughing helplessly.

But some absolutely absurd part of her wanted to be standing on one of those turrets listening to the bugler blowing his song of triumph and watching her knight ride up to the castle walls, cloak billowing, drawn sword in hand, smiling up at her in triumph and love.

There were definite disadvantages to being a dreamer. It could make one daft.

"I have not shown you anything of the park, have I," he said, "except the parterre garden and the empty east lawn. The walk about the lake is picturesque and can be done at a sedate pace in an hour or so or at a brisk trot in considerably less. The wilderness walk up into the hills behind the house is more rugged and takes a few hours to walk in its entirety. But it was carefully constructed and offers much variety for nature lovers as well as some pleasing prospects for those who like them."

"I would enjoy both walks," she said.

"We will do the longer one," he said. "Tomorrow?"

"I have promised to look in on three different committee meetings in the village tomorrow morning," she said, "and one in the afternoon. The Misses Laycock are coming to tea the day after with their young niece. She is Charlotte's friend, I believe."

"Might I make an appointment to go walking with you the day after, then?" he asked. "Most humbly? On my knees if necessary?"

She smiled at him. "I ought to make you do it," she said. "You did not do it when you proposed marriage to me. The day after tomorrow, then. I shall look forward to it."

"I believe," he said, "that if I had knelt to propose marriage to you, you would have kicked me in the head."

"Probably," she agreed.

He got to his feet, set his hat back on his head, and offered her his hand.

"Shall we go back to the house for tea?" he said. "I find that after imbibing cup upon cup of the stuff for the past three days, I now cannot do without it. Is it like alcohol, do you think? Have I become addicted to it? I cannot wait for Con to find out and Charlie and Hal."

"Tea would be lovely," she said, setting her hand in his.

And she meant it too. The day had brightened somehow since he came.

She was not sure if she ought to feel relieved or alarmed.

She wondered if heartbreak loomed somewhere in her future.

But she would deal with the future when it became the present.

19

THE following two days were busy ones in which Jasper scarcely saw his wife. He was tied up with farm and estate business—and with the men's committee for the fete. How he had got drawn into that he would never quite know, but there it was. Perhaps it was the fact that when Cornell had suggested rowing on the lake as a possible amusement for the men on that first visit made with Katherine, Jasper had suggested mud wrestling beside the lake. Apparently most of the men wanted more suggestions from him.

Katherine herself was never in one place long enough for him to find her—except at meals and in the drawing room during the evenings. She spent time with the housekeeper and the cook, and with the head gardener. She attended all the committee meetings in and about the village, except the men's. And she entertained the Misses Laycock to tea with Jane Hutchins, their niece, Charlotte's best friend. She invited the girl to join the house party. As she explained to Jasper at dinner that evening, their numbers had been made uneven by the fact that his cousins, offspring of Uncle Stanley, his father's brother, had agreed to come—two boys and one girl.

For two days the weather had been cloudy and blustery with a few light showers. But though the third day dawned cloudy again, by the time they set off for the planned wilderness walk, most of the clouds had moved off, and it promised to be a lovely day again.

"We will do the walk backward," he said, taking Katherine's arm as they left the house and turning her to the east. "Not that there is a forward or backward way of doing it exactly, but the tendency always is to start at the lake. The trouble with that is that there are so many places to stop and admire, very often one ends up merely circling the lake and missing some of the best parts of the walk."

"Through the hills among the trees?" she said. "Yes, I can imagine it is the best."

She was wearing a sprigged muslin dress today, pale blue on white, and her straw bonnet with blue ribbons. She looked delicate and pretty. The high-waisted style of dress that was currently fashionable was perfect for her figure, emphasizing as it did her slender grace as the gentle folds of the muslin softly molded her shape and sometimes showed the outline of her long, slim legs.

There was a glow of color in her cheeks and a sparkle in her eyes—something their servants and neighbors no doubt attributed to the fact that she was a new bride discovering the delights of the marriage bed when in reality it was probably due to the fact that she was busy with schemes that brought her pleasure.

He pursed his lips as he looked down at her.

They crossed the wide east lawn, soon to be the apple orchard, and he led her onto the path into the trees. It turned almost immediately to the north and ascended the gradual slope that would take them into the hills.

"You are unusually quiet this morning," Katherine said.

"I might have observed," he said, "that my prediction that this would turn into a lovely day has proved quite correct. I might even have added the words *I told you so*. But alas, you were reading your letter from the Duchess of Moreland at breakfast, so I made the prediction silently lest I disturb you. Now if I lay claim to it, you will probably accuse me of taking credit for something I did not predict at all. You are not a very trusting person, Katherine."

She had turned her head and was laughing at him.

"For the sake of peace between us," she said, "I will believe you."

He smiled lazily back at her.

"How lovely this is," she said. "Like an outdoor cathedral."

The trees were indeed tall and fairly widely spaced at this point, and the path was broad and straight despite the incline.

"This has always been one of my favorite stretches of the wilderness walk," he said. "I suspect that when the path was constructed, it was begun at the lake side and ended here. And that by the time the designer arrived here, he had run out of ideas and energy and interest. There are no follies, no seats, no prospects down to the house or out over the countryside. Just forest and hillside."

"And holiness," she said.

"Holiness?"

"I am not sure if it is the right word," she said. "Just unadorned nature, though I suppose the path is man-made. Just trees and the smell of trees. And birds. And birdsong."

"And us," he said.

"And us."

They walked in silence for a while, the sound of their breathing added to birdsong as they ascended more steeply into the hills behind the house and finally came to the rhododendron walk, the highest part of the trail, where there were several carefully contrived prospects and a few benches and follies. And the heady perfume of the blooms.

"Oh," she said. "Beautiful!"

"Better than the cathedral?" he asked her.

"But that is the wonderful thing about nature, is it not?" she said. "Nothing is better than anything else — only different. The parterre gardens, the cathedral section of the walk, this — they all seem best when one is actually there."

There was an ancient stone hermitage to one side of the path, complete with crucifix carved into the wall beside the doorway. It was not that ancient, of course. It was a folly. There never had been a hermit with sackcloth tunic and matted hair and beard, telling his beads from morning to night and existing on moldy bread and brackish water. They went and sat inside it on a stone bench that had been made more comfortable with a long leather cushion.

There was a view down across the east and south lawns to the village in the distance. The church spire was centered in the view. It all looked very rural and peaceful.

He took her hand in his.

"What would you be doing if you had not been

forced into marriage?" she asked him, reversing the question he had asked her a few days ago. "Where would you be?"

"Here," he said. "I promised to be home for Charlotte's birthday."

"And afterward?" she said. "Would you have stayed?"

"Perhaps." He shrugged. "Perhaps not. Brighton is a good place to be during the summer. The Prince of Wales is usually there, and he draws all sorts of interesting people. There is much company, much entertainment. I might have gone there."

"Do you *need* company, then?" she asked. She had turned her head and was looking at him.

He raised his eyebrows. "We all need company," he said. "And entertainment."

"Are you a lonely man, then?" she asked him.

The question jolted him. It was completely unexpected—and quite unanswerable. He answered it anyway.

"Lonely?" he said. "*Me*, lonely, Katherine? I have scores of friends and acquaintances. I always have so many invitations and activities to choose among, that making choices is a daily chore."

"And do you fear being alone?" she asked.

"Not at all," he said.

He had grown up essentially alone—with a mother and her husband and two sisters, with a houseful of servants and numerous neighbors, most if not all of whom had been kindly disposed to him. He had nevertheless grown up alone.

"People who live among crowds can be very lonely people," she said.

"Can they, indeed?" He laced his fingers with hers.

"And people who grow up in remote villages cannot be lonely?"

"There is a difference," she said, "between solitude and loneliness. It is possible to be alone and not lonely. And it is possible to be among crowds, to be a part of those crowds, and be lonely."

"Is this," he asked her, "part of the vicarage wisdom that you learned at your father's knee?"

"No," she said. "It is something I have learned myself."

"And are you," he asked her, "a lonely woman, Katherine?"

"Not often." She sighed. "I like being alone, you see. I like my own company."

"And I do not," he said. "Is that your inference? You once told me that I do not like myself. Is this why I must be lonely? Because I cannot enjoy the company of the only companion with whom I must spend every moment of my life?"

"I have annoyed you," she said.

Had she? He was not in the habit of allowing people to annoy him over trifles. He did not care for other people's opinions when they concerned him.

"Not at all." He raised their hands and kissed the back of hers. "Solitude holds no fears for me. I would just prefer company. Including present company."

"I think," she said, "I can be happy here."

"Can you?" he said.

"I love this place," she said. "I love the servants. And I like your neighbors—*our* neighbors. Yes, I can be happy here."

"Organizing fetes and balls and house parties and other social events?" he said.

"Yes," she said, "and just living. Just being here. Belonging here."

"And bringing up your children?" he said. "*Our* children?"

"Yes." She looked into his eyes, her cheeks slightly flushed.

"We could," he said, "begin immediately on those children—or on the first of them anyway—if you wish, Katherine. Although, on second thought, perhaps not *quite* immediately." He looked down at the bench, which, even with the leather cushion, was not very comfortable.

She laughed, though she continued to look into his eyes.

"I do want children," she said.

"And I *need* them," he said. "Or one son at the very least. So we are in agreement. We need to work on the first of those children. Almost immediately?"

She laughed again.

"It depends on your definition of *almost*," she said.

"*Almost* is to be three weeks long, is it?" he asked with a sigh.

"Yes," she said. "Do you not want children for their own sake, Jasper?"

He had never really thought of it. He thought now. Children of his own body. And Katherine's. Children who could be loved and nurtured. Children who could be hurt, who could have all the spirit crushed out of them. If he were to jump a hedge one month before his son was born and break his neck, would Katherine marry another man to bring him up?

There is too much potential pain in having children, he almost said aloud. *Too much risk.* But he would merely expose himself more to her with such words.

He raised their clasped hands again and tucked her arm beneath his.

"Daughters to look like their mother?" he said. "And sons to look like their...mother? Children to hold and love and play with and nurture? It is an appealing thought, I must confess. And now it is possible. I am married. Yes, I will have children with you, Katherine, not just because I need them, but because I want them."

Sometimes he was not sure himself whether he meant what he said to her or whether he spoke to impress or tease her. Though he never spoke with any serious intention to deceive. This wager was different from any other he had ever made. There was too much at stake in winning it—and though she did not know it, it *was* a double wager. Either they both would win, or they both would lose.

But oh, Lord, she believed him. Her lips had parted, and her eyes had brightened with tears that she quickly blinked away. And perhaps she was right. Perhaps he *did* mean what he had said. He had a sudden mental image of holding a baby as tiny as Moreland's—a baby that was his own.

Dash it all, he would be bound to drop it.

No, what he *would* be bound to do was love it. There would be no choice in the matter. No child of his was going to go unloved while he had breath in his body. Even a child who had just painted red, grinning lips and black arched eyebrows on all the stone statues along the balustrade about the roof or who had returned home with torn coat and breeches that he had forgotten to change out of after church before going to ride the waterfall—a strictly forbidden activity in its own right. He would love and love such a child anyway. He would probably take him back to the waterfall, in fact, so that they could ride it together, and take him—or her—back up to the roof to paint purple beards on all the statues.

Katherine had raised her free hand and was cupping his cheek with it. With the pad of her thumb she brushed something away from beneath his eye. Something wet.

Good Lord!

He jumped to his feet and stepped outside the hermitage. He moved back onto the path without waiting for her and plucked two blooms from the rhododendron bushes.

"Let me see," he said, turning to her as she came up behind him. "One to go here in the ribbon about the crown of your bonnet, I believe, and one to go ... *here.*"

He pushed the stem down inside the bosom of her dress, into her cleavage, using his finger to press it down firmly. She was warm and slightly moist there, and he felt such a stabbing of desire that he was surprised he had not got an instant erection and alerted her to the direction his thoughts had taken.

"Not that you need sweetening," he said. "But perhaps the flowers do. They will be sweetened by their proximity to you."

"Oh, well done," she said, her eyes twinkling. "That was one of your better efforts."

"Do I win any reward, then?" he asked. "A kiss, perhaps?"

But, as he had expected, she merely laughed.

Lord, that was not a *tear* she had wiped away, was it? He had rarely felt more embarrassed in his life.

He offered her his arm and they continued along the path, which began gradually to slope downward in the direction of the lake.

They passed the great, ancient beech tree at the end of the rhododendron walk and stopped to set their palms against the trunk and marvel at its great size and age. He looked beyond it, up the hill into the trees, which grew dense here. But there was nothing to be seen from here. And for today, he decided, he would keep her on the path. There would be time enough to come back—or not.

"There is a beach at this end of the lake," he said. "It is called a beach though, of course, there is no sand, and no ebb and flow of tides. But the bank was deliberately created to slope into the water so that one can sit picnicking there or paddle one's feet without toppling in over one's eyebrows. Or one can swim. We do not have any picnic fare with us, alas."

"We will paddle our feet instead," she said as they descended the slope and the trees thinned out and the sun beat down on them. "It has turned into a warm day and I am a little footsore after all the walking."

"Can you swim?" he asked her.

"I can," she said. "I learned as a child at Rundle Park, when we used to go over there to play with the Dews. I thought I had forgotten how, but I have not. I have swum at Warren Hall too."

"Then we will swim today," he said. "What better way to cool off after a long walk?"

"*Today?*" She turned her head sharply to look up at

him. "I cannot swim in this dress, Jasper. It is one of my best ones. And you cannot swim in those clothes."

They had come to a fork in the path. One branch would take them about the far side of the lake and up to the little cottage and the waterfall and so on around to the house side. The other fork went down to the beach and then on around to the boathouse and jetty. He turned down toward the beach.

"I suppose," he said, "unless you are very brazen, Katherine, you are wearing a shift beneath your dress. And stays too?"

"Of course," she said. And then she looked at him again, her eyes widening. "I am not bathing in my shift!"

"Without it, then?" he asked. "You need not fear being seen by anyone except me. And I have seen you unclothed before. It was by candlelight on that occasion admittedly. But I would wager you will look just as lovely in sunlight."

"Jasper!" She laughed nervously. "I am *not* swimming without my shift."

"With it, then," he said, "if you must be modest."

They stood on the sloping, grassy bank, looking out across the water of the lake. It was sparkling invitingly in the sunshine. The air was hot now that there was no shade.

"Come," he said, releasing her arm and turning her so that she faced away from him. "I will help you out of your dress and stays. I make a tolerable lady's maid when pressed into business."

"Oh," she said indignantly, "I am sure you *do*. But, Jasper, we cannot go swimming now. We have no towels. We have no dry clothes. We have no . . . *oh*!"

He had opened her sash and the back of her dress,

lifted it off her shoulders, and let it slide down to the ground. He tackled the tapes that held her stays together at the back.

"We will dry in the sunshine afterward," he said, setting his lips between her shoulder blades as he loosened her stays and dropped them to the grass before kneeling and rolling down her stockings.

Her shift covered her from the breasts to several inches above her knees. She looked tall and willowy and more enticing than any other woman he had ever set eyes upon as she stepped out of her shoes and stockings and turned to face him.

He was committed now. If he did not get himself into the lake water soon, he might well explode like a firecracker.

"Oh," she said, "this is not very proper at all."

The vicar's prim daughter in a skimpy shift and nothing else at all—a potently erotic mix.

He stripped off his coat and waistcoat and neckcloth with ungainly haste.

"For your husband to see you in your shift?" he said. "It is shocking indeed."

He pulled off his shirt over his head and sat down on the grass to haul off his boots before standing again and dragging off his pantaloons and stockings.

Should he shock her completely? But he hesitated for only one fraction of a moment before removing his drawers as well. How the devil had he managed to show no outer sign of arousal?

She bit her lower lip.

"The water will be cold," she said—a very weak protest indeed.

"Then we will warm it up," he said. "We will boil it

over its banks. I do not know about you, Katherine, but I am feeling very warm indeed. Are you coming?" He held out a hand for hers.

"I do not know." She glanced gingerly at the water. "I really do not think this is quite— Oh!"

He scooped her up in his arms and strode off with her. It might be unmannerly to interrupt a lady, but there were limits to a gentleman's powers of endurance.

It was horribly shocking. Not the coldness of the water—they had not reached that yet. But the fact that she was with a man in the outdoors in broad daylight, clad only in her shift while he was clad in nothing at all.

Nothing.

Of course, he *was* her husband.

This was all very shocking nevertheless.

And exciting.

And exhilarating.

And she was very warm indeed. She had not realized quite how hot the sun was.

He was wading into the water. A few drops splashed up onto her skin. They were *cold*. She laughed and clung to him and shrieked. He was surely not going to—

But he was.

And he did.

He dropped her.

She sank to the bottom like a stone and came up sputtering and fighting. She dashed the water from her eyes, gasped for air, and saw him still standing there, thigh deep in the water, his hands on his hips, laughing at her.

And looking so handsome and carefree that she could have wept.

Instead she doused him with water and, while he sputtered in his turn and shook the water out of his eyes, she dived under and swam as fast as she could out into the deeper water of the lake.

Two hands grasped her ankles and then slid up her legs until they reached her hips. They pressed her under. She performed some sort of somersault as soon as he released his hold on her, came up underneath him, and grasped one of his ankles and hung on.

It was not a good idea. The fight that ensued was an unequal one in which she spent far more time below the surface of the water than he did. She was soon gasping for breath in earnest. It did not help, of course, that she could not stop laughing whenever her head was above the water.

"You were right," she said when the fight came to a natural end after ten minutes or so and they were both floating on their backs, side by side. "We have warmed the water."

He turned his face and smiled at her and reached for her hand.

And it happened.

Just like that.

She fell in love.

Or realized that she had been falling in love with him for some time.

Or that perhaps she had always loved him, right from that evening in Vauxhall when she had thought that perhaps love was not safe, that perhaps it was the most dangerous thing in the world.

Love did not have to make sense. It did not have to

be worthy. It did not have to be earned. It did not have to woo.

It just simply *was*.

She closed her eyes, held loosely to his hand, and floated beside him as the world changed its course and settled around her again.

And he was not immune. Surely he was not. He had shed a tear earlier at the thought of having children with her. And now for several minutes he had simply frolicked with her, simply enjoyed being alone with her. He had been laughing and carefree, not hidden behind his habitual mask of hooded eyes and ironical teasing.

Surely he was growing somewhat fond of her.

Surely there was hope that disaster might after all turn to glory.

He let go of her hand and turned onto his stomach and swam a lazy crawl. She swam beside him, reveling in the sights she had of well-muscled arms and shoulders and back muscles, of tight buttocks and long, strong legs.

He was an incredibly beautiful man. *Not* that she had anyone with whom to compare him, of course.

And then he swam close to her again, lifted one arm across her back, and rolled her under him, his other hand sliding beneath her buttocks. She wrapped her arms about him and rolled them over, so that she was on the surface, he beneath—until he reversed their positions. And they rolled over and under until they were both breathless again and both smiling into each other's eyes.

They swam together to shore and emerged, dripping, onto the bank. Katherine squeezed the water out of her hair while he spread his coat on the grass, and then they lay down side by side, their hands touching. She was aware again of his beautiful nakedness as the initial feeling of cold at coming out of the water gave place to the bright warmth of the sun against her flesh.

He was her *husband*.

And she loved him.

And surely he loved her too. But that was foolishness. No, it was not. *Surely* he did.

She turned her head to find him smiling lazily at her.

"I have swum here a thousand times," he said, "but always alone until today."

"Your sisters did not swim?" she asked him.

"Goodness, no," he said. "It was strictly forbidden."

"Even for you?" she said.

He laughed softly. "Even for me. We will teach our children to swim here, Katherine—and then we will strictly forbid them to swim here alone."

"They will not need to," she said. "We will come with them whenever they wish."

"Or if we cannot," he said, "there will always be a brother or sister to accompany them."

"Yes." She smiled and draped an arm over her eyes. The sun was bright.

"Happy?" he said.

"Mmm," she said. "Yes. And you?"

"Happy," he said.

It seemed to Katherine that she had never been happier in her life. Just over a week ago she had walked into a marriage that she had expected to bring her nothing but misery. Yet now...

The sunshine was blocked, and she removed her arm to find him leaning over her.

"In love?" he asked. "Do you love me, Katherine?"

Of course I do. How the words did not escape her lips she would never know. But—

Do you love me, Katherine?

Not *I love you, Katherine*.

"Have you won your wager, do you mean?" she asked him.

He smiled slowly at her, knowingly, sure of her answer. Sure of *her*.

"Have I?" he asked her, his eyes full of amusement. "I will not hold it against you. But it is confession time. Have I won?"

She closed her eyes for a few moments.

She had been duped. He had been working hard today—just as he had worked hard that evening at Vauxhall. That mention of children, those few tears, their swim, this lying side by side in the sunshine—all part of an elaborate campaign.

And she was as green now as she had been that night.

This was not about love or even about affection and spontaneity and the enjoyment of a sunny afternoon and each other's company.

This was about a *stupid* wager.

She rolled away from him, got unhurriedly to her feet, and dressed as well as she could without assistance.

He was still lying naked on the grass.

"Katherine?" he said. "Let's forget that wager for a while. It was unsporting of me to mention it."

She wrapped the ribbons of her bonnet about her hand. She would not put it on. Her hair was still wet. She set off alone back to the house without saying a word or looking back. He could not hurry after her. He had to get dressed first.

Perhaps he would not have come after her anyway.

He would be berating himself for jumping his fences too early, for asking her just a little too soon.

Had he waited, she might have volunteered the information he wanted. She might have turned her head and told him that she loved him.

How excruciatingly humiliating that would have been.

She was as miserable as she had been happy just a few minutes ago.

He would never change.

They could never be happy together.

All the warmth and brightness seemed to have gone from the sun. It seemed only hot and glaring, and the route back to the house seemed interminable.

20

D A M N him for an idiot!

In the game of seduction his skills and his timing were unsurpassed.

In the game of love he was the veriest dunce.

He had asked her if *she* loved *him*.

Instead of telling her that *he* loved *her*.

He was worse than an idiot. Even an imbecile would have known better.

It ought not to have mattered that he still did not know quite what he was supposed to have meant by professing love for her. He ought to have done it anyway. And he had been feeling an affection for her that he had never felt for anyone else his whole life. He had been feeling relaxed and even happy—whatever the devil *that* meant. He had been feeling that all was well after all, that marriage was not all that bad. No, he had been feeling more positive than that. He had been feeling that his marriage was a good thing, that it was going to bring him a contentment he had never yet known, that it was going to bring *her* contentment too.

He was going to suggest that they consign that wager to the devil. Instead...

In love? Do you love me, Katherine?

And then, even worse...

Did I say something wrong?

He was an embarrassment to himself. If Con could have heard him or Charlie or Motherham or Isaac ... It did not bear even thinking of.

And the consequences were that for what remained of the week before Charlotte came home and all the guests arrived, they lived together like polite, amiable strangers, he and Katherine.

He could not think of a way of putting right what had gone wrong down at the lake. He could not suddenly blurt out *I love you,* could he? She might ask him what he meant, and then he would be left gaping like a fish with nothing to say. What *would* he mean?

And *she* made no attempt to put things right. She dived into plans and preparations for the house party and fete so that he hardly saw her. When he did, she was the vicar's daughter—the sort of prunish woman who would not even have known the meaning of the word *shift* if someone had asked her, let alone cavort about in one by a lake and frolic and shriek in the water with nothing on *but.*

He busied himself with his steward. The man took to looking at him every time he hove into sight as if he must be suffering from a touch of sunstroke.

Deuce take it, but this marriage business was nothing but trouble after all. Not that *she* had done anything wrong. He might at least have enjoyed feeling aggrieved if she had. But it was him. He had been an ass.

And Couch was starting to give him wooden-faced, sour looks. So were Mrs. Siddon and even Mrs. Oliver when he went down to the kitchen one day to steal an apple. Even Cocking, for the love of God.

Mutiny at Cedarhurst!

And if anyone thought that *that* was a contradiction

in terms—wooden-faced and sour, that was—then that person had not seen his upper servants when their eyes alit upon him.

Knowles was merely wooden-faced.

But the day of the expected arrivals came at last, and Jasper remembered the *and one other thing* that Katherine had mentioned when they were coming here from London. He had promised to convince her family and his that theirs was a happy, love-filled marriage.

Well, then!

He dressed with special care after an early luncheon. Cocking tied his starched neckcloth in a perfectly symmetrical knot. And he discovered when he went downstairs to the hall that Katherine too was looking her very best in a pale green cotton dress that fell in soft folds from its high waist, which was tied with a cream-colored silk ribbon. The hem and short, puffed sleeves were trimmed with narrower bands of the same ribbon. Her hair was arranged in soft, shining curls on her head with a few wavy strands arranged enticingly along her neck.

And she was smiling.

So was he.

That was the thing, though. They had smiled all week. How the devil his servants could have the gall to look sourly upon him, he did not know.

"I suppose," she said, "that if we stand here all afternoon, no one will come. But the minute we go about our business elsewhere, there will be a half dozen or more carriages bowling up the driveway."

"Perhaps," he said, "we ought to go and stroll in the parterre garden and pretend that we are expecting no one. Perhaps in that way we can trick at least one carriage into showing its face."

"A splendid idea," she said, taking his arm. "We are not expecting anyone, are we?"

"Never heard of him," he said. "Never expect to set eyes on him. And what a foolish name to have—*Anyone*. He could be anyone, after all, with a name like that, could he not?"

For the first time in a week he heard her laugh.

They stepped out of doors and descended the marble steps together to the upper terrace.

"I have heard," she said, "that he is a very bland gentleman with an equally bland wife. The sort one might pass on the street and hardly notice at all. Which is very unfair really. Everyone is precious and really ought to be noticed."

"Perhaps," he said, "he ought to change his name to *Someone*."

"I believe he ought," she said. "And then *everyone* will notice him, and his wife, because he will be *someone*."

Which silly nonsense set them both to snorting and laughing like a pair of idiots. It felt good to laugh again—with her.

"And just look," he said, pointing beyond the parterres. "While we have been deep in intellectual discussion, a carriage has come into sight—no, two."

"Oh," she said, gripping his arm more tightly, "and the first carriage is Stephen's. They are *here,* Jasper. And look, Stephen is riding beside it. Meg and Charlotte will be inside."

He released her arm in order to clasp her hand and lace their fingers. Then he tucked her arm beneath his again. She was glowing with excitement, he saw, and he felt an unfamiliar fluttering of . . . something low in his stomach. Tenderness? Longing? Both? Neither?

Actually, though, it was not a totally unfamiliar feeling. He had felt something similar on the beach that day.

Merton reached the terrace first with Phineas Thane, who could be no more than seventeen, if that, and had the spots to prove it. Merton's carriage was close behind them. Sir Michael Ogden rode beside the second carriage, which contained his betrothed, Miss Alice Dubois, as well as her younger sister and her parents, Mr. and Mrs. Dubois. Thane must have come with them.

Merton was off his horse in a moment. He threw a grin Jasper's way and then caught Katherine up in a hug and swung her off her feet and in a complete circle. She wrapped her arms about his neck and laughed.

Jasper did not wait for the coachman to descend from his perch. He opened the door of the carriage and set down the steps. He offered his hand to Miss Huxtable and smiled at her.

"Welcome to Cedarhurst, Miss Huxtable," he said.

"Oh," she said as she descended the steps, "I think that had better be *Margaret,* Lord Montford. Or, better yet, *Meg.*"

"In which case, Meg," he said, "I am Jasper."

She turned to Katherine, and they held each other in a wordless hug while Jasper turned back to the carriage. But Thane had already offered his hand to Charlotte, who was smiling at him and blushing.

Well, Jasper thought, already supplanted by a spotty youth. He helped Miss Daniels alight.

But Charlotte turned to him as soon as her feet had

hit the terrace, and she squealed and threw herself into his arms.

"Jasper!" she cried. "I have had *such* a wonderful time at Warren Hall. And really the journey here was not tedious at all, was it, Danny? There was Meg to talk to, and sometimes we let down the window and talked with Lord Merton, and then when we were changing horses at—oh, I cannot even remember where. It was three or four hours ago anyway. Along came the Dubois and Sir Michael and Mr. Thane, and we all came along together in one merry party. Oh, *Kate*! I have longed to see you again. And how lovely you look. But you *always* look lovely."

Jasper turned to greet the other new arrivals and to welcome them to Cedarhurst. After a few moments Katherine joined him and slipped her hand into his.

The guests were shown to their rooms, and Katherine and Jasper awaited the arrival of the others. They all came before tea, one after the other.

The Countess of Hornsby was in the next carriage to arrive with her daughter, Lady Marianne Willis, and not far behind them were Sidney Shaw and Donald Gladstone, riding side by side, and Sir Nathan Fletcher and Bernard Smith-Vane, one on each side of the carriage that brought the former's sister, Louisa Fletcher, and Araminta Clement. They had all traveled together.

Miss Hutchins came up from the village in the Reverend Bellow's gig and was immediately claimed by Charlotte, who had come running downstairs to meet her and take her to her room.

They both squealed before they disappeared.

And then, last to arrive, came Uncle Stanley with

Cousins Arnold, Winford, and Beatrice—aged seventeen, sixteen, and fourteen.

It all seemed a little like the infantry brigade, Jasper thought. All the gentlemen except Gladstone, and of course Dubois and his uncle, were years younger than himself. Miss Dubois and Miss Clement had already made their debut in society and therefore must surely be at least eighteen, but the other young ladies, with the exception of Margaret, were younger even than Charlotte. He felt like a veritable fossil.

He walked into the house with his uncle while Katherine took Beatrice's arm and Arnold and Winford fell into step on either side of them.

"It is good to be here again where I grew up, Jasper," his uncle said, "and to see you settled at last with a good woman. And despite all that foolish gossip in London, I do believe she *is* a good woman. Your father would be pleased."

Jasper raised his eyebrows but made no comment. He wondered if his father would look somewhat like Uncle Stanley today had he lived—slightly portly but still a fine figure of a man with all his hair. There was a definite family resemblance—as there was with the cousins. He had felt bitter through most of his life about their neglect—abandoning him and Rachel because they could not stand his mother's second husband. But it was foolish to remain bitter. It was time to mend fences.

And it struck him suddenly that if he had been born a girl, then Uncle Stanley himself would have inherited the title and property. Perhaps *he* had felt somewhat bitter too.

"It is good to have you here, Uncle Stanley," he said.

"I look forward to getting to know you better—and my cousins."

"You will be shown to your rooms," Katherine said, addressing them all when they were inside. "I am sure you will want to refresh yourselves. We will wait in the drawing room for everyone to come down for tea. Come when you are ready. There is no hurry today. Oh, we are *so* glad you could come. And, Mr. Finley, you look very much like Jasper. As do Arnold and Winford, particularly Winford."

"You will call me Uncle Stanley, if you will, my dear," he said.

"Uncle Stanley," she said, stepping up to Jasper's side and slipping her arm through his. "Family is so terribly important."

And then they were alone together, the two of them, though soon everyone would be coming for tea, and the next two weeks were likely to be hectic enough. There would be chance enough to avoid each other's company if they wished—though he *had* promised to give a good impression to their families.

"Well, Katherine," he said.

"Well, Jasper."

"Happy?" he asked.

"Happy," she said.

But the question and its answer brought to mind the next question he had asked down at the lake. And he could see that she had the same thought.

He patted her hand.

"We had better go up to the drawing room," he said.

"Yes."

*   *   *

It was very easy to feel happy, Katherine discovered over the next week or so, when one was mistress of one's own home, when that home was filled with guests and it was summertime and they could amuse themselves every moment of every day with walks and rides and picnics and a few excursions, with tours of the house and musical evenings and charades and a thousand and one other activities.

It was easy to feel happy when one was planning a combined birthday party and fete and ball and when the whole neighborhood was buzzing with excitement and pitching in to plan and help. And when all the houseguests were filled with enthusiasm too and could not wait for the day to arrive—except that it would be the next to last day of their stay and they were not at all anxious to return home.

It was easy to feel happy when one had family close by. It was not just her own family whose company she enjoyed. She delighted in Charlotte's enthusiasm and she loved sitting or strolling and talking with Jasper's Uncle Stanley, who told her tales of his own childhood at Cedarhurst, many of them involving his elder brother, Jasper's father.

But, oh, to have Meg at Cedarhurst! And to show Meg how well she was managing the household and how well she was hosting the house party and planning the fete! And just to be able to talk to her, to sit in Meg's room with her and just talk the old, familiar talk.

"Are you happy, Kate?" Meg asked her one day when they were sitting in her room. "Oh, I know you are enjoying these weeks, and I know you and Jasper have a fondness for each other. But is it going to be enough afterward? Kate . . . Oh, I do not know quite *what* to ask. Are you going to be happy?"

Katherine, who was sitting on the bed, hugged her knees to her chest.

"Meg," she said, "I *love* him."

It was the first time she had said it aloud. She had tried not even to *think* it since that day at the lake.

"Yes." Meg smiled. "I know you do, Kate. And does he love you? I believe he does, but one can never really tell with men, can one?"

"He will," Katherine said.

And *almost* she believed it. When they joked and laughed and talked nonsense together, when he pursed his lips sometimes when he looked at her, when he took her hand and laced their fingers together and held her arm to his side, even if it was done primarily to impress their guests—oh, then, sometimes, just occasionally, she believed that one day he would love her.

And, really, *love* was just a word. She would never demand that he use it. She would never allow herself to feel rejected and unloved if he did not. But she would *know*. When he loved her, she would know it.

When?

Not *if?*

Sometimes she was optimistic enough to say *when*. More often it was *if*.

"And what of you, Meg?" she asked.

"What *of* me?" her sister asked, smiling. "It was good to be back at Warren Hall, Kate. Though I missed you—even though I had Charlotte and Miss Daniels with me."

"The Marquess of Allingham?" Katherine asked tentatively. "Did you see him again after I left London?"

"He was at the wedding, of course," Meg said. "He took me driving in the park the next day, but we left for home the day after that."

"And has he *said* anything?" Katherine asked.

"By way of a declaration?" Meg asked. "No. I refused him once, remember."

"But that was more than three years ago," Katherine said.

"We are friends." Meg smiled. "I like him and he likes me, Kate. Nothing more."

Katherine would not press the matter further. But she did wonder about her sister's feelings. Close as they had always been as sisters, there *was* the age gap between them, and she had always been aware that she was not quite Meg's confidante. She doubted anyone was. Meg and Nessie had been close when they were younger, but Nessie had been married for a number of years, first to Hedley Dew and then to Elliott.

"Nessie is taking the children to Rundle Park for a few weeks," Katherine said, "for Sir Humphrey and Lady Dew to see them."

"Yes," Meg said. "They were always terribly fond of her. They were genuinely glad for her when she married Elliott. They told her, though, that she would always be their daughter-in-law and that they would consider any children of her marriage to be their grandchildren."

They smiled at each other.

"I am going to go with her," Meg said. "I will stay at the cottage in Throckbridge with Mrs. Thrush. It will be good to be there for a while and to see all our old friends."

"You must give everyone my love," Katherine said. "I am sorry there is no one eligible for you here, Meg. All

of Charlotte's guests are very young. We did think perhaps Mr. Gladstone would single you out for attention
since he is older than everyone else, but Sir Nathan
Fletcher has taken to monopolizing your company instead, and he is hardly any older than Stephen."

Meg laughed.

"He is a charming and eager boy," she said, "and I am
flattered by his attentions. I like him—as I do everyone
here. It is a happy group, Kate, and much of the credit
must go to you and Jasper. You are keeping us all well
entertained every moment of every day."

It was lovely to have Stephen at Cedarhurst too. He
was extremely popular, as he seemed to be wherever he
went. The gentlemen tended to look to him to take the
lead, and all the ladies gazed at him with thinly dis-
guised adoration. Had Katherine drawn his attention
to the fact he would have replied as he always did that
of course he was an *earl* and such an exalted title tended
to dazzle people. But it was more than that. There was
something...oh, what was the word? *Charismatic?*
There was something in her brother's very character
that drew people to him.

There was a joy for life in Stephen.

Charlotte was his favorite. Or he was hers. Although
all the guests mingled with all the others, more often
than not it was beside Charlotte that Stephen sat or beside her that he walked or rode.

It was easy to feel happy for these two weeks. And if
there was some apprehension about what would happen afterward, when all the guests had left and all the
excitement was at an end and life settled, as it inevitably must, into a fixed routine, then Katherine

firmly set aside her anxiety. That time would come soon enough. She would deal with it when it came.

Meanwhile she dreamed that perhaps Jasper would love her someday—even if he never said so.

Jasper could not remember a time when Cedarhurst had been so filled with guests, though his staff assured him that in his father's day and his grandfather's there had always been people coming and going and sometimes there had been great house parties that had brought every guest room into use.

He had been forbidden to mention his father when he was a boy. Strangely, it was one order he had obeyed—perhaps because he had not wanted to know any more about him than he already did. And perhaps because every servant had been forbidden to mention his name too. He was surprised to hear him mentioned now.

It happened one morning more than a week after the house party had begun, when he had wandered down to the kitchen in search of Katherine—she was not there—and had stayed to eat two currant cakes, fresh out of the oven. Someone mentioned the upcoming fete and someone else mentioned his father as the host of the last one.

"Did he even *attend* it?" Jasper asked. "He was a wastrel, was he not?"

At which Mrs. Oliver lifted the utensil she happened to be holding in her hand at that moment, a rather lethal-looking carving knife, and pointed it directly at his heart from no more than three feet away.

"I heard quite enough of that nonsense when Mr.

Wrayburn was alive," she said, "God rest his soul. But just because Mr. Wrayburn liked his Bible and his sermons and did not like liquor or dancing, that does not mean everyone who enjoyed a bit of fun now and then was the devil incarnate. *You* were not the devil, my lord, even though you was bad enough to grow gray hairs on the heads of everyone that cared for you. And your *papa* was not the devil either even though he liked his drink and his wild ways and, yes, even his women before he married your mama. At least there was laughter in this house while he was still alive, which there was precious little of after he died, Lord knows — and no one has ever persuaded me that the good Lord does not enjoy a good belly laugh from time to time. And if her ladyship, God bless her, is aiming to bring the laughter back, and even a bit of the wildness, then good for her, says I."

Her eyes fell upon the wicked blade of the knife she had been wagging at him, and she had the grace to lower it hastily. She was flushed and out of breath.

"And so says everyone in these parts," Couch added. "Begging your pardon, my lord, for expressing an opinion in your hearing unasked."

"That never stopped you when I was a lad," Jasper said. "I seem to remember growing heartily tired of hearing your opinion, Couch."

"Well," the butler said, looking somewhat abashed, "if you *would* tie the footman's wig to the back of his chair when he nodded off in the hall, and if you *would* ride down the waterfall when you were wearing your good clothes and tear holes in your coat and your breeches when they caught on branches and stones on your way down, you had to expect to hear my opinion, my lord."

"Let me hear it now again, then," Jasper said, grinning and sitting down on one of the long benches that stretched the length of the kitchen table and helping himself to an apple, into which he bit with a loud crunch. "Tell me about my father."

They both told him a good deal even though they exchanged a look first, as if even now they were afraid of breaking a rule set by a dead man. His mother's second husband had cast a long, dark shadow, Jasper reflected.

He could not stay in the kitchen for long. Charlotte had borne off the young people in gigs and on horseback to the village, where they intended to look at the church—probably very briefly if Jasper knew anything about young persons—before taking refreshments in the taproom at the inn. He had promised to show the gallery to Lady Hornsby and Dubois and his wife and give them a bit of a history lesson about his family and Cedarhurst. His uncle was going to join them too.

He had hoped that Katherine would accompany him—that was why he had been looking for her—but she had vanished, probably into the village for one of her committee meetings.

The young people had in no way been tired out by their outing, it appeared later at luncheon. It was decided that they would walk about the lake during the afternoon. They had been down to the water several times, to stroll along the near bank and to picnic there and take out the boats on one occasion, but they had never yet found the time to walk to the far side—or to take the wilderness walk.

"It is really very pretty on the other side," Charlotte explained. "There are lovely views from every point, and there are several places to sit and rest—including the little cottage, which is really just a folly. We will save the full wilderness walk through the hills for another day."

"I would think so too," Miss Fletcher said. "My shoes will be all worn out before I return home, not to mention my feet."

"You must allow me to escort you, then, Miss Fletcher," Thane said, his voice half cracking over the words, as the voices of very young gentlemen frequently did, "and you may lean upon my arm."

"Oh, *thank* you, Mr. Thane," she said, blushing while the younger Miss Dubois giggled.

Why did very young ladies giggle so much? And why did they do it almost without ceasing when other young ladies were with them—and even more so when there were young gentlemen within earshot? But Jasper listened to it all with an amused indulgence.

"Miss Huxtable," young Fletcher said, "may I have the honor of escorting you?"

The poor boy had been suffering from a severe case of infatuation for Margaret all week, even though he must be at least six years her junior and in no way her match in the looks department.

She smiled kindly at him. "It would be my pleasure," she said.

She was a kind lady.

"Shall *we* walk to the far side of the lake too, Jasper?" Katherine asked. "It is the one part of the walk we have not yet done."

All heads, it seemed, turned first her way and then his, as if his answer was of the utmost importance to them all. No one had forgotten the circumstances of their marriage, of course, when so little time had passed since their wedding. Everyone's eyes had been upon them for more than a week. They had done a great deal of smiling at each other, he and Katherine.

"We certainly shall, my love," he said. "Especially if I may have you on my arm."

"Of course," she said.

21

THE walk took them down the lawn to the jetty, around the grassy bank of the lake to their left, past reeds and a noisy family of ducks, into the trees on the far side, and onto the beginnings of the wilderness walk. Sometimes the trees enclosed them and offered a welcome shade from the sun. At others they opened out and afforded views of the water and the house. At one point it led to the tiny cottage at the top of the steepest part of the bank and the waterfall beside it.

Lady Hornsby and Mrs. Dubois had remained behind to sit in the parterre garden. Mr. Dubois had walked into the village with Mr. Finley to call upon a few former acquaintances of the latter. Everyone else had come on the walk, even Miss Daniels and the Reverend Bellow.

It took close to an hour just getting as far as the waterfall since there was so much to stop for and admire and exclaim over on the way and so many seats on which to sit to rest from their exertions. And at every moment there was a great deal of animated chatter and laughter to delay them even further.

"I am well aware," Jasper said to Katherine while Miss Fletcher and Miss Hortense Dubois were stretching their hands gingerly into the waterfall and then shrieking at their own daring and exclaiming loudly at the coldness of the water, "that this house party is for Charlotte's sake and that both she and the infants are enjoying themselves enormously. But I am an elder and bored almost to tears by it all. Are *you*?"

"Not at all," she said. "I like all our guests very much indeed and the surroundings are lovely and the weather is perfect. I daresay a curricle race to Land's End and back would be more to your taste."

"If you would come with me," he said. "Would you?"

"I am afraid not," she said. "I have no desire to break my neck and both my legs."

"Coward," he said.

"Besides," she said, "it would probably rain somewhere along the way and I would ruin a perfectly decent bonnet."

"No race to Land's End and back, then," he said with a sigh. "How about a private walk a little way up into the hills instead? There is somewhere I want to show you."

"Did I not see it all two weeks ago?" she asked as Charlotte shrieked and Thane bellowed and someone informed him that his sleeve was soaked and everyone shouted with laughter.

"No, you did not." He offered her his hand. "Come with me. No one will miss us—they are all too busy flirting with one another. And Miss Daniels is here to see that they do not get too enthusiastic about it."

"It seems very neglectful to abandon all our guests," she said. But it was a weak protest. She did not resist the pull of his hand, and he walked her briskly away from the waterfall in the direction of the fork in the path, one branch of which led down to the beach while the other climbed up into the hills. He took the latter.

He was feeling too restless for a walk at slower than a

snail's pace. His thoughts had been swirling around in his brain for several hours, and he felt in dire need of peace and quiet.

They walked rather briskly despite the upward slope until they reached the ancient beech tree at one end of the rhododendron stretch of the walk. He stopped there and leaned back against the trunk for a moment, still holding her hand.

"Winded?" he asked.

He could hear that she was. But she turned to look down at the view, which was admittedly rather splendid. It looked down on the paddocks and kitchen gardens behind the house and over the house itself to the parterre gardens, the lawns and driveway, the village in the distance, and a patchwork of fields stretching into the distance in all directions. Just a little higher, he had always thought, and they would be able to see the sea. He had tried climbing the tree once, but he had sprained an ankle and a wrist as a result and, worse, had scuffed a newish pair of boots so badly that even the combined skills of several servants had not been able to cover up his transgression.

They had been putting on a good front for their family and guests, he and Katherine. But there was still a reserve between them in private that had been there since he had made an ass of himself at the lake. She must think him a sorry wager-winner since there were no more than a few days left in their wager and he had made no real attempt recently to win it.

"Come," he said after they had their breath back, and he took her hand again and turned off the path to strike straight upward through dense trees until they had reached almost to the top of the rise and into the sudden, unexpected clearing that as far as he knew no one else had ever discovered. It was like a miniature meadow or dell, all lush grass and wildflowers, completely enclosed by trees. Coming here had always felt like walking into another world, in which he was entirely alone and in which time and troubles mattered not at all.

"My most secret retreat as a boy," he said, stopping at the edge of it. "I came here more often than I can remember, summer and winter."

He had been somehow afraid that it would be gone. It was years since he had been here last.

"It is always carpeted with snowdrops in the early spring," he said, "as if it had suffered its own private little snowfall. And with bluebells later on as if a patch of sky had taken refuge in the forest. I wish you could have seen it in the spring."

"I will," she said softly. "Next year and the year after. I live here, Jasper."

He knew somehow from the tone of her voice that she understood, and he felt foolish and grateful.

One thrush, perhaps disturbed by the sound of their voices, flew out of a high branch with a flutter of wings, and she tipped back her head to watch it soar into the sky.

"I have always had places like this of my own," she said, "though never anywhere quite so remote or more splendid."

He looked over to the far corner of the clearing and was surprised and relieved to discover that it was, of course, still there—a great flat slab of rock jutting out of the hillside, level with his knees when he was a boy.

"Ah," he said, "the stone is still there. My drea—"

He stopped abruptly.

"Your drea—?" she said.

"Nothing." He shrugged.

"Your dreaming stone?" she said.

Good Lord, she had got it exactly right. His dreaming stone.

"A foolish boyhood fancy," he said, striding away from her to take a closer look at it. It was covered with moss and twigs and other debris, and he leaned over to brush it off. "I was captain of my own ship here and lord of my own castle and navigator of my own flying carpet. I slew dragons and enemy knights and black-hearted villains of all descriptions here. I was my own favorite, invincible hero."

"As we all are in our childhood fantasies," she said. "As we *need* to be. Our games give us the courage to grow up and live the best adult lives of which we are capable."

Had the vicar taught her that?

He set one booted foot on the stone.

"And sometimes," he said, "I would just lie here watching the sky."

"Flying on the coattails of the clouds," she said. "And yet you scorned me when I told you that I dreamed of flying close to the sun."

"I was a child at the time," he said, lowering his foot back to the ground, "and knew nothing. It is here we have to do our living, Katherine. And not even here in this clearing or places like it, but down there in the world, where dreams signify nothing."

"Our lives ought to be lived in both places," she said. "We need both our retreats, our private places and our dreams, *and* our lives out there, where we make a difference to one another, for good or ill."

He must think quickly of something about which to tease her. He was not accustomed to serious conversation. And he felt too raw for one now. Why, then, had he brought her here? He might easily have got away on his own.

He had never brought anyone else here—until now.

She stepped up onto the stone, looked around the clearing from that higher vantage point, and sat down. She took off her bonnet and set it beside her, and then hugged her knees and lifted her face to the sky.

A few weeks ago she had worn lemon and blue for the lake and the sunshine. Now she wore her pale green cotton for the woods, as if she had known they would come here. A sun goddess there, a wood nymph here.

And then she looked suddenly dismayed.

"I am sorry," she said. "Am I encroaching upon what is yours?"

"*You* are what is mine, are you not?" he said, grinning at her. And he stepped up there too and sat with his wrists resting on his crossed legs for a few minutes before removing his hat and coat, spreading the latter behind him, and lying back on it, leaving enough room for her if she chose to lie beside him.

It was no good. She had not responded to that provocative claim of ownership, and he could think of nothing else with which to tease or mock her.

She glanced down at him, looked into his eyes, and then came down to join him, her head beside his on the coat. He felt himself relax. It was safe here. There had always been that illusion. It *was* an illusion, of course. He had always had to go back to the house eventually where he had been required to explain where he had been, why he had chosen to worry his mother so much with his long absence, why his lessons were not done or his Bible verses learned, why his clothes were dirty, why . . .

Well.

His body was relaxed, but his thoughts had a busy agenda of their own. He could not still them. He could not think of a single thing to say that would make her laugh or that would draw a spirited retort.

He was not himself at all. He ought to have come alone.

"He loved Rachel, you know," he said abruptly at last and felt like an idiot when he *heard* the words. He had spoken aloud.

"Mr. Gooding?" she asked after a pause. "Ought that not to be present tense? It seemed to me at our wedding breakfast that—"

"My *father*," he said, interrupting her. "She was more than a year old when he died, and he loved her. He adored her, in fact. He used to carry her all over the house, to the frequent consternation of her nurse."

She did not say anything.

"And he was excited about me," he said. "He had been out shooting with some other fellows on the day he died and was carousing with them afterward, after the rain started, when word reached him that my mother was having pains. He was riding hell bent for leather back home when he jumped that hedge instead of taking ten seconds longer to go through the gate. Perhaps he did not even notice that it was open. And so he died—and the pains were false ones. I did not put in an appearance until a month later."

Her hand was in his. Had he taken it? Or had she taken his? Either way, he was clasping it rather tightly.

He felt like a prize idiot. He turned his head and smiled mockingly at her, loosening his grip as he did so.

"It was just as well he popped off when he did," he said. "His second child would have been a colossal disappointment to him. You must agree with that, Katherine."

"Why do you speak of these things as if they are new discoveries?" she asked.

"Because they *are*," he said. "I had a chat with some of the servants this morning when I went down to the kitchen in search of you, and they told me all sorts of things I had never heard before. We were not allowed to mention my father's name, you know."

"Why?" She frowned.

"He was a rake and a libertine and the devil's spawn," he said. "When righteousness came into the house in the guise of my mother's second husband, his influence was to be forgotten once and for all. For the good of every one of us, family and servants. Come to think of it, maybe he would not have been disappointed. Maybe he would have hailed me as his true successor. Do you think?"

She ignored his flippancy.

"So you were told nothing of your own *father*?" Her huge, fathomless eyes grew larger.

"On the contrary," he said. "I was told something of him almost every day of my boyhood. He was the man whose seed had made me bad, irredeemable, incorrigible, and any number of other nasty things. I was as like him as two peas in a pod—as two *rotten* peas, that is. I would never amount to anything in life because I had his blood running in my veins. And everyone knew where I was headed after I died—downward, to be re-united with him."

"Did your *mother* not have something to say?" she asked.

"My mother was a sweet lady," he said. "Naturally placid, I believe, and very easily dominated. She needed always to have someone to tell her what was what. The servants claim that she adored my father. But after his death and my birth she collapsed into lethargy and a gloom that lifted only when Wrayburn took over her life and married her. She loved him, I suppose. She was also terrified of him, or at least terrified of displeasing him. Even after his death she would not say or do anything of which she thought he would disapprove."

"She did not love *you*?" she asked softly.

"Oh, she did," he said. "She undoubtedly did. She shed tears over me more times than I can count and begged me to be good and godly, to do all that my step-papa told me so that I would be worthy of his love too."

"And Rachel?" she asked.

"She was denied her youth," he said, "because the world beyond our doors was a wicked place and a girl's place was at her mother's side."

"Charlotte?"

"Ah, but she did not have the bad blood," he said. "And Miss Daniels came when she was still very young. She was also fortunate enough to be a girl. He was not much interested in her."

He felt more and more of an idiot. Why was he spewing out all this ancient history? He *never* spoke of his boyhood. He rarely even thought about it. He was certainly not looking for pity—perish the thought! He was just surprised that this morning's revelations in the kitchen had upset him so much, set the wheels of his mind whirling.

His father had loved Rachel. He had loved his own unborn self. He had been capable of love. He had died for love.

His thoughts were spinning so fast he felt downright dizzy.

"I think my father loved my mother too," he said. "He stopped womanizing after he married her."

She had their clasped hands raised, he realized. He could feel the touch of her lips and the warmth of her breath against the back of his.

"Only minutes before word was brought to him that my mother's pains had started," he said, "he proposed a toast to me. Son or daughter—he did not care which I was provided I was born alive and healthy. He actually said that, though he must have wanted a son. An heir."

She rubbed her cheek back and forth across his hand.

"The servants worshipped him," he said, "though they were by no means blind to his faults. Recklessness, according to them, was probably the worst of those."

"They worship you too," she said. "Though they are still not blind."

"I think," he said, "we might have been a happy family if he had lived."

He wished he could stop spouting drivel. When was he going to shut his mouth and keep it shut?

"But then," he said, "if things had not happened as they did, there would not be Charlotte, would there? She has always been very precious to me."

Devil take it, would someone *please* tell him to shut up?

"Strange that," he said. "She is *his* daughter. How can she possibly be dear to me?"

"Because she is herself," she said, "just as you are yourself."

"Katherine," he said, "stop me, please. There must be all sorts of skeletons in your cupboards too. Tell me about them."

"There are really none," she said. "My life has been privileged indeed. Oh, I have lived through the unspeakable grief of losing my mother when I was just a child and then my father when I was only twelve. They were desolate times—and that word does not begin to describe them. But I always had my sisters and brother, and none of us ever doubted that we were loved or wanted. Even though Meg gave up her future with Crispin Dew for us, she never made us feel that it had been a sacrifice for which she partly resented us. Indeed, I did not even know about it until a few years ago when Nessie told me. I was always so secure in the love of my family that I find it hard even to imagine being a child and not having that security. I cannot imagine anything worse than a child feeling himself to be unloved and unlovable. I cannot *bear* the thought."

Her voice had become thinner, higher pitched.

He could not blame circumstances for anything, though, could he? For making him who he was? That would be a sniveling thing to do. They were the circumstances with which he had been presented, and at any moment in his life—child, boy, or adult—the choice of how to think, speak, and behave had been his.

Still was.

He drew his hand from hers, raised himself onto one elbow, and smiled lazily down at her. It was time to recover himself.

"Has my sad story moved your tender heart, Katherine?" he asked, his eyes roaming over her face to come to rest on her mouth. "And is that heart smitten with love for me as a result? Are you ready to confess all? That I am one step closer to winning our wager? *Two* steps? Or that I have won it outright?"

He realized his mistake immediately. She would not view *that* as gentle teasing. It was too reminiscent of what had happened at the lake, by Jove. And it was unfair, dash it all.

Would he *never* learn?

But the words could not be unsaid, and all he could do was wait for her reply, his right eyebrow cocked, his eyelids hooded over his eyes, the corners of his lips drawn up into a half-smile.

One devil of a fine fellow.

God's answer to the prayers of lonely, lovelorn womankind.

Or perhaps not.

She raised one hand as if to set it tenderly against the side of his face. Instead, her open palm cracked hard and painfully across his cheek.

22

SHE rolled away from him, scrambled to her feet, jumped down from the stone, and strode halfway across the clearing before stopping almost knee-deep among the grass and wildflowers.

She had never in her life hit anyone. She had *slapped him across the face.* Her hand was still stinging. Her heart was pounding up into her throat and her ears, almost choking and deafening her.

She whirled on him.

"Don't you *ever* do that to me again," she cried, her voice breathless and shaking. "Not *ever.* Do you hear me?"

He was sitting up, propped on one arm while two fingers of the other hand were poking gingerly at his reddened cheek.

"I do indeed," he said. "Katherine—"

"You took me in," she said, "you *invited* me in, and then you slammed the door shut in my face. If you do not want me to have any part in your life, then shut me out altogether, stay hidden behind the wit and the irony and the hooded eyes and the cocked eyebrow. Go away. Leave me here to live my life in peace. But if you choose to let me in, then let me all the way in. Don't suddenly pretend this has all been about the winning of a stupid *wager.*"

She was panting for breath.

He gazed at her for a few moments, his lips pursed. Then he got to his feet and crossed the clearing to stand in front of her. She wished he were wearing his coat and hat. He was too disconcertingly . . . *male* in his shirt-sleeves and waistcoat.

"They were just a few random comments about my family," he said with a shrug. "Nothing to get excited about. I thought you might be amused by them. No, I thought you might be touched. I thought you might pity me. Is pity not halfway to love? I thought you might—"

Crack!

Oh, dear God, she had done it again—the same hand, the same cheek.

He closed his eyes.

"That *does* hurt, you know," he said. "And you have me at a disadvantage, Katherine. As a gentleman, I cannot retaliate, can I?"

"You know nothing—*nothing!*—about love," she cried. "You have *been* loved, and you *are* loved. You even *love* without knowing it. But you shut yourself away from it as soon as it threatens to break through the barriers you erected about your heart years and years ago lest you be hurt more and more until you could not bear even to live. Those days are *over* if you would just realize it."

He half smiled at her.

"You are lovelier than ever when you are angry," he said.

"I am not angry," she cried. "I am *furious!* Love is not a game."

Still that half-smile and the hooded eyes, which were

hooded indeed now. There was not even a glimmering of mischief or humor in them.

"What *is* it, then, if not a game?" he asked softly.

"It is not even a feeling," she said, "though feelings are involved in it. It is certainly not all happiness and light. It is not s-sex either, though I know you must be about to suggest that. Love is a connection with another person, either through birth or through something else that I cannot even explain. It is often just an attraction at first. But it goes far deeper than that. It is a determination to care for the other person no matter what and to allow oneself to be cared for in return. It is a commitment to make the other happy and to be happy oneself. It is not possessive, but neither is it a victim. And it does not always bring happiness. Often it brings a great deal of pain, especially when the beloved is suffering and one feels impotent to comfort. *It is what life is all about.* It is openness and trust and vulnerability. Oh, I know I have had life easy in the sense that there has always been unconditional love in my life. I know I cannot even begin to understand what it was like to grow up with very little love at all. But are you going to let that upbringing blight your whole life? Are you going to give your stepfather that power, even from the grave? And you *were* loved, Jasper, perhaps by everyone *except* him. All your servants and I daresay all your neighbors have always loved you. Your mother did. Charlotte adores you. I am going to stop talking now because really I do not know *what* I have been saying."

His smile was twisted, lifting one corner of his mouth higher than the other, and she realized that there was a great tension in him, that his facial muscles were not perhaps quite within his control. The two slaps had probably not helped either.

"If I can persuade *you* to love me too, Katherine," he said, "my life would be complete. Happily ever after. I will—"

"That wager!" She almost spat out the words. "I am mortally *sick* of that wager. I'll have no more of it, do you understand? It is over with. Done. Love is *not* a game, and I will no longer have any part in pretending that it is. The wager is obliterated. Null and void. Gone. Go back to London with your stupid wagers if you must and to your equally stupid gentlemen friends who think it fun to bet money on whether or not you can persuade a woman who has done nothing to offend any one of you to . . . to *debauch* herself with you. Even to allow it to happen up against a tree in a public pleasure garden. Go, and never come back. I will never miss you."

Oh, dear, God, where were the words coming from? Why had she had to bring *that* up again?

"I think," he said softly, "my wagering days are probably over. I hurt you dreadfully."

It was not a question.

"Yes, you did," she said, and burst into tears.

"Katherine." His hands cupped her shoulders.

But she would not collapse against him and cry her heart out. She beat her fists against his chest instead, sobbing and hiccuping and keeping her head down. Oh, how foolish she felt. Why this sudden hysteria? All that had happened a long time ago. It was ancient history.

"How *could* you?" she cried, gasping and sobbing as she spoke. "How *could* you do that? What had I ever done to you?"

"Nothing," he said. "I have no excuse, Katherine, no defense. It was a dastardly thing to do."

"All the gentlemen in that club must have known," she said.

"A goodly number, yes," he agreed.

"And now *everyone* knows," she said. "And it is too convenient to blame Sir Clarence Forester."

"Yes," he said, "it is. The fault was entirely mine."

She looked up into his face even though she knew her own must be red and swollen.

"How could you do that to *yourself*?" she asked him. "How could you have so little respect for yourself? How could you have so little regard for human decency?"

He pursed his lips. His eyes—wide open now—looked steadily back into hers.

"I do not really know, Katherine," he said. "I am not much given to introspection."

"And *that* has been deliberate on your part," she said. "Feelings must have been unbearable to you as a boy, and so you cut them off. But when there are no feelings, Jasper, there can be no compassion either—for other people or even for yourself. You end up treating other people as you have been treated."

She swiped the back of her hand over her wet nose, and he turned abruptly and strode back to the flat stone. He leaned down to his coat, drew a handkerchief out of a pocket, and came back to her, his hand outstretched.

She dried her eyes and blew her nose and balled the handkerchief in one hand.

"I am not going away," he said when she looked at him again. "This is my home and you are my wife. What I did to you three years ago was unpardonable, but unfortunately you are stuck with me. I am sorry about that. But I am not going away."

"Oh, Jasper." She looked at him, glad despite herself. *He was not going to go away.* "Nothing is ever unpardonable."

He pursed his lips and gazed at her in silence for a few moments.

"If the wager is off," he said, "is it *all* off? All the conditions too?"

"Yes," she said, and it was an enormous relief to say so, for of course she knew to *which* condition he referred. He was not going to go away, but their marriage as it was now was no marriage at all—thanks to that condition she had imposed on the wager during their wedding night.

She had missed him so much, which was a ridiculous thing when there had been only that one night. Not even a full night. He had slept in their private sitting room for much of it.

"Come to me tonight," she said, and felt her cheeks turn hot.

She dropped the handkerchief to the ground and lifted her hands to cup his cheeks. The marks of her fingers were still visible on the left one. And her face must look an absolute fright.

He took her hands in his and turned his head to kiss first one palm and then the other.

"Katherine," he said, "you cannot seriously expect me to hear that *yes* at one moment and *come to me tonight* at the next and be content to wait that long. You could not expect it of any self-respecting red-blooded male. Least of all me."

"But everyone would wonder where we had gone,"

she said, "if we were to disappear to our rooms as soon as we returned to the house. Besides—"

"Katherine," he said softly, and kissed her lips.

And of course she knew instantly what he meant, what he intended. She was aware just as instantly of sunlight and heat, of the chirping and whirring of unseen insects, of the call of a single bird, of the softness of grass and wildflowers about their knees. And of the smell of his cologne and his body heat and the feel of his lips against hers again. And of a welling of desire that engulfed her from head to toe.

She wrapped her arms about his neck and opened her mouth.

And somehow they were down on the ground, the grass waving above them, and all was hot, fierce embrace and labored breathing and urgent, exploring hands and mouths, and clothing discarded or pulled and pushed out of the way—until she lay on her back and his weight was on her and his face above hers, filled with a desire to match her own.

"Katherine," he murmured.

His waistcoat and neckcloth were gone. His white shirt gaped open at the neck to show the muscles beneath and the dark hair that dusted his chest. His pantaloons were opened at the waist. Her bodice was down below her breasts, her skirt up about her hips. Her legs were spread on either side of his, her stockinged feet resting on the warm, supple leather of his Hessian boots.

She twined her fingers in his hair, which was warm from the sun.

"The ground makes a damnable mattress," he said, "especially in the act of love."

"I do not care," she said, and lifted her head to kiss him, to draw him down onto and into her. She did not care that he must know he had won that stupid wager long before it had been abandoned. She did not care if he knew that she loved him. Love was vulnerable, she had just told him.

Ah, yes, it was.

But it was not to be avoided for that reason.

"Let me be noble." There was a smile in his eyes. "For once in my life, let me be noble."

And he rolled with her until he lay on his back. He had taken her legs in his hands and bent them so that she was kneeling on either side of his body. She set her hands on his shoulders and lifted her head so that she could look down at him. And he raised his hands and pulled out her hairpins until her hair fell down on either side of her face and onto his shoulders.

"Come," he said then, and he grasped her hips, lifted her, and then guided her down onto him so that she felt his long hardness slide into her wet depth. She pressed down onto him, clenching her inner muscles as she did so, and closing her eyes.

There was no pain.

And surely—oh, surely!—there was no lovelier feeling in the world. And in the outdoors too. She opened her eyes and was aware of the pinks and mauves of the wildflowers that bloomed in the grass all around their heads.

She closed her eyes again, relaxed her inner muscles, and lifted herself half off him for the sheer pleasure of pressing downward again and clenching her muscles once more. She did it again. And again.

Perhaps a minute passed—or two or ten—before she

realized that he lay still beneath her, that she rode him for her own pleasure. His hands were spread warm and firm over her outer thighs.

She opened her eyes once more and looked down at him. He was gazing back, and she knew that she was riding him to pleasure too, that there was a mutual delight in lovemaking no matter which of them it was who was making the primary moves. There was power in being a lover, man or woman. She smiled down at him as she rode on, and his lips lifted ever so slightly at the corners.

But there was pain too. Or, if not exactly a pain, then an ache that threatened to turn into pain. And a recklessness in continuing to lift herself off him only to impale herself on the pain again.

His hand came to the back of her head and drew it down, first to his opened mouth, and then to his shoulder. Then both hands went to her buttocks, grasping firmly and holding her half off him while he moved at last, driving hard and fast up into her until he pulled her down and stopped all movement so abruptly that she shattered without warning and cried out.

The insects chirped on. The single bird must now have alit on a branch somewhere close by and was singing its heart out. A piece of grass or the stem of a flower was tickling her ear. She could smell the vegetation, all mixed up with the fragrance of his cologne.

He had straightened her legs so that they lay flat and comfortably on either side of his. She could feel the leather of his boots again against her stockinged legs. She could easily, easily drop off to sleep.

He kissed the side of her face.

"I love you," he said.

For a few moments she let the words wash about her like a caress. She smiled.

"There is no need," she said then. "They are just words."

"Three of them," he said, "which I have never strung together before now. Shall we see if I can do it again? I love you."

She crossed her arms over his chest and lifted her head to look down into his face.

"There is no need," she said again. "They *are* just words, Jasper. You have said you will not leave me. We have resumed our marriage. Perhaps soon we will have a child and start our own family in earnest. And we will remain here for much of each year and make it home. We will work at our marriage to make it one that will bring us both contentment—and some pleasure too. It will be enough. It *will* be enough. You must not feel that you need to say—"

"I love you?" he said, interrupting her.

"Yes," she said, "that. It is not necessary."

"You cannot say the words to me, then?" he asked.

"Just to have you say that you had only pretended to agree to end our wager?" she said. "Just to hear you claim the victory? No, indeed. You will never hear those words on *my* lips, Jasper."

She smiled dazzlingly at him, and he pulled his lips down into a mock pout.

She laughed.

"Katherine," he said, suddenly serious again, "I am sorry about Vauxhall. An apology does not even begin to be adequate, but—"

She set two fingers across his lips.

"You are forgiven," she said. "And there is an end of it."

He kissed her fingers.

And then panic assaulted her as if from nowhere. *How long* had they been up here? How long ago was it since they had left the others down at the waterfall?

"Jasper," she said, rolling away from him and trying to lift her bodice and push down her skirt at the same time, "what are we *thinking* of? Everyone must be back at the house and waiting for their tea and no host and hostess in sight."

"Charlotte will be delighted to play hostess in our absence," he said, "and everyone will be fed. And if they believe our absence is due to a pair of lovers' unawareness of the passing of time, not only will they be quite right, they will also be charmed. Think of the stories they will be able to take back home with them to feed to the avid gossipmongers."

"My hair!" she cried. "I have no brush or mirror with me. However am I to put it up into any respectable style? I will have to cover it all up with my bonnet."

"No such thing," he said, getting up and adjusting his clothing before crossing to the stone, putting on his hat at a slightly rakish tilt, and picking up his coat and her bonnet. He wrapped the ribbons of the bonnet around one wrist and then hooked his coat over one finger of the same hand and slung it over his shoulder. He offered her his free hand. "Your hair is beautiful as it is. You may dart up to your room as soon as we get home and have your maid do it up properly."

She shrugged and took his hand. She was feeling too happy to argue, though she hoped no one would see her before she had had a chance to tidy herself in the privacy of her own room. She was feeling wonderfully lethargic after their lovemaking. She was feeling all tender inside, where he had been.

They walked home hand in hand, both of them looking sadly creased and rumpled, she saw when they came out of the trees and were walking past the beach. They had both better hope very fervently that no one saw them. In fact, they had better make for a side door rather than the main ones.

But as they climbed the slope of the lawn and drew level with the stables, Katherine could see that a carriage was approaching up the driveway—a traveling carriage, which surely did not belong to any of their neighbors.

She clasped Jasper's hand more tightly. It was more imperative than ever that they sneak off to a side door.

But there were two other people on the upper terrace—Jasper's Uncle Stanley and Mr. Dubois. And both gentlemen had seen them. Uncle Stanley had raised a hand to greet them. And the carriage was turning onto the terrace close by them. The occupants had doubtless seen them too.

It was too late to hide.

"Oh, dear," she said in dismay, "whoever can this be? Are you expecting anyone?"

But the carriage door was already open and the coachman was reaching up a hand to help someone alight.

Mr. Dubois was looking upward with amiable politeness.

Uncle Stanley was frowning.

And out stepped Lady Forester.

Closely followed by Sir Clarence Forester.

"What in thunder?" Jasper said.

Katherine might have turned and fled ignominiously if he had not gripped her hand more tightly and stridden forward with her. But he stopped in his tracks when the coachman turned to help yet a third passenger out.

An elderly gentleman whom Katherine did not know.

"God damn it all to hell!" Jasper exclaimed. "What now?"

23

L A D Y Forester and Clarence.

The bald-faced gall of it!

But before Jasper could express any of the outrage he felt . . .

Seth Wrayburn too!

"Be civil, Jasper," Katherine murmured to him. "Do, please, be civil."

After what the two of them had done to *her*? But God bless us, Seth Wrayburn! The man never stepped beyond the threshold of his own London house. Yet here he was in Dorsetshire, in company with Lady Forester and Clarence, of all people.

Jasper took himself in hand. What would more disconcert the latter two more than civility, after all?

"Ma'am? Sir? Clarrie?" he said in cheerful tones. "This is an unexpected pleasure."

It would probably have been obvious to an imbecile, of course, that it was anything but. He had been unable quite to unclench his teeth as he spoke.

"Pleasure you may call it, Montford," Wrayburn said, making no attempt to smile or to look anything other than thoroughly irritated. "I call it a decided *dis*pleasure, being dragged half across England over roads that are a disgrace and past tollbooths that seem to have sprouted up every half mile or so and being *talked* to every mortal inch of the way. I am not in any way pleased, I would have you know."

He frowned ferociously.

"We have come, Jasper," Lady Forester said, "to take dear Charlotte away to a home where she will be properly cared for and carefully guarded until her come-out next year. We have come—"

"If I have to listen to one more of your rehearsed monologues, Prunella," her uncle declared, cutting her off in the middle of a sentence, "I swear I will hire a post chaise without further ado and take myself off back to the sanity of my own home in London, and the whole pack of you will find the doors barred against you for the rest of my natural life. We have *come*, Montford, to settle this matter of Charlotte once and for all. Prunella and Clarence claim this is an unfit home, and they are like flies in autumn, the two of them, buzzing about one's head and trying to fly into one's mouth and up one's nostrils no matter how many times one tries to bat them away. I have come to see for myself. I shall see and I shall decide and then I shall go home and hope never to set eyes upon a single one of you ever again."

"Sir." Jasper found that his good humor was being restored. "May I have the honor of presenting Lady Montford to you? Charlotte's great-uncle, Katherine, Mr. Seth Wrayburn."

Katherine curtsied and Wrayburn looked at her fiercely. She was looking more than usually beautiful in her creased green dress and with her hair down and one long piece of grass clinging to a lock of it behind one ear. She also looked like someone who had been recently tumbled in the hay.

"And have you met Stanley Finley, my father's brother?" Jasper asked. "And Mr. Dubois?"

"An unfit home?" Uncle Stanley said, ignoring the introduction. He was looking thunderous. "An *unfit home* when my brother's own son is heading it with his new wife, who is the sister of the Earl of Merton? Unfit in what way, I would like to know?"

He had turned his frown upon Lady Forester and Clarence.

"Where is Charlotte," Lady Forester asked pointedly, "while her half brother and his new wife have been off ... *romping* together?" Her eyes raked over them with haughty contempt. "And where are all the houseguests, including all the *gentlemen*?"

Katherine spoke for the first time since she had murmured to him to be civil.

"They are at tea in the drawing room, I do believe, ma'am," she said. "All the very young people will be there with Charlotte as hostess for the occasion and Miss Daniels as her chaperone. Mrs. Dubois and Lady Hornsby will be there too—they have come with their daughters to stay with us. You must all be weary after your journey. Allow us to take you up there for some tea while rooms are being prepared for you. And welcome to Cedarhurst."

"I am surprised, Lady Montford, that you are prepared to appear in the drawing room before guests looking as you do," Lady Forester said.

"She does indeed look almost *too* charming, ma'am," Dubois said. "I quite agree with you. But indeed, my wife and I are charmed by the beauty of *all* the young ladies here and delighted with the good manners and breeding of all the young gentlemen. It was a splendid idea to gather them all together here in the country for a bit of summer fun. Life can be lonely and dreary for the very young."

"What makes this an unfit home," Clarence said, as usual speaking when he really ought to know that the best policy was to maintain a silence, "is that everyone knows Jasper's marriage is a sham, that he married only because society demanded it of him. And that he married a social upstart who is no better than she ought to be."

That did it!

Jasper released Katherine's arm and strolled forward until the toes of his boots almost touched those of Clarence, who could not step back because the carriage was still directly behind him.

"Clarrie," Jasper said in the soft, pleasant voice he reserved for those with whom he was not pleased at all, "you are a nasty little beast and I have a few scores to settle with you when the time is ripe. That time, for the sake of civility, is probably not yet, alas. But if the time is *not* to be now, you will apologize to my wife with abject humility so that we may proceed into the house and make you and your mama comfortable as we do with all our guests."

"You will make the apology, Forester," Uncle Stanley said, "if you do not want me to knock every tooth in your head down your throat."

"And make it quick, Clarence," Wrayburn said, sounding more irritated than ever. "I want my tea even if it *does* have to be taken in a roomful of people, most of them very young. *And* silly, I do not doubt."

Clarence looked at Katherine before allowing his eyes to slide off to one side of her.

"I am sorry, ma'am," he muttered.

Jasper moved his face half an inch closer.

"With *abject humility,* Clarrie," he said in the same quiet, pleasant voice. He was slowly swinging Katherine's bonnet by its ribbons.

"I beg you will forgive me, ma'am," Clarence said, his eyes darting at her and then away again. "What I said was uncalled for."

"How lovely it is," Katherine said before Jasper could object further, "that Charlotte is to have her family about her for her birthday the day after tomorrow. Do come inside, all of you. You look very weary, Mr. Wrayburn. May I take your arm?"

He still looked irritated, but he allowed her to do so and they proceeded up the steps. Jasper offered his arm to Lady Forester, raising one eyebrow as he did so.

So here he was welcoming Clarrie and his mother beneath his own roof. Because Katherine had asked him to be civil. And because they had had the forethought to bring Wrayburn with them.

Perhaps the moon was made of cheese after all.

Clarence had a new, quite unbecoming bend in his nose. If he did not want another, he had better learn to keep his tongue clamped between his teeth, by Jove.

Jasper hoped fervently that he would not do so.

Provoke me, Clarrie, he thought. *Please?*

But there had already been provocation enough. There was no need for more.

All there *was* need of was the right time and place.

The conversation in the drawing room had obviously been lively enough to prevent anyone from noticing the arrival of a new traveling carriage beneath the window. It was still merry with the sort of chatter and laughter only the very young were capable of producing.

Charlotte at first looked thunderstruck when she saw her aunt and cousin appear in the doorway. Then she got to her feet and hurried across the room.

"Lady Forester and Clarrie have come to join in your birthday festivities, Char," Jasper said.

Katherine noticed that Stephen had also got to his feet, his hands balling into fists at his sides, his eyes fixed upon Sir Clarence.

"Aunt Prunella?" Charlotte smiled at her and curtsied. "Clarence?" She nodded to him with an only slightly fading smile. "How lovely!"

"Charlotte?" Lady Forester looked about the room as if she were gauging the ages of all the gentlemen present. They paused for a moment upon Stephen. "We have come to rescue you."

Katherine caught Stephen's eye and shook her head slightly. But Meg already had one hand on his arm, and his hands had relaxed at his sides.

"And here is your great-uncle too, Charlotte," Katherine said.

"Great-Uncle *Seth*?" Charlotte's eyes widened, and then she smiled radiantly. "You have come to see *me*? You have come for my *birthday*?"

He looked sourly at her.

"So you are Charlotte, are you?" he said. "And a parcel of trouble you have been to me, girl, though I daresay you are not to blame for that. You are a pretty enough little thing."

She blushed.

"Oh, *thank* you, Great-Uncle," she said. "You must be tired. May I pour you a cup of tea?"

What she ought to have done was offer to introduce him to everyone else in the drawing room. But it appeared that she had done the right thing.

"One small splash of milk and two spoonfuls of sugar, slightly heaped," he said.

"Let me have the pleasure," Katherine said while Charlotte went darting off to the tea tray, "of introducing everyone to you, sir. And to you, ma'am, and to you, Sir Clarence, if there is anyone here you do not know."

She proceeded to do so even though outrage over the arrival of two of them warred for the main part of her attention with a terrible awareness of how she looked—and of how Jasper looked without his coat and with her bonnet *still* dangling from one of his hands. She did not believe she had ever felt more uncomfortable in her life. She also had a ghastly urge to burst into laughter. She dared not look anywhere near Jasper's face.

Civility, though, had been preserved. How they had managed it, she and Jasper, she did not know. But she felt somehow as if they had just passed one of the first great tests of their marriage and their position as lord and lady of Cedarhurst.

She could not pretend to be delighted by the unexpected, and uninvited, arrival of three new guests. She could not pretend that she had not been deeply insulted by the words Sir Clarence Forester had uttered out on the terrace. And she could not pretend either that for one shameful moment when Jasper had left her side to stride over to him, she had not hoped he would knock him senseless and evict him from his land without further ado.

But civility had called for better, and they had both risen to the occasion. She was proud of them both.

Katherine forced herself to relax as afternoon turned to evening—especially after she had finally been able to escape to her room to change her dress and repair her appearance. There was really nothing to which Lady Forester and her son could take exception. Almost all the female guests were girls more than young ladies. Almost all the male guests were well below the age of majority and were boys more than men. Even Sir Nathan Fletcher, who was a friend of Stephen's from university, was only twenty-one. Stephen himself was not quite that.

And the young people were very well chaperoned indeed. The Countess of Hornsby, Mr. and Mrs. Dubois, Uncle Stanley, Miss Daniels, not to mention Jasper and Katherine herself—all of them kept an eye upon their own charges and everyone else's. No, Lady Forester would have nothing about which to object.

She found something anyway.

It happened in the drawing room after dinner, just before the gentlemen joined the ladies. Someone in the group of young ladies that had gathered about the pianoforte mentioned the fete and the ball. The older ladies were gathered about the fireplace, conversing about something else.

"Mr. Shaw and Mr. Thane," Hortense Dubois said, "are going to join in the tug-of-war at the fete. I do not know if any of the other gentlemen will find the courage to join them. I can scarcely wait to see it."

"I would join in myself," Jane Hutchins said, "if I could be sure of being on the winning side."

There was a gust of girlish laughter.

"Girls—*ladies*—are not allowed," Lady Marianne said, pulling a face. "We might get *muddy*. Men have all the fun."

"But just imagine, Marianne," Araminta Clement said, "losing the pull and being dragged into a mud bath. *In* one's best dress."

"But everyone who is to be in the tug-of-war and in the mud wrestling," Louisa Fletcher said, "is to bring old clothes to wear. And then, if they get muddy—or *when* they get muddy if they are wrestling—they are to swim in the lake to clean themselves and change into their good clothes."

"*Not* on the bank in full sight of everyone, I hope," Beatrice Finley said, fanning her face vigorously with a sheet of music.

"Oh, my!" Alice Dubois exclaimed, a hand over her heart. "Perhaps I can persuade Michael to join the tug-of-war."

There was another flurry of girlish giggles.

"*Fete?*" Lady Forester said sharply from the other group of ladies. She looked at Katherine. "Fete? *What* fete?"

Katherine smiled.

"Jasper and I have decided to revive an old tradition of holding an annual summer fete and ball at Cedarhurst," she explained. "There has not been much time to organize it this year, but everyone for miles around has pitched in to help so we are able to combine it with the celebration of Charlotte's birthday the day after tomorrow."

Lady Forester's bosom had swelled.

"Ball?" she said. "*In the ballroom?* For girls who are not even *out* yet?"

"It will be the only room large enough," Katherine said. "All our neighbors will be attending as well as the houseguests. And all ages, too."

"There cannot be *that* many people of genteel birth living close enough," Lady Forester said.

"Everyone has been invited," Katherine said.

"*Everyone?*" Lady Forester's bosom swelled even further. But she was prevented from making any other comment by the arrival of the gentlemen from the dining room.

It was a few minutes before everyone had settled with their tea and Alice Dubois had taken her seat at the pianoforte with her betrothed standing behind her to turn the pages of her music. But as soon as everyone had settled and before the music could begin or any sustained conversation, Lady Forester spoke up again for all to hear.

"Uncle Seth," she said, "did you realize that instead of a discreet birthday party here the day after tomorrow for dear Charlotte's birthday, there is to be a *fete* and a *ball*?"

"I did not, Prunella," he said with a scowl. "But thank you for the warning. I shall be sure to spend the day in my room—with the window closed."

"Everyone is invited," she said. "*Everyone.* That includes tenants and laborers and shopkeepers and other such, I presume. And Charlotte is to be allowed to dance *in the ballroom* during the evening. Surrounded by riffraff. And there is to be *mud* wrestling and a *tug-of-war* over mud. Is *this* a fitting home for your great-niece and my niece and my dear dead brother's daughter?"

"Clarrie," Jasper said pleasantly, "there is room for another man or two on the tug-of-war teams, I believe. I daresay we can find you a place at the back of one of the lines—or at the front if you prefer."

"Uncle Seth," Lady Forester said, "my brother *banned* the annual fete when he married Charlotte's dear mother. He banned it because it was vulgar. But more than that, it was *sinful*. He took a moral stand and refused to have Rachel and Jasper and Charlotte exposed to something so wicked."

"I believe, ma'am," Jasper said, "you would wish our guests to understand that your esteemed brother had the state of Rachel's immortal soul in mind and mine when he announced the ban, but not Charlotte's. It would have been nothing short of scandalous if she had been in existence at the time, just after his marriage to my mother."

Mr. Dubois laughed aloud, and Mrs. Dubois silenced him with a pointed look. The young ladies all blushed and the young men looked interested.

"For the love of all that is wonderful, ma'am," Uncle Stanley said, sounding thoroughly exasperated, "what Wrayburn *did* do with his pious ways was kill all the joy that had ever existed at Cedarhurst *and* besmirch my brother's name. All in the name of a god of wrath I would not worship even if he heated up hell ten times over for my benefit."

"Our papa," Arnold Fletcher said from the far side of the pianoforte, his voice shaking slightly, "has told us so many grand tales of the Cedarhurst fetes that I can almost imagine that I had been at one. I cannot wait for the day after tomorrow."

"Katherine and Jasper have worked *very* hard," Margaret said quietly, "so that everyone in the neighborhood from the youngest child to the oldest grandparent can have a day of pure enjoyment."

There was a general murmur of agreement.

"It is too bad, Prunella," Mr. Wrayburn said, "when a man may not enjoy his after-dinner tea without being *talked* to and *appealed* to when he has said that he will make his decision in his own good time and with his own perfectly capable powers of observation. I'll be damned before I leave home again."

"Perhaps, Miss Dubois," Katherine said, "you will play for us now? You always do it so well. And, Jasper, I believe Lady Hornsby and Miss Daniels would like to play cards if there are two gentlemen wishful of joining them. Sir Clarence, perhaps? And Mr. Gladstone? Is anyone ready for more tea?"

Lady Forester pressed her lips together and said no more. Margaret sat beside her and engaged her in conversation. Mrs. Dubois joined them.

Katherine was standing by the window in her bedchamber later that night, brushing out her hair, when Jasper opened the door from the private sitting room without knocking. He had seen beneath the door that a candle was still burning.

She was wearing the nightgown she had worn on their wedding night.

Come to me tonight, she had said out on the hill.

Well, here he was.

He propped one shoulder against the door frame, his arms crossed over his chest, his bare feet crossed at the ankles.

This afternoon had been just an appetizer. He wondered if she realized that.

She smiled at him, and the brush stilled in her hair.

"Is this what women who are no better than they ought to be do to entice their lovers?" he asked.

"You ought to know the answer to that better than I," she said.

"Minx!" He pursed his lips and pushed himself away from the door frame to advance farther into the room. "Did that charge hurt you? And the accusation of being a social upstart?"

"I can be hurt," she said, "only by people I respect."

Which was probably as big a lie as she had ever told. It had made him see red.

"And you do not respect poor Clarrie." He took the brush from her hand, turned her to face the window again, and drew it down the back of her head and all the way to the ends of her hair at her waist. "I did not avenge you very thoroughly, did I?"

"I found myself wishing," she said, "that you would punch him in the nose, as Stephen once did, and hoping that you would not. It is precisely what Lady Forester and her like would expect you to do. I am glad you rose to the occasion and played the well-mannered host instead—though you *did* call him a nasty little beast. Which he is."

She laughed softly, and he drew the brush through her hair again.

"I *will* avenge the insult," he promised her.

"The baser part of my nature is glad to hear it," she said. "But there must be no violence here, Jasper. It would be unseemly. And it might be the very thing that will cause Mr. Wrayburn to decide that this is indeed an unfit home for Charlotte."

He set the brush down on the windowsill, moved the heavy column of her hair to one side, and set his lips against the back of her neck. She was warm and smelled of soap.

"Mmm," she said, lifting her shoulders.

"There will be no violence," he said. "*Not,* at least, anything anyone would classify as wanton viciousness. I have just the plan."

"Oh, what?" She turned to face him, all eager curiosity, the bloodthirsty wench, and, when he did not step back, she set her hands on his shoulders.

"You will know when the time comes," he said. "It will be quite unmistakable."

And reasonably satisfying since he could not in all conscience use his fists while Clarence was a guest in his home. *Quite* satisfying, in fact.

"But you are not going to tell me now," she said.

"I am not." He kissed the tip of her nose. "But *must* we talk about Clarrie Forester? I seem to recall that I had other plans when I came here."

"Did you?" she said. "What?"

He smiled at her and kissed her mouth softly as he grasped the sides of her nightgown and lifted it up off her body. Not to be outdone, she pulled free the sash that bound the waist of his silk dressing gown and it fell open. He was wearing nothing beneath it.

"This, I believe," he said, tossing her nightgown aside and shrugging out of his dressing gown.

"Ah," she said and set her hands on his shoulders again.

Whatever had once made him believe that he liked heavily voluptuous women best when there were slenderly curvaceous, long-legged women like Katherine in existence? With gold-flecked hair that smelled of soap?

He drew her against him and ran his hands down her back from her shoulder blades to her buttocks. He opened his mouth over hers and she kissed him back.

I love you, he had told her this afternoon, and she had told him there was no need to say the words. She did not believe that he meant them.

And did he?

Would he be in any doubt if he *did*? But did it matter anyway? He was committed to her happiness for the rest of his life. He might as well call it love. What else *could* he call it?

"Jasper," she said when he was kissing his way along her throat, "take me to bed."

He raised his head and smiled down at her.

"Ah," he said. "I had almost forgotten again. *That* is why I came to your room."

And he scooped her up in his arms and strode toward her bed.

He followed her down onto it after dropping her there.

"I love you," he said just before engaging her mouth with his own again.

"Oh, silly," she said.

Well. Monty the great lover—*silly!*

"There has to be punishment for that insult," he said.

"Show me." She pulled his head down to her own. She was laughing.

24

T H E great fear for the past month had been that the day of the fete would turn out to be a wet one. Many of the activities could be moved indoors, of course, and careful plans had been made for that eventuality. But it would not be the same. The day as Katherine had envisioned it would be effectively ruined.

What a relief it was, then, to awake early, to jump out of bed and hurry to the window and throw back the curtains to discover that the early morning sun was beaming down from a cloudless sky—and to know that other people in other rooms and throughout the surrounding countryside and in the village would be doing the same thing and feeling a similar happy relief and surge of excitement and joy to know that this was the day.

Katherine looked back over her shoulder to find Jasper squinting at her, his hands laced behind his head on the pillow. The sun was shining directly into his eyes.

"Oh, I *am* sorry," she said, pulling one of the curtains halfway across the window to put his face in shadow.

"No need," he said. "I *like* being awoken at the crack of dawn after a night of disturbed sleep."

She looked at the clock on the mantel. It was not quite six o'clock.

"Oh, I *am* sorry," she said again.

"About the disturbed night?" he said. "It was in a worthy cause. Or about waking me early? It means that there is a little more night left to be disturbed before it is time to get up. Or were you apologizing for standing there in the sunlight? And so you should apologize. Have you no modesty?"

She had been so anxious about the weather that she had forgotten to pull her nightgown on over her head as she got up.

"Oh," she said.

"If you are embarrassed," he said, holding back the bedcovers on her side of the bed, "you had better jump under here to hide yourself."

Which she did.

It was almost seven o'clock before they both got up. She had even dozed for ten minutes or so of that hour.

There was to be no dozing for the rest of the day. By the time they had got dressed and had a quick breakfast and stepped outside, there were already servants out there, carrying tables and blankets, and already a few committee members were arriving to set up tables and booths and exhibits and to mark out a racecourse and an archery range and a picnic area and everything else that would be needed during the day. Katherine stayed in the area of the house. Jasper strode off with a few of the men to inspect the mud pond that had been created at the marshy end of the lake. It was rather horrifying to think that there was to be mud wrestling and a tug-of-war there today. But it had made the fete irresistibly appealing to the men.

Men were funny that way.

By the middle of the morning most of the young guests were outside too, exclaiming with delight over all that had suddenly appeared around them, and choosing the activities in which they planned to participate. Several of them offered to help.

Charlotte was more excited than anyone else. This was her eighteenth birthday, and after today no one could deny that she was old enough to be considered a young lady. And *what* a birthday it was. She came and linked her arm through Katherine's while the latter was admiring the needlework table that Mrs. Bonner and one of her daughters was arranging with an eye for artistry and color.

"Kate," Charlotte said, squeezing her arm tightly. "I love you. I really, really do. And I know I have you to thank for all this—for the houseguests, for the fete, for the ball tonight. There has surely never been a birthday party to match this one."

"You are happy, then?" Katherine asked unnecessarily.

"I am happy," the girl said with a sigh. "I am even happy that Aunt Prunella and Clarence have come and Great-Uncle Seth, though he swore last evening that he would not come out of his room today. They are my *family,* and family is important, is it not?"

"It is," Katherine said, patting her hand.

"And Aunt Prunella cannot take me away from here," Charlotte said. "How could she when *you* have come here to be such a steadying influence on Jasper? You *are* happy, are you not?"

"I am," Katherine said. "*We* are."

And it was not even an untruth. Not for now, anyway. What would happen when the honeymoon was over, she did not know. That was undoubtedly what they were living through, she and Jasper. It could not last, this amity between them, this . . . Well, this *honeymoon*. But for now she was happy, and she believed he was too.

Charlotte was laughing.

"Jasper used to call her Aunt Prune," she said. "Was he not dreadful?"

"Indeed," Katherine said.

And then Charlotte went dancing off to link her arm through Stephen's, and they both went off to join some of the other young people.

Meg was helping Mrs. Penny arrange the baking items on a long table on the lower terrace.

There was no time for luncheon. There were too many last-minute details to attend to. But Katherine did not even realize she had missed the meal. Any minute now the outside guests would begin to arrive and there was only time to rush upstairs to change into her lemon yellow muslin with the blue sash and to have her hair properly styled beneath her wedding hat.

Jasper was standing propped by one shoulder in the doorway of her dressing room when she was ready to leave again, looking handsome and immaculate in blue and cream. He raised one eyebrow.

"It is to be my sun goddess today, is it?" he said.

She smiled and he offered his arm and led her down the stairs and out to the upper terrace, where Charlotte was already waiting. The three of them would greet all the visitors as they arrived.

"Happy, Char?" Jasper asked.

"Oh, I am," she said, turning a glowing face to him and wrapping her arms about his neck. "If I were any happier I would burst."

"Sounds messy," he said, patting her back. "Enjoy your

birthday anyway. This is all for you, Char. Katherine's idea. Blame her if you burst."

And if he thought he knew nothing about love, Katherine thought, watching him with his half sister, then the foolish man ought to see his face now.

And as good fortune would have it, Lady Forester was coming out onto the terrace with Clarence, and Mr. Wrayburn was coming out with Uncle Stanley and Lady Hornsby. They would all see the hug and the look on both faces.

Suddenly people on foot and people in gigs and two or three on horseback were approaching along on the driveway.

The outside guests were coming, and the fete was about to begin.

She was mistress of Cedarhurst, Katherine thought, and hostess of the revival of the annual fete and ball. Her husband was close to her, Charlotte between them.

Life felt very good.

The boats were out on the water—three of them—and there was a queue of people waiting to take them out. It had been decided not to have any boat races but merely to use them for recreation. There were children swimming and paddling at the beach end of the lake under the supervision of some parents and grandparents. There were people strolling about the lake, exploring the cottage folly and standing above the waterfall. The mud was ready for the wrestling and tug-of-war later on—much anticipated by the men and by a good number of the women too, Jasper suspected.

He left the lake behind him and strode up the lawn

toward the house. The archery competition had begun. There was a cluster of people on the lower terrace, looking at the baking and needlework and the wood carvings. There were people sitting in the parterre gardens or strolling about the gravel walks. There were people at the food tables on the low balcony outside the ballroom.

He was going to have to taste and judge the fruit tarts later on. But for now he strode across the upper terrace to the east lawn, where the races were to be run. In future years they would have to be located elsewhere, as the rose arbor and the apple orchard would fill this space.

A large crowd of very young children were playing a circle game, their hands joined. Katherine and Jane Hutchins were leading them. There was a burst of shrieking merriment as they all fell to the grass.

Jasper stood still, watching Katherine get back to her feet and brush the grass off her skirt. Her face was flushed and filled with laughter. She looked quite breathtakingly beautiful.

And then her eyes met his across the distance and her hands stilled against her skirt and her smile was arrested.

And he realized something like a hammer blow.

She had become as essential to him as the air he breathed.

Whatever the devil *that* meant.

He did not pause to consider the puzzle. He strode toward her, his hands at his back. He was equally unaware of the children who darted across his path and the adults who stepped out of it—and then paused to watch his progress.

He stood in front of his wife and noted how the sun brightened her face and glinted gold in her hair. Her wonderful, fathomless eyes gazed back into his. Except that they were no longer fathomless. He could see into their depths.

"I love you," he said.

And for the first time the words were involuntary. And for the first time he could see from the welling of tears in her eyes that she believed him.

He leaned forward and kissed her lips.

And was instantly aware of three things simultaneously—that he loved her more than life, that she knew it and returned his love full measure, and that the cheers and laughter and applause that erupted around them had nothing whatsoever to do with any game that was in progress.

Good Lord! Devil take it! Could he have chosen a more public setting for such an epiphany if he had tried?

He lifted his head and grinned at Katherine before turning and acknowledging the applause with a regal wave of his hand and a theatrical bow.

There was another burst of laughter.

But Mrs. Ellis was waving her arms purposefully at him. She was ready to start the races, and it was his job to fire the gun to begin each one.

"To be continued," he murmured to Katherine before he strode away.

It was truly amazing how many children lived in the neighborhood. Not that it was all children gathered for the races. There were many young people here too, including most of the houseguests, and all were in noisy high spirits. Perhaps it was as well that Lady Forester was sitting in the parterre garden with Mr. and Mrs. Dubois.

Indeed, it was a *very* good thing in light of what had just happened. A man informing his wife that he loved her and actually *kissing* her in public, for the love of God. Lady Forester would have swooned quite away if she had witnessed it.

There were all the usual races—simple footraces, sack races, egg-and-spoon races, hop, skip, and jump races, leapfrog races to name a few—but everyone enjoyed them as much as they ever did if the shouting and shrieking and laughter were anything to judge by. There were distinct advantages, Jasper decided, to being the host and stuck with the starting gun. Merton fell so many times during the sack race that finally he rolled to the finish line, only to be disqualified when he arrived there for not being on his feet. Thane got egg down both boots during his race and made matters worse by trying to clean the mess off with his handkerchief. Araminta Clement caught a foot in her skirt as she leapfrogged over Smith-Vane and they were both covered with grass when they finally left off their laughing and struggled to their feet. She had lost the race long ago to an exuberant Charlotte.

But there was the three-legged race still to be run. And there was a certain bright-eyed sun goddess, who had finished playing with the infants and was standing watching the races and applauding the winners.

He caught her eye, crooked one finger to beckon her, and handed the gun to one of the strapping young laborers from the home farm.

"My race, I believe, ma'am," he said when Katherine came close.

"The three-legged race?" she said. "Oh, dear." And she laughed.

The children under twelve ran it first. Then it was time for the adults.

Katherine laughed again as he tied his left leg to her right. To one side of them were Charlotte and Merton. On the other side were Margaret and Fletcher. Then there were villagers and country people—the serious contenders.

"Right," Jasper said, wrapping one arm about Katherine's shoulders while she set one about his waist. "We will do this on a one-two count, one being our bound legs and two our outside legs. We will take it slowly to start and then speed up. Got it?"

"Got it," she said, and laughed.

"We will start on a one," he said.

"That sounds sensible." She laughed again and he grinned at her.

A larger crowd was gathering, he noticed. Perhaps word had spread that Lord Montford was in love and was about to run the three-legged race with the object of that love, his wife, whom he had so brazenly kissed an hour ago.

"Oh, dear," she said, noticing the same thing, "look at the crowd."

And she laughed again.

He remembered then that during the month preceding their marriage, after he had pressed his suit on her, he had believed he had killed all laughter in her, all possibility of joy.

Was he after all to earn forgiveness? Not from her—she had already forgiven him. But from himself?

"It is time, my baroness," he said sternly, "to put on a good show."

Lady Forester was there, he saw, and—good Lord!—Seth Wrayburn, looking his usual sour self. It was doubtful he would look kindly upon a man who kissed his wife in full view of a large crowd of his guests and neighbors—and then ran a three-legged race with her.

"Take your marks," the laborer called—he was Hatcher, was he not? "Get set."

The gun fired with a loud pop.

Charlotte and Merton tumbled to the grass with a shriek and a shout. Margaret and Fletcher seemed just to have realized that they would have to hold on to each other if they hoped to proceed.

"One," Jasper said, and by some miracle their bound legs moved forward in unison.

"Two." Their outside legs moved past the bound ones.

"One."

She was laughing.

Most of the field was on the ground within two strides. What was left of it was soon left behind as they forged ahead to the finish line in perfect unison with each other, cheered onward by the crowd.

And then it struck Jasper that the first prize in the race was to be three guineas, nothing at all to him, especially as the money was his to start with, but a truly enormous sum to Tom Lacey, one of his laborers, who was coming along several paces behind them with his wife while three of their five children screamed encouragement from the sidelines and the fourth watched with wide eyes and thumb firmly lodged in his mouth and the fifth lay fast asleep in the arms of the eldest.

"Two," Jasper said, and their outside legs moved.

"Two—ah, I mean *one*."

But Katherine had already hesitated, and he had performed a little stutter step, and they tumbled to the grass a mere three or four strides from the finish line.

"*One* comes after two," she cried.

"No, it does not. Whoever did you have as a childhood teacher?" he asked her, tutting. "Three comes after two."

And they lay there laughing helplessly, their arms wrapped about each other as Tom and his wife jogged across the finish line, closely followed by Margaret and Fletcher.

The crowd was applauding loudly and laughing hard too at the spectacle their baron and his wife had just made of themselves—again.

Somehow they got back to their feet and hobbled the rest of the way to come in fourth out of a field of ten. Not bad. Merton and Charlotte were still about six feet from the starting line and down on the grass again.

Lady Forester was purple in the face. And, silly woman, she was talking to Wrayburn, who had brows of thunder. Jasper did not hear what she said. Strangely, he *did* hear her uncle's reply.

"You would not recognize simple fun, Prunella," he said, "if it reared up and bit you on the arse."

The lady would have swooned without further ado, Jasper guessed, if she could have trusted that someone would catch her. But Clarence was nowhere in sight, and Uncle Stanley was looking openly delighted.

"We could have *won*," Katherine said when she had

recovered somewhat from her laughter. She looked at Tom lift his wife from the ground after releasing their legs and swing her once about with a whoop while their children dashed up to them. "But I am very glad we did not. That was deliberate, was it not?"

"Me?" he said. "Deliberately losing a race? Do you have windmills in your head?"

"No," she said. "And I am on to you, Jasper Finley. I am on to you."

Whatever the devil she meant by that.

He bent to untie the bond that held their legs. He touched the soft flesh behind her knee in the process.

"Sorry," he said.

"Liar."

"Three guineas, girl," Tom was saying. "*Three guineas.*"

And he had dared to complain, Jasper thought, about the lack of freedom that wealth and position and property could bring to a man.

"I have some baking to judge," he said.

"And I have some needlework to judge," she said. "Shall we go together?"

It took them a while to get to the lower terrace. People who had kept a respectful distance earlier in the afternoon were suddenly eager to joke with them and tell them what a wonderful time they were having and beg them to please *please* make the fete an annual event again.

It was already late in the afternoon. The races had all been run, the archery competition was over, the exhibitions had been judged, and the prizes awarded. Most people had eaten and drunk their fill, either standing on the terrace with friends and neighbors or sitting in the parterre garden or on one of the blankets spread on the lawn. All that was left apart from the ball tonight and the simple enjoyment of the park for those who chose to stay instead of going home to change were the mud sports.

And those were to be, Katherine had come to realize, the highlight of the day. Everyone was going to watch the eight men who had entered the mud-wrestling competition and the tug-of-war that was to follow and would involve a large number of the men. Several of the houseguests had already changed from their best clothes for fear they might be on the losing team and be dragged through the mud.

Men really *were* foolish. But what did that make of the women who were eager to watch them?

Including her.

"Stephen," she said, when he came up behind her on the upper terrace and set an arm about her shoulders, "you are not going into the tug-of-war, are you?"

He had changed.

"But of course," he said. "I have chosen the winning side, and so there is nothing to fear."

She punched him lightly in the chest.

"It will serve you right," she said, "if it turns out to be the losing side."

But he only grinned, and she suddenly realized that perhaps many of the men secretly hoped that they *were* on the losing team.

"Are you enjoying yourself?" she asked. There had been so little chance during the past two weeks for private conversation with him.

"Enormously," he said, tightening his arm about her.

"You have done superlatively well, Kate, with both the house party and this." He gestured about them with his free arm. "You are happy?"

"Yes," she said.

He turned his head to look down into her face, his eyes searching hers.

"Dash it all." He grinned. "I was looking forward to breaking his nose."

She set the side of her head briefly against his shoulder.

"And what of you?" she asked. "You have hardly moved from Charlotte's side."

He did not immediately reply, and she looked up at him.

"There are problems with being Merton, Kate," he said. "Especially now that I have almost reached my majority. I am *eligible,* am I not? I see fellows like me all the time deliberately avoiding the ladies for fear of a leg shackle. But the thing is that I *like* ladies. I like Miss Wrayburn."

"But you are not in love with her," she said.

"Kate," he said, "I am twenty. She is seventeen— eighteen today."

"But you think she does love *you*?" she asked him.

"I don't know," he said. "I don't *think* so. She is a jolly girl, and I think she just likes me as I like her. But it has struck me that I have to be careful now just in case some lady should mistake friendliness for courtship. I would hate to break anyone's heart, Kate. I would hate to break Miss Wrayburn's, though I do not *think* she has a tendre for me. It is conceited of me, I suppose, even to imagine that there is a possibility that she might. But I *am* Merton."

"Oh, Stephen," she said, "you are such a very *decent* young man. I am proud of you. But you are not responsible for anyone's heart unless you have specifically laid claim to it. You must not hide from ladies and treat them coldly as so many gentlemen do. You must be yourself. Everyone will love you—and that will have *nothing* to do with the fact that you are the Earl of Merton. But everyone will come to understand that your heart is something precious, to be given to the lady who can win it—when you are considerably older than you are now."

"Ah, Kate." He chuckled. "It is wonderful to be a saint in my sisters' eyes. I do hope I will not be hurting Miss Wrayburn in any way, though, when I leave here. This house party has meant so much to her. And I really am very fond of her."

"And she of you," she said. "I doubt there is more than that, Stephen. She is looking forward to her come-out next year. I will make discreet inquiries, though, and set your mind at ease if possible."

He sighed. "Why do we always think we will be free and perfectly happy once we grow beyond the restrictions of childhood?" he asked her.

She stretched up and kissed his cheek.

"Oh, I say," he said, "we had better get down to the lake before we miss one of the wrestling bouts. Have you *seen* the mud hole, Kate? It makes a fellow envious of those wrestlers."

Katherine shook her head and made no comment.

25

"H o w are you enjoying the fete, Clarence?" Jasper asked, clapping a hand on his shoulder.

Clarence turned his head and looked suspiciously at him. It was probably the first time he had heard his full name on Jasper's lips. They fell into step together on their way down to the lake—almost everyone's destination since word had spread that the mud wrestling was about to begin.

"I see you did some shopping while you were in London," Jasper said. "Those are very smart clothes indeed, and I know many discerning gentlemen who would give a right arm for those boots."

They were white-topped and sported gold tassels. The rest of his clothes bordered on the dandyish too. His starched shirt points were high and in grave danger of piercing his eyeballs if he were to turn his head too sharply. His neckcloth was tied in an elaborate, artistic knot more suitable for an evening ball than for an afternoon fete.

"I visited my tailor and my bootmaker, yes," Clarence admitted. "One feels obliged to keep up with the latest fashions when one intends to mingle with one's peers."

"The ladies have had eyes for almost no one else all afternoon," Jasper said.

"I think you exaggerate," Clarence said, "though I

have drawn my fair share of attention, it is true. Some ladies appreciate a gentleman who knows how to dress well and how to behave with dignity and decorum and allow his inferiors to participate in the games."

"You are not going to join the tug-of-war, then?" Jasper asked.

"By no means," Clarence said.

Jasper squeezed his shoulder.

"I cannot tell you," he said, "how much it means to Charlotte that you and Aunt Prunella have given your time and suffered all the discomforts of the road in order to be with her as she celebrates her eighteenth birthday. We have had our differences over the years, Clarence, but I must express my gratitude to you for this. You are a good sort."

"Yes, well, Jasper," Clarence said, "we never would have had differences if you had always behaved as you ought. But it is my duty as one of Charlotte's guardians to be here today, and it is Mama's pleasure. Perhaps you have not always understood how very fond we are of my cousin."

Jasper kept a hand on his shoulder as they joined the crowd that had gathered about the mud pond, a safe distance away so that no one would get splashed. The eight wrestlers, all of them laborers from the farms, were stripped to the waist and barefoot—evidence of the depravity of the fete that Jasper could almost see Lady Forester storing away in her mind to be used later with her uncle, who was also present with Uncle Stanley and Dubois.

Arbitrary rules had been set for the wrestling. In each bout, the contestant who could send his opponent sprawling full length into the mud three separate times was the winner. Mud being what it was, it was not easy for any man to keep his footing in it for very long. The first round of bouts was over within ten minutes, but they were minutes of intense excitement for the crowd of spectators, who roared and squealed and groaned and cheered every time one of the men went sprawling and splashing in the mud. All eight were covered with it from head to toe before the round was over—and all eight went dashing off to swim in the lake before the semifinal round began among the four winners.

"Ah, this brings back happy memories of childhood summers, does it not, Clarence?" Jasper said rather loudly. "We had good times, though they were often happier for you than for me."

Clarence looked at him suspiciously.

It was not difficult to draw the attention of people who were merely waiting for the fun of the mud wrestling to resume. A number of people half turned to listen.

"Sir Clarence Forester," Jasper explained to them, "was younger than I, but he was always somehow more nimble and sure of foot. If ever we climbed a tree, it was always I who fell out and tore my clothes. And if ever we climbed to the balustrade on the roof of the house— it was considered unsafe for boys and so was forbidden, of course—it was always I who was not fast enough to get down before being caught."

He laughed.

So did a good number of the people close to them.

So did Clarence.

"But it was always your idea to climb, Jasper," he said. "It was only right that you were the one to be punished."

"And so it was," Jasper said, and laughed again.

Jasper had fallen out of the tree because he had dared Clarence to follow him up, and Clarence, standing on the ground, had pulled at his heel—before running home to tell on him. Jasper had been caught up on the balustrade because Clarence had run away and bolted the door leading down before running to tell on him.

Once a weasel, always a weasel.

The wrestlers were back for the next round. They had all learned something from the first round. This one lasted much longer as the slimy brown figures of the wrestlers pulled and pushed and clawed at one another and struggled to maintain their own balance. The crowd shrieked and moaned and cheered and jeered through it all. But inevitably there were just two men left standing in the end.

There was another break in the action while the four men loped off to dive into the lake again.

"Some of these men," Jasper said loudly enough for a large number of people to hear, "have about as much sense of balance as I have—which is not a great deal at all. Do you remember the time, Clarence, when we wrestled in the boat and I ended up in the water while you were left standing solidly on your feet? I learned my lesson that time. I do not believe I ever wrestled with you again."

He laughed.

So did a crowd of his guests.

"Yes, well, Jasper," Clarence said, puffing out his chest and speaking loudly enough for their audience to hear, "my father saw to it that I had the proper instruction in all the manly sports at a young age. You always thought to get your way with brute force, but brute force is never a match for practiced skill."

"Alas, that is true," Jasper said.

He had been about to take the boat out without first going back to the house to change out of his good clothes and to get permission, which would doubtless have been denied. He had been standing in the boat, about to sit down, his back to the bank. Clarence, standing solidly on the bank, had taken an oar and tipped him in.

"What other sports did you learn, Sir Clarence?" Hortense Dubois asked. "You must be very good indeed if you can defeat Lord Montford. He has a reputation for winning everything he tries—or so Mr. Gladstone was telling us just yesterday, was he not, Marianne?"

"Well," Clarence said, "I am handy enough with my fives, Miss Dubois. I have gone a few rounds with Gentleman Jackson himself."

"With *Gentleman Jackson,*" a young man from the village said. "I have heard of him. He is said to be one of the best."

"Not *one* of the best, young man," Clarence said. "The *very* best."

"Clarence is too modest, Miss Dubois," Jasper said, "to tell you how good he is at fencing. I take it you are still as good at it as you used to be, Clarence?"

"Well—" Clarence said.

Jasper clapped a hand on his shoulder again.

"Now don't be modest," he said. He grinned about him. A large crowd was listening now, including—at some distance—a wide-eyed Katherine. "Remember the afternoon when you routed me in every single bout?

And at the time you had only just *started* learning. I would say it was a good thing the rapiers were tipped or I would have looked like a fountain of blood. Sorry, ladies, that is not a pleasant image, is it?"

"Oh, do tell us about it, Lord Montford," Miss Fletcher begged. "I *love* to watch two gentlemen fencing. There is no more manly sight."

"I simply could not get past Clarence's guard," Jasper said. "Yet he could get past mine with ease every time. It was really quite lowering for me—but a grand display by Clarence. I daresay he was his fencing master's star pupil."

"Well," Clarence said, "he *did* say I was the best he had ever had, but he had been teaching for only five years or so at that time. Perhaps later he discovered someone who was better."

"I most certainly doubt it," Jasper said with a sigh.

"Devil take it," Merton said, exchanging a pointed look with Jasper, "if we had known Sir Clarence was coming, Monty, fencing could have been added as a sport for today. Is it too late?"

"I have no rapiers in the house," Jasper said. "You do not have any with you by any chance, Clarence, do you?"

"I do not," Clarence said, sounding rather as if he had almost swallowed his tongue. "Unfortunately," he added.

"*Very* fortunately for me," Jasper said with a laugh. "Of course, you were just as good with an oar."

"One can hardly fence with oars, Jasper," Clarence said, and looked about him, smiling at the laughter his words provoked.

"It would have to be something more creative than simple fencing," Jasper said. "Not a jousting match with oars while standing in the boats—that would put too severe a strain on my lamentably poor sense of balance. Although having to keep one's balance would add spice to such a jousting match, would it not? What is a little more solid than boats but not quite as solid as the ground?"

The head groom—the only person whom Jasper had taken into his confidence—spoke up on cue.

"There are these planks, my lord," he said, pointing to them. "The ones we set across the mud pit so that we could get right over it to add more water. They are eight inches wide."

"You are suggesting, Barker," Jasper said, aghast, "that Sir Clarence and I stand on one of those planks each—over the *mud*—jousting with *oars*? When I am wearing a *white shirt*?"

"It is a mad—" Clarence began, equally aghast.

"And against a *star fencer*?" Jasper added.

"I will wager, Monty," Merton said, looking very deliberately at him, "that you cannot win a bout but will be tipped ignominiously into the mud."

"Now wait a minute," Jasper said, holding up a hand. "This is foolish. I wish I had not said anything about Clarence's fencing skills. Much as I find any wager hard to resist, this one—"

"I will wager against you too, Jasper," Uncle Stanley said, looking at him with narrowed eyes.

And suddenly there was a chorus of voices, all urging this impromptu jousting bout between Lord Montford and Sir Clarence Forester. The two wrestlers who were returning from the lake ready for the final bout were almost forgotten.

Jasper held up a hand.

"Now wait a minute here," he said again. "For very pride's sake I will feel forced to take on the challenge and suffer a proper dunking in the mud for my pains. But perhaps Clarence is more sensible. Indeed, I am sure he is. And perhaps he does not allow pride to cloud his judgment as much as I do. Perhaps he will not mind if half the guests here believe he must have lost the skills he used to have. What do you say, Clarence? Do say no, old chap."

"If any nephew of mine proves to be such a sniveling coward," a thoroughly irritated voice said from the crowd, "I swear I will disown him."

Seth Wrayburn!

"Uncle Seth!" Lady Forester said. "Can you not see what is *happening* here? Do you not see that Jasper is deliberately—"

"Silence, woman," Wrayburn said. "Clarence? What is it to be?"

Clarence attempted nonchalance, but Jasper could see that the hands he clasped behind his back were trembling.

"If Jasper insists upon taking a mud bath and humiliating himself before all his houseguests and neighbors," he said, "then there is nothing I can do to stop him, is there?"

"Clarence," his mother wailed.

He threw her a drowning look, but she was powerless to save him.

Clarence had had his mother with him on the occasion of that ridiculous fencing match, when he was ten and Jasper was thirteen. Jasper, who had never had a fencing lesson in his life or ever even watched the sport, had lunged at him a number of times and would have speared his spine via his stomach each time if the rapiers had not been capped. But each time the hit was declared to be an illegal one. There were more rules in fencing, it had appeared, than there were stars in the sky. Clarence, in the meanwhile, had pranced about him like a damned flat-footed ballerina, and every time his waving rapier had whistled within a few inches of a contemptuous Jasper, his mother had declared it a hit and a wondrously skilled one at that—as well as being squarely within the rules, of course.

Everyone's attention turned to the wrestling, which was a worthy final and lasted all of ten minutes before Lenny Manning tipped Willy Tufts over his shoulder and headfirst into the mud to score a three-to-two victory.

The crowd went wild, Katherine presented Lenny with the ten-guinea first prize, laughing as she held her skirts well clear of him while she did so, and Lenny tossed the coins to his sweetheart before dashing off to the lake to wash and into the boathouse to don dry clothes. He would be the hero of the village for weeks to come, Jasper did not doubt.

The tug-of-war was to have been next as a grand finale to the fete. But no one had forgotten the jousting bout, and Barker stepped forward as soon as Lenny had disappeared to set the two specially cut planks across the mud—there had been no need to add more water to the mud, of course, because water flowed there from the lake. A few other men helped him to position them a suitable distance apart and to make sure that their ends were set firmly into the ground on either side.

There was a swell of excited anticipation.

Jasper removed his coat and his boots. Katherine

had come to stand in front of him. She was looking steadily at him.

"Hold my coat, if you will, my love," he said. "It would be a pity to ruin it. I would not need to remove either it or my boots, of course, if I could only be confident of not landing in the mud. Clarence need feel no misgivings, alas, though he may want to be overcautious anyway. Those boots would never be the same, would they, if he went in."

"If he removes them," Merton said, "he will be telling us that he is not so confident after all and I might change my wager. But I think my money is safe."

"I have every confidence in the world," Clarence said, and the silly idiot walked to the edge of the mud hole dressed in all his Bond Street finery.

Barker was fetching two oars.

"Whoever can knock the other off the plank and into the mud is the winner, then?" Jasper asked of no one in particular as he stood at the edge of the hole and frowned down into it. "I will try to make the bout last as long as ten seconds, but I cannot promise. If Clarence was that good as a boy, one can only imagine what he is like now. Should we perhaps just proceed to the tug-of-war after all?"

There was a loud chorus of protests, and Jasper took an oar from Barker's hand, stepped up onto one of the planks, and crossed it to the middle. Clarence followed him on the other plank. He almost lost his footing even before he was in position. What an anticlimax *that* would have been!

A hush fell over the crowd.

"Get set," Barker said.

Jasper raised his oar and touched it to Clarence's.

The gun fired.

Clarence swung wildly and would have taken Jasper's head off if the latter had not ducked out of the way. Jasper had to reach out smartly with his oar to hold it against Clarence's side and prevent him from falling off his plank. It would not do for him simply to *fall* in.

It was a game of thrust and parry for a while—or a game of cat and mouse—with Jasper blocking wild swings and administering taps and pokes that were sufficient to send Clarence swaying from side to side and back and forth and to cause his eyes to bulge with fright but were not designed to pitch him in too soon.

The crowd might as well be given a decent show to watch.

And Clarence might as well be made to wait before being put out of his misery—or into his misery.

But the fool must have thought that Jasper was finding it impossible to dislodge him. He grinned suddenly and began his silly dancing to impress the crowd. He held his oar in one hand like a rapier and prepared to spear Jasper in the stomach with it.

Jasper lowered his own oar as if in surrender, nudged Clarence's aside with one elbow, and caught his opponent just below one prancing knee.

Clarence performed a few desperate steps that were in no way balletic, flailed with both arms as if he were a windmill, roared with alarm, and then shrieked like a girl as he fell forward between the two planks and landed facedown and spread-eagled in the mud.

There was one companion shriek from the crowd—probably from Lady Forester—and one jubilant roar from everyone else.

Jasper discovered that he was liberally spattered with mud.

He found Katherine with his eyes and made her an elegant bow.

"For you, my love," he said aloud, though he doubted she or anyone else actually heard the words.

She read them on his lips, though.

She smiled dazzlingly.

"Thank you," he read on her lips. "My love," she added.

Jasper turned his attention to the brown, slimy creature that was wrestling with itself in the mud below him, presumably in an attempt to gain a footing. He leaned down and possessed himself of one of Clarence's slippery hands.

"Come on, old chap," he said. "I'll help you out and we will go for a swim. You are a good sport."

Clarence pawed at his muddy face with an equally muddy hand while the roar died down around them.

"That was deliberate, Jasper," he wailed. "I will never forgive you for this. Mama will never forgive you. Great-Uncle Seth will never—"

"Prunella," Seth Wrayburn said in thunderous tones, "I am not master here and so cannot give orders. But I would strongly suggest you take your sniveling apology for a son once he has cleaned himself up and convey him back to Kent. And it is my fervent wish that I never have to set eyes on either one of you ever again."

There was a smattering of applause from those gathered about him.

"Come on, Clarrie," Jasper said for his ears only. "Have some dignity. At least I have not broken your nose again. Let us go and get cleaned up before the tug-of-war."

"I cannot swim!" Clarence wailed—loudly enough to raise something of a jeer from the bank.

The tassels on his Hessians looked like two drowned rats clinging to the slime of his boots.

26

"HAPPY?" Jasper asked, smiling down at Charlotte as they waited at the top of the long line that was forming for the opening set of country dances at the ball.

She had been toasted more than once at dinner and wished a happy birthday more times than anyone could count in the course of the day. And now there was the final grand moment of celebration as she led the first dance of the evening with her brother.

"I am," she said. "Oh, I *am*, Jasper. I do not think anyone could possibly be happier than I am at this moment. I am so very glad that you and Kate between you were able to persuade Aunt Prunella to stay until tomorrow. Uncle Seth spoke out of turn after you pitched Clarence into the mud. He deserved it, of course, and I am very glad indeed that you did it—it was quite, quite splendid—but he *is* my cousin and Aunt Prunella *is* my aunt and I really could not bear any great unpleasantness on my birthday. Do you think Clarence *really* has a headache?"

"I would not be surprised," he said.

"Oh," she said, "all the *flowers*, Jasper. The ballroom looks like a garden. And it smells like one too. And look at how the mirrors multiply them all many times over."

He smiled at her.

Dressed all in white, she looked delicate and very

young—something that would doubtless dismay her were he to say it out loud. All her dances for the evening were already spoken for, though.

Next year she was going to be mobbed by suitors. He and Katherine were going to have a busy time of it keeping an eye on her.

"I am glad you have been able to reassure me about Lord Merton," she said, glancing at the orchestra, which was merely awaiting his signal to begin playing. But a few couples were still joining the line.

Katherine had had a word with him and he had had a word with Charlotte. How he would have despised such maneuverings even just a few weeks ago!

Charlotte liked Merton exceedingly well, she had told him. Jasper suspected that she was even a little in love with him—she had compared him to the sun again. But she did not really want him to be in love with her. She wanted to be free to enjoy the excitement of her first Season next year. And she still intended to reach the age of twenty—clearly some sort of magic age to her—before fixing her choice upon any particular gentleman.

Jasper had been able to assure her that Merton was far too young a gentleman to be considering matrimony.

And she was far too young.

"Ready?" he said.

She nodded, all wide eyes and eagerness.

He turned to nod at the leader of the orchestra, and the ball began. The first ball at Cedarhurst in his lifetime.

Katherine was dancing with his uncle. He caught her eye, and she smiled dazzlingly.

He raised one eyebrow and then winked at her.

To be continued, he had promised this afternoon. Soon now. He enjoined patience on himself and gave his attention to his sister.

The Cedarhurst ball reminded Katherine of the assemblies she had attended at Throckbridge during her youth, and she and Meg reminisced about them as they stood together between the first and second sets. There too everyone had attended, not just those of the gentry class. Such events, in her opinion, were far more entertaining than *ton* balls in London.

Even Mr. Wrayburn had come.

And Lady Forester had come, though she had pointedly ignored both Jasper and Katherine since before the tug-of-war—which had sent Jasper back to the lake along with Stephen and Winford Finley and the other nine men who had been on the losing team.

The second set was to be another one of country dances. Stephen had already claimed Charlotte's hand. Uncle Stanley came to claim Meg's. Katherine watched Jasper approach across the room, chatting with a few of the guests as he came, a look of open good humor on his face.

I love you, he had said this afternoon just as if he had not noticed that everyone out on the east lawn had paused to watch his purposeful approach to her and to listen to his words.

I love you.

They were words he had spoken before. But he had never spoken them in just such a way. Not for one moment had she doubted that he meant them this time.

And she still did not doubt though they had had scarcely a moment to themselves since then.

I love you.

He stopped in front of her now and smiled.

"You are not going to force me to dance again so soon, are you?" he asked her. "I do not know when was the last time I danced more than once at any ball, Katherine. And until this spring even once would have been once too often."

She smiled at him.

"I will waltz with you later," he said. "I will insist upon it, in fact. Husband's privilege. That will be *two* sets in one evening. A record breaker."

He grinned and she laughed.

"Oh, go," she said. "Go and play host with the card players if you must."

"That is not my point at all," he said. "I want to go for a walk. But only if you will come with me."

She ought not. Goodness, they were the host and hostess, and the ball had begun only half an hour ago. But everything was proceeding smoothly. Their constant presence was not strictly necessary. And there was a look in his eyes . . .

There was *always* a look in Jasper's eyes.

"Oh, very well," she said. "If it will make you happy . . ."

"It will make you happy too," he said, allowing his eyelids to droop over his eyes for a moment and his voice to drop half an octave. "I promise."

They crossed the floor together just as the music was about to begin and went out through the French doors onto the balcony.

"It was not much of a revenge, was it?" he said,

placing one hand over hers on his arm. "Was it even marginally adequate?"

"It was quite, quite splendid," she assured him. "It was *wonderful*. There was no violence. He was made to look like a fool, but he did it to himself. He might have fought and lost with dignity, but you knew he would not, and so you chose perfectly."

"Of course," he said as he led her across the balcony toward the steps down onto the lawn, "the whole thing would have rebounded upon me if *he* had knocked *me* in. And it might have happened."

"Never in a million years," she assured him.

"But perhaps in a billion?" He raised his right eyebrow and looked down at her. "Do you have so little faith in me, Katherine?"

"Besides," she said, "if he *had* knocked you in, you would have come up laughing and making a joke at your own expense, as you did after the tug-of-war. And you would have congratulated him."

"And felt like a prize idiot," he said.

"Yes, and that too." She laughed. "Did you hear me say thank you? I did say it. And I meant it. Thank you for avenging me so well."

The music was playing behind them—in *their* ballroom, at the summer ball, for the enjoyment of all their neighbors. It would be the first of many, but she knew she would always remember this one as being very special.

"Happy?" he asked against her ear as they turned the corner onto the upper terrace.

"Happy," she said.

There were a few people down in the parterre garden. But he led her across the terrace and across the

east lawn, where the races had been run this afternoon.
It was deserted now.

So was the beginning of the wilderness walk, the section of tall trees that she had likened to a cathedral.

They had not spoken for a while.

Their hands were joined, their fingers laced.

He stopped when they were among the trees, turned her off the path, and set her back against one of the sturdy trunks. He placed one of his hands beside her head. She could just see him in the moonlight that was filtering down from above.

"Déjà vu," he said softly.

And she remembered Vauxhall.

"I love you," she whispered to him.

"To be continued," he said. "And now, my love, we *will* continue—without an audience."

She had forgiven him.

He had pledged himself to love her and had done it.

He had promised himself that he would bring her to love him and she had just said she did.

He had made a friend of her.

He had avenged—to a certain degree anyway—Clarence's horrible insults.

They could, he supposed, proceed to live happily ever after—or at least happily. Actually he had no interest in happily-ever-after. It was on a par in his mind with the idea of going to heaven and playing a harp for eternity. It sounded dashed boring. Happiness, on the other hand, was a state much to be desired.

But he had still not fully atoned. Not really.

Somehow they had to go back to Vauxhall and put

it all right—create memories that would obliterate the old.

He lowered his head and kissed her, tasting her lips, teasing them apart, moving his tongue over the soft, moist flesh behind them, sliding it deep into her mouth.

All without touching her anywhere else.

Her palms were flat against the tree trunk.

"Shall we do it as it ought to have been done that night?" he asked her.

"It ought not to have been done *at all* that night," she said gravely.

"Quite right." He smiled at her—he could just see her face in the darkness. "Shall we do it as it ought to be done tonight, then?"

"Yes," she said.

He had never coupled with any woman while they were both still on their feet, he realized as he lifted her skirts and unbuttoned his breeches. Which was strange really when he considered all the times . . .

But he was not interested in any time that had not been with Katherine. Or any time that was not now.

It was not particularly easy. He stepped between her spread legs, held her firmly by the buttocks, half lifted and tilted her, bent slightly at the knees, and thrust upward into her.

Not easy, but dashed erotic, by Jove.

Her muscles clenched about him.

By Jove and by thunder!

She gripped his shoulders, arched her back so that her bosom was pressed against his chest, and tipped her head back against the trunk. Her eyes were closed, her teeth clamped on her lower lip.

He took her with swift, vigorous thrusts and no finesse at all until, after an almost embarrassingly short time, they both cried out and collapsed against each other.

It was perhaps, he thought in a moment of surprised clarity, the best sex he had ever had.

He found her mouth again as he leaned against her and they both relaxed.

"Katherine," he said, slightly breathless.

She looked into his eyes and smiled. She reached up one hand to push the hair back from his brow.

"I love you," he said.

"Yes," she said with a sigh, "you do."

They both laughed softly.

"You *do,*" she said, hugging him more tightly. "Oh, Jasper, I know you do. And I love you. I suppose I always have, though I would not have admitted it in a billion years if you had not loved me."

"Always?" he said, drawing back his head and looking at her in the darkness.

"I fell in love with you at Vauxhall," she said, "because you were dangerous. And I fell in love with you this year because you made me laugh and were so absurd. And then because . . . Well, just *because*. I do not know why."

"Because I had a wager to win," he said, "and went about it with consummate skill."

She laughed and lifted her face for his kiss.

"There was another half to that wager if you will remember," she said. "You insisted upon it. I am just as skilled as you."

"I would be an idiot of the first order if I tried

arguing with that," he said. "What is my forfeit to be? A lifetime of love?"

"Yes," she said.

"Ah," he said, "the same forfeit that I am going to exact from you."

"Very well," she said.

And they kissed again for long minutes, their arms wrapped joyfully about each other.

"Jasper," she said eventually, pushing him firmly from her, "we *must* be getting back. Whatever were we thinking, leaving everyone like this?"

"I believe," he said, "to put it bluntly, Katherine, and to risk putting you to the blush, we were thinking about sex."

"Oh, dear," she said. "I fear you are right."

They were halfway across the east lawn when she spoke again.

"I hope," she said, "there will be a child soon. It will make my happiness complete."

"I shall do my very best to see that it happens soon, then," he said. "I am always eager to oblige you."

"Perhaps I will be increasing by Christmas," she said, "or next Easter. I *do* hope so."

"Good Lord," he said as they stepped onto the terrace, "you must think me a dreadful slowtop, Katherine. I would say by the end of September at the latest, the end of August at the soonest."

"Oh," she said. "I will not hope for it so soon or I will be disappointed when it does not happen. I say Christmas."

"And I say the end of August," he said as they rounded the end of the house and approached the balcony.

"Don't tempt fate by saying that with such confidence," she said.

He wrapped one arm about her waist and turned her to face him.

"Listen!" he said, holding up one forefinger. "Do you hear it? Do you feel it?"

She stood very still for a moment, frowning in concentration.

Hear *what*?" she said. "Feel *what*?"

"It is quite unmistakable," he said. "I feel a wager coming on, Katherine."

Her face lit with laughter.

Katherine and Jasper had decided upon one waltz for the evening. *Only* one because they were well aware that most of their neighbors would not know the steps. But one nevertheless because they could not resist the chance of dancing it in their own ballroom.

Their reacquaintance earlier in the spring had really begun with a waltz.

They would dance it again, then, at Cedarhurst during the summer ball.

When they had planned it, though, they had not expected to dance it alone.

When a waltz was announced, a number of people held back, as was understandable. But a number of people took partners too, most notably those who had come from London. They stood dotted thinly about the ballroom floor while the musicians tuned their instruments and everyone, it seemed, spilled out of the refreshment room and the card room and came in off the balcony and up from the parterre garden.

Everyone seemed eager to watch the waltz being danced.

Katherine stood in the middle of the floor with Jasper, waiting for the music to begin. She surely had never been happier in her life. And it was a happiness that had more than one cause. It had been a perfect day for Charlotte, for Meg and Stephen, for all the houseguests and neighbors. They had revived a tradition that would surely continue for years to come. Life at Cedarhurst was going to be very, very good.

And she loved Jasper. He loved her. They had just *made* love quite scandalously against one of the sturdy trees on the wilderness walk. How inspired a choice of venue *that* had been on his part. She would never again be able to remember Vauxhall without having that particular episode of this evening superimposed upon it.

It had been perfect.

And now the day was to end with a waltz.

Could anything be *more* perfect?

The orchestra was ready. The music was about to begin.

Katherine placed one hand on Jasper's shoulder and set her other in his as his arm came about her waist and drew her as close as propriety allowed. She raised her face and smiled at him. He smiled lazily back.

The music began.

Katherine had no idea how many seconds or minutes passed before she realized that they were the *only* ones dancing, that the other couples had stepped back to join everyone else in watching them.

She looked, startled, into Jasper's face.

"This is *your* doing?" she asked.

"With *my* fondness for dancing?" he said. "Absolutely not."

But he grinned at her, and she smiled back at him.

"It would seem," he said, "that we are expected to put on a demonstration."

"Oh, dear," she said.

"And this is *not* the time," he said, "to look down to make sure I put on a left *and* a right foot when I was dressing for the evening."

"It is not," she agreed.

She looked about at all the familiar faces of family, neighbors, friends, laborers, and servants, at all the extravagant banks of flowers and greenery that had come from the hothouses and the gardens, at the candles in the wall sconces and the chandelier overhead, and at the man who held her.

All was color and light.

Like her life.

He twirled her about a corner of the floor and continued to twirl her down the center of the room while colors and light swirled and hands clapped.

Katherine laughed.

So did he.

"I have just remembered," he said, "I *did* put on two left feet."

ABOUT THE AUTHOR

MARY BALOGH is the *New York Times* best-selling author of *Simply Magic, Simply Love, Simply Unforgettable,* and *Simply Perfect,* a dazzling quartet of novels set at Miss Martin's School for Girls. She is also the author of the acclaimed Slightly novels, as well as the romances *No Man's Mistress, More Than a Mistress, A Summer to Remember,* and *One Night for Love.* A former teacher, she grew up in Wales and now lives in Canada. Visit her web site at www.marybalogh.com.

If *Then Comes Seduction* stole your heart,
get ready to fall in love with
the next book in Mary Balogh's series
featuring the extraordinary Huxtable family.

At Last Comes Love

MARGARET'S STORY

Available from Dell
May 2009

And make sure to be on the lookout for
the following book in the series . . .

Seducing an Angel

STEPHEN'S STORY

Available from Delacorte
June 2009

Turn the page for a sneak peek inside

At Last Comes Love

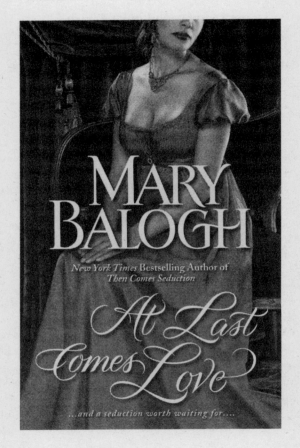

MARY
BALOGH

New York Times Bestselling Author of
Then Comes Seduction

*At Last
Comes Love*

...and a seduction worth waiting for....

AT LAST COMES LOVE

on sale May 2009

"The next set is forming," remarked a lady whose name Margaret had entirely missed, and the marquess extended a hand toward Miss Milfort.

With her peripheral vision Margaret became aware of a flash of scarlet off to her right. Without even turning her head to look she knew it was Crispin and that he was making his way toward her, perhaps to ask her to dance with him, perhaps to seek an introduction to the Marquess of Allingham, *who was betrothed to someone else.*

The ghastly truth rushed at her.

She was not engaged.

She was not about to be engaged.

She was thirty years old and horribly, irreparably single and unattached.

And she was going to have to admit it all to Crispin, who had believed that she *needed* his gallantry since no other man could possibly want to offer her his company. Her stomach clenched with distress and incipient queasiness.

She could not bear to face him just yet. She really could not. She might well cast herself, weeping, into his arms.

She needed time to compose herself.

She needed to be alone.

She needed...

She turned blindly in the direction of the ballroom doors and the relative privacy of the ladies' withdrawing room beyond. She did not even take the time to skirt the perimeter of the room but hurried across it, thankful that enough dancers had gathered there to prevent her from looking too conspicuous.

She felt horribly conspicuous anyway. She remembered to smile.

As she approached the doors, she glanced back over her shoulder to see if Crispin was coming after her. She was in a ridiculous panic. Even *she* knew it was ridiculous, but the trouble with panic was that it was beyond one's power to control.

She turned her head to face the front again, but she did so too late to stop herself from plowing into a gentleman who was standing before the doors, blocking the way.

She felt for a moment as if all the breath had been knocked from her body. And then she felt a horrible embarrassment to add to her confusion and panic. She was pressed against a very solid male body from shoulders to knees, and she was being held in place there by two hands that gripped her upper arms like a vise.

"I am so sorry," she said, tipping back her head and pushing her hands against his broad chest in a vain effort to put some distance between them so that she could step around him and hurry on her way.

She found herself gazing up into very black eyes set in a harsh, narrow, angular, dark-hued face—an almost ugly face framed by hair as dark as his eyes.

"Excuse me," she said when his grip on her arms did not loosen.

"Why?" he asked her, his eyes roaming boldly over her face. "What is your hurry? Why not stay and dance with me? And then marry me and live happily ever after with me?"

Margaret was startled out of her panic.

His breath smelled of liquor.

There had been no ball the evening after Duncan's interview with his grandfather. Not one single one. London positively teemed with lavish entertainments every day and night of the Season, but for that one infernal evening there had been nothing to choose among except a soiree that was being hosted by a lady who was a notable bluestocking and that would doubtless be attended by politicians and scholars and poets and intelligent ladies, and a concert with a program clearly designed for the musically discerning and not for anyone who happened to be shopping in a hurry at the marriage mart.

Duncan had not attended either but had been forced to waste one of his precious fifteen days. He had gone to Jackson's Boxing Salon yesterday afternoon when he might, he thought too late, have joined the afternoon promenade in Hyde Park to look over the crop of prospective brides. And today, when he *had* thought of going there, rain had been spitting intermittently from low gray clouds, and all he met were a few hardy fellow riders—all male—and one closed carriage filled with dowagers.

He had been reminded of those dreams in which one tried to run but found it impossible to move even as fast as a crawl.

But tonight there was Lady Tindell's ball to attend, and it was a promising event. According to his mother, who planned to be there, it was always one of the grand squeezes of the Season since Lady Tindell was renowned for her lavish suppers. Everyone who was anyone would be there, including, Duncan fervently hoped, armies of young, marriageable hopefuls who were running out of time in the Season to find husbands.

It was enough to make him feel positively ill.

He had not told his mother about his grandfather's ultimatum though he might have to enlist her help if he found himself unable to come up with a bride on his own within the next few days. His mother knew everybody. She would be sure to know which girls—and, more important, which parents—were desperate enough to take a man of such notorious reputation in such indecent haste.

He arrived late. It was perhaps not a wise thing to do when time was of the very essence, but earlier in the evening he had acquired cold feet—the almost inevitable consequence of having been forced to wait more than twenty-four hours to begin implementing his search—and had stayed at White's long after he had finished his dinner and his companions had left to go about their evening business, some of them to attend this very ball. He might have come with them and hoped to enter the ballroom almost unnoticed. Instead he had stayed to fortify himself with another glass of port—only to discover that fortification had demanded several more glasses of port than just one.

He did not have an invitation to the ball, but he did not fear being turned away—not after a few glasses of port, anyway. He was, after all, the Earl of Sheringford. And if anyone remembered the rather spectacular scandal of five years ago, as everyone surely would— well, they would undoubtedly be avid with curiosity to discover what had become of him in the intervening years and how he would behave now that he was back.

Duncan wondered suddenly if any of the Turners were in town this year, and fervently hoped not. It would not be a comfortable thing to come face to face with Randolph Turner in particular—the man he had cuckolded.

He was *not* turned away from the ball. But of course he had arrived late enough that there was no longer any sign of a receiving line or even of a majordomo to announce him. He stepped into the ballroom, having left his hat and cloak downstairs in the care of a footman, and looked about him.

He felt very much on display and half expected that after all there would be a rush of outraged persons, led by ladies, to expel him into outer darkness. It did not happen, though undoubtedly he *was* attracting some attention. He could hear a slightly heightened buzz of sound off to his right.

He ignored it.

It was indeed a squeeze of a ball. If everyone decided to dance, they would have to push out the walls. And if everyone decided to rush him ... Well, he would be squashed as flat as a pancake.

He had arrived between sets, but couples were gathering on the floor for the next one. Good! He would be able to view the matrimonial prospects at his leisure provided that buzz of interest to his right did not develop into a swell of outrage to fill the ballroom.

He could see Con Huxtable and a few other male acquaintances some distance away, but he made no move to join them. He would become too involved in conversation if he did and perhaps allow himself to be borne off to the card room. He would be willing enough, by God. He could feel his mood turn bleaker and blacker with every passing second. This ought not to be happening.

He had *not* planned to go wife hunting yet—or perhaps ever. He had *certainly* not planned to come to London any year soon.

How the devil was he to begin?

There were pretty women and plain ones, young ones and old ones, animated ones and listless ones—that last group being the wallflowers, he suspected. Most of them, indeed, were still standing on the sidelines, nary a partner in sight though the dancing was about to resume. He should probably concentrate his attention upon them.

It was one devil of a way to choose a bride! Pick the most bored looking wallflower and offer to brighten her life. Offer her marriage with a man who had abandoned his last bride almost literally at the altar in order to run off with her married sister-in-law and live in sin with her for almost five years. A man who had no wish whatsoever to marry but was being forced into it by the threat of penury. A man who no longer believed in romantic love and had never practiced fidelity. A man with an illegitimate child he refused to hide away in some dark corner of the country.

He had fixed his narrowed gaze upon a mousy-haired young girl who, if his eyes did not deceive him from this distance, had a flat chest and a bad case of facial spots, and who was beginning to notice his scrutiny and look decidedly frightened by it, when he was distracted.

A missile almost bowled him off his feet—something hurled his way in order to expel him after all, perhaps?

He clamped his hands about the two arms of the missile in order to save himself from landing flat on his back—what a spectacular reentry into society *that* would be!—and realized that it was a human missile.

A female human, to be exact.

Very female.

She was all generously sized breasts and delicious curves and subtly fragrant dark hair. And when she tipped back her head to apologize, she revealed a face that did the body full justice, by thunder. She had wide eyes and a porcelain complexion and features that had been arranged on her face for maximum effect. She was loveliness personified from head to toe.

He held her against him longer than was necessary— and far longer than was wise in such a public setting, when his sudden appearance was already provoking attention. But she would surely fall over if he released her too soon, he reasoned.

She had long legs—he could feel them against his own.

She was beautiful and voluptuous—and pressed by some happy chance to his body. Could any warm-blooded male ask for more? Privacy and nakedness and a soft bed, perhaps?

The only negative thing that could be said about her—on the spur of the moment anyway—was that she was not young. She was probably his own age, give or take a couple of years. That was not at all young for a woman. She was undoubtedly married, then. She must have been snaffled up off the marriage mart ten or twelve years ago. She probably had half a dozen children. A pity that. But fate was ever a joker. He must not expect his search to be *this* easily or happily concluded.

There was no ring on the left hand that was splayed over his chest, though, he noticed.

All of which thoughts and observations flashed through his head in a matter of moments.

"Excuse me," she said, flushing and looking even more beautiful, if that were possible.

She was pushing at his chest. Trying to get away.

There was no harm in being hopeful, was there?

"Why?" he asked her. "What is your hurry? Why not stay and dance with me? And then marry me and live happily ever after with me?"

He felt her body grow still and watched the arrested look on her face. Then her eyebrows arched above her eyes—and even *they* were lovely. It was no wonder some poets wrote poems to their ladies' eyebrows.

"Does it *have* to be in that order?" she asked him.

Ah. An intriguing answer indeed. An answer in the form of a question.

Duncan pursed his lips.

She had bowled him over after all—and rendered him temporarily speechless.

MARGARET almost laughed, though more with hysteria than with amusement.

What had he said?

And *what* had she answered?

Gracious heaven, he was a total stranger, and not a very reputable-looking one at that. Was anyone observing them? Whatever would they *think*?

His hands had loosened their hold on her arms though they still remained there. She could have broken away quite easily and hurried on her way out of the ballroom. Instead she looked up at him and waited to see what he would say next.

He had pursed his lips, and his very dark eyes—surely they could not be literally black?—gazed steadily and boldly back at her.

He appeared to be quite alone. Some instinct told Margaret that he was not the sort of man with whom she ought to be talking, especially without a formal introduction. But here she was standing very close to him, her hands splayed on his chest, his clasping the bare flesh of her upper arms between her sleeves and her gloves. And they had been standing thus for more seconds than any ordinary collision ought to have occasioned. They ought to have sprung apart, both embarrassed and both apologizing profusely.

Oh, goodness.

She pushed at his chest again and, when he still did not release his hold on her arms, she dropped her own to her sides. Her back prickled. Half the *ton* was somewhere behind her. Including her family. And including Crispin Dew. And the Marquess of Allingham.

"I am afraid it does," the stranger said at last in answer to her question. "If I dash off immediately in pursuit of a special license, you see, and then someone to perform the ceremony, this particular set will surely be over by the time I return. And someone else will have discovered you and eloped to Scotland with you and left me clutching a useless document. If we are to both dance and marry, it must be done in that order, I am afraid—much as I am flattered by your eagerness to proceed to the nuptials without further delay."

How very outrageous he was, whoever he might be. Margaret ought not to have laughed—she ought to have been offended by the levity of his words, absurd and quick-witted though they were.

But she laughed.

He did not. He gazed intently at her and dropped his hands to his sides at last.

"Dance with me now," he said, "and tomorrow morning I will procure that special license. It is a promise."

It was a strange joke. Yet he showed no sign of finding it amusing. Margaret found herself shivering slightly despite the fact that the smile lingered on her face.

She really ought to run from him as fast as her feet would carry her and keep the whole width or length of the ballroom between them for the rest of the evening. Her own words had been very indiscreet. *Does it have to be in that order?* Had she really spoken them aloud? But his answer, alas, proved that she had.

Who on earth *was* he? She had never set eyes on him before tonight. She was sure of that.

She did not run.

"Thank you, sir," she said instead. "I *will* dance with you."

It would be better to do that than run away simply because the Marquess of Allingham, whose hand she had refused three separate times, had chosen to betroth himself to someone else. And because Crispin was at the ball, and she had told him she was betrothed.

The stranger inclined his head and offered his arm to lead her out to join the other dancers. It surprised Margaret to discover that the dancing had still not begun. That collision and the bizarre exchange of words that had followed it must all have happened within a minute or two at the longest.

The arm beneath her hand was very solid indeed, she noticed. She also noticed as she walked beside him that her initial impression of his physique had not been mistaken. His black evening coat molded a powerful frame like a second skin. His long legs looked equally well muscled. He was taller than she by several inches, though she was a tall woman. And then there was that harsh, dark, almost ugly face.

It struck her that he might be a frightening adversary.

"It occurs to me," he said, "that if I am to be granted a special license tomorrow, I ought to know the name of my bride. And her place of residence. It would be mildly irritating to pry myself away from my bed at some ungodly hour of the morning only to have my application denied on account of my inability to name my bride or explain where she lives."

Oh, the absurd man. He was going to continue with the joke, though his grim face had not relaxed into even the suggestion of a smile.

"I suppose it would," she agreed.

The orchestra struck up with a lively country dance tune at that moment, and after a short spell of dancing together they moved away from each other in order to perform a series of steps with the couple adjacent to them. When they came together again, it was with the same couple, and there was no chance for private conversation, absurd or otherwise.

This was really very improper, Margaret thought. As he had just reminded her, he did not know her and she did not know him. Yet they were dancing with each other. How on earth would she explain the lapse to Vanessa and Katherine? Or to Stephen? She had always been a stickler for the social niceties.

But she discovered that she did not much care. She was almost enjoying herself. The marquess's announcement—and his assumption that she already knew—had seriously discomposed her. So had the appearance of Crispin. But here she was dancing and smiling anyway.

And there was something definitely amusing about the joke the stranger had set in motion.

How many ladies could boast of meeting a total stranger and being asked to dance with him and marry him—all in one breath?

Her smile widened.

"*Might* I be permitted," the stranger asked her when they were dancing exclusively with each other again, "to know the name of my prospective bride?"

She was tempted to withhold it. But that would be pointless. He could quite easily discover it for himself after they had finished dancing.

"I am Margaret Huxtable," she told him, "sister of the Earl of Merton."

"Ah, excellent," he said. "It is important to marry someone of impeccable lineage—important to one's family anyway."

"Absolutely, sir," she agreed. "And you are . . . ?"

But she had to wait another couple of minutes while the pattern of the dance drew other couples within earshot again.

"Duncan Pennethorne, Earl of Sheringford," he said without preamble when they were alone again. "The title, I must warn you before you get too excited about marrying it, is a courtesy one and therefore of no real value whatsoever except that it sounds good—and except that it is an indicator that a more real and illustrious title is to follow if and when the incumbent should predecease me. The Marquess of Claverbrook, my grandfather, may well not do so even though he is eighty—or will be in two weeks' time—and fifty years my senior."

He had offered a great deal more information than she had asked for. But it was surprising she had not met him before. And yet . . . *The Earl of Sheringford*.

Something tugged at the corners of her memory, but she could not pull it into focus. She had the impression that it was something not too pleasant. Something scandalous.

"And where," he asked, "may I come to claim you to-morrow, Miss Huxtable, marriage license in hand?"

She hesitated again. But it would take him only a moment after he had left her to discover it for himself.

"At Merton House on Berkeley Square," she said.

But the joke had continued long enough. As soon as the set was at an end, she decided, she must put as much distance between herself and the Earl of Sheringford as she possibly could. She did not want to encourage him to continue to be as bold and familiar with her as he had been thus far.

She must make some discreet inquiries about him. There was *something* there in her memory.

Crispin, she could see, was talking with Vanessa and Elliott. It still seemed unreal, seeing him again like this after so many unhappy years. She had not expected ever to see him again after his marriage. She had expected him, she supposed, to settle in Spain with his wife after the wars were over. Or at Rundle Park.

"Miss Huxtable," the Earl of Sheringford asked her, bringing her attention back to him, "why were you flee-ing the ballroom in a panic?"

It was a thoroughly impertinent question. Did he know nothing of good manners?

"I was not *fleeing*," she told him. "And I was not in a panic."

"Two bouncers in a single sentence," he said.

She looked at him with all the hauteur she could muster. "You are impertinent, my lord," she said.

"Oh, always," he agreed. "Why waste time on tedious courtesies? Was he worth the panic?"

She opened her mouth to deliver a sharp retort. But then she closed it and simply shook her head instead.

"Was that a *no*?" he asked her. "Or a *you-are-impossible* gesture?"

"The latter," she said curtly before they were separated again.